THE
SECRETS
OF THE
WILD
WOOD

THE
SECRETS
OF THE
WILD
WOOD

TONKE DRAGT

Translated by Laura Watkinson

PUSHKIN CHILDREN'S BOOKS

Pushkin Children's Books
71–75 Shelton Street
London, WC2H 9JQ

Copyright © 1965, *De geheimen van het Wilde Woud*
by Tonke Dragt, Uitgeverij Leopold, Amsterdam
© illustrations Tonke Dragt
English translation © Laura Watkinson 2016

The Secrets of the Wild Wood was first published as *De geheimen van het Wilde Woud* in the Netherlands, 1965

First published by Pushkin Children's Books in 2015
This edition first published in 2017

N ederlands
letterenfonds
dutch foundation
for literature

This book was published with the support of the Dutch Foundation for Literature.

10 9 8 7 6 5 4 3 2 1

ISBN 978 1 78269 195 2

Designed and typeset by Tetragon, London
Printed by CPI Group (UK) Ltd, Croydon, CRO 4YY

www.pushkinpress.com

Contents

"The sun goes down in the sea, in the water," said the Fool. "I shall tell my brothers, because they don't know. Or is it a secret?"

"There are no more secrets now," said Tiuri, as he walked to the cabin with the Fool.

The Fool stopped and wrinkled his brow. "No more secrets?" he said. "They call me the Fool, but I don't believe that there are no more secrets left."

Tiuri looked at him with new respect.

"Yes," he said. "You're right. I am free to tell my secret now, but of course there are still lots of other secrets. The secrets of the Wild Wood, for instance, and all kinds of other mysteries. Some of them we have never even heard about. And others we shall never understand."

"I'm not sure I know what you mean," said the Fool.

The Letter for the King, Part Eight

Prologue

Winter in the Wood

The cawing of a crow broke the silence. The bird flew up to perch on a branch, a patch of black against all the white and grey. Snow came swirling down from the tree in a fine powder.

Sir Ristridin stopped, wrapped his cloak more closely around him and wondered if the crow had any significance for him. Was it a sign? A portent of danger? He wryly thought how much he had changed, that a bird could make him pause, nothing but a hungry creature in this bitterly cold winter.

It seemed like an age since King Dagonaut had summoned him and said, "I have heard strange rumours about the Wild Wood, about robbers and dangerous bands of men, about woodland spirits and Men in Green. I want you to investigate and find out which of those rumours are true – you, the trustiest of my knights-errant. And I need you to go there immediately, as many dangers in those parts could threaten our kingdom."

Ristridin had ridden out, accompanied by Sir Arwaut and twenty men. Now he was walking through the forest on his own, but he knew he was not truly alone. He kept thinking about what his friend, Edwinem of Forèstèrra, had once said to him, "You *must* go to the Wild Wood, for a knight should know his own land, and that

11

means all of King Dagonaut's territory. I remember from the old stories that there was once a wide road leading through the forest to the west, to the Kingdom of Unauwen. Why did your people allow it to become overgrown? If you clear that road once again, if you cut it open, the creatures that shun the daylight will flee. It will also be another route between our two lands: the kingdoms of Unauwen and Dagonaut."

Edwinem had been a knight in the service of Unauwen, the noble king who ruled the lands to the west of the Great Mountains. He had been murdered by the Red Riders – not here, but in another forest. Red Riders from Eviellan, the dark land to the south... Unauwen and Eviellan were at war, even though the ruler of Eviellan was actually a son of King Unauwen – his youngest son, yet his greatest enemy. Edwinem had fought in that war, but in the end he had been treacherously slain, within the sovereign territory of King Dagonaut.

The flapping of wings stirred Ristridin from his thoughts. The crow flew away, and Ristridin walked slowly onwards. The snow crunched beneath his feet, and small branches and twigs cracked and snapped as he passed. There were no other sounds to be heard. He felt like a traveller in the Land of the Dead. This was the Wild Wood, where Dagonaut ruled, though the king himself had never set foot inside the forest and did not know what secrets it concealed. *And what will become of me?* thought Ristridin. *Now that I have discovered those secrets, will I ever get out of here alive and tell others what I know?*

Somewhere out there were villages and cities, houses and castles, where people lived in peace and quiet, ignorant of such wildernesses as this. Ristridin wondered if he would ever reach those places. *I must!* he thought, but he felt tired and old.

Again he stopped. He saw footprints in the snow. Lots of footprints! Others had passed straight across the track in front of him...

But he was alone. Where was he now? It had been many days since Ristridin had crossed the Black River, and he had been wandering for a long time. He had beaten a path through thorny bushes and tangled branches, in snow, in mist and ice. Islan should lie somewhere to the east of him now, not too far away – Islan, the lonely castle on the open plain, surrounded by forests. That was where he planned to go.

Who had left those fresh footprints in the snow? Was he already that close to Islan? Or had he taken a wrong turn? Was he lost? He looked up and saw a web of bare branches and twigs, with the silvery sky between them.

As Ristridin walked on, he felt as if he were being followed and watched. His lean face was grim and alert, and his hand rested on the hilt of his sword. He sought the way to Castle Islan.

Castle Islan... where the civilized world began. If Ristridin reached the castle, he would be able to travel onwards from there. Then he would once more ride a horse; then he would see his friends again.

He had made a promise, an agreement with his friends. In the spring they would meet at Castle Ristridin by the Grey River, the home of his forefathers. His friends were all knights – no, one of them had not yet been knighted, but perhaps by now the ceremony had taken place. Tiuri, son of Tiuri, had proven himself worthy of becoming a knight by successfully completing his mysterious mission: taking a most important letter to King Unauwen.

PART ONE

SIR IDIAN

1 TRAVEL PLANS

Sir Tiuri rode Ardanwen, his black horse, down the muddy path beside the Blue River. Not so long ago, its surface had been covered with ice floes, but now the water could flow freely once again. The river was high and tumbled along. Far away, in the mountains, the snow must be melting. Tiuri raised his head and took a deep breath. Although the air was still cold, it felt different today. The fields and trees to his right were still bare, but the birds swooped happily through the sky above, because they knew it too: winter was over! Soon travellers would be setting out along roads and tracks. Tiuri himself was keen to be off on a journey and to leave Tehuri, his father's estate, where he had spent the past few months.

He gazed into the distance, towards the south. There, some days' journey away, was Deltaland, a marshy country situated around the mouth of a river. To the west of that land lay Eviellan, a realm that was ruled by a wicked man. Tiuri had no desire to travel to that particular place. But on the Grey River, which formed the border with Eviellan, was a castle he had often thought about, even though he had never been there: Castle Ristridin, the ancestral home of the knight-errant who shared its name, Ristridin of the South. Sir Ristridin had headed into the Wild Wood in the autumn of the previous year, but in spring he would return to his castle, to meet up with his friends once again, and he had invited Tiuri to join them.

Tiuri reined in his horse and spoke out loud, "And I mean to go there. As soon as possible. Tomorrow!"

Ardanwen twitched his fine ears as if he understood what his young master was saying. Tiuri patted the horse's neck. "Are you

17

longing to roam the land again too, like you used to?" he whispered. "Like Sir Edwinem?" And Tiuri thought to himself: *I want to be a knight-errant, too. Later, when Father's old, I shall live at Tehuri. I'll always return here. It's my home, after all. But I want to see more of the world before then. And who knows? Perhaps King Dagonaut will have need of me, and I will be able to prove myself worthy of being his knight.*

Tiuri turned his horse and rode back to Castle Tehuri, which he could already see ahead of him in the distance.

Before long, Tiuri was riding over the drawbridge, which was kept lowered in this time of peace. The gatekeepers welcomed him back to the castle. The two Tiuris, father and son, were dearly loved. The elder Tiuri was known as "Sir Tiuri the Valiant", a name he had earned long ago, in days of war. His son was the youngest of Dagonaut's knights, and the only one who was allowed to carry a white shield; that was because of the great service he had performed for Unauwen, the ruler of the kingdom in the west.

As Tiuri jumped down from his horse in the courtyard, a boy of around fifteen came running over to him. It was Piak, his best friend, who was also his squire.

"Hey, Tiuri!" Piak called. "Where have you been? I was playing chess with your father and when I looked up, you'd disappeared!"

"I had to get out for a while," Tiuri replied, "and so did Ardanwen. The weather's changed."

He led the horse into the stable. That was a job he always did himself. No one else was allowed to touch Ardanwen, except for Piak.

"Yes. I could smell a change in the air too," said Piak, walking alongside him. "I went up to the top of the tallest turret, and everything smelt so different and new."

Tiuri smiled. Piak was still fond of high places, even though it was just castle towers now instead of the mountains that were his home.

"So now we can set off on our journey," Tiuri said.

"Journey? Journey? Now? Nonsense!" said Waldo, the old stable master. "What utter nonsense!" he repeated. "March is far too cold to travel. And April's too unpredictable. You really should wait until May."

"But May might be too mild," said Tiuri with a smile.

"And June could be too sunny," Piak added.

Waldo shook his grey head. "You young people are always in such a hurry," he said. "Hasty, reckless, never content to be where you are." He looked sternly at the two young men, his master's son and the boy's best friend. It was not a fitting way to address a knight and his squire, but they would always be children to the stable master, who had known Tiuri's father since he was just a little boy. "At least wait until the first day of spring," he continued. "You've only just returned home. Why would you want to run the risk of getting lost, breaking your neck, being murdered by brigands, or catching a cold and getting rheumatism from sleeping by the roadside?"

"But Waldo," said Tiuri with a smile, "you'd grumble even more if we stayed at home and never rode out at all."

Waldo grunted, but his eyes were friendly. "That's as may be," he said. "But you should know, Tiuri, son of Tiuri, that there's no need to go out searching for adventure. If it's your destiny, adventure will find you. Before you know it, you'll be in all sorts of trouble that you never asked for!"

"You're probably right," said Tiuri. "But we're not just riding out on a whim. Sir Ristridin of the South invited me to come to his castle in the spring."

"Sir Ristridin doesn't have a castle, does he?" said Waldo. "I thought he was a knight-errant, without lands and possessions."

"That's true," replied Tiuri. "The lord of the castle is actually Sir Arturin, Ristridin's brother, but it's also Ristridin's home, whenever he stops to rest from his travels."

"Some men are fools, handing over their castles to others, just so they can go wandering about," said the old man in his usual grumpy

19

tone. "Fine then, so it's Sir Arturin's castle. And that's where you're going? You and your friend?"

"My first journey as a squire," said Piak. His brown eyes sparkled at the thought of the adventures he might have. "And it's not far from the Great Mountains," he added longingly.

"It's even closer to the Wild Wood," said Waldo. "Well, I suppose it's your decision. We have a wood here, too, and it's far more beautiful and agreeable than that dangerous forest. Let's just hope Sir Ristridin has made it back in one piece."

When Tiuri had been knighted, after his journey to the Kingdom of Unauwen, King Dagonaut had told him he would not call upon his services for a while. First he should return home with his parents, to Castle Tehuri, and take some time to recover. Tiuri didn't think he needed any, but he was keen to go home, as he hadn't been there for so long. Piak went with him, of course. At Tehuri, Tiuri and his father taught Piak a great deal about everything a squire needs to know. Tiuri's parents had become very fond of him and treated him like their own son.

Tiuri had also learnt a lot. His father took him riding around his estate, preparing him for the day when Tiuri would take charge of the castle and surrounding countryside.

Autumn had flown by. In the winter, the cold, with its snow and frost, had often kept the residents of Tehuri inside the keep. It had been a quiet few months. Hardly any travellers had ridden over the drawbridge to request hospitality, and there had been very little news from the outside world. The young men had not been bored, though. In spite of the icy weather, they still went outside, and there was always something to do indoors. Tiuri and his father played chess together, for instance, and Piak had also learnt how to play, but he never managed to beat his friend. Tiuri was a skilful opponent and a match for his father.

Yet in those winter months, a feeling of restlessness sometimes came over Tiuri. He was Sir Tiuri now, but nothing happened in peaceful Tehuri that might put him to the test.

He would think back to his journey to the Kingdom of Unauwen to the west of the Great Mountains. It was so hard to reconcile all that he had learnt and experienced on that journey with the facts of his everyday life at Tehuri. Far away, in the west, Unauwen's knights could be waging a fierce battle against their enemies from Eviellan. He had no idea what was happening, as news from that part of the world never reached Castle Tehuri.

Sometimes he was struck by a sudden longing for the City of Unauwen and the Rainbow River, and for the other places he had visited. His thoughts turned to far-off Mistrinaut too, where Lady Lavinia lived. When would he see her again?

There were other people he was keen to see, like Sir Ristridin, who had ridden with Arwaut and his men to the Wild Wood, because of the strange stories that were told about that place.

And now that he could feel spring in the air, Tiuri was more certain than ever that he wanted to do as he had once resolved and travel the land as a knight-errant, like Ristridin. His first step would be to accept Ristridin's invitation and to go to the castle by the Grey River. Piak would go with him, of course. He felt the same way as Tiuri.

2   CASTLE RISTRIDIN

Now Sir Tiuri was riding along the Grey River, on Ardanwen, of course, the black horse whose name meant Night Wind in the old language of the Kingdom of Unauwen. The young knight had a helmet on his head and a sword hanging at his side, and the tunic over his armour was blue and gold, the colours of Tehuri. His shield, though, was white, like those of the knights from the west. Tiuri was proud of that shield and so he had taken it on his journey.

Piak rode beside him, on a horse as brown as his own hair. Anyone who had known him before, when he still lived up in the mountains, would hardly have recognized him now that he was a squire.

Old Waldo had been proved right; the weather had stayed cold, and that had not made their journey any easier. But now their goal was close. They saw castles and strongholds on both sides of the river, "watching and spying on one another", as Piak put it. The water was all that separated them from Eviellan, the land of the evil Red Riders, where the knights carried shields of black or red. They had seen no sign of any inhabitants of Eviellan, though.

"They pay no attention to us," a knight had told them at a castle where they stopped for the night. "Eviellan's eyes are focused only on the Kingdom of Unauwen. I have heard rumours of a great battle that was fought there, but I do not know the outcome."

Tiuri had asked if there was any news of Sir Ristridin. Was he already back at his castle? But the knight, like everyone else they had encountered along the way, had been unable to answer that question.

"We'll find out soon enough," said Piak, when they spotted distant towers that could only be Castle Ristridin. "All of these castles look so alike, don't they? Big and made of stone, with thick walls and battlements. I don't like them much, although they can be quite pleasant inside." He let go of the reins for a moment and rubbed his hands, which were blue with cold. A little later, he called out, "Look! I can see something else in the distance over there. Mountains!"

Yes, far to the west of them rose the hazy summits of the Great Mountains, almost indistinguishable from the grey clouds above.

"We're riding along the Third Great Road to the west now," said Tiuri. "It leads through a mountain pass and into the Kingdom of Unauwen."

"And we travelled along some of the First Great Road last year," said Piak, "past Castle Mistrinaut. So where's the Second Great Road?"

"The Second Great Road," replied Tiuri, "has practically disappeared. It's been overgrown by the Wild Wood."

"I can see a forest, too," said Piak. "Do you think that's the Wild Wood?"

"I don't think so. I've heard it's more to the west."

"Sir Ristridin may be able to tell us more about it soon," said Piak. "Do you know I almost feel like I know him? Even though I've never met him in my life. You've told me so much about them, about Ristridin and Bendu, and Arwaut and Evan. See, I remember all of their names."

"And we're going to meet Sir Arturin, too," said Tiuri, "Ristridin's brother. I don't know him either, but he's to be our host."

They reached the castle towards evening. The lookout at the top of one of the towers had sounded his horn to announce their arrival. Creaking, the drawbridge came down. As they rode across, one of the doors in the gate opened slowly and a group of four armed guards appeared.

"It seems they don't just let their guests wander in, eh?" Piak whispered to Tiuri.

Tiuri greeted the guards. "We come as friends," he said, "and we ask for hospitality. Sir Tiuri, and Piak, his squire."

"Sir Tiuri?" repeated one of the guards. "So you've not come from the west? But you're carrying a white shield, like a knight of Unauwen, and you're far younger than I believed Tiuri the Valiant to be."

"I am his son," said Tiuri. "Tiuri with the White Shield. I am here at the invitation of Sir Ristridin."

"Sir Ristridin!" cried the guard. "Do you bring news of him?!"

"No," said Tiuri. "Has he not returned?"

"Not yet," replied the guard.

"But he was supposed to come here in the spring."

"That's true," said the guard, "but he has not yet arrived. Sir Bendu is also waiting for him; he arrived the day before yesterday. Please enter, Tiuri, son of Tiuri. I shall have your arrival announced to Sir Arturin."

Soon the two friends were standing before Sir Arturin, the lord of the castle, who greeted them warmly. "Welcome, Sir Tiuri," he said, "and you too, young squire. A fire burns in the hearth, and food is ready. I also welcome you in the name of my brother, who I believe invited you here."

Tiuri didn't think that Sir Arturin resembled his brother Ristridin at all. He was shorter than the knight-errant and nowhere near as lean; they just shared the same curly hair.

Now another man came over to Tiuri and Piak, a large, dark-haired man with a beard.

"Sir Bendu!" cried Tiuri.

"The very same," the man said, shaking Tiuri's hand. "It's good to see you again, Tiuri. And I note that what I predicted has now come to pass: you are a knight, as is only right and proper." He turned to Piak, who was standing there, looking a little awkward. "And who might you be?" he asked.

"This is Piak, my best friend," said Tiuri. "He was my guide through the mountains and my travelling companion in the Kingdom of Unauwen. Now he is my squire."

Bendu shook Piak's hand, too, so firmly that Piak winced. Then Bendu spoke to Tiuri, "Do you bring news of Ristridin?"

"It's been a few months since I saw him," Tiuri replied. "Just before he went to the Wild Wood."

"Oh," said Bendu, clearly disappointed.

"As you can see, he has not yet returned," said Sir Arturin. "But he is no longer in the Wild Wood either."

24

"He isn't?" said Tiuri. "So where is he? And what happened to him in the forest?"

"We know very little about it," replied Arturin. "And we have no idea of his whereabouts now. He left the Wild Wood in the winter; a messenger from Islan brought me the news. Castle Islan is close to the Wild Wood, as you probably know. Ristridin passed by the castle and asked the lord there to send messages to King Dagonaut and to me. He intended to travel on to other parts, where there was more for a knight to do. He said the paths in the Wild Wood were dead ends or led to ruins of towns and villages that were abandoned long ago."

"That may be so," said Bendu, "but I still think he could at least have said where he meant to go. Does the Lord of Islan truly have no idea?"

"I wrote him a letter," said Sir Arturin. "He replied to say that was all he knew. Ristridin did not even enter his castle. He was in a hurry and heading eastwards." Arturin fell silent, a frown on his face.

"Why not to the south?" said Bendu. "He had a mission to carry out there!"

"A mission?" repeated Tiuri. Then suddenly he understood. Like Bendu, Ristridin had sworn to punish the Black Knight with the Red Shield – the leader of the Red Riders and the man who had murdered their friend Edwinem. That knight fought with his visor closed. No one knew who he was or what he looked like.

"Have you just returned from Eviellan?" Tiuri asked. "What happened there? Did you find the Knight with the Red Shield?"

"Did I find him? I can't tell you how many such knights I found!" Bendu replied gruffly. "Eviellan is full of knights, and most wear black armour and nearly all of them have red shields. Whenever I met such a knight, I called him to account for Edwinem's death – but they all denied knowing anything about it. I fought twelve duels but, unless I am very much mistaken, I did not defeat the man I was looking for."

"They must have been very pleased to see you in Eviellan," said Sir Arturin in a slightly sarcastic tone.

"They were certainly happy to see the back of me," said Bendu. "But that will not hinder me in my search for that dishonourable knight! I am here now because it is what Ristridin and I agreed, and I hope he will soon accompany me to the south. Two men will have more chance than one of finding that murderer."

"You will never succeed," said Arturin. "The King of Eviellan will expel you from his land as an undesirable outsider. That is at least what I would do were I in his place. Why do you personally feel the need to avenge Edwinem's death? That is surely the responsibility of the men from the west. Edwinem was a knight of Unauwen, was he not? So let King Unauwen punish his murderer!"

"Sir, I do not like your words!" growled Bendu. "Edwinem of Forèstèrra was my friend. It does not matter to me that he came from a different country! Ristridin, Arwaut, Evan and I have sworn to avenge his death, and I certainly intend to keep my word."

"As you wish," said Arturin, shrugging his shoulders. "But perhaps you are the only one who has not yet forgotten that oath – or rather, who has not realized its futility. The four of you went your separate ways months ago, as there were more important things to do. I suspect you will have to continue your quest for revenge on your own. Ristridin and Arwaut are not here, and Evan has not yet arrived either."

"A man who forgets his oath loses his honour," said Bendu.

Tiuri and Piak looked at each other. It seemed as if the two knights were about to start arguing. However, Arturin put an end to the discussion by inviting his guests to sit by the fire and drink a glass of wine with him.

Soon it was time to dine. Many of the castle residents came to join them, and Tiuri and Piak were introduced to Arturin's wife and to their young son, who shared his father's name. Sir Bendu did not say another word. He was generally taciturn and never particularly jovial, but now he really seemed to be brooding over something. Perhaps that was why Tiuri found the atmosphere in the room so gloomy. Piak was also sitting too far away. As a knight, Tiuri had been seated close to the lord of the castle, while his friend was with the other squires and servants. Tiuri wasn't pleased about the seating arrangements, but it was a custom that knights rarely abandoned.

Towards the end of the meal, Bendu seemed to muster his energies. He started talking about the Wild Wood again and wondered why they had heard nothing from his nephew Arwaut.

"I think he must have gone with Ristridin," said Arturin. He said he had received just one letter from his brother, dated on the eleventh day of the wine month, October, of the previous year. The message had been brief ("Ristridin has never been much of a writer," Arturin explained). Ristridin had written to tell him that the knights had found a robbers' hideout somewhere between the Green River and the Black River. "They were living in some old ruins," Arturin told them. "Ristridin and his men fought them and overpowered them. Then the robbers were sent as prisoners to King Dagonaut, along with a message that Ristridin, Arwaut and their companions were all fine. The letter to me was a copy of that dispatch. It also said the knights were planning to head deeper into the forest, to the west, to look for the Men in Green."

"The Men in Green?" asked Tiuri. "Who are they?"

"The Men in Green," replied Bendu, "live between the Green River and the Green Hills. That's what the woodcutters and hunters say, and I once heard it from a monk, too. Some people say they're very tall and beautiful, while others claim they're squat little monsters, like gnomes. That's why I don't believe they exist. As far as I know, a person is either big or small, not both at the same time."

"Perhaps they're not people," said Arturin. "Who knows what might be living out there in those wildernesses where no godly man has ever set foot?"

27

Bendu looked sceptical. "Whatever the case, there is no way Ristridin met them," he said. "Otherwise he would certainly have let us know! In fact, nothing of any import could have happened... as is evident from the fact that we have received no word from him."

He looked at Arturin as if waiting for him to agree.

However, the lord of the castle remained silent and frowned down at his plate. "Well," he said finally, "there is nothing we can do but wait for him to return, as he promised he would."

"Let us hope he does not take too long about it," muttered Bendu.

Tiuri looked at Arturin, then Bendu, and thought: *Yes, let's hope he gets here soon. The mood is not going to improve until Sir Ristridin comes home.*

3   KNIGHTS OF KING UNAUWEN

A few more days went by, but still Ristridin did not return.

Sir Arturin did his best to make the wait as pleasant as possible for his guests, taking them out for rides and keeping them occupied with games and conversation. But no matter how cheerful he pretended to be, the mood of anxious anticipation persisted.

One afternoon, it seemed as if winter had come again. There was rain and hail, and the wind howled around the castle. In the great hall, though, the fire blazed merrily in the hearth. The lady of the castle and her maids sat spinning at one side of the fireplace. Piak stood in front of the fire, playing with Arturin's son and a couple of dogs. Tiuri and Sir Arturin were seated on the other side of the fireplace with a chessboard between them. Bendu, though, could not settle. He kept pacing up and down, then stopping by the spinning wheels to talk, or looking at the chess game, or crouching down beside the dogs.

Then the sound of a horn made them all look up.

"Visitors!" said Sir Arturin, as he moved one of his bishops.

"I'll go and see who it is," said Bendu, and he strode from the room.

Sir Ristridin? thought Tiuri, looking down at the chessboard without noticing that he could take Arturin's bishop.

None of them could concentrate on what they had been doing. Apologizing, Arturin stood up and followed Bendu. His wife told her maids to make sure the guest rooms were ready.

"Shall we go and take a look?" said Piak, jumping to his feet.

"Me too! Me too!" said little Arturin.

With the boy between them, the two friends headed into the corridor outside the great hall. The large arched windows had a good view over the courtyard. They stood together, looking out, and Piak lifted young Arturin onto his shoulders.

"I can see them!" the boy cried.

Yes, there they came. It was a whole procession, men on horseback... knights. The rain made everything a little hazy, but the knights' shields were clear enough. White shields!

"King Unauwen's knights!" cried Piak. "I can see two of them. And soldiers, too."

Servants hurried to help the guests dismount and to take care of their horses.

"There's Father!" called the little boy. "And Sir Bendu. Are the knights coming to see us?"

"Yes, I think they must be," said Piak, lowering Arturin back down to the ground. "They'll be here any moment."

Just minutes later, the two knights entered the great hall, accompanied by their squires and Arturin and Bendu. The younger of the two knights gave Tiuri a friendly nod.

It was Evan!

Sir Arturin introduced the guests. "Sir Evan," he said, "and Sir Idian."

29

Tiuri did not know Sir Idian, and he was rather puzzled that this knight had kept his helmet on so that his face could not be seen. He was tall, however, and had a proud bearing. There was something captivating about his voice, too, even though he spoke no more than a greeting.

"This is Marvin, Evan's squire," Arturin continued, "and this is..."

"Currently the squire of Sir Idian," the man said, interrupting Arturin. "But usually... court jester to King Unauwen." He threw back the hood of his travelling cloak, spraying droplets of water all around, and gave an elegant bow.

"Tirillo!" exclaimed Tiuri.

"Tirillo!" cried Piak.

"Indeed. Tirillo arrives as a traveller in the rain," said the merry jester.

"And as a victor in the battle," said Evan.

"So there really has been a battle?" asked Arturin.

"We fought at the Southerly Mountains," replied Sir Idian.

"And defeated the armies of Eviellan," added Evan.

"We only held them off," the jester corrected him. "Now they're resting and licking their wounds. Soon they'll be on the march again. If you stand on top of the mountains and look into Eviellan, you'll see nothing but soldiers and army camps. This was merely a skirmish, my dear Evan."

"What sombre words," said Arturin. "I thought jesters were meant to make people happy."

"Jesters merely confront people with the truth," said Tirillo, "and usually it sounds so improbable that they can't help but laugh. We try to remain in good spirits in spite of threats from sinister quarters, rather than closing our eyes to danger."

"Have you been guarding your borders closely?" asked Sir Idian.

"As always," replied Arturin. "Although recently there has been no sign of Eviellan."

"That proves what fools they are in Eviellan," said Tirillo. "There are no mountains here. They have only to cross a river. No, they cannot possibly be so stupid. And for that reason I believe the opposite must be true: the enemy in the south is crafty and cunning. Be wary, Sir Arturin, Lord of Castle Ristridin by the Grey River!"

"My thanks for your wise counsel," said Arturin, a little abruptly. Then he asked his guests if they would like to put on dry clothes. They were keen to do so, and the party left the room, accompanied by Arturin and his wife.

But Evan looked back for a moment at Tiuri and said, "I'm glad you're here. Later we will have much to tell each other."

The candles had been lit in the great hall. Only Tiuri, Piak and Bendu were sitting there now, waiting for the others to arrive.

"So now Evan's here," said Bendu. "And I hope Ristridin and Arwaut will come soon. Then we'll all be together again."

Tiuri sat beside the chessboard, staring blankly at the pieces. "Sir Evan made it in good time," he said. "Do you know Sir Idian?"

"No, I've never met him before," replied Bendu. "I don't recognize his name either. But he must be a powerful lord; you should have seen how respectfully his men addressed him. The jester is a friend of yours, isn't he?"

"Yes, I met him last year in the Kingdom of Unauwen," said Tiuri.

"He's really nice," said Piak.

"Nice? Then I am not a good jester," said Tirillo, as he entered the room, followed by Sir Arturin. "Jesters should be nuisances. We are supposed to taunt and provoke people."

He sat down opposite Tiuri and asked, "Whose move is it?"

"Mine," replied Tiuri. "Yes, it's white's turn."

"Then play!" commanded Tirillo.

Tiuri took the black bishop, and said, "Now it's Sir Arturin's move." He leant back comfortably, planning to ask the jester all kinds of questions. But the jester put one finger to his pointed nose and stared down at the chessboard.

"Please, go ahead and make my move for me," said Arturin.

"My thanks," said the jester, moving a piece. "And now it's your move again, Tiuri."

Tiuri wasn't really in the mood for playing chess. "How are affairs in the Kingdom of Unauwen?" he asked.

"Much the same as you see here," replied Tirillo. "White against black; the knights of Unauwen against Eviellan. Bishops confer, knights gallop, castles are besieged. Good and evil attempt to checkmate each other." He looked at the chessboard with a smile. "It's been a long time since I last played," he said. "These black and white squares bring back all sorts of memories for me."

Tiuri soon realized, however, that the jester had not forgotten how to play. In just a few moves, Tirillo had taken three white pieces and said, "Your mind's not on the game, Sir Tiuri!"

Tiuri had to admit he was right. He would far rather have been talking to the jester and asking him questions.

"The conversation can come later," said the jester. "It will happen naturally, when we're all sitting together. Now please be so kind as to concentrate on our game."

So they went on playing.

The lady of the castle entered the room, with Evan and Sir Idian. Evan came over to talk to Bendu and Piak, while Sir Idian stood and watched the game of chess.

"You can check him in three moves, Tirillo," he said, "unless Sir Tiuri has thought of the only way to save his king. Then maybe he could even put yours in danger."

Tiuri tried to work out what that move might be.

"Why don't you play for him, Sir Idian?" suggested Tirillo. "You have not sat across a chessboard from me for many years."

Tiuri looked up at the knight, who had now removed his helmet. His hair gleamed like gold in the candlelight, and his face was young and friendly.

"I'm afraid I will not be playing chess for now," he said.

Tiuri stood up and said, "Then, please, help me. Take my turn for me."

Sir Idian smiled. He sat down and made a jump with the last white knight. Then he explained his move to Tiuri.

Tiuri listened and watched Idian's hands as he spoke. On one of his fingers, a beautiful ring glinted. Tiuri had seen other rings like it before. There were only twelve of them in the whole world and King Unauwen had given them to his most loyal paladins. Tiuri had never heard of Idian before, but he must be a knight of great renown.

A quarter of an hour later, the chessboard had been forgotten. Sir Arturin's guests were busy telling one another their news. Evan was the only one who planned to remain at the castle until Ristridin returned. The others had merely accompanied him for some of the journey. Sir Idian meant to return soon to the Kingdom of Unauwen, while Tirillo was travelling to the north to talk to King Dagonaut as an envoy from the kingdom in the west.

"An envoy?" said Bendu, his expression suggesting that he thought it strange for a jester to be chosen for such a task.

Tiuri was about to speak up on his friend's behalf, but Tirillo silenced him with a wink.

"In these times of danger, it is wise to strengthen the bonds of friendship between our two lands," said Sir Idian. "We have a dangerous enemy in the south."

"Eviellan is your enemy. I have seen little good about that land," said Sir Arturin, "but we in the Kingdom of Dagonaut are not at war."

"Do you feel safe?" asked Tirillo.

"We never let up the watch at our borders," replied Arturin. "But I must say we have had no difficulties with the south since the present king has been in power. And the feud between him and your king is nothing to do with us in Dagonaut."

"I disagree!" said Tiuri indignantly. He felt so closely connected to the kingdom in the west. Did he not carry a white shield, given to him by King Unauwen?

"And so do I!" agreed Bendu. "The King of Eviellan is a villain, as everyone knows."

Sir Idian's expression shifted, as if a shadow flitted across it.

"He is as much a villain as his knights with red shields," Bendu added.

"There is only one knight with a red shield whom you regard as your enemy," Arturin said to him, "and that is because he murdered Edwinem – heaven rest his soul. Edwinem was a subject of King Unauwen and therefore an enemy of Eviellan, but you have chosen to avenge him because he was your friend. You have said so yourself."

"That is true," growled Bendu. "But," he continued, "is it possible to trust a country that is inhabited by such knights and ruled by such a treacherous man?"

"I do not trust Eviellan either," said Arturin. "But there is peace between that land and our own, and I hope it will remain so."

If only Sir Ristridin were here, thought Tiuri. *He sympathizes with those beyond our borders.* Ristridin's homeland was the Kingdom of Dagonaut, to the east of the Great Mountains – but the world was larger than that. No one who had travelled to the Kingdom of Unauwen, on the other side of the mountains, would ever forget that land. And Eviellan should never be forgotten either, but for entirely different reasons.

Tiuri looked at Sir Idian and his companions, in the hope that they would say more. But they remained silent.

4 TWO KNIGHTS FROM THE SOUTH

Ristridin did not appear the following day either. Bendu grumbled, "I do not understand where he could be. If he has left the Wild Wood, he has no reason whatsoever not to keep to our agreement. I think I shall go to Islan. Perhaps someone there can tell me where he went."

"I haven't been here that long myself," said Evan. "Who knows how soon the sound of horns might announce the arrival of our friends?"

"Well, I certainly hope they come quickly!" said Bendu.

"As do I," said Sir Idian. "I should like to meet Sir Ristridin, but I cannot remain here for long."

It was evening again, and Sir Arturin and his guests were sitting together in the great hall. Tiuri and Sir Idian were playing a game of chess, at Idian's request. That gave Tiuri a chance to study him. He was intrigued by the knight. The man had said little, but his presence could always be felt – it was in the way he paid attention when he listened, the occasional calm remark he made, the expression on his face. He was not as young as Tiuri had initially thought; fine lines around his eyes suggested he had lived longer, and those years had perhaps been difficult ones. His eyes were dark and appeared dreamy and distant at first. However, when they looked at a person, they proved to be very penetrating, and Tiuri felt that Idian knew far more about him than the other way around. He wondered why he was so curious about this knight. *I know nothing about him at all!* he thought. *He hasn't spoken a word about himself. But perhaps that's why...*

He had noted that Idian was clearly the leader of the visitors from the west. His authority seemed perfectly natural, and not just because he was the oldest of the three and wore King Unauwen's ring on his finger. However, Evan and Tirillo had told Tiuri nothing about their companion. In fact, when Tiuri thought about it, he realized that they'd avoided every question about him. There was definitely something mysterious about this Sir Idian.

Tiuri was roused from his thoughts as Sir Idian looked right at him and said, "I am only one of King Unauwen's many paladins."

Tiuri did not know how to respond, but the other knight turned his gaze to the chessboard and quietly added, "How pleasant it is to be in a peaceful castle and to play a friendly game of chess. And yet – though this may sound strange – it somehow feels as if I am doing more here than just playing chess."

Tiuri still said nothing, but no answer seemed to be expected.

Tirillo came over to them and spoke in a whisper, "Now time seems to stand still and..."

His words were interrupted by the sound of horns.

"Ah, it would seem I am mistaken," said the jester. "Time is knocking at the very gates of this castle! Guests, events, travellers in the darkness!"

"Ristridin and Arwaut? Could it be them? At last?" said Bendu.

However, the gatekeepers brought other news. "Two knights from the south have crossed the river," they reported to the lord of the castle. "They have requested shelter."

"Knights from the south?" repeated Arturin.

"From Eviellan?" asked Bendu. "Are they carrying red shields?"

"Yes, my lord," came the reply.

"Then we shall not let them in!" cried Bendu. "Knights with red shields! How dare they? Tell them I shall come outside and measure my strength against theirs!"

Sir Arturin placed his hand on Bendu's arm. "You must remain calm," he said. "They are asking for shelter and, as Lord of Castle Ristridin, I cannot refuse."

"Have you forgotten that Edwinem, too, was once your guest?" shouted Bendu. "He was murdered by a knight such as those."

"And which knight was that?" said Arturin. "You have no more idea than I. And the laws of hospitality should be sacred to you, too, Sir Bendu."

"Do not forget that you already have guests!" cried Bendu. "And those guests are knights with white shields, the mortal enemies of those men at the gate!"

Arturin had no response to that. He looked anxiously at his other guests, who had listened to all of this in silence.

Tirillo walked over to join the knights and asked, "What is the problem?"

"I'm sure you must have heard," said Bendu. "Two knights from Eviellan want to enter the castle."

"Which lord may close the gates of his castle to those who request hospitality?" said the jester.

"Yes, but..." began Arturin.

"But *you* are already here," Bendu added, looking at Sir Idian.

"And what of it?" Sir Idian replied calmly. "This is neutral territory, is it not? In this castle, enemies may meet in peace. Let them enter!" He smiled at Bendu and said, "Your challenge can wait until they have left the castle."

"So you do not mind?" asked Arturin.

"Whether my lord minds or not is of no import," the jester replied on Idian's behalf. "He says, 'Let them in.' To which I would add, 'Do not leave them waiting out there in the cold.'"

Sir Arturin and the guards left the room and headed to the gate.

"There's going to be trouble!" said Piak.

"Oh no, we shall all remain perfectly calm," said Tirillo. "As for me, I have to say that I enjoy coming face to face with my enemies. I find that they're so very different from me! They have arms, legs, eyes and a mouth..."

"And a heart," added Idian.

Bendu looked unhappily at Tirillo, then Idian. Sir Idian stood up and paced the room, as if considering his course of action.

"My lord," Tirillo said to him, "do you wish us to withdraw, or should Evan and I converse with the new guests?"

"Stay here, in this room," replied the knight, "and wait to see what happens." But Sir Idian himself slowly walked away, stopping at the door to look back. "I shall remain nearby," he said, and then he left the hall.

Piak leant over to Tiuri and whispered, "Are you as keen as I am to find out more about Sir Idian?"

So his friend felt the same way! Tiuri had no time to answer, though, as Sir Arturin returned, followed by two knights in black armour with red shields.

"Allow me to introduce you," he said. "Sir Melas of Darokítam and Sir Kraton of Indigo."

After the servants had helped the newly arrived knights out of their armour, silence fell as the men glared at each other.

Tirillo was the first to speak.

"I know you, Sir Kraton," he said, "from a long time ago, when you were still Lord of Indigo."

"I still consider myself Lord of Indigo," said Sir Kraton gruffly. He was a large man with a sombre face.

"Indigo no longer exists," said Evan.

"The Castle of Indigo on the White River is a ruin," said Sir Kraton. "Your soldiers destroyed it."

"Because you rose up against your king, Unauwen," said Evan.

"Because I remained loyal to my lord, the King of Eviellan!"

"You were born in the Kingdom of Unauwen, not in Eviellan," said Tirillo. "You once carried a white shield, if I am not mistaken. Are you so eager to bear different colours?"

"I have chosen red," Sir Kraton answered abruptly, "and that is enough for me. I have no need for the entire rainbow, like some... jester." He turned to Melas and said something to him in a strange language. "My friend knows only a little of your tongue," he said. "It is perhaps just as well that he did not understand the words of Tirillo, the king's fool."

"The king's paladin!" Evan exclaimed.

"One does not need to carry a sword and a shield to be a knight," Tiuri added.

Sir Kraton looked at Tiuri and Evan. "Tell me, who are these young boys?" he asked. "Surely they are not knights?"

"Sir Evan from the west, and Tiuri, knight of Dagonaut," said Arturin, who now also sounded annoyed.

"I have never heard of Evan," said Kraton, "but Tiuri..." He cast a hostile glance at him.

Tiuri knew the knights of Eviellan must see him as an enemy, even though he was a citizen of a neutral land – or at least they would if they knew about the vitally important letter he had once carried to King Unauwen.

Sir Bendu eyed Kraton with suspicion, as Arturin glanced uneasily from one knight to the other. Then he called a servant to bring wine in honour of the new guests, in an attempt to improve the atmosphere.

The wine was brought and poured, but the men all watched one another closely over the rims of their goblets. The knights from Eviellan said nothing, while Arturin made light-hearted remarks in a futile attempt to lift the hostile mood.

"Let's talk about the weather!" Tirillo finally cried. "Sun and rain treat us all equally. Even in Eviellan there is a full moon every month."

"Pah! Only a moonstruck fool would suggest such a topic of conversation," Sir Kraton sneered. "I have other matters on my mind than the moon, full or not. Wind and weather cannot sway me."

"And yet you are such a poor weathercock," said Tirillo. "First facing west, then spinning to the south."

"I once had a golden weathercock on the tallest tower of Castle Indigo," said Kraton. "Whatever became of it? One day, though, that tower, and my ruined castle, will be rebuilt. That is what I dream of every night, moon or no moon."

"Do you ever dream about Castle Forèstèrra?" asked Tirillo. "Or Ingewel? The knights who lived in those castles were slain by you and your kind."

"The fool's words grow ever wiser!" mocked Kraton. "How can a war be fought without deaths?" He said something else to his silent companion. Sir Melas laughed and drank down his wine. Kraton did the same and had his glass refilled. Then he turned to Bendu and Arturin.

"I do not know what stories the gentlemen from the Kingdom of Unauwen might have told you," he said. "I'm sure they will have informed you that my master, the King of Eviellan, is wicked and evil. And that his opponent, the crown prince, the son of Unauwen, is noble and good. That is what they have said, is it not? But did they tell you that the King of Eviellan is also a son of King Unauwen and that the princes are twin brothers? Why should one become crown prince and have everything? Why should the other receive nothing, merely because he was born a little later?"

"You have it all wrong!" interjected Evan. "The hostility did not begin with the crown prince. His brother has always been jealous of him."

"There can be only one successor to the throne," said Tirillo.

"Your ruler started the war," said Evan. "He was given every chance, but he would not obey his father and he threatened the life of the crown prince. His own brother!"

"Gentlemen," said Arturin, almost pleading with them, "please behave as guests in this peaceful place. Come to a truce, in both words and deeds!"

"I would like nothing more," said Kraton, holding out his glass for more wine. "Sir Melas and I are here for reasons of peace. We travel as envoys from our king to pay a visit to King Dagonaut."

"You too?" said Bendu.

"Then we can travel together," said Tirillo with a smile. "My destination is the same."

"Does King Dagonaut need cheering up?" Kraton said sarcastically. "No matter. You are welcome as a travelling companion. We intend to propose that King Dagonaut should form an alliance with Eviellan."

Tirillo laughed. "And I am to ask King Dagonaut to form an alliance with Unauwen," he said. "It should be interesting if we go to see him together!"

Sir Kraton did not deign to reply. He drank his third glass, filled it again, and said to Bendu, "I do not wish you to delay me when I leave. I swear to you on my honour as a knight that I did not kill Edwinem of Forèstèrra. So it would be foolish of you to start your duelling again."

"Allow me to be the judge of that," said Bendu coldly.

"Where is your friend? What's his name again? Sir Ristridin of the South?" Kraton continued. "I should have liked to meet him."

"He went to the Wild Wood," replied Bendu.

"The Wild Wood?" repeated Kraton.

"Yes, but he is elsewhere now," said Arturin. "He is heading here. We expect him soon."

"What on earth was Sir Ristridin doing in the Wild Wood?" asked Kraton.

"A man needs to know his own country," said Tirillo.

"Ristridin found nothing of interest in the Wild Wood," said Arturin. "He left the forest in the winter."

"Oh, now I understand," said Kraton. "I heard rumours that he was roaming around Deltaland."

"Deltaland?" cried Bendu. "But where? And when?"

"I know nothing about that," replied Kraton. "I heard only rumours. And I can't remember who told me. It may not be true."

"Deltaland is not so far," said Arturin.

41

They talked about Deltaland for a while before the conversation petered out.

I hope they leave soon, thought Tiuri. He was watching Tirillo, the only one who might cheer up the company if he chose to. But the jester was arranging the pieces on the chessboard and appeared to be paying no attention to anything else. Bendu stood up and started pacing once again. Sir Kraton poured himself another glass of wine. He had already had quite a few and it seemed that he was planning to keep on going.

He soon became talkative again, making caustic remarks at the expense of Evan and Tirillo. They did not respond, which of course provoked Kraton all the more. Finally he cried out, "What has become of King Unauwen's famous paladins? A timid little boy and a court jester, that is all I see! You did say they were knights, did you not, my host?"

"As indeed they are," replied Arturin, "and I would ask you to..."

Kraton interrupted him. "There was another knight, a knight with a white shield!" he shouted. "I don't mean Tiuri – he's one of King Dagonaut's men. But there is a third knight from the west here in this castle. You mentioned his name, Sir Arturin, when you so kindly allowed me in. Where is that knight?"

"I do not know," said Arturin.

"We have come here with open visors!" cried Kraton. "At least Evan and Tirillo have come to meet us. Why has the other knight not done the same? Could he be hiding?" He stood up and looked around as if issuing a challenge.

Sir Melas tapped him on the elbow and muttered something, but Kraton paid no attention to him. Bendu pursed his lips and looked as if he were struggling not to attack Kraton. Arturin seemed angry. Evan and Tirillo were silent.

"Could he be hiding?" repeated Kraton.

Tirillo looked up from the chessboard. For the first time, he appeared a little concerned.

"And what business is that of yours?" said Evan haughtily.

"None whatsoever, my friend," answered Kraton. "I merely wish to shake his hand. That's if he dares to come out here! Who is he? What is his name?"

The room fell silent for a moment. Then Tirillo said, quietly, but clearly, "Sir Idian."

Kraton frowned and rubbed his forehead as if he were trying to remember something. But then he shouted out loud, "Well, I challenge this Sir Idian to appear, so that my friend and I may greet him!"

He lifted up his empty glass and smashed it to the floor.

"Sir Kraton!" Arturin exclaimed angrily.

"Sir Idian!" Kraton shouted again.

Tirillo also stood up, crossed his arms, and looked at Kraton, then at the door. It swung open and Sir Idian appeared in the doorway. He seemed very large as he paused there before slowly entering the room. His arrival had a dramatic impact on the knights of Eviellan.

Sir Kraton grasped the edge of the table and his face froze. Sir Melas jumped to his feet so quickly that his chair fell over, and for a moment it seemed as if he were about to kneel. Kraton grabbed hold of him and hissed, "No, no, stop!"

Sir Idian halted in front of them. His expression was serious, almost severe.

"Make no mistake," he said. "I am not the man you take me for. They say we are very similar, my brother – the King of Eviellan – and I."

"The crown prince!" whispered Kraton.

5   PRINCE OF THE WEST

Now Tirillo spoke: "Sir Idian, or rather Prince Iridian, eldest son of King Unauwen, crown prince, Lord of the Seven Castles, vice-regent of the kingdom in the west."

They all stared at the prince. Yes indeed, he looked like a mighty lord!

"I shall never mistake you for your brother," said Sir Kraton, slowly and almost with difficulty. "My apologies. Now that I know who you are, I understand why you preferred not to show yourself."

The prince shook his head. "Perhaps it would have been better if I had stepped forward immediately, Sir Kraton," he said. "But what could I have said? You already know what I think of you. You will never mistake me for my... for the King of Eviellan. But I was your rightful lord in the Province of the Rushing Rivers and your king is my father, Unauwen."

"I have chosen the King of Eviellan as my master," said Kraton in a challenging tone, but he could not look Idian in the eye.

"You have made the wrong choice, Sir Kraton," the prince said with a quiet sigh.

"That may well be, my lord," replied Kraton, "but it is my choice and I shall stick with it."

"So be it," said the prince. "Just one more thing, Sir Kraton and Sir Melas. You will inform your king of our meeting. Tell him I will never be able to forget that he is my brother, but that I will resist him with all of my strength! He has no claim to our father's throne and he is fighting his war for hate and vengeance alone."

"Has he then no reason to hate and to wish revenge?" said Kraton.

"No," said the prince sternly. Then he continued, "And yet it pains me when I think how all the evil that he does weighs most heavily upon him. He has such a burden to bear! Even now I would still like to make peace with him, but for the sake of my father's subjects I must fight him, unless, of course, he changes. Tell him that as well."

"And if he were to change, would he be welcomed back into your father's kingdom?" asked Kraton.

"Yes," replied Idian. "But he may not enter Unauwen as a prince, nor as the King of Eviellan."

"How, then?" shouted Kraton. "As a beggar perhaps? A penitent? That is something he will never do!" He took a step back and grudgingly bowed. "I shall convey your words to my king, Your Highness," he said, "although I do not think he will listen." He beckoned to Melas, who also bowed, and the two men left the room.

"Your Highness," began Arturin.

"Allow me to be Sir Idian while I am here," said the prince. He sat down, and those who looked at him did not dare to speak, as his face was so desperately sad.

But after a short while, Tirillo softly asked, "What now, my lord?"

Sir Idian awoke from his reverie. "It is probably good that I have spoken to this knight," he said. "And to answer your question, Tirillo, our paths will soon part. I am returning to our homeland. I now know what I wanted to know."

"It also seems best to me that you should return," said the jester. "And as soon as possible, my lord! I do not trust those knights with the red shields." Bendu nodded vigorously. "Now that they know who you are," continued Tirillo, "they may send a message to their compatriots to pursue you and attack you."

"Have no fear for my safety," said Sir Idian.

"But I am afraid for your safety," said Tirillo. "You are the hope of our kingdom, the successor to King Unauwen."

"What would become of us if something were to happen to you?" said Evan.

"I have a son..." began Sir Idian.

"Your son is still a child," said the jester. "Truly, my lord, you must leave without these knights noticing. One of us will keep them talking until you have slipped away from the castle."

"Fine," said Sir Idian with a smile. "Then you must be the one who keeps them talking, Tirillo. That's certainly a job you can be trusted with."

"I am at your service, my lord," said the jester.

Idian rose to his feet. "Hear now my commands," he said, prince once again instead of knight. "You, Tirillo, will travel to the City of Dagonaut tomorrow to argue for an alliance with the king of this land."

Tirillo bowed.

"Farewell, then," said the prince. "Until we meet again."

They shook hands. Then Tirillo turned around and quickly walked away.

"And you, Evan, will remain here until Sir Ristridin returns," the prince continued. "I wish to hear what he has to say, and you shall bring me news. However, you may not stay away for too long. I expect you back in my city in a month's time."

"I will obey, my lord," said the young knight.

Then Prince Iridian turned to Tiuri and Piak.

"You are not subjects of my father," he said, "and yet you are connected to our land with an unbreakable bond. You once did us a great service and Sir Tiuri even carries a white shield. Remain loyal to King Dagonaut, but do not forget Unauwen. Be on your guard against Eviellan and do as your conscience tells you."

The two friends bowed. Tiuri said only, "Thank you, my lord," and Piak found himself unable to speak. But his eyes said the same as his friend's: *I shall never forget Unauwen or Prince Iridian!*

"Sir Bendu," the prince said now, "you will surely wait here for your friend Ristridin, and what you do after that you cannot yet know. You are seeking a knight with a red shield, but whether you find him or not, I know you will always fight against evil. Should Ristridin not return, you must look for him rather than your enemy, as Ristridin is your friend and his mission may have taken him to strange places."

Finally, he turned to Sir Arturin. "I thank you for your hospitality," he said. "If I might give you a task, it would be one you have performed faithfully for many years: guard your borders. Perhaps you will not agree with me when I say this, but it is possible that

46

you may ultimately have to pick sides, that you will have to become involved in the fight, whether you want to or not."

Arturin also bowed. "I hope it does not come to that, Your Highness," he replied. "But if it should be so, I will fight on the side of right and good."

Then the prince took his leave of them and, in the company of Arturin, he went to say farewell to the lady of the castle and to prepare for a swift departure.

"It's such a shame he has to go!" said Piak. "Now we finally know who he is, and I would have liked to get to know him better."

"Hush!" said Tiuri. "Sir Kraton and Sir Melas mustn't notice anything."

"That jester will make sure they don't," said Bendu. "But you're right. Prince Iridian is a most interesting man. What do you think of his words about Ristridin? Does that rude oaf Kraton know more than he's saying? Ristridin was in Deltaland, he said, but he claimed not to know where, when, why or under what circumstances. I intend to tackle that gentleman! I will not allow him to continue his journey until I have had a word with him." But the expression on his face said it was more than just a word that he wanted.

6   TO ISLAN

Prince Iridian and his company left that same evening, without the knights from Eviellan realizing.

The next morning began with an exchange of words between Bendu and Sir Kraton. Having heard that the prince had left, Kraton seemed most upset. "Was he scared we would betray him?" he asked. "But we are men of honour and on neutral ground!"

"Prince Iridian is a knight," said Bendu. "He is scared of nothing. He is also a wise man, and so he has learnt that he must beware of treachery, particularly when Eviellan is near. Of course, you know how Sir Edwinem came to be killed."

"Will you stop bringing that up?!" cried Kraton.

"Fine," replied Bendu. "I shall not mention it again until we are at the gate, at the moment you leave."

"I do not accept your challenge," said Kraton firmly. "I have already sworn to you on my honour as a knight that I had nothing to do with the death of Edwinem of Forèstèrra. So you would lose your honour if you were to attack me. I am an envoy and a negotiator and as such I am protected."

Arturin spoke up now. "Bendu," he said. "Sir Kraton is right. As long as he is travelling through our land as an envoy, you may not put any obstacle in his way."

"Ha! That's a fine shield to hide behind," said Bendu with a sneer.

"When I return, I would be pleased to oblige you," said Kraton. "I am no coward." And he didn't look like one either.

"Perhaps, Bendu," said Arturin, "you would do better to abandon the idea of duels for now and to act upon your other plan. You were intending to go to Islan."

Sir Kraton frowned as he looked at Bendu, then Arturin, before turning to Melas, who was standing beside him. They briefly spoke to each other in the incomprehensible language of Eviellan. As they talked, Bendu's expression grew darker and darker.

Kraton saw the look on Bendu's face and said, "As far as my companion is concerned, Sir Bendu, there are witnesses who can swear that at the moment of Edwinem's death he was at Darokítam, his castle on the other side of the Grey River."

Melas added something, loudly and angrily.

"He says," translated Kraton, "that he has no wish to remain in this land any longer. He intends to return to Darokítam immediately. And he would like to show you his shield, Sir Bendu, with the deep dent you knocked into it. It happened in Eviellan, during one of your many fights with knights who had the misfortune to carry a red shield."

Bendu turned red and Arturin brushed his hand over his mouth as if trying to hide a smile.

"Then I have nothing more to say to you," said Bendu brusquely. "But wait, there is one more thing I should like to ask, Sir Kraton, if I may."

"Go ahead," said Kraton.

"You said yesterday that Sir Ristridin is in Deltaland. Could you tell me anything more about that?"

"I have already told you I know nothing about it," replied Kraton. "It was a rumour, but there are so many rumours. I can no longer remember who told me."

"And Sir Melas," asked Bendu, "does he know anything about it? Darokitam is close to Deltaland, and almost all of Deltaland belongs to Eviellan."

Kraton corrected Bendu. "We have not conquered any part of Deltaland," he said. "We have only entered into an eternal alliance with them." Then he turned to ask Melas the question.

But Melas shook his head.

"Fine. Well, that's all, then," Bendu said grimly. "Travel in peace. I shall say 'until we meet again', rather than 'farewell'."

That was the last thing Bendu said to the knights from Eviellan before they left. Sir Melas did indeed head back to the south, but Kraton rode to the City of Dagonaut. He did not travel alone; Tirillo accompanied him to the same destination. It is unlikely that the knight and the jester found each other pleasant travelling companions.

The farewell to Tirillo had been altogether friendlier. The jester had been unable to promise to visit on his return journey, because he would reach his king's city much sooner by the First Great Road to the north. "But I shall also say 'until we meet again'," he said, "and I shall add 'farewell'."

He had a little more to say to Evan: "My dear boy, please do not look so worried. Go with Sir Bendu to Islan, or wait here for your friends."

"I know there is nothing else I can do," replied Evan, "but still I am uneasy about the prince. If he had not instructed me to wait for Ristridin, I would travel after him."

"The Third Great Road is completely safe at the moment," said Tirillo, "and our Sir Idian can take good care of himself."

Then Arturin made a suggestion. "I could send some of my men after him," he said, "with orders not to turn back until they are sure no further danger can threaten him."

This proposal was gratefully accepted, and Evan's squire, Marvin, went along with Arturin's men.

After Tirillo's departure, Evan was the only remaining guest from the Kingdom of Unauwen.

The next day, Bendu decided to go to Islan and he asked Tiuri, Piak and Evan if they wanted to accompany him. "I plan to stay there for two or three days," he said, "so we will be back within the week. If Ristridin and Arwaut return in that time, well, then they can just wait for us!"

The three of them were very much in favour of travelling with Bendu, and Arturin agreed with their plan.

"It's a shame I have to stay at home," he said. "I should like to speak to the Lord of Islan, because I have not seen him for a long time. But I do not like to leave my castle, and Sir Fitil also travels rarely."

Tiuri asked, "Is Sir Fitil the Lord of Islan?"

"Yes, he is," replied Arturin. "His name was once widely known, but for years now he has lived, almost forgotten, in his castle on the plain between the forests." He turned to Bendu. "If anything out of the ordinary happens here, I'll have word sent to you. And you must let me know if you intend to stay away for longer."

"We shall return within the week," said Bendu. "And we shall depart soon. So we should reach the edge of the forest by this evening and be in Islan by tomorrow afternoon."

Half an hour later, four riders left for the north: Bendu, Tiuri, Piak and Evan.

"This reminds me of last year," said Evan. "Then, too, we flew along the roads and Bendu chose to take the lead, just as he is now."

"But then Ristridin and Arwaut were with you," said Tiuri, "instead of Piak and me."

"And we were clad in the grey armour of mourning," Evan continued. "Perhaps Ristridin and Arwaut have had other, stranger adventures since then."

"And perhaps we are riding towards an adventure of our own!" cried Piak.

"You are in for a disappointment," said Bendu, reining in his horse. "You don't know Islan. It's a place fit for a hermit, so lonely and isolated. There won't be anything of interest happening there."

PART TWO

—

THE DAUGHTER OF ISLAN

1   RED QUIBO'S TALE

As evening fell, the four travellers found shelter at the small inn in the woodcutters' village at the edge of the forest.

"We'll be early to bed," said Bendu after dinner. "We have to be on our way before dawn."

"You'll have another quick glass of wine before you head upstairs, won't you?" said the innkeeper as he started to clear the table. "There are plenty of people in this evening, all from the village. They've come to see you. We don't often have knights like you staying here."

Tiuri, Evan and Piak looked at the other guests, who were sitting together at a long table and watching them curiously.

"I don't feel like going to bed yet," said Piak.

"Me neither," said Tiuri and Evan at the same time.

"Ah, you young people! You have no sense!" said Bendu. "But I don't mind staying here for a little longer. Let's go and sit with the others. Perhaps we might hear some news."

Everyone at the long table was pleased to welcome them, and soon the conversation was in full flow. Bendu explained that he and Sir Arturin were waiting for Ristridin and his companions to return. However, none of the villagers had heard any news about the knight-errant. When they found out that he'd gone to the Wild Wood, they shook their heads.

"Why would anyone want to do that?" one of them said.

"That forest is enchanted," said another. "I wouldn't dare to cut down any of its trees."

"Ah, you fool!" said the innkeeper. "Sir Ristridin is a knight. A man like him is scared of nothing! He has had more adventures than you could imagine. And I'm sure these knights here also have a tale or two to tell. Isn't that right, Sir Bendu?"

Bendu muttered into his beard.

"How boring life would be without knights," the innkeeper went on pensively. "Whatever would we have to tell each other stories about?"

"I know other folk who can spin a good yarn," said one of the villagers. "Like Red Quibo, for instance. Hey, where is Red Quibo?"

"Oh, he'll be here soon enough," said someone else, with a laugh. "There's no way he'll go to bed without his little nightcap."

"Red Quibo's been into the Wild Wood," said the innkeeper.

"And what does Red Quibo have to say about it?" asked Piak.

The door opened and a hoarse voice called out loudly: "Who is taking my fine and florid name in vain?"

A scrawny young man entered the room. He was dirty and unkempt, and his fiery red hair stood up in spikes. With large, clumsy steps, he walked over to the table and sat down opposite Piak.

"That was me," said Piak. "I've heard you have a good story to tell."

"Story? Story?!" cried Red Quibo. "It's no story! What I have to tell is the truth, the pure truth, the truth as pure and as potent as..."

"As brandy," said the innkeeper, helping him.

"Exactly! As brandy. Pour me one, please! I'm sure these fine gentlemen are paying, eh?"

"Hm," said Bendu, "if you tell a good tale."

"I can only tell a good tale when I've had something to drink, noble sir," said Red Quibo with a smile.

Bendu gestured to the innkeeper. "Go ahead, then," he said. "Drinks all round, on me."

The innkeeper went around with a bottle and a flagon, and everyone cheerfully raised their glasses to drink to Bendu's good health.

Red Quibo made use of the opportunity to pour another glass for himself, which he soon emptied.

"You should bear in mind," said the innkeeper, when the excitement had died down a little, "that the truth of Quibo's stories decreases with every glass he drinks."

"That is a lie!" cried Red Quibo. He looked around and jabbed his finger at the chest of the first person he saw. It was Tiuri. "Sir knight," he said. "I am a maligned man, a misunderstood man. Do you understand?"

"I understand," said Tiuri, as seriously as he could.

"I know I'm better at telling my story when I've had a drop to drink," continued Red Quibo. "And I always hope they'll finally believe me. But do they? No! So then I have another one to make me even more convincing when I tell them what happened to me. And do they believe me then? No, they still don't. And then..." He fell silent, picked up the nearest glass, which happened to be Tiuri's, and emptied it. "They're scared," he said, almost in a whisper. "Scared... Yes!" he suddenly shouted at Piak, so loud that he made him jump. "Scared... of the truth!" He lowered his voice again as he continued, "And it isn't a pleasant thought that just a few miles from here the Wild Wood begins, where paths are overgrown by wild plants, where creepy creatures crawl all around you, where the wailing of wind in the tangle of branches wakes you at night..."

He looked around at the others, his piercing eyes glinting in the flickering light of the oil lamp above the table. He cracked the knuckles of his lean and filthy fingers. Almost in a monotone he continued: "I used to go there, even as a boy, although my parents had forbidden it. I dared to go because I had never cut down a tree in the forest, or picked a flower, or even snapped a twig. I walked along paths until they became dead ends, I watched animals as they came to drink from the pool, and I followed the Forest Brook, deeper and deeper into the trees..." He stopped his tale to ask the innkeeper for a refill. After swirling the brandy around his glass for a moment, he took a swig and continued: "I will not tell you everything. You might end up believing it and then you wouldn't sleep tonight or even the next night. I won't talk about the rustling in the reeds and the surreptitious sounds coming from who knows where. Or about the gnarled branches with beetles gnawing away, nor about the stealthy steps I heard, and the slithering snakes and the furtive feet... But then the Forest Brook led me to the Unholy Hills." He downed his brandy, wiped his lips and nodded.

"The Unholy Hills," he repeated. "And unholy is what they are! You go round and round in circles, and when you think you've finally found the way, it's suddenly gone, and when you think you're going back, you're actually going forward. As you walk on, you go more and more astray, deeper and deeper into the Wild Wood. There, in the valleys among the Unholy Hills, many skeletons lie beneath a thick layer of leaves... white bones on the dark moss, those who went astray and never found their way back to the path again. I have been there. I did not want to go, but I found myself there anyway, and I have not been the same man since."

He turned to the innkeeper. "How long was I gone?" he asked.

"Over a month," he replied and, for the benefit of his new guests, he added: "He came back twice as thin as he is now and talking like a drunk man. But then he always does that."

"You be quiet!" cried Red Quibo, suddenly angry. "Let me be drunk if I wish. I was not drunk when it happened, and that's all I'm going to say."

"Oh no, please, go on," said Piak. "Tell us more. What happened to you in the Unholy Hills? What a name! That alone is enough to give anyone goose bumps."

"Nothing happened to me," said Red Quibo abruptly. "I walked round and round in circles, and finally I got out. But I was on the wrong side, very deep in the forest, somewhere in the west. There was nothing there, no sign of civilization. I walked – no, I stumbled – onwards. The animals fled from me, and I was alone... all alone...

Then, suddenly, nearby, I heard loud cheers. Yes, people cheering! Do you understand what that meant? You're walking in a forest, the first human being who's been there for centuries, and then you hear cheering, happy cheering on the other side of the trees right beside you! I nearly dropped down dead with shock. My heart must have skipped three beats! The cheering was accompanied by the sound of hoofs, someone laughing, something clinking, someone shouting. When I'd recovered a little, I tiptoed towards the sound and peered through the bushes to see a clearing and men jousting. I could see knights in full armour, riding fierce and fiery horses. They had red plumes on their helmets, and the light on their lances and swords flashed before my eyes. A crowd watched, cheering them on. They were standing all around the sides of the clearing and sitting in the trees, dressed in red and green and black.

"As I watched, though, I realized I was seeing something that was not meant for my eyes. These were not people! Perhaps they were the spirits of those who had lived long ago in places where trees now grow. I have heard that here and there are still ruins of their cities. And I knew they must not see me, or they would strike me blind. I crept back, slipped away and left that place. And after a long time, with the help of heaven or my lucky stars, I found the way back through the Unholy Hills... the way back to civilization. But it wasn't easy – oh no!"

Quibo stopped to pour himself another glass.

"Many paths led from that place," he continued in a quiet voice. "But I will not tell you what I found there or how I wandered and strayed, for many days. If I did, I would have to talk until tomorrow and I am too tired for that. But in the middle of those Unholy Hills is a shallow valley, a gloomy vale with a dark pool. Poisonous mushrooms grow there, grey and sickly pale. But whatever is green withers in that place, and whatever blooms wilts..." He sat up straight and continued, almost as if he were reciting a poem: "There is a slope, a hill, a den that seems like a grassy bank, covered with plants and

59

turf... an opening within it like a darkened eye... a hole in the roof sending smoke to the sky..."

"What else?" asked Piak.

Red Quibo looked at him and started laughing. That broke the tension. Glasses clinked and people began to murmur.

Quibo dipped a finger into his glass and then licked it. "That's it," he said, grinning at Piak. "The rest is for you to guess."

"You stopped at just the right moment," said Bendu. "You have told a good tale, but I must agree with the landlord that your story does sound rather unlikely."

"Why shouldn't it be true?" said Piak. "I couldn't make up something that strange!"

"Didn't you go inside the den, Quibo?" asked Bendu.

"Would you have dared?" replied Red Quibo.

"Me? Most definitely," said Bendu. "But I'm convinced I'd have found nothing in there. Not even a fire that was sending up smoke!"

"No smoke without fire," said the innkeeper.

"Ah, but there *is* such a thing as smoke without fire!" cried Quibo.

"For sure. The smoke of your imagination," said Bendu.

"The smoke of what once was..." whispered Quibo, "the mysterious smoke of what is past and gone... Look, now my glass is empty, but the glow of what was in it still warms my body!"

"It certainly does," said one of the other guests with a laugh. "Now heed Red Quibo's warning. Drink in moderation and stay away from the Wild Wood!"

"Just a glass or two won't do you any harm," said the innkeeper. "But it's true that you're well advised to steer clear of the Wild Wood."

"Oh, but that's not true!" said Tiuri. "You have to investigate, find out which of the stories are genuine and which are not, try to solve its mysteries..."

"Nonsense!" said Red Quibo. "You will never solve those mysteries because they are not your mysteries to solve. We have no business

60

in that forest. I'll never go back there again. I've had enough for a lifetime."

Tiuri gave him an inquisitive look. He didn't really know what to think about Red Quibo's tale. *He seems to believe it himself,* he thought. *But that doesn't mean it has to be true.*

Can those who disappeared long ago come back to life in lonely places where once they dwelt? It was a strange thought to have in this lowly but cosy inn.

"So? Have I changed your mind?" asked Red Quibo.

"I... I still think Sir Ristridin was right, and so was King Dagonaut, when they wanted to discover what was in the Wild Wood," said Tiuri.

"And when you've found out, what then?" asked Red Quibo. "Do you want to lie awake every night? That is if you're lucky enough to be able to lie awake... Don't you remember what I said about the mournful valleys in those unholy, hateful hills?"

"Hey, stop it," said Piak. "You're just trying to scare us."

Red Quibo stood up. He looked a bit shaky on his legs.

"Brave knights cannot be intimidated!" he cried. "They dare to go into the forest, like Ristridin of the South. Others, though, stay safe indoors, by the fire, like Sir Fitil of Islan."

"Mind your tongue," said the innkeeper.

"I'm not speaking ill of the Lord of Islan, am I?" cried Red Quibo. "He once took many a step inside the Wild Wood. They even say he can wander the Unholy Hills without going astray. But now he knows what's what and he stays inside his castle, nice and quiet, and laughs at those who fret and worry. As he is so right to do."

"These knights are on their way to Islan," said the innkeeper, nodding at Bendu and his companions.

Red Quibo looked at each of them in turn and started laughing again.

"Are you a friend of Sir Fitil's?" he asked Bendu.

"That would be overstating it," Bendu replied. "I last saw him years ago."

Red Quibo turned his gaze on Tiuri, Piak and Evan. "And you are all heading to Islan, too?" he asked. Without waiting for an answer, he continued, "But not to see Sir Fitil, I should wager... No, I am certain of it! Good heavens, with the sun and the moon and a thousand stars together, three young men, all with the same goal! What do they seek beyond the palisades and peaks, within the mighty walls of Islan? A beautiful maiden with honey-blonde hair and hands as white as snow, with eyes like lakes in the moonlight... a girl like a May rose, as slender as the vine."

"That's enough drink for you, Quibo!" the innkeeper said sternly.

"May I not drink to Islan's daughter? A toast to the fairest lady in the Kingdom of Dagonaut! The Daughter of Islan! Isadoro, Lady Isadoro of the pale plain beside the dappled forest, the green-dappled Wild Wood in the west!" cried Red Quibo and then he stopped, out of breath.

"I was not aware that Sir Fitil had a daughter," said Bendu soberly.

Then Tiuri remembered the daughter of another lord: Lavinia of Castle Mistrinaut. Lavinia with her long dark plaits and her eyes like stars. In his bag, right at the bottom, he carried her glove. No one knew about it, not even Piak.

Red Quibo had sat down again and was talking to Bendu. "Take good care of those young men, so quickly aflame, so often in love!" he said. "Ah, let me have just one more drink. Then I shall drink to you, knights, and to all the secrets – the inextroca... inoxtrica... um... unfathomable secrets of the Wild Wood, so strange but true!"

2   CANDLELIGHT AND HARP MUSIC

At first sight, the Plain of Islan did indeed seem pale and dull, but anyone who looked closely could see that was about to change. New blades of grass poked through the soil, and white bellflowers blossomed by the side of the road. Buds were on the trees and the dark, ploughed farmland would not be bare for much longer.

It's spring, thought Tiuri. *Finally it's really spring!*

And there was Castle Islan – a strange, outlandish building, half stone, half wood, surrounded by palisades and moats.

It was some time before the four travellers were admitted to the castle, as it took a while for the drawbridge to be lowered and the gate opened.

But finally the captain of Sir Fitil's guards, a particularly grim-looking man, led them to the castle's living quarters. He took them into a large hall, with rough stone walls and a ceiling black with soot. A wooden staircase led to a gallery, with various doors opening onto it. Three spotted dogs came bounding down the stairs, wagging their tails, followed, more slowly, by the lord of the castle himself. Holding out his hands in welcome, he walked to meet his guests.

"Well, well," he exclaimed jovially. "So they haven't forgotten us in lonely Islan! Welcome, welcome! Sir Bendu, if I'm not mistaken." He slapped the knight on the shoulders as the dogs whirled about his feet. "It's good to see unfamiliar faces for a change!" he continued. "I was starting to feel like a hermit." He gave a booming laugh.

Sir Fitil looked nothing like a hermit. *He'd need to be a lot thinner*, thought Tiuri, *with a beard*. Sir Fitil, though, was stout, perhaps even fat. His face was ruddy and clean-shaven, and his hair was blond and thinning at the temples. He looked very merry and his stature ensured that he cut a fine figure in his long robe of peacock-blue velvet.

Now he turned his small, bright eyes on the other three members of the party. "And here we have two knights of King Unauwen!" he said, raising his eyebrows. "Welcome, welcome! What brings you here, from your distant land?"

"Only one of our number comes from the west," said Bendu, "and that is Sir Evan. Tiuri is a knight of King Dagonaut, even though he carries a white shield."

63

Tiuri also introduced Piak to Sir Fitil.

"We come from Castle Ristridin," Bendu continued. "Sir Arturin sends you his greetings."

"Arturin," repeated Fitil, twitching his eyebrows again. "How is he? Is that why you travelled here, to bring me his greetings? Or have you come for another reason? To visit me, perchance?" Again, his laughter boomed around the hall.

"We are glad you have welcomed us so warmly," said Bendu, "and we should like to stay for one or two days. But we also have something to ask you. You can probably guess what it is."

Now Sir Fitil raised his eyebrows so high that his forehead turned into a mass of wrinkles. "I am not very good at guessing," he replied. "What could I, the hermit of Islan, have to tell you? However, you may ask whatever you wish. I am at your disposal." He placed his hand on the head of one of the dogs, which was trying to jump up. "Calm down, Baro!" he ordered.

The grim-looking man-at-arms, who had waited in silence, gave a cough.

"I'm coming, Hamar," Sir Fitil said to him. He turned back to the four travellers. "My house is yours, knights and squire," he said. "I hope you will stay longer than a couple of days! But I must briefly excuse myself. If you go up the stairs and open the first door, you will find my daughter. Her name is Isadoro. She is the mistress of this castle and she knows of your arrival. As your hostess, she will undoubtedly give you a better reception than I have! I shall join you shortly." He bowed, and left the hall with his dogs and the man-at-arms.

His four guests climbed the stairs and knocked at the door.

"Let's go in," said Bendu when they heard nothing. He did exactly that – and the others followed him.

Then they stopped in their tracks and looked around in surprise. The room was so very different from what they'd seen of the castle so far, not bare and forbidding, but filled with splendour and opulence.

There were colourful tapestries on all the walls; soft animal skins on the floor; beautiful, carved furniture; and fine plates and glasses on the table. It was rather dark in the room, as the only light came through the green panes of two narrow windows. As they surveyed the room, a curtain at one end slid aside, and a young woman appeared, with a candle in her hand.

Tiuri held his breath.

Isadoro, the Daughter of Islan, looked just as Red Quibo had described her – a girl like a May rose, with honey-blonde hair and hands as white as snow. She wore her hair loose, and jewels sparkled on the band around her head. Her dress was a pale green, with wide sleeves. She stood motionless for a moment, beautifully silhouetted against the deep purple of the curtain. Then she came to greet them, with a smile on her face. "Welcome," she said, "to Islan." Her voice was gentle and melodious.

She put the candle on the table, shook hands with her visitors and gave each of them a kind word of welcome. Then she offered to take their shields and assist them with their helmets, but they said this was not necessary.

Then Evan pulled back a chair for the lady. She sat down and the visitors joined her at the table. Then she enquired where they had come from and where they were going. "I dare not presume," she added, "that Islan was your actual destination."

"And yet it is, my lady," said Bendu.

"If we had known what it was like here and who lived in this place, we would have come far sooner," said Evan, giving her a meaningful look.

"You, sir, are a knight of Unauwen," she said. "Why have you come here, from your land on the other side of the Great Mountains?"

"I am a friend of Sir Ristridin," replied Evan, "and I..."

"A friend of Sir Ristridin?" she said, interrupting him. "But surely you do not seek him here?"

"We know he has been here," said Bendu.

The lady rose to her feet. "That was months ago," she said, "but I can still remember it well." She walked to a window, opened it and leant out. The last light of the sun made her cheeks glow and lent a rosy gleam to her hair. "Winter had come early," she continued, "and there was snow on the fields. I was standing at the window and I saw him approaching on foot through the snow. He looked like a real knight, tall and proud, even though his green cloak was torn and his face weather-beaten."

"Ristridin," said Bendu quietly.

Lady Isadoro stared outside as if she could still see the scene before her. "He blew on his horn," she continued, "and my father went out to meet him. They spoke for a time." She turned away from the window and went back to join her guests. "He did not want to enter the castle," she said. "He was in a hurry and had to travel onwards. He rode to the east, into the Forest of Islan."

"Rode?" repeated Bendu. "But he was on foot."

"My father gave him a horse," said Lady Isadoro quickly.

"Was he alone?" asked Bendu.

"When he arrived here, yes," she replied, "but not later. Men on horses came after him from the direction of the Wild Wood. I do not know how many – maybe ten, maybe twenty. They waited for him near the castle, and when Ristridin had spoken to my father, they followed him."

"Do you think it was Arwaut and his men?" said Evan.

"Do you know who they were?" Bendu asked Isadoro.

"What are the colours of Sir Arwaut?" she asked.

"Green and red."

"One of the riders had a shield of green and red," she said. "In fact, I think many of them were clothed in green and red. But they did not stay long and did not come inside, but rode swiftly with Sir Ristridin to the east."

"Did he say nothing about where he was heading?" asked Bendu.

"Or mention where he had been?" said Tiuri.

"He came from the Wild Wood and asked my father to send a message to the king and to his brother Arturin. Did you hear nothing of it?"

"Yes, we did hear of it," replied Bendu. "But that message was brief. Sir Ristridin agreed to meet us this spring at the castle by the Grey River. So far he has not appeared, and so we should like to know more about the plans he had last winter."

"My father can tell you exactly what Sir Ristridin said to him," said Isadoro. She paused for a moment before continuing, slowly and somewhat hesitantly: "Although... I think... there was something mysterious about it..."

"Why's that?" asked Bendu, leaning forward and looking at her. As she moved her head, one of the jewels on her hairband twinkled like a star in the flickering candlelight. "He was in such a hurry," she said, almost in a whisper, "and he did not say where he was going. I'm sure about that. But there are people who live nearby, close to the Forest of Islan, who saw him going by. I heard from them that he was on his way to the south, but not to Castle Ristridin."

"So where was he going?" asked Bendu.

"Perhaps none of it is true," said the lady. "But I heard he was going to Deltaland."

"Deltaland? Deltaland again!" said Bendu.

"Deltaland," repeated Isadoro. "Where exactly does that country lie?"

"To the south-east. It shares a border with Eviellan," replied Tiuri.

"Why would Ristridin go to Deltaland?" asked Bendu.

"I have no way of knowing," said the lady. "Perhaps I should not have told you, as I do not know if it is true. Sir Ristridin did not mention it to my father and I did not speak to him myself."

She looked at each of them in turn. Her eyes were like deep pools, sometimes almost black, and then green or blue. "Why are you so worried about Sir Ristridin?"

"We are not worried," said Bendu. "We just want to know where he is."

"No, you are worried about him," said Lady Isadoro calmly. "But Ristridin is a knight of renown. He is sure to return. Are you afraid he might not?" She stared intently at Bendu.

"Oh, no, no," he replied a little impatiently. "It's just that..." He fell silent.

"Sir Kraton also mentioned Deltaland," mumbled Evan.

"And who," asked the lady, "is Sir Kraton?"

"A gentleman from Eviellan," replied Bendu, "and therefore not to be trusted."

"Not to be trusted," said the lady. "Because he comes from Eviellan?"

"Of course," said Bendu.

"I know little about all those lands so far from here," she said apologetically. "I should like to hear more about them, but we are so isolated here and hardly anyone ever passes this way. That is why I am so delighted by your visit." She stood up. "But I am neglecting my duty as your hostess!" she continued. "I have not offered you anything to eat or drink, or asked if you would like to rest. Let me show you to your rooms, so that you may remove the dust of your journey. And in the meantime I will have some food brought to the table."

She took the candle and led them to the guest quarters. The rooms were just as beautifully and opulently furnished as the hall they had left. There was a small room for Bendu and a larger one for Evan, Tiuri and Piak to share. "I'll see you soon, when we dine," said the lady as she left them.

Piak looked at the huge four-poster beds and carefully stroked the velvet curtains.

Evan sat down in one of the comfortable armchairs and sighed. "It is a long time since the tumult of the fray felt so far away," he said.

Evan had fought in a battle only recently. He had said little about it and Tiuri wondered now what memories he had of that experience. He looked at the calm face of the young knight. How would it feel if your country were at war, if you had to set out to kill or be killed? Tiuri would have liked to know, but he didn't dare ask. Evan didn't seem the type who would enjoy talking about it, and now was certainly not the right moment.

"She's like a fairy of the forest," the young knight continued.

"Who? Lady Isadoro?" asked Piak.

"Who else?" said Evan. "I say 'fairy', because she hardly seems real. Fairies can just suddenly disappear into thin air, you know."

"I think she's real enough," said Piak. "But she's very beautiful, I'll give you that."

Evan laughed. "You seem almost reluctant to say so," he said.

"Well, um... I didn't mean anything by it," said Piak. "But I think Lady Lavinia is at least as beautiful as Isadoro. Don't you, Tiuri?"

To his annoyance, Tiuri could feel himself blushing. He tried to hide his face from Evan. "Yes," he replied reluctantly. "But she's completely different."

"Lavinia?" asked Evan.

"Yes! Lavinia!" said Piak indignantly. "The young lady of Castle Mistrinaut. You surely must remember her, Sir Evan."

Tiuri agreed with him. How could anyone forget Lavinia?

But, when he was looking at Lady Isadoro, Tiuri hadn't given much thought to Lavinia himself.

They ate in the company of Sir Fitil and his daughter; the other residents of the castle apparently ate elsewhere. "I am sorry I have nothing more to tell you about Sir Ristridin," said Sir Fitil. "I can only repeat his message to you. Give me a moment to think and I might remember it word for word. He was most insistent that I passed on his exact words, you see."

He moved his eyebrows as he slowly recited: "*From Sir Ristridin to King Dagonaut, with respectful greetings. No dangers found in the Wild*

Wood. All the paths are dead ends or lead to ruins of towns and villages that were abandoned long ago. So, in winter, I shall travel to other places, where there is more for a knight to do." Then he looked at them and added, "The same message went to Sir Arturin."

"And that's all?" asked Bendu.

"That's all," said Sir Fitil. "Your friend appeared to be safe and sound. He was in the company of a group of riders in green and red. They came along later and rode with him."

"To Deltaland?" asked Bendu.

Sir Fitil raised his eyebrows. "Where did you get that idea?" he said.

"I told them, Father," Lady Isadoro interjected in a quiet voice. "That's what some people said."

"Ah, people say so many things," said Sir Fitil. He looked at Bendu. "Now you know as much as we do," he said. "That really is everything."

"Tomorrow I should like to ride along the road that Ristridin took," said Bendu thoughtfully. "To the east. Perhaps that will give me some clue."

"Yes, you must do that!" said the Lord of Islan cheerfully. "And I shall go with you."

Tiuri said, "Let's start our ride at the Wild Wood, where he came from."

"That's too far for one day," said Sir Fitil. "Besides, what can the wood tell us? There's not a soul living there, and Ristridin left because nothing was happening."

"I hear you have often been into the wood," said Tiuri.

Sir Fitil filled his plate again. "In the past, yes, when I was young," he replied. "I took pride in wandering through the forest without going astray."

"So you never got lost?" asked Piak.

The Lord of Islan twitched his eyebrows again – it seemed to be something of a habit. "Oh, very occasionally," he said. "But I never found anything out of the ordinary. Sometimes I'd startle a young bear or come across a wild boar – nothing more dangerous than that. That's why I never understood what Sir Ristridin thought he might find there. He really should have asked my advice before going into the wood."

"It was on the king's orders," Bendu said sternly. "And Sir Ristridin and my nephew Arwaut found and routed a band of robbers to the north of the Black River."

"Oh, yes, there," said Sir Fitil. "But that's not so unusual. I was afraid Sir Ristridin might be looking for gnomes!" He laughed his loud laugh and then turned his attention to the food.

"Do not jest about such matters, Father," said Lady Isadoro, shivering. "I am afraid of the Wild Wood. It is so dark and lonely – truly a place where the Little Folk might dwell."

"As far as I am concerned, they may keep it," said Bendu scornfully.

Soon after that, Sir Fitil looked around the table. "Have you finished eating?" he cried. "Am I to assume you've had enough?"

"Most certainly!" said Piak.

"Then let us end our meal," said the lord of the castle, "and retire to the Round Chamber. It is actually my daughter's domain, but it's cosy and that's where she keeps her harp. Perhaps, Isadoro, you would like to play and sing something for our guests."

In the Round Chamber many long white candles burned in tall brass candlesticks.

Lady Isadoro sat by her harp. Behind her was a tapestry, with intertwining flowers and plants, in ochre and azure, emerald and rose red. The four guests sat around her. Sir Fitil took a seat in the background, with the dogs at his feet.

The lady ran her hands over the strings; they were pale and white with slim, pointed fingers. Her hair gleamed like gold. As he looked at her, Tiuri tried to picture Lavinia's black plaits, but he did not find it easy.

71

"Shall I sing?" said Isadoro, a little shyly.

Lavinia had sung as well, but she had not played the harp. The sound was like the pattering of raindrops or the babbling of a brook.

Tiuri felt a strange lethargy taking hold of him. All he could see was the lady and the images that her song brought into his mind.

Isadoro sang:

I heard tell of a city of stone,
that stood by rivers wide.
That once was so, but is no more,
for there, by riverside,
there now stand only trees.
Dreams, schemes... Who may go near?

"Do you really want to sing that song now, Isa?" asked Sir Fitil, knitting his nimble eyebrows. "It's far too long and dreary."

The lady shook back her hair. "Would you like something else?" she said, sounding a little hurt. "That's fine."

She waited for a moment, and then strummed the harp and began again, this time playing very light and fast:

A young knight wandered far and wide
through valleys, over mountainside.
'Whither goest thou, knight so good?
To the field or to the wood?
The bright field or the darkest wood?'
A young knight wandered wide and far
by light of sun and light of star
his hair gleamed like the purest gold.
'Whither goest thou, knight so bold?
To the wood or to the wold?'
'Let me wander, let me roam.
My journey takes me far from home,

I shall guard my honour as I should, –
in the field or in the wood,
The bright...'

Sir Fitil pushed back his chair. "Why choose that song?" he said, interrupting his daughter. "Of all the songs you know?!"

"But it's about you!" said Isadoro.

"Exactly!" grumbled Sir Fitil. "And such an old song is better forgotten. I'm not the sort of man to sing songs about."

Tiuri stared in surprise at the stout man in his chair piled high with cushions, at the wrinkles on his forehead, at his thinning hair. And yet he had once been that wandering knight, young and blond like Evan. He turned his gaze to the lady again, who was looking at her father, a wry smile on her lips.

"Then you must tell me what I should sing," she said calmly.

"Any song you like," said Sir Fitil, peering down at his feet. "But, please, not that one."

The lady bowed her head and played again. She sang a number of songs, but the atmosphere of enchantment was gone and soon the guests retired to bed.

3   ON THE EDGE OF THE WILD WOOD

Tiuri awoke early. He got out of bed quietly and began to get dressed. Piak opened one eye and asked sleepily, "Is it time to get up?"

"I'm ready," said Tiuri, "but you can stay in bed for a bit longer if you like."

"I had such a strange dream," mumbled Piak. "About Sir Bendu and little men in green and..."

"About *what*?" came Evan's voice, sitting up in bed.

"Sssh!" said Piak. "No, too late! I've forgotten."

Tiuri left the room. It really was very early and he saw no one about. Bendu was apparently still asleep, and there was no sign of Sir Fitil and his daughter. And yet people were awake in the castle, as he could hear footsteps and the murmur of voices.

He walked around until he found himself in the gallery, where he stopped and looked down into the hall, with his elbow resting on the wooden balustrade. Two servants were busily sweeping the room.

"The master was up before the sun this morning," said one of them. "That doesn't happen very often!"

The other man laughed. "You're right. He usually prefers to stay beneath his covers," he said.

Then they spotted Tiuri and looked guilty.

A moment later, the lord of the castle himself came into the hall, his hair tousled and his cheeks bright red. As always, his dogs ran alongside him. He spotted Tiuri immediately. "Good morning!" he called cheerily. "And I really do mean that. This is most certainly a good morning. Marvellous weather for a ride! I've just come from the stables. What a fine horse you have, Sir Tiuri. Not the friendliest of creatures, though. It barely allowed me anywhere near."

"Oh, Ardanwen won't harm you," said Tiuri. "It's just that he obeys only one master."

"And that's you!" said Sir Fitil. "Oh, I love fiery horses. That gives me an idea – perhaps we should hold a tourney tomorrow." He waved at Tiuri and went on his way.

Tiuri turned around and headed into the great hall. Breakfast was ready, but no one was there yet. One of the windows was open, the same one Lady Isadoro had been standing at yesterday when she'd told them about Sir Ristridin. Tiuri looked outside, but could see little more than a wide tower and a high palisade. So this couldn't have been the window through which Isadoro saw Ristridin approaching...

A quiet sound made him turn around. It was the person he had just been thinking about: Lady Isadoro, her skin whiter than ever in a moss-green gown.

He bowed, wished her good morning, and then fell silent. He felt a little shy in her company, even though he hardly wanted to admit that even to himself. Isadoro, though, was in a talkative mood. She wanted to find out all about him: where he lived, where he'd been, what he'd done. Had he often visited the City of Dagonaut? Had he spoken to the king? Had he seen any tournaments? Or taken part in them?

As Tiuri talked to her, he forgot his shyness. Isadoro was a good listener; she was interested in what he had to say.

"You cannot imagine," she said, "how wonderful it is to hear all these things. I would so love to visit the capital, but Father does not wish to leave Islan and I can't abandon him. I am all he has since Mother passed away."

"Do you ever feel lonely, Lady Isadoro?" asked the young knight.

"Yes, at times I feel very lonely, Tiuri. May I call you Tiuri?"

"Of course you may, my lady."

"Please call me Isa. None of this 'Lady Isadoro' or 'my lady', just Isa," the Daughter of Islan said with a smile.

Isa. Tiuri liked the sound of her name: short, light, elfin – Isa. Tiuri thought they were both around the same age. So he could see Isa as a friend, instead of as a beautiful, mysterious lady who made him feel tongue-tied. He looked at her. Why was she smiling? She wasn't laughing at him, was she?

"Good morning. I'm not disturbing you, am I?" asked Piak's clear voice. He was standing in the doorway with what Tiuri thought was a disapproving look on his face. That was nonsense, of course. Piak had absolutely no reason to disapprove of anything – and yet Tiuri suddenly felt a little guilty.

"Not at all, and good morning to you," said the lady. "Are the others coming, too? It's time for breakfast. Father's up and about already." She gave Piak a smile that was just as friendly as the one she'd recently given his friend. "Sir Tiuri has told me a great deal," she continued. "You must be proud to be his squire."

"I certainly am," said Piak. "Did he tell you about his journey to the land of King Unauwen?"

"No. No, he didn't tell me about that," she replied, giving Tiuri what appeared to be a look of reproach.

"It was a long journey," said Piak. "I was with him for some of it. We saw so many places! Castle Mistrinaut, for instance."

"Castle Mistrinaut?" said Isadoro.

"Didn't Tiuri tell you about it?" asked Piak with a mischievous glint in his eye.

"There are lots of things I didn't mention," Tiuri said. "How can I have told her everything? We've only just met!"

"You met all kinds of nice people at Castle Mistrinaut, too, didn't you?" Piak persisted.

Tiuri was becoming annoyed with him. Did Piak really have to start on about Lavinia again now? He was allowed to talk to another young lady, wasn't he?

"Like, Sir Ristridin, for instance," said his squire.

Fortunately, Bendu, Evan and Sir Fitil arrived at that moment. Piak didn't say a word to Tiuri and Isadoro during breakfast. They were sitting opposite each other and Tiuri kept glancing over at her. But he was thinking about Lavinia. Her face, which had faded a little in his memory after he'd seen Isadoro's, now came back clearly to him. She was so different from the Daughter of Islan. He knew he'd never have felt that self-conscious sitting opposite Lavinia.

After breakfast, Bendu said again that he wanted to ride in the direction Ristridin had taken a few months before.

"To the Forest of Islan, then," said Sir Fitil. "I shall go with you, although I think there is little point. But it is little enough trouble to ask a few questions of the people who live there."

"Are you coming, too?" Bendu asked Evan and Tiuri.

Evan nodded, but Tiuri said he'd actually prefer to head towards the Wild Wood. That was where Ristridin had come from, after all.

"Oh yes," said Piak. "I dreamt about the Wild Wood last night. It was full of little men in green."

"And, of course, you want to go and catch them now," Bendu teased him.

"No, you already did that," Piak pointed out. "You were in my dream, too!"

"What strange dreams a man can have," Bendu growled. Then he added, "So if you and Tiuri head to the west, today we can take in Ristridin's known route."

"That's a good plan," said Tiuri.

"You're not going into the Wild Wood, are you?" said Isadoro, sounding shocked. "You're sure to get lost!"

"Isadoro's right," said her father. "Sir Tiuri and his squire can go there, but they must stay on the paths, because it's so easy to get lost. And do not ride into the Unholy Hills... But that's too far for a day's ride, anyway."

"The Unholy Hills, we've heard of them," said Piak. "Are they really that close?"

"Oh, you can wander around those hills for days," said Sir Fitil. "If you're determined to go into the Wild Wood, then take the road to the old hunting lodge. That's the road Ristridin came along."

And so they all had something to do – except for Lady Isadoro, who pouted and asked if she was expected to stay at home alone.

"Come with us," said Evan.

Piak looked at Tiuri as if hoping his friend would not say the same. But Tiuri paid no attention and repeated Evan's words.

"No, no," said Isadoro. "I am not fond of the road to the east, and I never go to the Wild Wood."

"You could go with us now," said Tiuri.

"Or... I could always stay here," said Evan.

Tiuri opened his mouth to say the same, but then he changed his mind and held his tongue.

"No, I don't want you to do that," said Isadoro, friendly but firm. "You are not staying away for long and I have much to do here. Go, all of you, and enjoy your ride."

"Come along now," said the Lord of Islan. He went over to his daughter and said a few quiet words to her.

Soon after that, he left, with Bendu, Evan and his dogs.

Then Tiuri and Piak headed to the stables. As they were leading their horses across the courtyard, Lady Isadoro walked up to them.

"Are you really going?" she called.

"Yes, Isa. You don't mind, do you?" said Tiuri.

She came closer and replied, "No, no, it's fine. It's just that I don't like the thought of..." To Tiuri's surprise, she suddenly stepped back. Then he saw why: she'd been startled by his horse, which was a little restless.

"Ardanwen won't hurt you," he said.

"Is that his name? Ardanwen?" she asked, still looking nervous.

"Yes, it means Night Wind. Really, he won't do anything."

"You can stroke him if Tiuri doesn't mind," said Piak.

"He looks rather spirited to me," said Isadoro. "No, don't let him come any closer."

Piak gave her a withering look, but Tiuri just smiled. "There is no better or more loyal horse," he said.

"Oh, I believe you," replied Isadoro, but she made sure to stay at a safe distance.

Piak climbed up onto his horse. Then Tiuri said, "Isa, what was it that you didn't like the thought of?"

"What do you mean?" she said.

"You just said that..."

"Oh, nothing," she said, shaking her head. "Wait. I'll go and fetch my cape. I'm coming with you. Tell the stable lad to saddle my horse." She turned around and walked away, quick and light on her feet.

"Why does she have to come?" grumbled Piak.

"I hope you're going to behave yourself!" snapped Tiuri. "What do you want me to do? Am I supposed to tell her to stay at home? You could try being a little more... knightly towards her!"

Piak went red. "I'll leave the chivalry to you, Sir Tiuri," he replied.

"Well, you can at least be polite," said Tiuri abruptly.

Lady Isadoro rode a dapple grey. She wore a white cape, lined with bright red, and a small cap of green velvet on her long hair. Together, they rode to the Wild Wood, Tiuri on her right, and Piak on her left.

The sun was shining and a mild breeze blew from the south. After a while, they could see the Wild Wood very clearly and, beyond it, mighty summits, hazy blue, violet and white.

"The mountains!" cried Piak.

"They're still a long way away," said Isadoro, "although one would not think so today. Even Father has never been there."

"How long would it take to reach them?" asked Piak.

"I once heard of a man who wanted to travel to the mountains," Isadoro told them. "He entered the wood in good spirits and wandered around for weeks. And finally... finally he saw light shining through the trees. He was so delighted! *I'm almost there*, he thought, but when he reached the edge of the wood, he realized he was back where he'd started... He was on the Plain of Islan! And the mountains were still just as far away."

They all laughed.

"But did that really happen?" asked Piak.

"Well, it certainly could be true!" Isadoro said seriously. "There's no place you can lose your way as quickly as in the Wild Wood." She gave a shiver. "I'm scared of it," she continued. "It was once much closer to Islan than it is now. The trees came right up to the castle. Father had many of them chopped down, but sometimes I dream they are surrounding the entire castle and I can hear the rustling of leaves outside my window. Oh, Islan is such a lonely place! That's why it makes one think such strange thoughts." She shot a glance at Tiuri and a smile lit up her face as she added, "But with you, Sir Tiuri, and your brave squire, I would dare to ride anywhere."

They rode past small farmsteads and barns, and people at work in the fields greeted them. But the closer they came to the Wild Wood, the quieter their surroundings became, and there were no more houses in sight. The road grew narrower, and Piak had to ride behind Tiuri and Lady Isadoro. It was almost midday by the time they reached the edge of the forest. They could no longer see the mountains, and the wood didn't actually look all that wild.

"It's just like any other forest," said Piak, sounding rather disappointed.

"That's because it's spring," said Isadoro. "There are only very few leaves now, and they're still young and pale green and bright, don't you see? Anyway, it only becomes truly wild once you venture into it." She reined in her horse and pointed ahead. A red ruby sparkled on her finger.

Like a drop of blood, thought Tiuri, but he didn't think it a very good comparison.

"Look," said Isadoro, "what a pretty little patch of grass. Shall we stop and rest there for a while?"

Tiuri and Piak were not tired, but they got down from their horses, and then Tiuri helped Isadoro to dismount. The grassy patch was a small meadow at the edge of the trees, full of sunlight, with yellow flowers growing all around.

Isadoro was about to take off her cape and spread it on the ground, but Tiuri beat her to it and put down his cloak instead. She sat upon it and asked him to join her. Piak fetched the bag of food and drink.

"If we're resting, we may as well have something to eat," he said.

Before long, he leapt to his feet and suggested they should be on their way. Isadoro wanted to stay a little longer, though. "Then, if it's all right with the two of you, I'll go and scout ahead," said Piak, disappearing into the forest.

"Don't stray from the path!" Isadoro called after him.

Tiuri lay on his back in the sun, with his eyes closed. He could feel himself growing sleepy. It really was time to get up and ride on, but he was so comfortable lying there and it was so peaceful... He smiled. And this was the infamously terrifying Wild Wood!

But then his smile vanished. He could hear something – was it nearby or in the distance? Footsteps! Eyes still closed, he imagined someone peering at him from the bushes. If he were to open his eyes, he would see him, if only he knew in which direction to look. He held his breath... Something brushed against his cheek, tickling him.

He sat up with a start, and found himself looking into Isadora's smiling face. She was still holding the blade of grass that she'd used to tickle him.

"I thought you were asleep," she teased.

Tiuri looked around. There was no one hiding in the bushes. Of course not! And the footsteps must have been Piak. But then why did Ardanwen raise his head and snort so restlessly?

"What's wrong?" asked Isadoro.

"Oh, nothing," mumbled Tiuri, a little embarrassed. "I must have been almost asleep. I think I was dreaming."

"What about?"

"I can't remember," Tiuri began. But then he said, "Maybe... about you, Isa?"

The lady leant back, still with her gaze on him. Her eyes were green, with long, dark lashes. They seemed to be speaking to him, to be asking a question that could not be uttered with words. Tiuri leant towards her.

Then he was startled by the sound of Piak's voice.

"Tiuri, Tiuri! Come here!"

Isadoro looked down and turned her face away. "Your friend is calling you," she said.

Tiuri sighed impatiently. If only Piak had called him just a little later.

"Tiuri!" came his voice again, loud and urgent.

"You don't think anything's wrong, do you?" Isadoro said anxiously.

"No, I'm sure it's fine," said Tiuri. He jumped up and shouted, "Piak, where are you?"

Yes, there *was* something moving in the trees. He nodded at Isadoro, who was still sitting on his cloak, and ran into the forest. Piak came to meet him.

"Is something wrong?" asked Tiuri.

"N-no," replied his friend. "Not... wrong."

"So why did you call me?" said Tiuri, feeling rather annoyed.

"I wanted to show you something," said Piak, and more quietly he added, "Have you encountered anyone?"

"Encountered anyone? No," said Tiuri. "Why?"

"I saw someone," replied Piak, "or perhaps I should say that I saw something. At least... I thought I did. It felt like someone was watching me from behind the trees. When I went over to take a look, I heard rustling and..."

Tiuri thought of the vision he'd had a few minutes ago.

"And?" he said. "What happened then?"

"Then? Nothing!" said Piak. "I thought I saw someone walking away, but I'm not certain."

Tiuri looked around. The leaves of the trees were trembling in the wind. There were patches of light in the undergrowth, and birds chirping. "Do not mention any of this to the lady," he said. Then he headed back to the little meadow.

Piak followed him.

Isadoro was impatiently waiting for them. "So what was the problem?" she asked.

"Piak just wanted to show me something," replied Tiuri.

"Yes," said Piak. "I found a stone. I walked down the path for a while and then it split in two. One path went straight on..."

"That's the way to the old hunting lodge," said Isadoro.

"The other was much narrower," Piak continued, "and that was the path I took. And that's where I found the stone. There were words on it."

"What did they say?" asked Tiuri.

"That's the problem – I don't know," said Piak. "Will you come and take a look? It's nearby. And we were planning to go into the wood anyway, weren't we?"

Tiuri realized that he hadn't been thinking about the purpose of their ride at all. "Yes," he said, "we need to follow the road that Sir Ristridin came along."

"Sir Ristridin came from the old hunting lodge," said Lady Isadoro. "The other path leads to the Unholy Hills."

4   YELLOW FLOWERS

They headed into the forest on foot, with Piak leading the way. The path was easy enough to follow and it was covered with a thick layer of dead leaves, which muffled their steps. Tiuri stayed alert, but he didn't see anything unusual.

Isadoro said, "We can take a look and then ride to the old hunting lodge. But I can tell you now that you'll only see pine trees and bushes there."

"Does your father ever go hunting here?" asked Tiuri.

"He used to, but that was a long time ago. The hunting lodge isn't used these days. When Father goes hunting now, it's in the Forest of Islan."

Piak pointed ahead. "It's this path," he said. "We're nearly there."

He walked on, but Isadoro hesitated. The path was not only narrow, but also extremely muddy. There were big puddles everywhere.

83

"Do I really have to go on?" she said, smiling yet clearly reluctant, as she glanced down anxiously at her clothes, which were indeed most unsuitable for a walk in such surroundings.

"Are you coming?" called Piak. He'd already gone on ahead of them.

"I'll carry you!" offered Tiuri.

"Fine," said the lady. "If you really want to."

Tiuri picked her up. Isadoro was light, but still he could feel his heart thumping away as he carried her onto the path. She had put one arm around his neck and her hair lightly brushed his cheek. He wondered if he would have kissed her, before, if Piak had not called out to him. What had that question in her eyes meant? He held her tightly and hoped the rest of the path would be just as muddy.

"Ha, finally! There you are!" cried Piak.

Tiuri almost missed his footing, but managed to stay upright. Carefully, he put Isadoro down, avoiding Piak's eyes, and looked for the stone.

He spotted it at the side of the path, where it sank at an angle into the boggy ground, grey, old and partially covered with moss. But the letters, which must have been carved into it long ago, were still clearly visible. Tiuri leant forward to decipher them. However, the words they formed were unfamiliar to him.

Isadoro began to speak. "It's a signpost, and this is what it says." She continued in a singsong voice:

You who come as an enemy,
retrace your steps
or may the Wood devour you!
You who come as a friend,
tread this path in peace
and may you reach your goal,
may you not go astray
and may the Spirits of the Forest watch over you!

Then she walked up to the signpost and sat on it as if it were a throne. "My father found this stone when he was still a boy," she told them, "buried under creepers and dead leaves. He had it placed upright here as a reminder of days gone by. Someone later translated the words for me."

"Who?" asked Piak.

"Someone I once met," replied Isadoro, and there was something evasive about her expression.

"How old do you think the stone must be?" asked Piak.

"Hundreds of years ago there were castles where the trees now grow," said Isadoro. "That's what the chronicles and legends say. Knights and princes lived there, who had come from afar, from beyond the Great Mountains..."

"From the Kingdom of Unauwen," whispered Piak.

Lady Isadoro shrugged. "Who can say?" she said. "Those days exist only in stories now, stories that not everyone believes."

Tiuri realized the words on the stone might well be written in the old tongue of the Kingdom of Unauwen, which was still used by some as a secret language.

"This is what they say," said Lady Isadoro. "In a castle on the Black River lived a knight who loved peace. But war stalked the land and enemies pressed in on every side. So the knight said he wished to be left alone and swore never to leave his castle again. And trees began to grow around his castle and to hide it from people. But there were paths that led there, and he had them marked with signposts like this one. As the years went by, the paths became overgrown and closed up, and he died all alone and was forgotten. His castle, the Tarnburg, became a ruin, entangled deep within the forest. But they say the knight's ghost still haunts the place. People call him the Master of the Wild Wood." She stopped talking and sang another fragment of the song she'd begun the night before:

I heard tell of a fortress grim
by mountains and by rivers wide.
That once was so, but is no more,
for there, by riverside,
there now stand only trees.
Dreams, schemes. Who may go near?

Tiuri and Piak stared at Isadoro as she sat on her strange perch, the bottom of her white and red cape falling across those ancient carvings.

But suddenly she leapt to her feet and said, "I mustn't sing that song here! We should go."

Tiuri picked her up again and they headed back along the path in silence.

As they approached the meadow, they heard the sound of hoofs.

"Put me down," said Isadoro.

Tiuri did as he was told. He had continued to carry her even after they'd left the muddy path.

A rider dressed in brown and yellow was approaching. It was the grim-faced captain of Sir Fitil's men.

"Hamar!" Isadoro exclaimed.

The man-at-arms reined in his horse. His expression was even grimmer than usual. "Lady Isadoro," he said, politely but sternly, "you know your father does not allow you to go out alone."

"My dear Hamar," said Isadoro, "I am not alone! Look, Sir Tiuri and his squire are accompanying me."

"Sir Tiuri and his squire know their way in the Wild Wood even less well than you," replied Hamar. "When I heard which direction you'd ridden in, I immediately came after you. That's what your father would have ordered me to do had he been at home."

"Sir Tiuri and Piak wanted to ride to the old hunting lodge," said Isadoro. "Father knows about it. And I thought I could go with them."

"Does your father know about that, too?" asked Hamar, still politely, but with an expression that clearly said he wasn't planning to let Isadoro dismiss him.

Isadoro seemed to realize that, because she smiled and said, "Ride with us, Hamar, and do not let us out of your sight!"

Hamar bowed his head. "Thank you, my lady," he said.

They walked back to the horses. Tiuri was the last one to mount his horse. As he did so, he gave a gasp of surprise. Little yellow flowers had been woven throughout Ardanwen's bridle!

"Look at this!" cried Tiuri. "Who could have done it?"

"How strange!" exclaimed Piak.

"Your horse has certainly made itself look very fine," said Hamar.

Tiuri leant forward to take a closer look at the flowers. There was no way it could have happened by chance, as they were so neatly woven into the leather.

"Who did this?" he said, looking at the others.

"Well, it wasn't me," said Piak.

Grim Hamar grinned scornfully at the thought that he might have come up with such an idea. Then he looked at his mistress. She was staring in amazement at the yellow flowers that stood out so brightly against Ardanwen's gleaming black coat. She slowly shook her head.

"Well, someone must have done it!" Tiuri cried.

"You really don't need to ask," growled Hamar, his eyes still on Isadoro.

"It wasn't me," she said, but it didn't sound very convincing. "Come on, let's go to the hunting lodge," she said as she rode off.

Tiuri caught up with her. "Did you do it, Isa?" he asked quietly.

She frowned and replied, "Hamar's right. There are some things you shouldn't ask about."

"But..." Tiuri began, but then he fell silent. He really didn't know what else to say. Isadoro seemed just as mysterious as the stories about the Wild Wood.

Now they were riding along the path in the direction Sir Ristridin had come from. Of course, there was no sign he had ever passed that way. Any trace had been wiped out after such a long time, and there were no people living anywhere around who might have been able to answer their questions.

"What are we actually doing here?" asked Hamar, when they stopped.

"I don't know," Isadoro said with a sigh. "It's so dark and gloomy!"

The abandoned hunting lodge was dilapidated and covered with moss; its doors were closed and the windows nailed up. It was surrounded by tall, dark pine trees and brushwood that was dry and old. The path came to a dead end there.

"Look, some branches have been snapped," said Piak, pointing. "Do you think it might have been Sir Ristridin?"

"It could just as easily have been an animal," said Hamar. "There are wild boars around here."

"Oh, let's go home, shall we?" Isadoro pleaded.

There was little else they could do than grant her wish. There was no chance of finding any sign of Ristridin here.

"And what if we had found something? What then?" said Tiuri to himself, as they rode back to Islan. "Ristridin has already left the forest." He felt annoyed and dissatisfied.

The yellow flowers were starting to wilt and he wondered again what they could mean. Piak had not woven them into the bridle, because he surely would have said so. Hamar had not done it either; the very thought was ridiculous. So it must have been Isa. But why would she deny it?

Oh, of course, he realized, *she's embarrassed.*

"Every flower has a meaning," said Isadoro's voice beside him, as if she had guessed his thoughts.

"A meaning?" asked Tiuri.

"In some cases, the names speak for themselves," she replied. "Rue, heartsease, forget-me-not... For others, you need to know the language of the plants. Rosemary for remembrance, violet for modesty..."

"What about this one?" asked Tiuri.

"They're primroses," she said. "And primroses mean..." She looked right at him. Then she whispered, "I want to speak to you, alone."

She urged on her horse and rode ahead of him towards the castle.

"So it was her!" said Tiuri to himself. He was about to chase after her, but thought better of it. She had said enough and apparently no longer wanted to ride with him. She had never ridden very closely beside him, even though she had allowed him to carry her.

Why did he still feel so uncertain?

It was only as they arrived at the gates of Islan that the answer came to him.

Isadoro was so scared of Ardanwen that she didn't dare to approach the horse. So it could not have been her who wove the yellow flowers into the bridle!

5 In the Lady's Garden

"All we have heard is what we already knew," said Bendu as they ate dinner. "Ristridin rode to the east through the Forest of Islan."

"And we heard more talk of Deltaland," Evan added. "Ristridin and his men stopped to rest for a short while at a hunters' cabin at the edge of the forest. A hunter who was there at the time heard them talking about Deltaland. But he didn't hear enough to give us any leads. Do you have anything to tell?" he asked Tiuri.

"No," Tiuri replied after a moment of hesitation.

Evan looked at him curiously, but did not ask any questions.

"Then we must soon return to Castle Ristridin," said Bendu.

"But not right away!" exclaimed the Lord of Islan. "You have only just arrived."

"We can wait another day," replied Bendu. "But I am sure you understand that we do not wish to stay away too long from the place where we are to meet Ristridin and Arwaut."

"Of course, that's perfectly clear," said Sir Fitil. "Then please remain here tomorrow as our guests. We shall do something enjoyable, a tourney with jousting, tilting at rings and the like. My best men can take part and my daughter will present the prizes. Then I shall hold a grand farewell meal, with singing and music, so you will not be quick to forget Islan."

"I'm sure we won't do that," said Bendu. "And the young men will certainly appreciate such festivities." Bendu himself did not seem particularly interested.

Tiuri was not in the mood for a celebration either, even though, like the others, he said it sounded most entertaining. He couldn't stop thinking about the yellow flowers and he kept wondering if Lady Isadoro had lied to him. And, if so, why? But she could have overcome her fear of Ardanwen and that meant she must have something important to say to him. He needed to talk to her alone, as soon as possible.

As they rose from the table, he was able to whisper to her quickly. "Isadoro, were those flowers yours?"

"Yes," she whispered back.

Tiuri noticed that her father was keeping an eye on them, and Isadoro could see it, too. "Tomorrow, in my garden," she added quickly before turning away from him.

The rest of the evening he spoke to her only in the company of others, and not a word was said about the flowers.

Tiuri lay awake for a long time. Evan was breathing quietly and Piak seemed to be asleep as well. But then he sat up, got out of bed and went to perch on Tiuri's bed.

"Hey, Tiuri," he said quietly. "Are you in love with Lady Isadoro?"

Tiuri did not reply.

"I know very well you're not asleep!" whispered Piak.

But Tiuri really didn't know how to respond to Piak's question. Was he in love with Isadoro? He thought about her all the time and kept seeing her in his mind, but there was something else mixed in with his emotions: distrust.

"Whether you're in love with her or not, you mustn't believe everything she tells you," said Piak. "She's acting as if the flowers were her idea, but that's not true! She doesn't even dare to stroke Ardanwen!"

"I know," said Tiuri.

"Oh. Well, I'm glad to hear that," said Piak. "So what now?"

"Hush!" whispered Tiuri. "I've told you that I already know. And tomorrow I'll speak to her, and ask her straight out what's going on..."

"Straight out? You can't even think straight when she's around," sniffed Piak. "She's beautiful enough, but she's as tricky as a... as a..." Then he fell silent because he couldn't think of a good comparison.

"Ah, stop talking so much," said Tiuri wearily. "But I will tell you this: tomorrow I'm going to the Wild Wood again. If she didn't do it, I want to know who did."

"Back to the forest?" whispered Piak. "But there's that tourney tomorrow."

"I'll go early, alone, and make sure I get back in time," said Tiuri.

"On your own? Can't I come with you?" asked Piak.

"Yes, you can come," replied Tiuri.

"So we're going together?" asked Piak, stressing the final word.

"Yes, together," said Tiuri.

Evan turned over and gave a sigh.

"And now I'm going to sleep," said Tiuri. "Goodnight, Piak."

Piak climbed back into bed and soon nodded off, but it was some time before Tiuri fell asleep.

Even so, like Piak, he was up and about before dawn the next morning. But when they went into the great hall, they found Lady Isadoro had risen even earlier. The three of them ate breakfast together.

"Tiuri and I would like to go for a short ride," said Piak. "That's all right, isn't it?"

"Of course," said Isadoro. "Where are you going?"

"Oh, we'll see," replied Tiuri.

But Piak said defiantly, "To the Wild Wood."

"That far?" she said. "You know we're having a tourney later. Don't tire yourselves and your horses, and make sure you're not back too late." She didn't seem at all guilty or concerned. In fact, she looked happy, and she kept giving Tiuri meaningful glances.

When they'd finished breakfast, Tiuri told Piak to go ahead to the stables. As for himself, he followed Lady Isadoro to the garden.

They walked along corridors and through rooms, up and down stairs, across courtyards and through gates.

Castle Islan is another place where it would be easy to get lost, thought Tiuri. Isadoro had told him it was very old. Once there had been a wooden house on the same spot, of which only a few parts remained, and then a stone castle had been built, and every lord who had lived there had added something new. There were many courtyards, with rooms around them, all kinds of towers, and various ramparts and moats surrounding the castle.

The garden was on the south side of the building, completely enclosed by high walls, with just one small door. Isadoro unlocked it with a key that hung from her belt, and said, "No one may enter this garden without my permission."

They went through the door and Tiuri took in the scene with surprise. Here, in this sheltered spot, spring was in full bloom: small, delicate trees like bouquets of blossom, bluebells and crocuses blooming in the grass, and creepers of rich green. Gravel paths led around the garden, and there were benches and pots of shrubs dotted about.

"This is my garden," said Isadoro. She almost looked like a pretty flower herself.

They strolled along the paths. Isadoro showed Tiuri the plants, told him their names and related little stories about them. Tiuri listened, but he was waiting for her to start talking about more important matters.

They sat down on a bench and Isadoro said, "Whenever I am tired or angry, or when I am feeling lonely, I always find comfort here. But it is more pleasant to be able to share this place with someone." She looked at Tiuri with a melancholy smile. "You probably feel it's too quiet here," she said. "You are a knight and you must dream of adventures and thrill at the thought of tourneys and banquets."

"Oh, no," said Tiuri. "Well, not all the time. I haven't been a knight all that long, you know."

"Tell me about the journey you went on last year," said Isadoro.

"Ah," said Tiuri, "but isn't there something you wanted to say to me?"

"What would you like me to say?" she replied vaguely. "Look, a butterfly! It's the first one I've seen here." She spoke cheerfully now. "Do you think it will settle on my finger? That will bring us good luck!" She stood up and chased after the butterfly. The green sleeves of her dress fluttered and her blonde hair rippled.

Tiuri would have preferred to forget his plans and stay here with the lady in her garden. But was it really the right time for such a carefree game? He had to find out what was going on – and what she was hiding from him. Tiuri stood up and walked over to her.

Isadoro had stopped beneath a big, gnarled tree in a corner, close to the wall, and was leaning against the trunk, her eyes fixed on a barred window in the wall.

"Gone," she said flatly.

"Gone? Who's gone?" asked Tiuri.

"The butterfly. I can't see it anywhere. Can you? It was supposed to bring us luck."

But Tiuri didn't look for the butterfly; he was gazing at Isadoro. She held out her hand and he took it in his. Was she crying? He leant towards her and kissed her, first on her eyes, then on her lips. He simply could not help himself. And she put her arms around his neck and responded to his kiss. He felt as if a dance of fiery butterflies were whirling all around him, but when he opened his eyes, he saw only her eyes, green, blue, like pools in a forest.

"Oh, Isa..." he whispered.

She laid her finger on his lips. "Hush," she said quietly. "Hush, hush!"

Far away, somewhere beyond the wall, they heard Piak's voice: "Sir Tiuri!"

Tiuri heard him, but he did not listen. Arm in arm, close together, he and the lady walked through the garden and sat down once again. Isadoro leant against him, and he played with a lock of her hair, his head full of conflicting thoughts. He wanted to kiss her again, but the question that was bothering him still remained unanswered. Or did it no longer matter?

"Isa..." he said hesitantly.

"Yes, Tiuri?" Her voice was soft and sweet.

"I... you, you were going to tell me something else... You wanted to speak to me in private... Why?"

"Oh, Tiuri," she said with a sigh. "I don't remember."

"But I'd really like to know," he said.

"So much more can be said without words, Tiuri," she said with a smile, laying her hand on his chest.

And suddenly Tiuri felt like a prisoner, bound with invisible gossamer threads. He was tempted to kiss Isa once again, but at the same time he wanted to explode at her in anger. He did neither, but instead said, loudly and clearly, "Isadoro, was it you who wove those yellow flowers into Ardanwen's bridle? Just tell me, yes or no."

She pulled her hands away, hurt or annoyed, and said, "Are you bringing that up again?"

"Yes or no?" repeated Tiuri. He didn't want to speak to her that way, but he had to know.

"Yes!" she said defiantly, but her attitude had changed. She seemed tense, almost afraid.

"But how could you have done it," said Tiuri, "when you were scared of Ardanwen?"

"Don't you believe me?" she asked angrily.

No, thought Tiuri, but he said: "I... I have my doubts."

"Then you can just keep on doubting me," she said indignantly and stood up. "I will answer only once. And I am starting to have my doubts about you, too – your behaviour towards me is most erratic!"

"Isa..." Tiuri began.

"Do not attempt to apologize," she said haughtily as she walked away.

Tiuri went after her. "Forgive me, Isa," he said, "but this really matters to me! Come with me to see Ardanwen, and then I'll be sure, and..."

"You still distrust me!" she shouted. "But I refuse to go with you to see your precious horse!" And she covered her face with her hands and burst into tears.

Then Tiuri really did feel miserable. He put his arms around her and tried to soothe her, "Isa, dear Isa!"

She pulled away and turned on him like a fury, tears still trickling down her cheeks. Before he knew what was coming, she'd viciously

95

slapped him in the face. She looked startled by her own action and her face turned pale.

Tiuri turned on his heels and left the garden.

6 THE ROAD TO THE UNHOLY HILLS

Tiuri fixed his eyes on the ground as he walked to the stables, where Ardanwen was saddled and waiting. He jumped up onto his horse and rode away, past courtyards where people were busy working, through gates and across bridges. He almost didn't see Piak, who had been waiting for him beside the outermost gate for some time.

"Hey, Tiuri!" Piak called. "Tiuri, what's wrong?"

Tiuri reined in Ardanwen. "Wrong?" he said. "I... um... nothing. Nothing's wrong."

"Where are you going?" asked Piak, half surprised, half angry.

"Just out for a ride," Tiuri answered brusquely, and then he reluctantly added, "To the forest. Were you waiting for me?"

"Yes, I was," said Piak. "But you can forget about it! If you don't need me, I've changed my mind about going."

"Oh, do come," said Tiuri, suddenly feeling ashamed. "Of course you should come, Piak."

"No," his friend replied. "I'd rather not. Goodbye!" He turned around and walked away.

Tiuri watched Piak go, wondering if he should call him back. He really wanted to be alone for a while, and yet he felt unhappy with himself after he'd left the castle and was heading to the Wild Wood.

Ardanwen didn't keep to a trot; no, he raced onwards, and still he couldn't go fast enough for Tiuri. He wanted to escape from the garden of Islan, from Lady Isadoro. He did not trust her, but he could feel her kiss tingling on his lips even now. And he knew that he had to do something: if the primroses weren't from her, he needed to find out who had woven them into Ardanwen's bridle.

"I'm afraid she's making a fool of me!" he called to Ardanwen. He could shout as loud as he wanted, because there was no one else for miles around. "I don't want to be in love with her, but I am! Oh, Ardanwen, it's all so difficult!"

There was the spot where he'd sat with Isadoro the previous day. Was something moving in the bushes at the edge of the forest?

Tiuri dismounted and rubbed down his steed. He hadn't galloped so wild and so fast for a long time. "If only you could speak," he whispered to his horse. "You know more about this than I do." Ardanwen lowered his neck and twitched his fine ears.

"Come on," said Tiuri, heading slowly along the path to the old hunting lodge. Again he was seized by doubt. Wasn't he a fool for coming here alone to look for... but what exactly was he hoping to find?

At the fork for the Unholy Hills he pulled on the reins and stopped to look around.

On the ground, in the mud, lay a yellow flower.

Tiuri jumped down and picked it up. There were no other primroses nearby and this one had been picked just recently. He put his arm around Ardanwen's neck and looked down the path. No sign of any movement. Something rustled in the undergrowth. A few birds darted up and flew angrily chattering over his head.

"I think we should head in this direction," he said, and that's what they did.

Just after the signpost he saw another flower and so he kept on riding. "Who is waiting for us, there, beyond the bend in the path?" he said quietly to Ardanwen. "Someone seems to be luring us to the Unholy Hills."

The path was narrow and winding, so he could not move quickly, and he also wanted to take some time to look around. He saw silvery-trunked birches and gnarled pine trees; he saw squirrels and partridges and he spotted a fox darting across the path, red tail flashing. The land was undulating, and he passed a few tracks leading off to either side. He saw no human beings, and yet it felt as if someone were keeping pace with him. Although he kept thinking he could see a figure beside him, it only happened when he was facing straight ahead. Whenever he turned to find out what was there, he saw no one.

Finally, he stopped and jumped down from his horse.

The track was so narrow now that it was indistinguishable from the side paths; the wood had become much denser. He realized he would have to take care not to get lost, and he didn't like the thought of being lured in any deeper. He had found no more flowers. Whatever creature was waiting for him – he was almost certain something was there – would have to come out of hiding now. He peered in every direction and called out: "Who seeks me?" Then, more quietly, he continued, "And what is it that I seek?"

There, in the trees, something was moving, walking! Was it a person? It dashed and darted and then disappeared behind a thick tree trunk.

Tiuri remembered the stories about woodland spirits... did they exist? And did they have any power to harm humans?

"I come as a friend!" he called, remembering the words on the signpost. He left the path and walked to the spot where he had seen the creature.

Behind the thick tree trunk he found no one, but he saw a few snapped branches and trampled leaves. He glanced around and realized he'd lost the path. On every side he saw the same: trees! He couldn't be in the Unholy Hills already, could he?

Luckily he caught a glimpse of Ardanwen and ran towards him. But his horse was not alone. Someone stood beside him... a man!

The man did not run away when Tiuri stepped out onto the path. He pressed himself against the horse and turned to look at Tiuri.

Tiuri stopped, frozen in astonishment.

He was a wild-looking man, dressed in little more than a shabby sheepskin. His arms and legs were bare and sunburnt, and his face was framed by a thick mop of brown curls and a tangled beard. That face had a pair of round blue eyes, which Tiuri had once known as childlike and happy, but which now looked at him with fear... fear, and also hope.

Tiuri gasped. "Marius!" he exclaimed.

Part Three

The Fool in the Forest

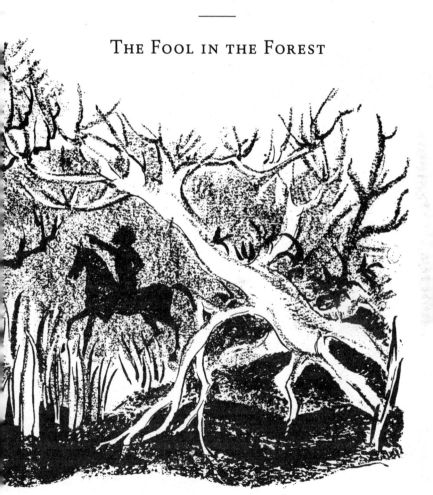

1   An Old Friend

Tiuri had first met Marius on his journey to the Kingdom of Unauwen. "I am the Fool in the Forest," he had told him. "The Fool in the Forest, that's what they all call me, the woodcutters and the charcoal burners, and my father and my brothers call me the same. But my mother calls me Marius."

Tiuri and Marius had become friends. That had been months ago, in a very different forest.

"Do you remember me?" asked the Fool. "Do you still know my name? Don't say it out loud! I know you, too. You are a traveller, a rider, and now I call you knight."

Tiuri went to greet him. "Marius!" he said. "However did you end up here?"

"Sssh!" said the Fool. "My cabin is far away and no one can find me now. Not even you, but I saw you and searched for you. I saw you, knight and rider, on your black horse. But you were not alone. Are you alone now, alone with me in this Wild Wood?"

"Yes," replied Tiuri. "I found your flowers and I came back to look for you."

"Beautiful flowers for a beautiful black horse," said the Fool, stroking Ardanwen, who calmly submitted. "I wanted to call out to you and to talk to you. But I couldn't speak out loud and tell you I was there. So I called you with the flowers instead and I told your horse that he must return with you – with you, knight and rider. Did you come here for me, truly for me?"

"Yes," said Tiuri. "I truly came for you." He looked in concern at the Fool. His friend had changed. He had grown thin, and his eyes seemed full of unshed tears. "What has happened,

Marius?" he asked. "How did you come to be here and whatever's wrong?"

"Sssh!" said the Fool again. "I am happy to see you. Do you remember me bringing you food?"

"I certainly do!" said Tiuri with a smile. "And I remember visiting you in your cabin."

The Fool's tears suddenly began to flow. He hid his face in the horse's mane.

"Oh, Marius! Do tell me," said Tiuri, laying his hand on his friend's shoulder. "What is it? Don't be sad. I'll help you."

The Fool raised his head. "I left the cabin," he said, his voice trembling, "far, far away." He wiped his nose and continued, "I didn't want to leave, but they came and said to my brothers, 'You're coming with us.' My brothers went and I had to go, too, but I didn't want to."

"Who came and why did you have to go with them?" asked Tiuri.

"Shh!" whispered the Fool. "They came and I had to go with them, and that's how it was. It was a long time ago, and my mother doesn't know where I am. And I don't know where I am either." He looked like he was about to start crying again.

"Calm down, Marius," said Tiuri. "It won't be hard to find the cabin again, you know. I'll take you there if you don't know the way."

The Fool started to laugh through his tears. "Would you do that, sir knight?" he asked. "Would you do that and do you know the way? The cabin is so far." Then his face clouded over again. "You can't go there," he said. "You mustn't. They'll find us and they'll capture us. They'll seek us and they'll catch us..."

"But who are you talking about?" asked Tiuri.

The Fool looked around. "They are not here now," he whispered. "But they will return. They were here last night, in that house, there."

"Where? And who do you mean?" asked Tiuri.

The Fool pointed.

"In the old hunting lodge? But no one goes there now," said Tiuri. "And you..."

But the Fool wasn't listening. He was peering down the track toward the Unholy Hills. Then he turned back to Tiuri and said, "Come with me, rider. Climb on your horse and ride back. Climb on your horse. I will go with you. Quickly!"

He broke into a run, constantly glancing back over his shoulder. Sometimes he went alongside the path as if he were scared he might be seen, and then he would step back out into the open to beckon to Tiuri. Tiuri could do nothing but follow him, still confused and wondering what exactly had happened to the Fool. Who were the "they" who had taken him against his wishes, and who were not here now but could return soon? Did they exist only in his friend's imagination, or were they a real, living danger?

Danger... But there was nothing out of the ordinary to be found in the Wild Wood, unless you believed in creatures like the Men in Green. And yet... *Does Isa know anything about this?* he thought. *Is there some secret hidden in this wood after all?*

"Marius!" he called softly.

The Fool turned back and came to walk beside him. "What is it?" he asked. "What do you want, knight and friend? You are my friend, aren't you?"

"Of course I'm your friend," said Tiuri, as he brought Ardanwen to a stop and dismounted. They had reached the signpost.

The Fool sat down beside the stone and huddled up, as if trying to hide. Tiuri crouched beside him.

"Now you have to tell me everything," he said.

The Fool looked at him with wide eyes. "I'm frightened," he whispered.

They waited in silence for a short while. Tiuri felt a strange shiver run down his spine. He sat down beside the Fool, leant back against the stone and peered around. But the wood didn't look frightening at all. Quite the opposite, in fact – it was nothing but pretty and full of the green of spring.

The Fool began to speak. "I'm not allowed to tell anyone. 'Keep your mouth shut,' they said. 'Or we'll beat you to death.' I mustn't say anything." He looked unhappily at Tiuri.

"Now listen to me, Marius," Tiuri said firmly. "No one is going to do anything to you while I am here. Do you hear me? You really can tell me everything!"

"But I don't want to, Friend," whispered the Fool. "You don't know who they are. You don't know them." He took hold of Tiuri's hand. "Do you remember what you said to me before?" he continued. "When you were riding to the place where the sun goes down? That they were looking for you and they wanted to hurt you because of your secret! You said no more than that and I told no one about it. No one! This is a secret as well and I'm not even supposed to know it myself! 'Ask nothing and say nothing,' they said to me. They're still looking for me and they'll be looking for you, too, if I tell you."

"Let them look for me!" said Tiuri. "Please tell me, Marius! You're talking in riddles. Who are 'they'? Are there many of them? Or few? Where are they? What do they want?"

The Fool gave a sigh. "Do not ask, do not ask, sir knight!" he said. "You are a valiant knight, and you are my friend. I have seen other knights, but they did not see me, no, no, never. They did not see me and they did not speak to me." He furrowed his brow and continued slowly, "I saw a knight, but he was not as fine as you. His cloak was green, but it was ragged, like a poor man's clothes. That's strange, don't you think, for a knight?"

Tiuri nodded. He said nothing. He dared not say a word, as he feared the Fool might stop talking.

"He had a sword, just like you," said the Fool. "And a shield. Do you have a shield, too?"

"I do," replied Tiuri.

"What colour is your shield? The other knight's was... What colour is yours?"

"White," said Tiuri.

"White. That's beautiful, white," said the Fool contentedly. "White. Like snow. But it hadn't snowed yet when I saw him..."

"What colour was his shield?" asked Tiuri.

"That knight's shield? Green and grey and white," replied the Fool. "No, not white... What's that colour called again? Silver! His cloak was green, and his shield was silver, green and grey. He had been fighting. Have you ever fought?"

"I have," said Tiuri. "But this knight, was he young or old, or..."

"He had a beard, like me," said the Fool. "But his hair was turning grey. I saw him very clearly, but he didn't see me. He knelt down and cried."

"He cried?" repeated Tiuri incredulously.

"Ah, do knights never cry?" asked the Fool. "I've cried. Don't you ever cry? My brothers call me a fool when I cry. They get angry and they laugh at me. You won't be angry if I cry, will you?" He looked anxiously at Tiuri.

"No, no, my dear Marius," he said. "I don't think you're a fool at all! I'd just like to know why that knight was crying."

"He knelt down," the Fool said again, "with his face in his hands, like this. He said something, but I didn't hear what it was. And he took his sword, like this" – Marius made a gesture as if giving a salute – "and he cut into the tree. He scratched into the trunk – signs like these." He put his finger on the letters of the stone signpost.

"Then what happened?" asked Tiuri eagerly.

"Then he walked away," the Fool replied. "He walked to the river. He crouched, and he crept, and he looked. But he didn't see me."

"And then?" asked Tiuri.

"Then? He ran away. I didn't see him again. Gone." The Fool was silent for a moment. "I ran away as well," he said. "They looked for me, but they didn't find me. But I couldn't find the cabin again."

Tiuri thought: *Ristridin? Did he see Ristridin? The description fits, but...* He couldn't imagine it, Sir Ristridin crying – no, with his face hidden in his hands. Ristridin, taking his sword and carving symbols into a tree trunk...

"Marius," he said, "where did you see that knight, and when?"

"I... I don't know," said the Fool. "I..." He jumped to his feet.

Tiuri stood up, too. "Answer me," he said urgently.

"I don't know if I'm allowed..." whispered the Fool. "They, they said... But he..." He gulped.

"Was the knight one of the men who took you?" asked Tiuri.

"No, no," said the Fool.

Tiuri leant towards him. "I think I know that knight," he said quietly. "And, if so, he's a friend of mine. A friend, Marius, just like you. That's why I need you to tell me everything you know about him."

"I don't know anything," whispered the Fool. "That's what they always tell me: 'You are a Fool and you know nothing, and you talk nonsense!'"

"Where did you see him when he was carving letters in a tree?"

The Fool thought for a moment and pointed to the north. "Far from here, in the wood," he replied. "I truly don't know where, sir knight. I have travelled for so long. But it was close to the dark river."

"The Black River?"

The Fool nodded vigorously. "Yes, the Black River," he said.

"And when was this?"

The Fool thought again. "The leaves were brown," he replied, "and some of the trees were almost bare. But it was not yet snowing."

So it must have been last autumn, thought Tiuri and he asked, "Were no others with him? Knights? Horsemen?"

"Sssh!" said the Fool. "No, he was alone. All alone. But he was not alone in the wood." He shivered and added anxiously, "They haven't killed him, have they?"

"Oh no, no," said Tiuri. "But I am glad you have told me this, Marius. You do not need to be afraid. I shall help you. I only want to know if there are dangers in this wood."

"What dangers do you mean? The animals? I am not afraid of the animals," said the Fool. "But I am afraid of others, even with you, knight and friend. Even with you and your black horse."

"We need to know the dangers we face, Marius," said Tiuri. "The better we know them, the less we have to fear them."

"Yes, but I do not know them myself, knight who keeps asking question after question!" the Fool argued. "They told me nothing. They just shouted or laughed at me."

"The Men in Green?" guessed Tiuri.

"Shh!" whispered the Fool. "The Men in Green are always on the lookout and they hear so much. But they never speak." Then he took Tiuri's hand and he pleaded with him, "I don't want to talk about this wood! I just want to go back to my cabin. You said you were going to help me, didn't you? What do I have to do?"

"Come with me," said Tiuri. He realized he was going to have to leave the Fool in peace for a while. He really did seem very upset. Suddenly Tiuri felt himself becoming angry at the mysterious creatures that were to blame. Poor Marius, who would not hurt a fly!

They slowly walked to the edge of the wood. The Fool stopped for a moment and pointed towards the hunting lodge.

"They were there, in that house, last night," he said. "Were they looking for me? What do you think, Friend?"

"The old lodge is never used these days," said Tiuri, half speaking to himself.

"I saw light inside," whispered the Fool.

"Did you?" Tiuri whispered back. "So who was there?"

"They came from every direction," said the Fool. "But I couldn't see them very well in the dark. I saw their shadows. I heard their voices. Were they looking for me?"

"I don't think so, Marius," said Tiuri, "but I can't know for sure. Let's go over there and take a look."

"No!" said the Fool, and he seemed so horrified that Tiuri didn't dare to insist.

He looked at the path. He could tell that horsemen had ridden along there, but it could have been the tracks that he and his companions had left on yesterday's ride. How much longer ago it seemed!

At the edge of the forest they stopped in the meadow with the yellow flowers.

"Marius," said Tiuri, "were you here yesterday, watching us?"

"Yes," replied the Fool. "You were sitting there, with the lady."

"The lady. Do you know her, Marius?"

The Fool shook his head. "No," he said. "She is beautiful. I would be too scared to speak to her!"

"Have you ever seen her before?"

"No," replied the Fool. He picked a flower and wove it into Ardanwen's bridle. "Pretty, isn't it?" he said, looking at Tiuri with a devoted smile. "Who is the lady? Has she enchanted you, knight and traveller?"

Enchanted! Yes, Tiuri realized, *you could call it that.* Isadoro had enchanted him. But right now it felt as if the enchantment had lost much of its power – even though he still found it difficult to fathom his feelings for her. Was she just a fickle young woman who wanted to make a fool of him? Was she the lady Evan believed her to be, more like a woodland fairy, barely an ordinary mortal at all? Or was she something entirely different? Whatever she was, she had lied about the flowers.

"Why do you say nothing, Friend?" asked the Fool.

Tiuri returned to reality. Here was someone who had more need of his attention. "You are coming with me, Marius," he said. "Come on, climb up onto the horse. Ardanwen is strong enough to carry us both."

"Is that his name? Ar-dan-wen, your black horse?" said the Fool. "I know your name, too – Tiuri. But I call you Friend."

"Come on," said Tiuri. He suddenly remembered that he should have been attending Sir Fitil's festivities. How long was it since he had left Islan? The sun was already in the south, and it was still quite some way to the castle. He was sure to be late, a most impolite way for a guest to behave. Yet he could not regret his decision, not now that he had met the Fool.

"Where are you going?" the Fool asked. "I don't want to go that way. No!"

"Don't be like that, Marius," said Tiuri, a little impatiently. "We are going together. There's a castle that way, where there are friends of mine."

"You have many friends," said the Fool. He climbed onto Ardanwen's back, clumsily, but he managed. Tiuri climbed up in front of Marius, who wrapped his arms around his waist. And off they rode to Islan.

"You have many friends," repeated the Fool. "I do not. I have only you, rider, knight."

"My friends will be your friends, too," said Tiuri. "I know my squire, Piak, is going to like you."

Piak! he thought. *He'll be furious with me – and rightly so!* He sighed. Soon he would be at Islan, and the thought of facing Isadoro again was a worrying one.

2 A Celebration Disrupted

Islan's drawbridge was down, the gate was open, and flags flew on poles all around the castle.

As Ardanwen arrived with his double load, a large number of horsemen went riding into the main courtyard. Tiuri recognized Evan as one of them, but he did not see Piak.

"Who lives here?" asked the Fool.

"Sir Fitil," replied Tiuri, "with his daughter, Lady Isadoro."

"And all those men, too?" said the Fool. "Then I do not want to go there." He let go of Tiuri and jumped down from the horse. "What are you doing?" cried Tiuri.

"I shall wait for you outside," said the Fool. "I don't want to go inside, not with all those knights and horsemen. I shall wait outside for you, or by the wood. No one can see me there."

Just then, two people came out of the castle and walked towards them. "There he is!" one of them cried. It was Bendu and Piak.

The Fool was about to run away, but Tiuri jumped down and held onto him. Soon, Piak and Bendu had joined them.

"Well, a fine knight you are!" Bendu said gruffly. "Is this a habit of yours, not showing up when everyone's expecting you?" Then he turned to look at the Fool. "And who's this?" he asked.

The Fool tried to hide behind Tiuri.

"Don't be scared, Marius," he said. "This is an old friend of mine," he added to Bendu. "I met him in the wood."

"Whatever made you decide to ride all the way to the wood?" said Bendu. "The festivities are almost over. Well, you're here now and you'll just have to make your apologies."

"I shall explain everything later," Tiuri began, but then he fell silent. How much could he say?

"Don't tell him anything!" the Fool whispered. "Say nothing, Friend."

"Who is this wild man of the woods?" asked Bendu.

"They call me the Fool," Marius said, half timid, half defiant. "I am the Fool. Everyone says so. But my mother calls me Marius and so does he."

"The Fool in the Forest!" exclaimed Piak. It was the first time he had spoken.

"Yes, he was the one who put the flowers in Ardanwen's bridle," said Tiuri.

"Flowers?" repeated Bendu with a puzzled look on his face.

"That really doesn't matter now," Tiuri said hastily. "What matters, Sir Bendu, is that Marius saw Ristridin in the Wild Wood."

"He did? When?" cried Bendu.

The Fool hid behind Tiuri again. "Why did you have to tell him?" he wailed. "Why?!"

"Marius," said Tiuri, "this knight – Bendu is his name – is the best friend of the knight you saw in the forest."

"They're all best friends! All of them!" said the Fool. "I do not know them, your friends. I know only you, and I will speak only to you! And you say too much, Sir Tiuri, far too much. You even talk about the Men in Green."

Bendu listened with impatience. "I fear you also say too much," he said to the Fool. "But what do you know of Sir Ristridin?"

"Who is Sir Ristridin?" asked the Fool. "I don't know. I don't know!"

"Calm down," said Tiuri soothingly. "The knight you saw carving signs in a tree. Do you remember?"

Bendu turned to the Fool and questioned him in his usual gruff tone.

That only scared the Fool even more and the longer his answers were, the more confused and evasive they became.

"What a lot of nonsense!" Bendu finally blurted out.

Tiuri said angrily, "You are frightening him, Sir Bendu! Please ask him no more questions. I shall talk to him." He turned to the Fool and tried to calm him, but with little success.

"I know, I know!" said the Fool. "I talk nonsense. Everyone says so." He continued to babble almost unintelligibly about the "men who are coming back" and the "Men in Green".

At those words, Bendu really did lose his patience. "That's all we need," he sneered. "The Men in Green, in the depths of the forest, flying from tree to tree."

The Fool stared at him. "Yes, yes! That's exactly what they do!" he said. "You have seen them!"

That was enough reason for Bendu to dismiss all the Fool had said as truly foolish nonsense. "Right," he said brusquely. "I'm going to see the champion crowned. And if you think it at all important, Tiuri, you might also wish to show your face." And Bendu strode away.

"You mustn't be scared of him, Marius," Piak said to the Fool. "Sir Bendu is often a little rough-spoken, but he doesn't mean any harm."

The Fool wiped a tear from his eye. "You all talk too much," he mumbled. But Piak seemed to have made him feel a little better.

"Then, for now, we shall be silent," said Tiuri. "Come on, let's go to the castle. We'll talk more later."

But the Fool refused to take a single step in that direction. "I am not going in there," he declared.

The sound of applause came from the castle.

"I'll wait for you, outside or in the forest," said the Fool. "I'll wait for you. And this friend," he added, nodding at Piak, "can come, too. But I'm not going in there." Then he turned and ran away.

Tiuri went after him. "Marius!" he called.

The Fool stopped and looked at him. He seemed much calmer now. "I won't forget," he said. "I'll wait for you."

Tiuri realized he could not persuade him. "Fine, then," he said. "I'll see you again tomorrow. And I'll take you back to the cabin."

The Fool smiled. "You are my Friend," he said and started walking again.

Tiuri frowned. Should he really let Marius out of his sight? The Fool was older than Tiuri, but in many respects he was like a child.

"He's different, not like other people," he said quietly.

"Yes," Piak agreed. "You're right."

"I owe you an explanation," Tiuri said to his friend.

"Never mind," he replied.

"I rode off without..." Tiuri began.

"Without me," said Piak, interrupting him. "Oh, maybe it was just as well."

They made their way to the castle. Soldiers had appeared in the gateway and were watching them.

"What's this story about Sir Ristridin?" asked Piak.

"I'll tell you later," replied Tiuri. "First the festivities."

"No one had any idea where you were," said Piak. "Except perhaps for Isadoro. I think Sir Fitil was angry, but he still kept laughing long and loud. And Sir Evan won the ring-tilting contest."

A large crowd was gathered in one of the courtyards. As Tiuri and Piak entered, everyone was cheering Sir Evan as the victor of the games.

Lady Isadoro was standing with Evan on a platform. She placed a wreath on his head and declared, "To Evan the victory! And good luck to him!"

Everyone cheered and Tiuri felt a pang of jealousy. So the enchantment was not entirely gone; he wished Isadoro had looked at him the way she was looking at Evan now. He was annoyed that what had happened between them seemed to have made little impact on her.

Then Sir Fitil came over, accompanied by Bendu.

"You have missed out on the fame and the honour!" he cried with a booming laugh. But his expression was not unkind.

"My lord," said Tiuri, "I offer you my apologies. It was truly not my plan to remain away from your festivities so discourteously. I believed I would return in time, but..."

"You met a friend," the lord of the castle said, completing his sentence for him. "I just heard the news from Sir Bendu. A rather peculiar fellow, I understand."

"Oh no, not at all," said Tiuri. "A little strange perhaps for those who do not know him well. He was in trouble."

"Where is he?" asked Sir Fitil, frowning and narrowing his eyes.

"He didn't want to come inside," replied Tiuri.

"The poor chap's not quite right in the head, is he?" said Sir Fitil.

"No. That's not true," said Tiuri indignantly.

"Fine, fine!" said Sir Fitil breezily. "A knight must stand up for his friends, Sir Tiuri! Ah, I see my daughter has spotted you, too."

Tiuri followed his gaze. Isadoro was staring at him. He bowed to her, feeling rather uncomfortable.

Evan was beside her and people were crowding around them, so Tiuri could not go to her.

"The prodigal son has returned!" cried Sir Fitil. "And the best part of the festivities is yet to come: the fatted calf has been killed! Fine food for one and all! Let us head inside, sit down for our feast and raise a glass of the best wine from my cellar!"

His words were greeted by cheers and all the guests followed him as he entered the castle.

Long tables had been set up in the hall, and laid with pewter cups and glasses and bowls full of all kinds of bread. Two cooks were at work beside the big fire, where meat was roasting on a spit. Colourful banners hung on the walls and vases of blossom were dotted around the room.

Musicians arrived with their lutes and trumpets. They climbed the steps into the gallery, where they took their places and began to play. They were a little out of tune, and Isadoro, who was sitting with Evan in the place of honour, laughed and covered her ears. One of Sir Fitil's dogs began to howl, which didn't improve the sound, and it was chased from the hall with much hullabaloo. By then everyone was seated and they waited in silence as the lord of the castle began the feast with a prayer and a blessing. Then the guests tucked in, trying to make themselves heard above the music. Before long Sir Fitil beckoned the musicians to join them at the table. "You must have worked up an appetite!" he cried. "And even more of a thirst! Isadoro, I shall send for your harp. You must play something for us."

The guests, most of whom were soldiers in Fitil's service, clapped their hands, and Evan, still wearing his victor's wreath, laughed and said something to the lady.

But Isadoro did not laugh. She looked at her father and said, "No," so abruptly that it was almost rude.

For a moment it seemed as if Sir Fitil would respond in anger, but then he laughed and shouted, "Isadoro does not like to play this early in the evening. Let us remain patient and sing something while we wait – but not with our mouths full, of course!" He started the song himself, in his deep voice:

> *Gathered here together, all good friends,*
> *all good friends...*

The sound of a horn outside made him break off his song. "Aha, the gate is still open. Another guest at our feast!" he cried. "The more the merrier!" And he ordered his servants to go around with the wine once again.

A man appeared in the doorway, dirty and dusty from a long ride.

Sir Fitil saw him first. "Welcome, welcome!" he called. "Celebrate with us in honour of Sir Evan and Bendu and of... of all who are guests here or who live in my castle. Come in, sit down!"

The man came closer, walking unsteadily, as if he were very tired, but he did not sit down. He opened his mouth and said something that could not be heard above the hubbub in the room.

"Sit down, sit down!" cried Sir Fitil.

The man spoke again. "Sir Bendu..." was all Tiuri heard.

"Hey, everyone! Be quiet for a moment!" called Sir Fitil.

Now they could all hear what the man had to say.

"I come from Sir Arturin at Castle Ristridin with a message for Sir Bendu and his companions."

"Has Ristridin returned?" asked Bendu, standing up.

"No," said the man. "There has been... They came from Deltaland. They've invaded! They've invaded our country."

"Invaded?" repeated Fitil.

"An invasion from Deltaland," said the messenger. He took a deep breath and leant with one hand on the table. "Sir Arturin sent me here as soon as he heard," he added, haltingly. "I rode

117

without stopping. I'm sure no one has ever covered that distance so quickly..."

Bendu and Sir Fitil stood up at the same moment and went to the messenger. "Here," said Sir Fitil. "Have something to drink." But the messenger wanted first to tell his news.

"It happened the day after you left," he said to Bendu. "An army of fierce warriors crossed the border from Deltaland, close to Castle Warudin. The Lord of Warudin attempted to counter the attack and sent messengers in every direction. My lord, Sir Arturin, was equipping his men when I left. I was immediately sent here. Another messenger will follow with more news."

"An invasion from Deltaland," said Fitil. "Deltaland! I thought they were all sleeping."

"Eviellan is behind it, of course!" cried Bendu. "Deltaland and Eviellan are one and the same, as everyone knows. Do you see now that they are not to be trusted? I have always said so. And yet at the same time they have sent Sir Kraton to negotiate with King Dagonaut."

"Deltaland..." muttered Evan. He and Tiuri looked at each other.

Tiuri knew Evan was thinking the same as him, and maybe Bendu was, too. Yes, he was indeed, because now he said, "But why should we be surprised? We have often heard mention of Deltaland in the past few days." He turned to the messenger. "And you've heard nothing from Arturin's brother, Sir Ristridin?"

"Nothing, my lord," the messenger replied. "He has been away for a long time. That's true..." He eagerly took the glass that Sir Fitil held out to him, as he had nothing more to report.

Silence descended upon the hall. The celebration was over. The news had put an end to their joy.

Then Bendu spoke. "We must return immediately," he said grimly. "First to Castle Ristridin, and then onwards to face the enemy."

"I must send men, too," said Sir Fitil. "I shall call them together at once."

Lady Isadoro came to stand beside him. "What exactly does this mean?" she asked.

Bendu shrugged. "A brief skirmish," he said. "Or war."

At these words, silence fell once again.

It was Bendu who broke the silence for a second time. "Well," he said, "I'm so sorry about this turn of events. Sir Fitil, you will understand that we must leave."

"Of course," said the Lord of Islan. "I hope my men will be ready to leave with you."

"They could follow on a little later," said Bendu. "That might even be better. Then you'll hear from the second messenger how many men are needed."

He headed up the stairs and to his room.

Evan slowly removed the victor's wreath from his head. "I'll ride with you to Castle Ristridin," he said, "and then I hope I'll know enough to decide what I need to do."

"What do you mean?" asked Tiuri.

"My country has to hear this news as well!" said Evan.

"And what should we do?" Piak asked Tiuri.

"You must come, too!" said Evan. "What is there for you to do here?"

"There's a promise to keep," replied Tiuri. "And also... But I'll tell you about that later."

3 PARTING WAYS

"Well, I think you're a fool if you do not come with us!" Bendu said to Tiuri. "Our land, the Kingdom of Dagonaut, is under attack! Do you understand? Why did you become a knight – surely it was to fight against evil, whether that means Eviellan or Deltaland! And now you want to go off gallivanting with that friend of yours, that halfwit?!"

"Marius," Tiuri corrected him abruptly.

"Marius, if that's what you want to call that fool," continued Bendu. "But if you do, you're an even bigger fool yourself! The man can wait a little while, can't he?"

"He is unhappy," said Tiuri, "and he believes that people are pursuing him."

There were four of them in the room. Bendu was ready to leave; he stood glaring at Tiuri. Evan was packing his last few belongings. Piak sat cross-legged on his bed, looking anxiously at his friend.

"Fine, he's unhappy," Bendu went on, "and of course you can help him. But we have more pressing duties now. Oh, I know what you're thinking about, Tiuri! All that muddled nonsense about Ristridin. So, what do you want to do about it? Are you going to inspect every tree in the Wild Wood in an attempt to find the one Ristridin wrote something on? That's if he ever did! As if he would sit crying in the forest – Ristridin, of all the men I know! When did that fool of yours see him? In the autumn, you say, by the Black River. Well, that could actually be true. Ristridin, Arwaut and their men encountered and defeated some robbers there, and that was in the autumn, between the Green River and the Black River. That's what Ristridin said in his first message, the only letter he wrote. Fine, then maybe these robbers are the mysterious men who are chasing your fool. But that's still not the end of the story! Our friends left the Wild Wood quite some time after that, in the winter – because there was nothing happening there. And those robbers have been defeated, as I already said."

Bendu fell silent. He did not often speak for so long at once.

But Tiuri said, "Marius says they're still there. Last night there were even people in the old hunting lodge. There is something else in that forest!"

"Yes, Men in Green," muttered Bendu, "who fly from tree to tree. At least that's what your friend says. Ristridin reported that there was nothing of any interest in the Wild Wood. Which one would you rather believe?"

"We did not speak to Ristridin ourselves..." Tiuri began, but then he stopped. Bendu completed his sentence for him: "We only received his message via Sir Fitil, Lord of Islan. But it would appear that you favour the ramblings of a fool over the word of a knight of King Dagonaut."

Tiuri blushed. "That's not what I meant!" he cried.

"Then I should like to know what it is that you meant," growled Bendu. "Well, I've said my piece, and it's up to you to make your own decision." He turned away, picked up his bag, and made ready to leave.

Then Evan said, "I have something to add, Sir Bendu." He looked at Tiuri and continued, "They invaded from Deltaland... Twice we have heard that Sir Ristridin went to that place."

"That's right," said Bendu. "Ristridin was aware of that danger sooner than we."

"What I was wondering," Evan continued, "is exactly how he found out about it. First he was in the Wild Wood, where he drove out the robbers, and where otherwise there was nothing or no one. From there he went with great haste to Deltaland. So who was it who told him to go there?"

"How should we know?" Bendu said impatiently.

But Piak said quietly, "Might he have found out about it in the Wild Wood?"

"So there must be something or someone in there after all," said Evan.

"Those Men in Green again!" said Bendu with a sigh. "Evan, don't tell me you're going with Tiuri, too!"

"No, I'm not," replied Evan. "I feel that I should go to the south, and then head towards the enemy or to my own land as a messenger. But I think Tiuri should go ahead with his plan. First of all, he should help Marius. Many men will go to the border, as the news of the invasion will soon be known throughout the land. As we fight the enemy, we should not forget that others may be in even greater need of our help."

It seemed to Tiuri as if Prince Iridian were speaking with Evan's voice; the prince could have said those very words.

"And," concluded Evan, "If Marius can tell Tiuri more about Ristridin, it could only be of benefit."

"I can tell," said Bendu, "that you have not spoken to this Fool yourself."

"Tiuri knows him better than you do," was all Evan said in reply.

Bendu turned to Tiuri. "I do not agree with your decision," he said, "but still I give you my best wishes." He shook Tiuri firmly by the hand. "Are you ready, Evan?" he asked.

"Yes, we can leave," Evan replied. "So must I bid you farewell, Tiuri?"

"Yes, Evan," came Tiuri's reply.

"Yes, Sir Evan," Piak said, too.

"Then leave with haste, and do not say too much about what Marius has told you," Evan advised him. "Others might take it the wrong way."

What did Evan mean? Tiuri wondered, after Evan and Bendu had departed on their journey to Sir Arturin's castle. Because others might react as Bendu had done? Or for a reason that was so vague and nebulous he didn't want to go into it...? If the Fool had told the truth, what was he to make of Ristridin's message? No, he must not speak about it. Marius had also said the same.

But still he told Piak exactly what had happened on the way to the Unholy Hills. Piak was such a trusted friend. Even so, he said hardly anything to him about what had happened in Lady Isadoro's garden. He could barely even bring himself to say the name Isadoro. Somehow she made him feel guilty. Soon he would leave and he was not looking forward to the farewell.

I want to run from her and I want to stay with her, he thought. Circumstances had conspired to allow him to leave Islan, but still he was not content.

The path he had chosen did not truly appeal to him. How much easier it would have been to simply go with Bendu and Evan, even if that meant heading into battle. "I shall win no renown and honour on the way to the Fool's cabin," he mocked himself. "At best people will think me foolish, as Sir Bendu did." But the thought of Marius, the Fool, made such concerns vanish. *If I do not help him, I am worth nothing*, he thought to himself. And he tried to banish all thoughts of Sir Ristridin from his mind.

Besides, Piak thought he was doing the right thing, and so did Evan. So what was he worried about?

"I have heard you intend to go travelling with that peculiar friend of yours," said Sir Fitil the next morning. "Is your presence not required at the border?" His tone was so obviously scornful that Tiuri blushed, partly because Isadoro was also there.

"A knight must prove his courage in battle," the lord of the castle added.

But a knight must also help people! However, Tiuri did not respond to Sir Fitil's words. All he said was, "My friend is lost and I have promised to take him back to his home."

Sir Fitil's eyebrows shot up. "And where exactly," he asked, "is this home? Do you know the way?"

"In the Royal Forest," replied Tiuri.

"Oh, so that's where it is," said Sir Fitil. "Then you must head north and take the Second Great Road at Stoneford. You can only travel along it in an easterly direction from there, first along the Black River and then along the Green River. The Royal Forest begins on the other side of the Green River." His tone was friendlier now.

"Thank you, Sir Fitil," said Tiuri.

"And where is this friend from the forest?" asked Sir Fitil.

"He said he'd wait somewhere outside for me," replied Tiuri.

"A most peculiar arrangement," mumbled Sir Fitil. "Well, I have no right to interfere with your plans."

Tiuri looked him in the eyes and was shocked at what he saw there. *Sir Fitil is furious*, he realized. *Is that because he thinks I'm a coward as I want to go to the north while the battle is in the south?* It would not have surprised Tiuri if Sir Fitil had forbidden him to leave, but a moment later he was wondering if he had only imagined it. The lord laughed, slapped him on the back, and cheerfully wished him a good journey.

"I shall have the gate opened for you," he said and left.

Then Lady Isadoro turned to Piak, who was standing silently beside Tiuri.

"Does Sir Tiuri really wish to go?" she said. "Then tell him he must take the wide, open roads, and pay no heed to any of the strange tales that people sometimes tell."

"My lady, he is standing right before you," said Piak. "You can tell him yourself!"

"No," said Isadoro. "Sir Tiuri does not believe my words. His heart is filled with distrust of me."

Tiuri had no idea how to respond, and neither did Piak. She looked at each of them in turn. "There is nothing I can say to ease your suspicion," she continued, "but, and you must believe me, do as I have said! Go to the north, but better to the south. Travel to the east, but avoid the west." She spoke forcefully, her voice trembling a little.

"Isadoro, why?" whispered Tiuri.

But she shook her head and did not respond.

"The gate is open. My men are about to leave for Deltaland!" said Sir Fitil, as he came back into the room. "Would you like to join them, Sir Tiuri? Yes or no?"

"No, thank you," said Tiuri firmly.

He followed Isadoro's gaze and saw fear in her eyes. She was afraid of her father! Was that the reason for her puzzling behaviour?

"Other messengers have arrived," said Sir Fitil. "Knights and men-at-arms are coming from all directions to face the enemy from Deltaland – from Arturin's castle, from Mirtelan, from Warudin and Griudin."

"Are they?" said Tiuri vaguely. His mind was on Isadoro.

"Melas of Darokítam will send help from the south," continued Sir Fitil.

"Melas of Darokítam? From Eviellan?" cried Piak. "Help for Deltaland, I'm sure."

"No, help for us," said Sir Fitil. "Eviellan is on our side."

Both Piak and Tiuri were most surprised to hear this news.

"Sir Arturin's messengers are in the courtyard," said Sir Fitil. "You can ask them yourselves if you do not believe it. They have just arrived and wish to return to Castle Ristridin soon." He waited for a moment and then added with a sneer, "So your help will not be needed, which I am sure will come as a relief. You may stay here if you wish. Guests are always welcome."

"No!" said Isadoro loudly. Now there was not a trace of fear in her voice. She looked angry.

Tiuri was baffled.

"Come with me," said the Lord of Islan. "And I shall bid you farewell."

Tiuri turned to Lady Isadoro and held out his hand, almost pleadingly. She placed her hand in his. Tiuri tried in vain to read some kind of message in her eyes. Then he bowed and kissed her hand.

In the courtyard, in the sunshine, stood Sir Fitil's men, all in chainmail with tunics of brown and yellow – the colours of Islan. They were heavily armed, with swords and lances, bows and arrows. Tiuri and Piak spoke briefly to the messengers from Castle Ristridin and heard once again that Eviellan was to send help. The messengers asked if they wanted to travel with them, back to the castle by the Grey River.

"Perhaps Sir Ristridin has returned home by now," one of them said hopefully. "We could certainly use him in battle."

However, Tiuri and Piak kept to their plan to head to the north. And so they said farewell to Islan. They had chosen their path.

4   STONEFORD

The friends did not head north immediately. First they had to find the Fool, who was waiting for them nearby. The question was, though, exactly where he might be.

"He'll be somewhere close to the forest," said Tiuri.

"Then I wonder if we'll find him," replied Piak with a doubtful look on his face.

"I'm sure he'll find us," said Tiuri. "But Piak, you really do want to come with me, don't you?"

"You know I do! I'm your squire!" Piak said.

They urged on their horses and cantered until they reached the trees.

"We're here!" shouted Piak with his hands cupped around his mouth. "Sir Tiuri with the White Shield, and his squire!"

"Hey, be quiet!" said Tiuri. "There's no need to go shouting our names."

"Do you think others might be listening?" asked Piak.

"I don't think anything," said Tiuri. "I've noticed that thinking doesn't seem to get me anywhere." He sighed. "I'd rather wait and see," he added.

Then they rode slowly along the edge of the wood, listening and looking as they went. But no one appeared.

"Let's get off the horses and have something to eat," said Piak after some time.

So they did, and they had not been sitting there for long when a voice quietly called, "There you are, two riders, two travellers, and here am I!" The Fool stepped out of the forest. "You came, Friend!" he said happily. "You did not forget. Do you know the way home to my cabin?"

"Come sit with us, Marius," said Tiuri, "and eat. This is Piak."

"Yes, I know him. He's your squire," said the Fool. "Do you carry his shield, his white shield?"

"Sometimes," replied Piak with a friendly smile. "But not all the time. It's rather heavy, you know."

"I can carry it, too," said the Fool. "I am strong, very strong." He eagerly took the bread that Tiuri offered him and gobbled it down as if he had eaten nothing for days. But then he became uneasy. He kept looking around and asking when they would be on their way.

"Right now," said Tiuri, jumping to his feet. "We have only two horses for the three of us, but Ardanwen will just have to carry two for some of the time. And we can take it in turns to walk."

They rode along the edge of the forest at first and then took a narrow track that led to the wider road from Islan to Stoneford. The journey was an easy one. The Fool no longer seemed as frightened, and he and Piak soon became good friends. He did not say a word about his experiences in the wood, and Tiuri thought it better not to ask any questions for the time being.

From Islan to Stoneford was about a day's ride, but as the sun set they could still see no sign of the place. It grew dark and still they pressed on. The Fool was sitting on Ardanwen's back. He kept looking around and saying quietly, "Aren't they going to come after us? Aren't they looking for us? It's night time now."

"I'm afraid we're going to have to sleep by the roadside," said Tiuri, who was leading his horse by the reins. "I can hardly see my hand in front of my face."

"I can see something!" said the Fool a little later, peering straight ahead. "Look, a house!"

It was a moment before Tiuri and Piak saw it, too. Yes, there was a building. Narrow strips of light shone through shutters that weren't quite closed. When they reached it, they saw it was probably an inn. A sign hung above the door, but they could not read the name. There were no other buildings nearby, as far as they could see.

Tiuri knocked on the door.

"Are we going inside?" the Fool asked anxiously.

"Perhaps we can spend the night here," said Tiuri. "That's better than outside, don't you think, Marius?"

"No... or yes, maybe," said the Fool.

Tiuri knocked again.

"I wonder if anyone will answer," whispered Piak.

Just then, they heard wheezing and coughing. The door opened and a man said, "Come on in."

"Good evening," said Tiuri. "May we spend the night here?"

"This is the Silent Inn," replied the man, "and yes, you may spend the night here. Not that I have many guests. Times are hard." He showed them the stable and then led them into the small and shabby tavern.

"Ah, so it is fair to say that the late evening brings fine folk," he said, taking a good look at them. "Greetings, sir knight. And to you too, squire and manservant, if I am not mistaken."

"Three friends," said Tiuri.

The man chuckled and was overcome by a coughing fit.

"Ah, I'm not long for this world," he said cheerfully, as soon as he got his breath back. "Would you like something to eat? If I have anything in, that is. I don't expect guests these days."

"If you have something to spare, yes, please," said Tiuri.

"I'm hungry," said the Fool, nodding.

The innkeeper placed a dented cup and a jug on the table, invited them to sit and left the room, coughing all the while. It turned out that he did have some food, as he soon returned with a bowl of cold barley porridge and a long brown loaf. He filled the cup with beer, sat down with his guests and watched as they ate. He was dishevelled, with his dirty apron and his grey stubble, but seemed friendly enough.

"Is this Stoneford?" asked Tiuri.

"Well, you could say that," came the reply. "Stoneford's actually on the Black River, and that's a good half hour's ride from here. But the Silent Inn is the only inn hereabouts."

"Is Stoneford a village?" asked Piak.

"Ha, a village!" sniffed the innkeeper. "I wouldn't call one and a half houses a village. You can cross the river there, but it won't do you much good, because there's just the Dead Stone on the other bank and, after that, nothing."

"The Dead Stone?" repeated Piak.

"Nothing?" said Tiuri.

"Well, I say nothing, but what I mean is the Wild Wood," explained the innkeeper. "But I reckon places you don't go to don't really exist."

"What is the Dead Stone?" asked Piak.

"It's a stone," said the innkeeper, "on the other side of the Black River. They sometimes call it the Black Stone, too, even though it's grey, and green in parts from all that slimy moss." He grimaced. "There's no one who'll dare to go there at night," he continued. "That place is so haunted. Even in the daytime, people avoid it."

"Is that true?" asked Piak.

Tiuri looked rather anxiously at the Fool, who was staring at the innkeeper with big, frightened eyes.

The innkeeper coughed. "On my oath it's true," he replied. "A traveller was once murdered there, and even worse things have happened. But I'd rather not talk about that after sunset."

Piak opened his mouth to ask more, but Tiuri silenced him with a look.

The innkeeper, however, didn't need any more questions. "Yes, it's an evil place indeed," he nodded. "There's a curse on it. They say that every ill wish spoken at the Dead Stone will come true – but it's also really dangerous for whoever makes the wish." He regarded his guests with a look of contentment on his face. He seemed to think his story very ordinary indeed and not in the least bit frightening. "That's why the road comes to a dead end there," he added. "I mean the Second Great Road to the west. It was the Dead Stone that killed the road." He chuckled again, which set off his cough.

Tiuri looked at the Fool, who was sitting remarkably quietly. Fortunately they'd finished eating and so he asked if they could go to bed.

The innkeeper took them to a grubby room with a large bed. He said he hoped there were no fleas and then wished them a good night's sleep.

His wish did not come true. The three travellers slept badly, because the bed was hard, and every now and then something made them itch.

"And to think that only yesterday we were lying in those wonderful beds at Islan," sighed Piak.

Islan! Once again, Tiuri started thinking through everything that had happened there. Most of all, he thought about Isadoro. He suddenly felt worried about her. Was she unhappy? Did she feel like a prisoner in her father's castle? He thought she must. As he pondered, he fell asleep and dreamt about rescuing Isadoro from Islan, and racing on Ardanwen across wild landscapes with Isadoro in his arms. As he was about to kiss her, though, he saw that she was not Isadoro, but Lady Lavinia of Castle Mistrinaut. That only filled him with joy and he was just leaning in towards her when a cry awoke him.

It was the Fool, talking in his sleep. "I can hear them!" he groaned. "They're coming, on horses. They're trampling everything underfoot. Help!"

Tiuri gently shook him. The Fool sighed and mumbled, "I truly don't know," and then was silent.

I don't know either, thought Tiuri, as he turned over and closed his eyes. But it was no good. All kinds of thoughts were nipping away at him like fleas. He felt so very far from the confident Sir Tiuri who had left his father's castle in such high spirits.

The three travellers were glad to leave the inn the next day, although the innkeeper said he was sorry to see them go.

*

They soon reached the Black River. The village of Stoneford was indeed small, just a few shabby houses huddled together. It seemed that the villagers did not see many travellers and that they didn't really want to see them either. When the trio tried to buy bread from a place that appeared to be a shop, the owner looked at them as if they were mad. Then he held up two loaves of bread and demanded an outrageously high price.

"Isn't that rather a lot?" said Tiuri in a chilly tone.

"It's not too much, sir knight," said the merchant gruffly. "Don't buy it if you think it's too expensive. But I should tell you that bread is precious here. We barely have enough to eat ourselves."

"So it would seem," said Tiuri to himself, as he looked at the merchant, and he paid without haggling.

The man became friendlier then and tried to sell other things to him. It wasn't only food that he sold, he said, but also clothes, wicker baskets, axes, knives, and plenty of other wares.

Tiuri said no at first, but then he spotted a pair of boots and realized that the Fool could do with some. And so Marius was given a rather faded pair of trousers and the boots, which he was delighted with – so delighted that he thought it a shame to wear them.

Soon after that, the three travellers took the Second Great Road to the west. The Fool was wearing his new trousers, but carrying the boots in his hand.

"They're much too fine to walk in," he said. "I'll save them for when I have cold feet."

Tiuri and Piak looked at the river. The water was dark, perhaps because there was so much mud in it, and the banks were lined with thick, old trees.

"Look, it's really shallow there," Piak pointed out.

"That's the ford, where you can wade across the river," said Tiuri.

"Shall we cross to the other side?" Piak suggested.

A man with an axe, who was just walking by, heard his words and said, "I wouldn't do that if I were you."

"Why not?" asked Piak.

"You can figure that out for yourselves," he said in an unfriendly tone, and he walked on along the road towards the point where it reached a dead end.

Piak gazed across to the opposite bank, which seemed to be calling to him. "Just for a moment," he said.

Tiuri felt the same. He turned to the Fool and said, "Are you coming, too, Marius?"

"I go where you go, Sir Tiuri," he replied. "Is that the way home?"

"We still have far to go," said Tiuri.

"Far, far, far," sighed the Fool. "We won't be there for a long time. I feel it. I know it."

"We're only going to take a quick look," said Tiuri, "and then we'll travel on along the road."

Up on their horses, they were soon across the river. They rode a short way through tall reeds and then came to a clearing with a large stone in the middle.

"The Dead Stone," whispered Piak. He jumped down from his horse and walked over to it. As he reached out his hand to touch the stone, he changed his mind. He mumbled something: "'Now retrace your steps or may the Wood devour you...' Do you think this could have been a signpost, too?" he asked Tiuri, who was standing beside him.

"There are no words on it," said Tiuri.

"Yes, but there's a thick layer of moss. And all those strange brown marks. What could they be?"

It looks a lot like blood, thought Tiuri, but he did not say so out loud.

Piak walked around the stone. He seemed fascinated.

"So you can speak an ill wish here," he said. "Do you think a good wish would come true as well?"

"Maybe you could even use your wish to destroy the stone's evil power," said Tiuri, only half joking.

"Shall I wish something?" said Piak.

132

"No, don't do that," said Tiuri, and although his tone was light, he meant what he said. "What if the stone twists your wish and turns it into something bad?"

Piak nodded. "It could do..." he said pensively.

Then he looked around. "Hey," he cried. "Where's Marius?"

Two paths began at the clearing with the Dead Stone. One went to the north, while the other ran along the Black River to the west. That was where they found the Fool. He was sitting on the ground and staring at the water, twirling the curls in his beard.

"Can you hear what the water's saying?" he asked. "Can you hear how it flows? It comes from far away, from there – it comes from the Wild Wood. I *know* this river."

Tiuri sat down beside him and said, "Yes, Marius, this is the Black River, the river where you saw that knight."

"That wasn't here," said the Fool. "It was deeper in the forest. I know where it was."

"You know where it was?" asked Tiuri. "How far from here?"

The Fool furrowed his brow. "One day?" he said. "Two days, maybe three? It was dark there, and there were leaves floating on the water."

"Oh, can't we go and look for the place?" asked Piak. "Don't you really want to find out what Sir Ristridin wrote on that tree as well?"

Of course Tiuri did! But he gave a doubtful frown. He remembered Bendu's words, "Are you going to inspect every tree in the Wild Wood...?" Was there any chance that the Fool could ever find that place again? And how long would it take?

On the other bank, the man with the axe stood watching them. Then he disappeared into the forest and soon they heard the sounds of woodcutting.

"I had to chop down trees, too," said the Fool. "Chop down trees, because I'm strong. My brothers are strong, too. But where are they now?"

"Yes, where are they?" asked Piak.

"I don't know," whispered the Fool. "I ran away..." He paused before adding, "Oh, and I was at the Owl House, too."

"The Owl House?" Tiuri and Piak repeated.

"That's where it was!" said the Fool. "At the Owl House! I sheltered there when it snowed but later they came looking for me and so I went to the other side of the water. The Owl House."

"What about this Owl House?" asked Piak.

"Where that knight was, that knight with his sword. It was near there... there was a road there. But I never walk on the roads."

"Is the house by the river?" asked Tiuri.

"Yes, by the river," replied the Fool. "That way." He pointed to the west.

"Do you think this path leads there?" Piak said to Tiuri. "A path always goes somewhere... maybe to a house."

"It's possible..." said Tiuri. "Does anyone live in the house?" he asked the Fool.

"Yes," he replied.

"Who?" asked Tiuri.

"The owls, of course," replied the Fool. "It's an Owl House."

"Owls!" exclaimed Piak. "You mean actual birds live there?"

"Yes, birds," said the Fool. "That's what owls are. Birds."

Tiuri stood up. "Marius," he said, "do you mind if we go down this path for a bit? I'd really like to see this Owl House, and the tree where the knight knelt down."

"Because it's what you want, Friend," replied the Fool. "But I wouldn't want to go to that place again myself, no, no, never."

"Then we shall take you home to your cabin instead," said Tiuri.

But then the Fool stood up, too, and said, "No, no! Go to the Owl House first, Friend, and then to my cabin. I have to go past the Owl House if we are going to the cabin."

"That's not true!" said Tiuri.

"Yes, it is," said the Fool. "Don't you understand? From the cabin I went to the Owl House and from the Owl House I went deeper into the wood, much deeper. Then I ran away and went back to the Owl House. I wanted to go home to the cabin, but then they came, and I had to escape to the other side of the water. And that's what happened."

He placed a hand on Tiuri's chest and added, "Let's go to the Owl House, and then from the Owl House to the cabin. I won't be afraid with the two of you there, truly I won't."

"It could be close," said Piak.

"Fine, we'll do it," said Tiuri. "Down this path. But not too far. If we haven't found anything by tomorrow evening, we'll turn back."

"Then come with me!" said the Fool, picking up his boots. "Come with me, knights, friends. I know the way!"

"Wait a moment!" cried Piak. "Shouldn't we go and buy some more food first? We need to take enough supplies with us."

"Fine, if you want to do all the carrying," said Tiuri with a smile. "But remember we're not venturing too far into uncharted territory, eh?"

5   ALONG THE BLACK RIVER

The horses were still fresh and moved quickly along the path, which was fairly wide. Ardanwen did not tire, even with two riders on his back, Tiuri and Piak this time. The Fool, who was the heaviest, rode Piak's horse. The boots were on his feet now.

After about an hour, the path narrowed, and soon it was no more than a narrow track through the high, coarse grass. Still the horses walked calmly onwards, although more slowly than before.

The trees were thick and old and grew in strange and twisted shapes. And the longer they rode, the denser the undergrowth became. Many of the bushes had evergreen leaves, and some towered above their heads. They hung over the river, dragging their branches in the slowly flowing dark water.

"Now I understand why this river's called the Black River," said Piak. "Ow!" he added, as he banged his head on a prickly branch.

The bushes were so dense now that they could barely make their way through.

"Is this even still a path?" Tiuri wondered out loud. "I don't think so."

"There's something over there that looks more like a proper way through," said Piak, pointing.

"But that would mean moving away from the river," said Tiuri. "Oh, but let's give it a try. We really can't carry on along here."

After a while, they realized that the new track also ran parallel to the river, but it too became increasingly difficult to ride along. Leading their horses, they proceeded on foot. The Fool took off his boots again, as the ground was becoming boggy and he thought it a shame to get them dirty.

"Phew!" said Piak finally, dropping down onto the trunk of a fallen tree. "What a terrible path."

"It isn't a path at all!" said Tiuri. "The real path came to a dead end ages ago."

The Fool sat down beside Piak and said, "Bad ground here, bad ground. But soon there's a real road."

"Are you sure?" asked Tiuri.

"Certain, very certain," replied the Fool. "I can tell by the river. This is the dark river, and by the Owl House the road runs along the dark river."

"I hope you're right," said Tiuri.

"Don't you believe me, don't you believe me, Friend?" said the Fool, sounding very upset. "But I say nothing to you that is not true!"

"I believe you, Marius," Tiuri reassured him. "I only hope the Owl House is not too far and that it is possible to reach it by following the river. I don't plan on leaving the river. We'd get lost in no time."

"That is true," nodded the Fool. "I got lost, too, often. But I won't get lost with you."

*

Am I doing the right thing? thought Tiuri, as they went on their way. *Wouldn't it have been better to take the open roads to the Royal Forest, where the Fool belongs? Was Bendu right? Was Isadoro right? Bendu thought I shouldn't travel with Marius at all, Isadoro said I shouldn't travel to the west, and her father thought me a coward. No one, except for Piak and perhaps Evan, thought I should believe the Fool. Well, if his stories are nonsense, then nothing bad can happen to us in this forest. But then, if he's right, we could be heading into danger...*

Then, suddenly, he sank down into the mud. It came up over his ankles.

"The trees are wider apart here!" called Piak.

"But it's getting more and more like a bog," said Tiuri. "I'm afraid we're going to have to turn around and go back."

"Oh no, let's walk on until at least this evening!" said Piak. "We can always go back tomorrow. Besides, you said we had until tomorrow evening."

They trudged onwards, wading through puddles, stepping over branches, stumbling through mud, and cutting themselves on sharp grass.

"The Owl House is further than this," said the Fool.

Would Isadoro have believed him? Tiuri wondered. *She warned us, but why?* It must have something to do with the wood. And yet she had claimed she never went there. He couldn't work out which of her words were true and which were not. The day before yesterday he had been with her in her garden, and he had kissed her and imagined he was in love with her. Now he was walking in a wilderness, with his heart full of doubt.

He looked up. Through the branches, he could see the sun in the west. It was already getting late.

"Oh, urgh, what are those nasty-looking worms?!" exclaimed Piak.

"Bloodsuckers," said the Fool.

Piak looked in horror at one of the creatures, which had latched onto his leg. He was about to rip it off, but the Fool shouted, "No, no! Don't do that! The bloodsucker will drop off when it's had enough."

"Enough what?" asked Piak feebly.

"You can spare a drop or two of blood for a little creature like that, can't you?" said Tiuri encouragingly. "It's not going to kill you, you know!"

"I think you were right, Tiuri," said Piak. "This really isn't a proper path."

"But we'll keep on going until this evening," said Tiuri. "That's what you wanted to do."

"Of course," said Piak, a little embarrassed. "But I didn't know then that such nasty little beasts existed. Poor horses, you're getting attacked, too! Well, I suppose no one ever comes here, so it must be a feast day for these bloodsuckers."

Tiuri laughed. "You always have to look on the bright side, eh?" he said.

After some hesitation, the Fool decided to put his boots back on.

When they reached a spot that was relatively dry, they made a fire and had something to eat. Then they took the blankets from under the horses' saddles and settled down for the night. At Tiuri's suggestion, they took it in turns to keep watch, as they were in unfamiliar territory.

The next morning, they woke up feeling damp and cold. They discussed what to do and decided to stick to their initial plan: to keep going until that evening.

The surroundings didn't change as they walked with their horses over boggy ground and between twisted trees. Mosquitoes and bloodsuckers plagued them with their attacks. In the afternoon, Tiuri said, "I'm afraid we're not going to make much more progress this way. All we've done is waste a couple of days."

The Fool glanced around wildly, tugging his beard and shaking his head. "Bad ground," he mumbled. Then he pointed at Ardanwen. "Look!" he cried. "Look at the black horse. He knows the way!"

Ardanwen had indeed set off in a different direction.

"He'll find the path," said the Fool.

"He's moving away from the river," said Tiuri.

"But we can't follow the river now anyway," said Piak.

"That's true enough," said Tiuri. "All right, just a short distance, then. I trust Ardanwen."

"Beautiful black horse," said the Fool. "Wise black horse, show us the way!"

6   The Owl House

"He really is leading us far from the river," said Piak after a while. "Although, I have to say, I'm rather enjoying it. Finally solid ground beneath my feet. And we're free from those bloodsuckers!"

Tiuri didn't reply. He was taking a good look around and trying to memorize the surroundings, so he'd be able to find the way back later.

"Hey, look!" cried Piak. "There are flowers here. I'm glad to see them. At least I feel like I'm walking in a normal wood now." And he began to sing a happy song.

"Sssh!" said the Fool.

"What's wrong?" asked Piak.

"Don't talk so loud, Friend!" said the Fool. "Don't sing so loud! They might be able to hear us now."

"We can go back right away, if that's what you want, Marius," said Tiuri kindly.

"N-no," replied the Fool. "It would be mad to go back now, wouldn't it? Why did we keep on going? It wasn't just so we could turn back! And you are a knight. You have a shield and a sword."

Tiuri suddenly felt the heavy burden of his responsibility for Marius, who had such faith in him.

Ardanwen calmly started to graze.

"Look, he's given up, too," said Piak. He walked past the horse and let out a muffled cry. "There's a track here!" he said excitedly.

The others followed him – yes, it was a track, a narrow one, but most definitely a track.

"Was it made by people?" Tiuri wondered aloud.

"Animals have paths, too," said the Fool. "Fox tracks, deer tracks. But this is not an animal's path."

"Ardanwen, you're a marvel!" cried Piak. "Now we can keep on going, can't we?"

"Until nightfall," said Tiuri.

He reckoned that the track ran north-east to south-west – and south-west was the direction they wanted to go in. Then they'd probably come out by the Black River again.

The Fool looked around, twitched his nostrils, and said, "Hush, friends and travellers, walk softly! I have been here before, not alone, long ago... Look carefully, tread softly!"

His mood took hold of Piak and Tiuri. They hardly even dared to breathe as they moved cautiously onwards, first on foot and then on horseback.

Birds chirped in the trees, and they spotted two deer, which stared at them in surprise.

Then, late in the afternoon, they did indeed come to the river.

"This is the way," whispered the Fool. "This is our way, friends. Do you hear the reeds rustling beside the dark water? Take care. There's a stream flowing across the path here – jump over it. You can drink this water. It tastes better than the water from the river. Come on, keep walking, horses. Keep going, friends."

As the sun was setting, they came to a building – or rather, a ruin.

"The Owl House!" said Piak.

It had been a large house once, made of stone, but now most of it had collapsed. What was still standing was dilapidated and overgrown. The roof was almost completely gone, and the windows were just holes in the crumbling walls. A wide flight of steps had once run down to the river, but little of that remained either.

In silence, the travellers headed for the building and, after some hesitation, they stepped inside. They entered spaces that had once been halls and chambers, and walked among tall ferns and over dense moss instead of across floors with tiles and rugs. When they looked up, they could see the fiery red sky. There were not only windows in the thick walls, but also alcoves, where they thought they could spot the occasional movement.

"Owls," said the Fool. He pointed everything out to Tiuri and Piak as if he were the owner of the house. "You mustn't go upstairs," he said. "It's dangerous. And look, there's the well. There's still water in it, and it's really deep. Go and see."

It was a most suitable place for spending the night. When it was dark, they sat around a fire in one of the rooms and ate a very light meal.

"We should have just enough food for the journey back to the Dead Stone," said Piak. "Or are we travelling onwards to the cabin from here?"

"We shall have to ask Marius," said Tiuri. "The path we followed came from the north-east. That's the direction of Marius's cabin. Isn't that right, Marius?"

The Fool did not reply. He was staring intently ahead, as if trying to catch a sound.

Tiuri couldn't hear anything. No, there was something: rustling, flapping above his head. "It's the owls," he said.

"Yes, the owls," the Fool nodded absently, but it wasn't the owls that seemed to be worrying him.

Tiuri was in a strange mood. There was something sad about the thought that people had once lived in this place where they were now sitting, and had felt happiness or sorrow. But nothing of them remained; this ruin was the only reminder of their existence.

"And in ten or twenty years' time, even this ruin may have disappeared," he whispered, half to himself.

Piak answered him. "Out there, out in the marsh, it felt as if we were somewhere no one had ever set foot before," he said. "And here we're in a wood where once there were people, but now they're all gone. That's almost creepier, don't you think?"

"Yes," said Tiuri. "We should just go to sleep."

The night that followed was like no other night Tiuri had ever spent anywhere. He could hear the constant flapping of the owls, and sometimes he saw their round, staring eyes flickering in the glow of the smouldering fire. It occurred to him that maybe they were not owls at all, but spirits in the shape of birds with ragged feathers, sighing and bewailing their fate.

7   THE MAN IN GREEN

The sun chased away Tiuri's gloomy thoughts, even if few of its rays reached the travellers. Still it cast patches of light on the ground, on the leaves, and on the dark river. Tiuri and Piak took another walk around the rooms of the Owl House, silently hoping to find some traces of people. But there were none.

The Fool was in low spirits. He stood close to Tiuri and said quietly, "They're not here yet, but they will come. They are sure to come. Here or there."

"Can't you tell us now who 'they' are?" asked Tiuri.

The Fool shook his head. "I don't know," he said. "They are not here yet and soon we will go home to the cabin."

"Along the path we came from?" asked Tiuri.

"Yes, you know the path, sir knight!" said the Fool, a little more

cheerfully. "But first I shall show you the tree, the tree you're looking for."

The path ran on westwards along the Black River, and that was
the direction the Fool took them in. He himself avoided the path
as much as possible, keeping parallel to it whenever he could. Tiuri
and Piak rode along the track, which grew wider and wider.

"It's strange," said Piak. "I'd expect the track to become narrower,
the deeper we go into the forest."

"The paths in the Wild Wood are dead ends," murmured Tiuri, "or
lead to ruins of towns and villages that were abandoned long ago."

"What did you say?"

"I'm repeating the words of Sir Ristridin's message," replied Tiuri.
"Hey, where's Marius gone?"

"Over here!" came a voice. "Ride on, friends, ride on. Now you
are riding again to the place where the sun sets, Sir Tiuri. But not
too long, not too long. I don't want to go on for too long."

"It's further than I thought," said Piak a while later. The Fool, who
had disappeared into the undergrowth, reappeared and waved at
them, holding a muddy root in each hand. "I found food!" he said
proudly. "Come here, and we'll rest on the grass where no one can
see us. And then I'll take you to where you want to be."

Marius still seemed very sure of his ground, thought Tiuri, as he
chewed on the bitter, hard root. He sat leaning against a tree, with
Piak and the Fool lying nearby in the grass and the horses grazing
alongside them.

And then, suddenly, he saw a Man in Green.

He was sitting on a branch of the tree right in front of him. Tiuri
froze. He could hardly believe his eyes! He saw a big, tanned man
with a dark blond beard; his close-fitting clothes and the cap on his
head were in various shades of green. There he sat, perfectly at ease,
as if the branch were the most comfortable seat in the world. One

143

leg was tucked under him, and in his hand he held a bow. And he was watching them very closely indeed.

"Who are you?" Tiuri managed to say as he sat up.

Piak and the Fool followed his gaze and saw the man, too. He bared his teeth and then rose – incredibly quickly. One moment he was standing upright on the branch, and then he turned and made a leap that took him to the next tree. Before the three travellers' astonished eyes, he swung from branch to branch, and within just a couple of seconds he had disappeared. Only the rustling in the trees revealed that he was moving into the distance.

Tiuri and Piak jumped up and went after him. The Fool cried out, "No, don't do that, don't do that!" but still he followed them. Before long, though, they stopped, peered around, and then looked at one another. There was no sign of the Man in Green.

"So they do exist," said Piak.

"Yes, you saw him," said Tiuri.

"Was it actually a person?" asked Piak.

"I think so," replied Tiuri.

"Well, he's certainly at home in the forest," said Piak. "He darted through the branches like a squirrel!"

"Don't follow!" whispered the Fool. "Don't go on. They don't want us to see them. They don't want to speak to us!"

"Was it men like him who took you?" asked Piak.

"All they do is watch," said the Fool. "Quiet! Look out!" He turned and ran.

Tiuri and Piak went after him, determined now to hear the full story.

The Fool gave them no opportunity to ask questions, though. He stopped and said quietly, "Here. It was here. Now I remember. Nearby!"

"What?" said Tiuri.

"Hush," said the Fool. "The tree, of course." And he disappeared into the undergrowth.

8 THE TREE

"We're sure to get lost now, Tiuri!" muttered Piak, as they tried to keep up with the Fool.

The Fool looked back at them. "We're close to the dark river, friends," he said, "and I know the way."

A little later he stopped and took hold of their hands. "I was sitting here," he whispered. "I was sitting here and I saw... A knight by that tree..." He let go of their hands and pointed.

Tiuri felt almost as if he should be able to see the knight, but there was no one there. He saw the tree, though, strong and sturdy, surrounded by tall ferns.

Slowly, almost hesitantly, he went closer. As he pushed the ferns aside, he saw nothing on the trunk. He did not waste any time feeling disappointed, though, but walked around the tree, where there were indeed signs carved into the bark – letters, words, names...

Tiuri stood and read them, and then read them again... three times, four.

Piak gasped as he came to join his friend, staring incredulously at the message that had been carved into the tree trunk months ago.

IN MEMORY OF

SIR ARWAUT

AND ILMAR

AND ALL OUR FAITHFUL MEN

SO TREACHEROUSLY SLAIN BY ENEMIES

MAY THEY REST IN PEACE

MAY THEIR DEATHS BE AVENGED

I SHALL NOT FORGET THEM

RISTRIDIN OF THE SOUTH

9 The Sound of Drums

"Dead..." whispered Piak. Tiuri made the sign of the cross and bowed his head.

"Dead?" asked the Fool quietly. "What is wrong? What do those signs say?"

Tiuri laid one hand on his shoulder. "You have helped to reveal a terrible secret, Marius," he said. "Sir... Sir Ristridin has written here that his friends were killed by enemies."

"Ah," sighed the Fool.

All three of them stood in silence.

Enemies... thought Tiuri. And Arwaut, Ilmar, and others have been killed! He realized then that they had indeed been heading into danger, but if they had not done so, he and his friends would never have found out what had happened to Ristridin's party, and everyone would have gone on believing there was no threat in the Wild Wood and that all the paths were dead ends. Tiuri sprang into action.

"Quick! Come on!" he said. "Come with me!"

He took a few steps to the river. Then he asked the Fool, "Marius, do you know the way back to the horses?"

"Yes," he whispered.

"Then go there! Quickly!" ordered Tiuri, also in a whisper. He studied the tree one last time and then followed the Fool, who was already running away.

"Why the hurry?" asked Piak.

"Don't you see it could be dangerous here?" said Tiuri. "We have to get back to civilization as quickly as possible and tell them what we have found. Sir Ristridin, Sir Arwaut, Ilmar and their men were ambushed and defeated by enemies. May God grant that Ristridin escaped! These enemies are probably the same ones the Fool keeps mentioning. Who knows where they might be now? And I fear the three of us will be no match for them."

"But we must let people know!" exclaimed Piak.

"Exactly. Luckily there are three of us, so at least one of us should get out of the wood alive."

"Oh, Tiuri," said Piak. "You're being so gloomy."

"I'm just trying to see the situation as clearly as possible," said Tiuri. "There is something here that we are not supposed to know. Oh, Arwaut, Ilmar..."

"Who is Ilmar?" asked Piak.

"Ilmar was Ristridin's squire. I really liked him," replied Tiuri. "He was the same age as me," he added under his breath.

They walked on in silence until they reached their horses.

"They're still here," said Piak with relief. "Even though that Man in Green saw us."

And he could still be looking at us now, thought Tiuri, but he didn't say that out loud. First they had to try to get as far away from this place as possible, and head back to the east. Later, in a safer place, they would be able to talk more. But there was one thing he still needed to say.

"Listen carefully," he said. "It is our duty to tell King Dagonaut what has happened here in the Wild Wood. Do you understand, Marius? Sir Ristridin's friends have been killed and Sir Ristridin himself has disappeared. And King Dagonaut needs to know about this. I hope we can leave the wood without encountering any difficulties, but if anything happens, at least one of us needs to reach our goal."

"If what happens, sir knight?" asked the Fool anxiously.

"If enemies find us, each of us must try to escape – to run away, Marius – and to take the news to the king."

"To the king," repeated the Fool.

"And now let's go," ordered Tiuri. "Marius, take us to the Owl House, but don't use the path."

The Fool was so happy to be given this task that he forgot his fear for a moment. "No one will find us, Friend," he said, and again he led the way.

Leading the horses by the reins, Tiuri and Piak followed him silently. It seemed like hours before they saw the Owl House ahead of them. Tiuri decided that they would pass behind the building and find a place to hide for the night some distance away in the forest.

"We mustn't go too far from the river," he said, "but it seems better to avoid the paths. We can't make a fire later, either."

"It's already getting dark," whispered the Fool. "I shall listen carefully and warn you if they are coming."

"Marius, now you really do have to tell us who they are," said Tiuri a little later, after they had taken cover in a small hollow.

"Wait," said the Fool. "Listen!"

"It must have been your enemies who killed Sir Ristridin's friends," Tiuri continued. "You surely realize they have to be punished!"

"Sssh, listen!" whispered the Fool.

From far away, very vaguely, a sound came to them. Or was it just the pounding of their own hearts? Then it was gone... All they could hear was the wind in the trees.

"Wait," said the Fool once more.

And yes, there it was again. It wasn't their imaginations, they really could hear it – a dull and regular thud... The sound of drums!

After a while, it stopped, but then it began again. It was so threatening and ominous in the night.

"It's them," whispered the Fool, when all was silent again.

"Are they coming here?" asked Piak, so quietly it could barely be heard.

They huddled together in the darkness, unable to see one another. Keeping perfectly still, they listened. There it was again! No, it wasn't coming closer – but it wasn't moving away either.

"They're in the trees," said the Fool.

"Who?" whispered Tiuri.

Again they waited in silence until the drumming died away.

"The drums," the Fool told him quietly. "The drums are in the trees and they speak to one another. But I don't know what they say."

"Is it the Men in Green who are drumming?" asked Tiuri.

"Maybe," replied the Fool. "But maybe others. Many creatures live in the forest... Bad men in strange clothes, and men in coats of metal who have no faces..."

"No faces?" repeated Piak with horror in his voice.

"Helmets," whispered the Fool. "All you can see is their eyes, wicked, angry eyes."

"Closed visors," murmured Tiuri.

"They came to my cabin," the Fool told them, "and they said to my brothers, 'Come with us.' I had to go too, and I didn't want to, but you know that. They took us with them, me and my brothers, far, deep into the wood... The path along the dark river is long, much longer, and that's where they live. And there are other paths. But sometimes they tied something over my eyes so I couldn't see. I did see some things, though. I saw the Owl House and other houses of wood and stone."

"Is that where they lived?" whispered Piak.

"Not in the Owl House, but in other houses," said the Fool. "And I saw the Men in Green sitting in the trees. They look at you and then they're gone. They run beside the water with long spears in their hands, sharp spears..."

"But what are they doing in the wood?" asked Tiuri.

"I cannot say," replied the Fool. "They told me nothing, nothing, Friend! They wanted to make more paths, and my brothers and I had to cut down trees for them. We weren't allowed to leave, and no one is allowed to know that they are there. That's what they said. 'Keep your mouth shut,' they said, 'or we'll beat you to death.'"

Tiuri could feel him shivering. "And then you ran away?" he asked quietly.

"Not for a while, Friend," said the Fool. "I was scared. They were bad men. At first I was too scared, but then I had to go. I knew I'd die if I stayed..." His voice was trembling. "I ran away, one night," he continued. "They didn't notice at first, but then they came after

149

me, cursing me, looking for me, but they didn't find me." He paused before concluding, "That's it, my friends. That's all I know. It's not the first time I've heard the drums! I was in the woods for a long, long time, walking, hiding, waiting..."

Then Piak grabbed hold of Tiuri. "What's that?" he whispered. "Light!"

Tiuri was startled for a moment, but then he said, "It's just the moon rising."

"Phew," sighed Piak. "I'm jumping at everything."

All three of them held their breath and listened to the mysterious sounds of the night. They could no longer hear the drums.

Then Tiuri spoke up. "The second message from Sir Ristridin was false!" he said. "The message Sir Fitil passed on to us..."

"So do you think Sir Ristridin ever went to Islan?" asked Piak.

"That is indeed the question," whispered Tiuri, and then he stopped speaking. He was trying to imagine what part Sir Fitil had played in all of this. Had he lied? Did he know more than he'd said? Had he, a knight of King Dagonaut, been a traitor? Or was he in fact a victim of betrayal? Sir Fitil, who had wandered through the Unholy Hills without getting lost... how far had he travelled into the forest?

Then Tiuri remembered the story of Red Quibo, who claimed he had seen a ghostly tournament. "Were they actually people, not spirits, not some fantasy creatures?" he wondered aloud. "So where do they live? Where are their houses?"

The Fool, beside him, sat up straight. He could see him vaguely now by the light of the waxing moon. The whites of his eyes gleamed.

"They live there, and there," he whispered, pointing to the west and to the south.

The Unholy Hills lay somewhere to their south. And, according to the Fool, there had been people at the old hunting lodge.

Tiuri thought about Isadoro. He had to admit to himself that she could have known more about it, too. That would go some way to explaining her behaviour. After all, she had done everything she could to convince him there was nothing in the Wild Wood, and yet at the same time she had also warned him about it. He sighed. These were only vague suspicions, puzzles to which he had no answer. But in any case, Islan was not the place they should go for help. Their goal had to be King Dagonaut himself, the man who had ordered Sir Ristridin to go to the Wild Wood.

The Fool spoke again, almost in Tiuri's ear: "Their Master, their Lord and Master, lives at the end of the dark river," he said. "Or is it at the beginning? Far, far, where the sun sets. There are mountains there and the sun goes down behind the mountains. He lives in a castle, the Master of the Wild Wood..."

A shock went through Tiuri. How did that song go again, the song Isadoro had sung?

I heard tell of a fortress grim
by mountains and by rivers wide.

"That once was so, but is no more..." he said out loud.

"Quiet!" whispered the Fool. "They said he lives beside the other river, too, in a cave..."

"Which river?" asked Piak.

"Who?" asked Tiuri.

"The Master of the Wild Wood," said the Fool.

"Who..." said Tiuri and Piak at the same time.

"I don't know, my friends," whispered the Fool. "They spoke so quietly about him, never out loud. He was their Master and he told them what to do. But I never saw him, no, no, never."

"The other river, could that be the Green River?" asked Piak.

"Yes, the Green River. I know that river, too," said the Fool. "They fought there, the men who live in the wood, and other men. First I heard the drums, both far and near... Then they came – knights, riders. Other men jumped out of the bushes, out of the trees... And they fought!"

"Why didn't you tell me this before?" asked Tiuri.

"I don't always remember everything at the same time, Friend," replied the Fool. "I'd really like to forget about it all. I'm only remembering this for your sake. They fought, but I didn't want to watch, and so I ran. I'd already got away by then. And later, by the dark river, I saw one of those knights again... your knight, the one with the green cloak and the green and grey and silver shield."

Ristridin, thought Tiuri. So that's what had happened: Ristridin and his companions had first defeated the robbers who lived between the Black River and the Green River. That must have been somewhere to the north of the Dead Stone. Then they'd gone to the west, deeper into the wood, to look for the Men in Green. They'd found them, and perhaps others. In any case, they'd been attacked by enemies, and none of them had ever returned to civilization, except perhaps for Ristridin. Tiuri wondered again if he had really been to Islan. It was so unlikely, almost impossible, that Ristridin would have been there and then, without saying anything, would have ridden onwards to... Deltaland.

Deltaland... did all of this have something to do with the invasion?

He pulled his blanket more tightly around himself and shivered, and it was not just because of the cold. The Fool had fallen asleep. He was groaning and mumbling, caught up in some bad dream or other. "Stop thinking now," Tiuri said to himself. "You're not going to figure it out, and you need to be fresh tomorrow."

He had his own troubled dreams, about Ristridin and Ilmar, about Arwaut and the Men in Green. He heard the sound of drums again, mingling with the soft, sweet voice of Lady Isadoro as she sang. But Isadoro was on the side of the enemy. He dreamt of fierce horsemen, and he himself rode ahead of them, sometimes as their leader, sometimes as a fugitive. But, in truth, nothing at all happened, all night long.

10 ENEMIES

Tiuri looked up. The sky was clear, the sun had just risen, and dewdrops were glistening on the leaves. Piak had climbed a tree so that he could look out over the area.

"No trouble in sight," he announced when he was back down on the ground. "But that's not saying anything, because you can't see much more than the treetops up there. The Owl House isn't far. I could see one of the chimneys."

"We'll try to keep walking parallel to the river," said Tiuri. "I hope we'll find Marius's path again. Do you know where it comes out?" he asked the Fool.

"Which path?" he replied.

"The one the black horse Ardanwen found," Piak explained.

The Fool wrinkled his forehead. "It goes on through the wood," he said, "but there are other paths there, too, and I don't know all of them."

"But that's the way you came from your cabin," said Tiuri.

"Yes, yes, that way, Friend," said the Fool. "But we took detours, and it was a long time ago."

Tiuri held back a sigh. "How long does it take to get from the Black River to the Green River?" he asked.

"I don't know exactly, Friend," said the Fool apologetically. "More than a day, maybe even a week."

"Hadn't we better take the same route as we did on the way?" asked Piak.

"Yes, that seems safer to me, too," said Tiuri. He pointed to the south-east. "The Black River's over there," he said, "so let's go that way. But I'd rather not travel along the path right now." He turned to the Fool and added, "We're going to see the king first, Marius, and then back home to the cabin."

"I knew it, I knew it," said the Fool. "I'll go wherever you go, my friends. You know better than I do."

"Just as well it's not summer yet," said Piak, trying to be cheerful, as usual. "Then everything would be even more overgrown."

He was right. It was already bad enough. Undergrowth, creepers and prickly bushes made the going very difficult. Occasionally, Tiuri and Piak had to take out their swords to hack a way through.

"I never imagined we'd end up using our good swords for this!" Piak remarked.

Sometimes they had to change direction, as the path ahead was not clear, and by midday they weren't sure they were going the right way at all. Piak climbed up another tree, but all he could see was "one great big mess of green", as he put it – and no sign of the Black River. They were hot, tired and miserable, and felt hungry and very thirsty.

Piak opened the bag of provisions and closed it again. "We should wait to eat until we have some drink to wash it down," he said.

Soon after that, the Fool said, "Ah, here comes our drink, my friends!"

And yes, there was a stream, where they could quench their thirst. They did not eat yet, though, but first walked for a way along the stream, because, as Tiuri realized, "it has to flow into the Black River."

He was right. After a while, they came out onto the track Ardanwen had discovered.

"This is the stream we crossed on the way," said Piak. "It was close to the Owl House. So we haven't made much progress!"

"But we're not lost, and that's something," said Tiuri.

"Let's take a short rest," said Piak. "We can eat and I can dangle my feet in the water." He took off his shoes and did just that.

"I'm going to take a look around and see if everything seems safe," said Tiuri, after he'd finished his bread. "Perhaps we can go along the track for a way. Then we can ride and we'll move faster."

He peered down the path in both directions. There was no one in sight. But someone might easily appear around a bend at any moment.

"We should just keep under cover, don't you think, and walk parallel to the path?" he said to Piak and the Fool, who had both followed him. "And then back through the marsh, and onwards from there."

Piak pulled a face, but still nodded in agreement.

"We can get on the horses now, though," said Tiuri. "Piak, come up with me on Ardanwen."

They rode into the wood that ran between the path and the river. Then Piak suddenly gave a little gasp.

"Wait a moment," he said. "Oh, I'm such an idiot! I've left our bag of food behind." He jumped down from Ardanwen's back. "I'll just fetch it," he said. "It's down by the stream. You two ride onwards. I'll be back soon and I'll catch up with you." He ran off and soon disappeared from sight.

Tiuri and the Fool rode on very slowly. Marius raised his head and sniffed the air, as if he could smell something strange. Then he looked at Tiuri and said, even though there was nothing to see, "They're coming!"

"How..." Tiuri began and then he heard sounds, somewhere behind him – clinking, a voice in the distance... It wasn't Piak – where had he got to?

"Away!" he ordered the Fool, but Marius hesitated.

"Come on!" Tiuri urged Ardanwen onwards. The horse sped forward and started to canter, breaking twigs and branches and swerving to avoid tree trunks. He glanced back; luckily, the Fool was following him. But Piak, where was Piak?!

He had no choice, though. Danger was close at hand, and he had to flee.

Then a number of helmeted men loomed out of the undergrowth. They tried to block his way with lances and spears. Ardanwen reared up.

"Danger!" cried Tiuri. "Danger! Flee! Flee!" He drew his sword.

He heard the Fool shriek somewhere behind him. Then there was a yell; it sounded like Piak. And meanwhile he fought to defend himself. He managed to shake off the men, and Ardanwen took

155

him to the path in just a few leaps. There was more shouting and the sound of hoofs. And then he saw the Fool; other men, dressed in green, had pulled him from his horse. And along the path, more enemies came riding towards them from the direction of the Owl House. But he did not see Piak.

"Flee! Flee!" he shouted again, as he prepared to make a rescue attempt, although he wondered if he shouldn't be trying to get away himself. But Marius was so anxiously crying for help!

Tiuri drove apart his friend's attackers, but by then the horsemen had reached them. The ensuing fight was a short one. Tiuri defended himself valiantly, but he was no match for such superior numbers. Within just a few moments, he and the Fool had been overpowered. Their enemies surrounded them: soldiers in chainmail, and rough fellows in ragged clothes, and men dressed in green with black caps on their heads. Ardanwen whinnied in anger at being held fast by so many hands. The Fool whimpered softly.

But Piak was nowhere in sight. Tiuri prayed he had escaped.

"A knight with a white shield!" cried a fierce-looking man, bringing his face very close to Tiuri's. Tiuri couldn't help taking a step back.

A murmur spread throughout the others.

"Sir Tiuri and his squire!" cried a horseman in brown and yellow, who had just joined them. He did not raise the visor of his helmet, but his voice sounded familiar to Tiuri.

Brown and yellow. Weren't they the colours of Islan?

"Whatever possessed you to attack me?!" began Tiuri. "Highway robbery is forbidden in the Kingdom of Dagonaut."

A few of the men laughed mockingly. "We are no robbers," said a man dressed in green, who was clutching Tiuri's shield and sword.

"You are our prisoner," added the fierce man.

"No, he is *our* prisoner," said the horseman in brown and yellow.

"No, we are taking him with us," said the fierce man. "Those are our orders."

"Where to?" replied the horseman.

"To where our path takes us," said the man wearing green. And, grabbing hold of Tiuri, the fierce man shouted, "Come with me!"

"Islan!" cried Tiuri, but the soldier in brown and yellow withdrew and the other men pressed more tightly around him. The Fool huddled up to Tiuri, still whimpering.

"Shut your mouth," one of the enemies barked.

"Leave him alone!" said Tiuri. "He is my friend and... squire. Release us this instant!" Then he stopped. The expressions of the men around him made it clear that they wouldn't even contemplate letting him go and he didn't want to humiliate himself by demanding something he would never get.

Then he and the Fool were taken, along the path, back to the Owl House.

As long as Piak has escaped! thought Tiuri. Who were these men – and had he really seen one of the men of Islan?

There was the Owl House. A number of horses stood on the grass in front of it, all decked out in red. As they approached, three men appeared at the gate, standing out brightly against the dark opening behind them.

Tiuri's steps became slower and he felt as though an ice-cold hand had gripped his heart. Three soldiers in red, with blood-red plumes on their helmets.

"It's them!" he heard the Fool gasp out beside him.

Them... the Red Riders! Tiuri knew them only too well. How they had hunted and pursued him when he was on his way to King Unauwen with the letter! Many of them had been defeated by Sir Ristridin and his friends. But there were still more of them – all cruel and wicked men. Red Riders from the land of Eviellan! They stood, shoulder to shoulder, waiting for Tiuri.

He glanced around. Nothing but enemies, and silent forest. And again he thought: *Just as long as Piak has escaped. Please, God, let Piak have escaped!*

PART FOUR

PIAK

1 To the East

Piak soon found the bag of food. He hung it over his shoulder and was about to go back, when he heard voices – not Tiuri or the Fool. Startled, he peered through the undergrowth and saw a number of men coming along the path from the direction of the Owl House. He leapt back and headed eastwards through the forest, as quickly as he could without making a sound. He had to warn Tiuri, because what he'd seen of the men didn't look good.

But it wasn't long before he had another fright; he heard more people coming from that direction. Then a cry rang out: "Danger!" It was Tiuri shouting: "Danger! Flee! Flee!"

Then there came a shriek from the Fool and the sound of hoofs on the path.

Piak cried out, too. He started running towards his friend, no longer worrying about being silent, but still instinctively avoiding the path. Riders soon came thundering by; he had no idea how many.

Again he heard Tiuri call out, "Flee! Flee!"

He's calling to me, Piak thought, and he stopped, knees shaking. *One of us has to escape to tell everything to King Dagonaut.*

Should he run? The sounds he could hear – the clashing of swords – made his breath catch in his throat. Flee? And abandon Tiuri and Marius?

He carried on. Slowly, cautiously, he approached the spot where his friends had been ambushed. He could see something... He crouched down, crept closer, and surveyed the scene. He saw a troop of armed men, and Ardanwen, whinnying at being held captive. But where were his companions?

Someone cried out, "A knight with a white shield!"

Piak jerked to his feet, only to drop back down again. He felt all kinds of emotions at the same time: powerless fury, fear for his friends, frustration that he could not help them. What could he do on his own against all of those soldiers? He was also scared for himself, but he didn't want to run away for that reason. And yet he knew he had to escape, because of what Tiuri had said: "At least one of us needs to reach our goal."

Then he noticed more men approaching – riders. They came to a halt close to him. Piak didn't move a muscle; he didn't even dare to look. He did hear something, though: "Sir Tiuri and his squire." And then Tiuri's voice: "Whatever possessed you to attack me?!"

A tear came into Piak's eye. His friend was still alive!

Then the enemies spoke, but he caught only a few words. "You are our prisoner..." – "Where to?" – "To where our path takes us..." And louder: "Islan!" Was that Tiuri again? Very cautiously, Piak raised his head; the men on the path had started to move. Some of them looked like robbers, but there were also soldiers there, and men in green clothes and black caps. He caught a glimpse of Tiuri and the Fool; they appeared unharmed. Then they were led away, out of sight. They all disappeared in the direction of the Owl House.

Piak was about to stand up, but then he saw that a few soldiers had remained behind – riders in brown and yellow. With closed visors. *The cowards*, he thought, as he ducked back down and peered out at them.

They were talking. "What now?" one of them asked.

"His squire's not with him," said the other.

Now it's my turn! thought Piak. *If they take a good look around, they're sure to spot me!* He closed his eyes, even though he knew that wouldn't help. Thoughts flashed through his mind: *What should I do? Stay lying here? Jump up and run away?*

The sound of pounding hoofs thundered in his ears. It came closer, before moving away.

"Why did you..." said one. But he didn't hear the rest. He could hear the other one more clearly: "Quick! Spread out! Look for him! Find the squire!"

He knew that loud voice and also the brown and yellow colours. Islan!

"The last man who spoke was Hamar," he said to himself, cautiously getting to his feet. "So it is indeed Islan!"

There was no one else around. If he wanted to escape, he'd have to attempt it now – run to the east, fetch help... He had to, even though every step would take him further away from Tiuri. *Why me?* he thought.

He quickly crossed the path. As he did so, someone called out, "Hey! Who's there?"

Piak started to run. They'd seen him. Yes, he was being followed! He fled through the forest, constantly glancing back.

Then he had to stop. He'd come to the Black River; just a few steps through tangled reeds separated him from the river that he needed to follow to get out of the wood. Behind him, he heard his pursuers getting closer. Any minute now they would reach him – and he couldn't swim.

No, Piak couldn't swim, and the river was dark and seemed deep. In desperation, he ran onwards, dived into the reeds and crouched at the water's edge.

Twigs cracking, footsteps coming closer... Piak held his breath, clung on to a clump of reeds and lowered himself into the river. The water crept up his body – it was ice cold as it embraced his chest and his neck. When he felt mud beneath his feet, he let go. The water came all the way up to his lips. For a moment, he panicked and grabbed at the clump.

"Calm down," he said to himself. "You can't drown here." Then he moved carefully through the water, along the bank, and stopped, dead still, hidden beneath overhanging reeds. Close by – it seemed like almost directly above him – he could heard his pursuers, the men of Islan.

He heard what they were saying, "Why don't you ask for *their* help?"

"Then we'll get blamed for letting him escape. Now at least they don't know. Besides, Sir Fitil wants them at Islan."

"So what about the other two?"

"*They* took them with them, into the wood, as you know. There's nothing we can do about that. *Hoo-hoo-ooh!*"

The unexpected cry startled Piak. An answer came from the opposite bank.

"Any sign?" called the man on Piak's bank.

"No, nothing!" came the reply. "Is the path well guarded?"

"*Yoo-hoo-hoo!*"

"Quiet, then! Do your duty."

The water was so cold! Piak didn't dare to move a muscle. *And soon I won't even be able to move at all*, he thought. *My whole body's gone numb.*

He shifted his foot, sank into the mud, and almost went under. Something slimy brushed against his arm.

But, finally, he could no longer hear his pursuers and so he ventured back up onto dry land. He walked eastwards along the river, trying hard to keep his teeth from chattering. The path was guarded and it seemed safer here beside the water. *If only I could swim*, he thought. Yes, that was the first thing he'd have to learn, even though he didn't like water – right at that moment, he detested it.

He went on walking for a while until he heard his enemies again. They seemed to be coming after him along the river. His first impulse was to flee to the north, but that was where the path was – and the guards. He shuddered as he realized there was only one good hiding place: back into the river, into the cold, dark water...

He made himself invisible beneath the overhanging vegetation. His enemies didn't find him there, but, as he climbed back out and went on his way, he muttered to himself, "There's no way I'm doing that again! I'm not cut out to be a fish."

But he knew he would do it again if he had to – indeed, he soon found himself wading along the river, sheltered by the dense growth on the bank. After a while, he noticed that the bottom was becoming softer and the bank was lower. Some way downstream they appeared to merge and, where the ground should have been dry, it was boggy. It was just as well that his enemies were nowhere around as he came ashore with much splashing and struggling.

I'm back at the marsh, he thought. *Now I have to try to find the same route back as the way we came. At any rate, they won't be as keen to come after me on this awful ground. At least I hope they won't...*

He really wanted to rest for a moment, but he decided to keep on walking for as long as it was still light. Maybe walking would warm him up; he was still shivering with cold. He chose his path carefully. Marshes can be dangerous places and he didn't want to be surprised by his pursuers.

Piak didn't allow himself to stop for a rest until the day was coming to an end. He thought there was no one else around, and he was glad of that. But the surroundings felt more gloomy and dismal than ever. The twigs seemed to be pointing at him with their twisted fingers; countless eyes appeared to be spying on him from the bushes. He was still freezing and his clothes clung to his body.

He opened up the bag, which was soaked through. The bread had turned to mush and looked unappetizing. He took a couple of reluctant bites and moulded the rest into a ball.

"This will have to keep me going for a while," he said to himself. On the way there, it had taken two days to get from the Dead Stone to the Owl House. They'd had the horses, but still they'd walked most of the way. *I want to be at Stoneford by tomorrow evening,* he thought. *That should be possible! And I'll keep going now for as long as I can see.*

He headed onwards in the reddish twilight, wondering where his friends were now. They had been captured and taken away, deeper into the forest... not killed. But who knew what might happen to them? Would he be able to rescue them if he escaped? Would help – if he found any – come quickly enough? Wouldn't he have been better off following them and trying to come up with some plan to free them?

"Why am I the one who's still walking around free?" he said to himself. "Why didn't I get caught? Tiuri should have been here instead! He'd have a much better idea of what to do. He's a knight!"

How he'd been looking forward to travelling together with Tiuri! It had all gone so very differently than he'd imagined. Something had come between the two of them at Islan. Maybe his friend hadn't felt it, but Piak certainly had. Then when they'd headed into the wood with the Fool, everything had returned to normal, but that journey had ended so unhappily! His friends were in danger. He'd been separated from them and now he had to go onwards – or rather, back – all by himself.

It was getting darker and colder. Something jumped into a puddle – splosh! Frogs began to croak. The trees transformed into shadows, and it became more and more difficult to press on. Finally, shivering, he dropped to the ground.

Piak couldn't sleep. He tossed and turned. The wood was full of sounds, much more so than when he'd spent the night there with his friends. But he must have fallen asleep, because when he awoke with a start he saw that it was getting light. He swallowed a lump of bread with difficulty, as his throat was sore. Then he continued his journey through the marsh.

There was one thought in Piak's mind: *I must reach Stoneford today!* All his attention and effort were focused on completing that journey and evading his pursuers. He paid barely any attention to the bloodsuckers, and when he became tired he ignored that too.

That afternoon, he was startled by the sound of voices. He heard men talking. It sounded like they were on the other side of the water, but if they crossed the river...

Piak took a detour to the north, even though that meant he wouldn't reach the path that ran along the river to Stoneford, but he didn't want to run the risk of being seen. He thought he must have almost reached the end of the marsh, and hoped he wasn't mistaken. As he could still hear the voices, he moved away from the river. The ground beneath his feet became firmer, and he sighed with relief. "At least that's over and done with," he said to himself.

It was only at that point that he realized it was actually a fine day, and he would probably make it to Stoneford before too long. He knew that people lived there and he might be able to ask them for help. By then he'd be on the Great Road and surely no one would dare to attack him there. Piak looked around. There was no sign of anyone following him. Now he just had to get back to the river.

"Don't let me be lost," he prayed. "Let me find Stoneford."

Where had that river got to? How long had he been walking? The sun was already low – he was going in the right direction, wasn't he?

Then another path crossed his way. Was it a sign of civilization or one of the dangerous ways into the wood? Piak hesitated. If he went right, he'd probably come to the Black River. He'd have to risk it.

He could feel now just how far he'd walked; his legs seemed to be made of lead. "Just pretend they feel fine," he said to himself. "One foot in front of the other. One, two..."

Before long, he reached a clearing where a large stone stood. The Dead Stone!

2   FROM THE DEAD STONE TO THE NORTH

According to the innkeeper of the Silent Inn, this was an evil place, but still Piak was pleased to see it. The Black River was here, and Stoneford! He was exhausted, but that didn't matter. He'd escaped from the wood in one piece, and he'd done it quickly, too.

As he approached the river, he saw that there were people on the other side. But when he reached the riverbank, he realized he wasn't out of danger. Among those people were soldiers in brown and yellow – the men of Islan, who were looking for him!

Piak swayed on his feet. They had seen him, too, and lined up on the opposite bank. One of them shouted an order and stepped forward. Hamar!

Piak took a few steps back and knew with absolute certainty that he had no strength left to flee. Hamar crossed the river and some of the others followed him. All was lost! And yet Piak could not surrender until he actually dropped.

He turned and ran back to the Dead Stone. He stopped, gasping, a misty haze before his eyes. Swaying, he reached out his hand and grasped onto the stone that he hadn't even dared to touch before.

He leant against it, hating himself for his weakness. He felt better now, but his legs were powerless. He couldn't take another step.

"Stop!" called Hamar. "He's over here!"

Piak saw the soldiers coming. He couldn't see them very clearly, though... was it already so dark? They were all talking at once and Hamar said, "Come here!"

Is he talking to me? he thought. Why didn't they just grab him? And why was he just standing there? He had to escape! But he couldn't let go of the stone, the Dead Stone!

Quietly, as though from afar, he heard a voice inside, "They say that every ill wish spoken at the Dead Stone will come true..."

That was it! His only chance, if he had the courage and the strength.

Piak took a deep breath and stood up straight, still leaning against the stone. He shivered as he pressed his fingers more firmly against it. Then he looked at the soldiers and said, "This is the Dead Stone. And by this Dead Stone I speak an ill wish against anyone who attempts to touch me..."

"Come here!" shouted Hamar, stepping forward. But the others remained silent and did not move.

"Dead Stone!" cried Piak. "I speak a curse against anyone who captures me. May he become a captive himself, hunted through the Wild Wood!"

Hamar backed away and shouted, "Shut your mouth!"

"That is my ill wish," said Piak, drawing his sword.

Would it help? The soldiers said nothing, but he could feel it: they were scared, terrified... just as he was himself.

"Come here," said Hamar again, but he sounded unsure of himself now. "Come with us. My master wishes to speak to you..."

Now or never! thought Piak. He let go of the stone and ran – away from the river and from the soldiers.

He headed back onto the path he'd just come from. Then he fled to the north, back into the wood. Racing onwards as if his feet had wings, he was amazed that he could do it. Was it really him, Piak? Had he really spoken a curse at the Dead Stone? He didn't look back, even though he thought he heard footsteps behind him. It was almost completely dark and ahead of him he saw the path, narrow and straight, leading into deeper darkness.

Were they following him? Or had the curse saved him, even though it was supposed to be dangerous to speak such an ill wish in that place? But perhaps that was true of all such wishes. *I had no choice*, thought Piak.

His pace slowed, as the last of his strength left him. He stepped off the path and stumbled through the undergrowth, where he tumbled into a hollow, landing on dry leaves, and then lay there. It was like sinking into the depths. And Piak fell straight to sleep.

When Piak awoke, it was pitch dark. He tried to sit up, but he couldn't. His whole body ached, and his limbs were stiff. He lay there for a while and opened his eyes as wide as he could, but the darkness remained impenetrable. Anxiously, he made another attempt to sit up. The leaves beneath him rustled, and he broke out in a cold sweat. He felt so strange, and ill. Perhaps the Dead Stone had enchanted him and harmed him somehow. How could it be so very dark? Where was the light of the moon? Finally, he managed to sit up and he listened to his own frantic breathing.

I need to keep going, he thought. *But where to?* he wondered. *To King Dagonaut*. But where was King Dagonaut? Where was he himself? In the Wild Wood, to the north of Stoneford.

"That place is so haunted..." Who had said that again? Piak sank back down and curled into a ball. He imagined someone or something walking past his hollow. Any moment now, others would come, stand around him, surround him...

With a jolt, he sat up again. Was he still in the wood? Wasn't he in some far more terrible place, locked away somewhere as dark as night? He reached his hands into the leaves – yes, they really were leaves, some of them dry and crisp, others moist with earth. He touched something else – his sword, the sword King Unauwen had given him. Tiuri had once told him that you could hold your sword like a cross. Tiuri... That was it, he had to help Tiuri. But how? He couldn't see anything, and his thoughts were confused. He grasped his sword just beneath the hilt and tried to murmur a prayer. But before he'd finished, he fell back to sleep. He dreamt of the Great Mountains in the west, where the air was fresh and you could see for miles around.

When Piak woke again, the birds were already starting to chirp. He picked up his sword and his bag and scrambled out of the hollow. He still felt stiff and sore. He would soon be on his way, but first he had to know where he was going. "I need to make a plan," he said to himself, "and to keep to it precisely." He couldn't go back to Stoneford. But where would he end up if he kept on going? *I should eat something first*, he thought. *Food always helps*. But he could only get down a little of the remaining bread. He realized he was more thirsty than hungry.

To the north of the Black River was the Green River, which was where the Royal Forest began. "That's where you need to go, Piak," he whispered to himself. "You have no other choice... to the north, no matter how far it is." He struggled to his feet. "Then you have to try to find that path back. As far as I remember, it went in the right direction."

It was possible that they would come after him, now that it was light. During the daytime, ghosts and curses were not as frightening. Even though his pursuers might follow him, he was glad it was daytime. He looked for the path and soon found it. As he walked onwards, he did as he had done the day before: simply one foot in front of the other, one, two... After a while, the stiffness started to go away. He managed to walk at a brisk pace and without stopping for a moment.

Far in the distance, he heard a dog barking. As he thought of Sir Fitil and his men, he tried to walk even faster. Then the path narrowed and he had to take care not to trip over roots and stumps.

The dog in the distance barked again. Piak looked around. Nothing to see. But still he started to run. He raced along until he got a stitch in his side and was forced to rest.

Then he realized he'd be better off leaving the path for a while, so that anyone who was pursuing him would be unable to find his trail. He covered a long distance, crawling, falling and standing back up again, more than actually walking. When he reached a stream, he sat down to drink. Then he waded through the water for some way. "They won't find my scent now," he said to himself with satisfaction.

He felt that he could venture back out onto the path; he would make better progress there, with less chance of getting lost. But no matter how hard he searched, he couldn't find the path again.

As he looked around at a wood that appeared to be getting wilder and more hostile, he tried not to give in to his panic. It seemed more and more like a place where people did not belong. He climbed up into a tree and sat on a high branch, trying to find his bearings. But when he set off again, he wasn't at all certain that he was heading in the right direction. Maybe he was just going around in circles; maybe he'd be trapped in this wood forever.

But that meant Tiuri and the Fool would have to stay there forever, too.

He had no idea exactly how long he'd been wandering around in the wood.

The bread was finished on the first day and after that he chewed on the occasional piece of bark. Later, the feeling of hunger went away and he had only one wish: to lie down and sleep. But the thought that he had to go on kept him on his feet. *I have to get to the Green River, to civilization... to the king... tell him about Tiuri... the tree, and Sir Ristridin...*

Sometimes he thought he could hear people chasing him, but it could have been his imagination. He saw wild animals, which ran away from him, but he thought he saw other things, too. Creatures that looked like living tree trunks beckoned to him with claw-like hands, and strange little grey monsters seemed to flee as he passed. The whole wood started to dance before his eyes, and he stumbled and had to grit his teeth and struggle to his feet. But he got back up, over and over again. It didn't occur to him that he might be ill. Stubbornly he ploughed on, shivering with cold, and then burning with heat.

Evening fell, but the nightmares in his sleep mirrored what he saw during the day.

Then morning came – and he found himself on a path.

A path! But which one? He was vaguely aware that he had to go to the north. Rays of sunshine fell through the trees. If that was the east, the path would probably lead him to the Green River. Fine. Onwards, then.

When it was evening again, and he lay down to rest, his head felt a little clearer. *If I don't reach the Green River soon*, he thought, *I'll never get there. But it could be nearby, perhaps just a few steps away.*

It wasn't completely dark; the moon was shining through the branches. He could easily walk for a little longer. Before long he was following the path again, slowly feeling his way. Ahead of him, he could see that it was becoming lighter. And the trees were such a strange shape... No, they weren't trees...

He went closer – and found himself standing before a gate.

Piak wasn't even surprised. He walked on, through the gate, and stopped again.

In front of him was a clearing in the forest, with lots of buildings in it. It was an entire city: houses, walls, towers, stairs – all illuminated by moonlight. The city was white and black, eerily white, with black shadows between. It was a dead city, dilapidated and abandoned, the houses in ruins – and yet still mighty and beautiful.

Piak stood for a while, just staring. He felt that he should know what this city was, but he could not remember anything. He had found something he hadn't been looking for, but right at that moment he could no longer remember what exactly it was that he had been looking for.

A dead city, a forgotten city...

Then one of the shadows broke away from the others, a shade that moved and came towards him.

Piak was seized by fear. He turned and fled back through the gate and into the forest. As his foot caught on something, he fell. And everything went black.

3   THE GUARDIAN OF THE FORGOTTEN CITY

Someone was singing in a low, rough voice:

I heard tell of a city of stone,
that stood by rivers wide...

Who's that singing? thought Piak.

The voice continued:

> *That once was so, but is no more,*
> *for there, by riverside,*
> *there now stand only trees.*
> *Dreams, schemes...*

"Calm, calm," said a soothing voice above the song, a different voice. "Hush now, go to sleep."

Who... thought Piak and then he realized he had been singing himself. He opened his eyes and looked up into a face he didn't know. As he tried to focus, the face blurred, but he didn't have the strength to be afraid.

"Come, just sleep," said the voice again. A cool hand touched his forehead.

But it was *a human voice...* thought Piak. Now he could see the face clearly again – a long face, with a thin beard that made it seem even longer, and dark-rimmed eyes that looked at him with concern. Beside the face was a flickering light.

"Who...?" began Piak.

"Sssh! You have nothing to fear," said the face. "You are tired, you have a fever, and you need to sleep. Sleep! Soon you will wake up well."

Piak closed his eyes. He could still hear the voice speaking. "I am the Guardian of the Forgotten City and I will remain by your side. Sleep!"

When Piak looked up again, he saw a flock of birds against a mottled white and grey sky. He looked at them in astonishment. No, they weren't flying – they were painted on a vaulted ceiling. He noticed then that he was lying on a bed or couch, and covered with furs. He was in a small, round chamber, with an open door. A ray of sunlight fell into the room, so it must be daytime. Piak felt too drowsy to wonder where he was and how he'd got there. He felt so comfortable, so peaceful and safe.

A tall, thin man came into the room and said cheerfully, "Aha, so he's awake. How do you feel?"

Piak recognized him. "The Guardian of the Forgotten City," he said.

"Ah, so you can remember that much," said the man, sitting down on the bed beside him. "Or you can call me Adelbart. But I understand that the Forgotten City was not unknown to you, the city of stone that stood by rivers wide. Well, actually, the rivers are poetic licence. They're not really that close."

"Which rivers?" asked Piak. "Where am I?"

"This city lies between two rivers: the Black River to the south, and the Green River to the north."

The Green River! That was where Piak had to go! He sat up really quickly, but then noticed, firstly, that he was dizzy and, secondly, that he had no clothes on.

"Lie down!" said the man who was called Adelbart. He gently pushed Piak back down and covered him up. "Your clothes are outside in the sun. They were a bit of a mess. And as far as you're concerned, when I found you, you were in a pitiful state, so there's no way you can go running off yet."

"Yes, but... I have to keep going, to the Green River," Piak weakly protested. "I... I have no time to lose."

"Time is not yours to lose," said Adelbart. "And if you lose your life, then you will have no time at all. Please, be calm. Soon, if heaven is willing, you will be able to get up and go wherever you want. I'll even help you if needed. Wait there."

He stood up and left the room. A moment later, he returned with a bowl and a spoon. "Could you eat something?" he asked, sitting down on the bed again. "This is soup, nourishing, good soup, even if I did cook it myself."

It smelt delicious, and Piak realized that he could indeed eat something.

"I'll feed you," said Adelbart, holding out the spoon.

Piak felt himself becoming stronger with every mouthful, and when the bowl was empty, he said, "Now I really could..."

"No," said Adelbart, kindly but firmly. "You were singing and talking all night. First you need to sleep and then we'll talk some more."

"How did I get here?" asked Piak. "Am I in the... the Forgotten City? Who are you? What day is it, and what's the time? And the Green River, how far is it from here?"

"That's an awful lot of questions all at once," said Adelbart. "But fine, I shall answer them, or you might not be able to sleep. You are in the Forgotten City – Terraverdis is its old name – and no one lives here, except for me. I saw you coming last night, but when I approached you, you fled as if the devil were after you. A little later, I found you by the gate, in a dead faint. It's about ten o'clock in the morning now and the Green River is nearby. There are your answers. Now sleep tight."

Piak wanted to reply, but he fell asleep before he could figure out what he wanted to say.

When Piak woke again, he didn't know how long he had been sleeping. It was still light and Adelbart was sitting on a bench near the door, looking at a sword. Piak watched him and wondered what kind of man he was. He looked a little strange, with his long, sallow face and his sunken eyes. His clothes were colourful but ragged, and he had various weapons hanging from his belt. The Guardian of the Forgotten City looked up and nodded at Piak.

"Well?" he asked.

Piak stretched and gave a deep sigh. "I feel fine," he said and he sat up, this time without any difficulty.

"Then we can talk," said Adelbart, getting to his feet. "Your clothes are at the foot of your bed, but you should stay lying down until I've brought you some food. Here's your sword – a magnificent weapon! How did you come by it?"

"It was given to me," replied Piak. "By King Unauwen."

"By King... Unauwen?" Adelbart repeated in amazement. "Who are you?"

"My name is Piak. I am the squire of Sir Tiuri with the White Shield."

"Most impressive!" said Adelbart. "But come, I'll prepare some food for us. I'm feeling rather hungry myself." He left the room.

Piak stood up and started to get dressed. He was still a little shaky, but the thought of his friends was now tugging at him. He had already lost so much time! *I don't understand how I came to collapse*, he thought with annoyance. *I never get sick. Maybe it was because of the Dead Stone. Or could the water of the Black River be to blame?*

Buckling on his sword, he walked to the door and looked outside. He saw a courtyard, surrounded by walls that were almost entirely hidden by wild creepers. A few scrawny chickens were scratching about, and Adelbart was bent over a log fire in one corner. It all looked very different from the city he had seen last night. Last night... Or was it longer ago? He had to move on as soon as possible!

Adelbart looked up and called, "The food's ready!"

A few minutes later, they were sitting together in the round chamber and tucking into soup and a chicken leg. Piak proved to have a huge appetite. "That's a good sign," said Adelbart with satisfaction.

Then he wanted to find out how Piak came to be in the wood. "No one's been here for months," he said. "I know you want to go to the Green River – but why? What exactly are you seeking?"

Piak hesitated for a moment before answering. After all, no matter how friendly Adelbart might seem, he knew nothing about him, this Guardian of the Forgotten City in the Wild Wood. "I have to go to the City of Dagonaut," he said finally. "Is that far from here?"

"Well, yes, it's quite a way," replied Adelbart. "About a week from the Green River – that's if you're a fast walker."

"That far?" said Piak. "Isn't there somewhere nearby where I could get a horse, or a castle with a knight who can be trusted?"

"A knight who can be trusted?" repeated Adelbart. "To be honest, I've never really trusted knights that much. I'm not on such good terms with those fine gentlemen, you understand. I prefer to hide away in my city, ever since Sir Ristridin and his friends did their damage here."

Piak almost dropped his soup bowl. "Sir Ristridin?!" he exclaimed.

Adelbart froze. "Do you know him?" he asked.

"Yes... no... I've never met him," replied Piak. "But I've heard a lot about him." He took a good look at Adelbart and asked a little uneasily, "But you know him, don't you? How? He... He's not an enemy of yours, is he?"

"In a sense, yes, he is," said Adelbart slowly. "But don't be concerned," he added. "Just enjoy your soup. I'm not going to hurt you, not after I've nursed you all night." He looked pensively at the chicken leg in his hand before continuing, "Last year I was living here with a band of friends... Until Sir Ristridin and his men came along and drove us out. Nearly all my friends were captured and, as far as I know, sent to the capital. I had a lucky escape because I happened to be out hunting some distance away. I hid in the forest and didn't return here for a while."

"But... but what had your friends done?" asked Piak, although he thought he already knew the answer to that question.

"Eat up your soup! We were robbers, and this was our base. A fine place... no one ever dared to follow us here... until Sir Ristridin came."

"Oh," said Piak, not knowing what else to say.

"Sir Ristridin doesn't know what I look like, and I know him only from a distance," said Adelbart. "So I find it hard to judge whether I should consider him my enemy or not. What do you think?"

"I don't know either," said Piak hesitantly. "But you do know that highway robbery is..." He fell silent.

"Illegal and immoral," said Adelbart, completing his sentence for him. "I know." He threw his chicken bone onto the floor. "I've always been a wastrel, a good-for-nothing," he continued. "A jack of all trades and master of none. That's what my mother used to say. I never planned to become a robber, I truly didn't. But I just couldn't hold down a job. Finally I went to a monastery. That was the last resort, I thought. I have a rather contemplative nature, you see, and I hoped I might like it there. But I found that boring, too, so I ran away. I ended up in the wood, where I fell in with the robbers. They were a fine bunch of fellows! So I joined up with them and I found I liked their way of life: completely free, and no griping or groaning. As far as the robbery part was concerned – well, a man has to make a crust somehow, eh? I didn't join in very often. I cooked for us all, and guarded the city. It was me who showed them this place. I discovered the city years ago on one of my long walks." He looked at Piak with an apologetic smile. "So now I've told you almost my whole life story without you asking for it," he said. "And all because of Sir Ristridin. So you know him, then?"

Piak looked at him thoughtfully. He felt that he had nothing to fear from this man and was surprised to realize that he actually found it hard to see him as a robber. He'd always seen such people as the epitome of evil, but there was nothing wicked about the Guardian of the Forgotten City.

"I still haven't thanked you," he said.

"Oh, don't start that!" said Adelbart. "What was I supposed to do? Just leave you lying there? I'd rather you told me what you have to do with Sir Ristridin. Is he the reason you're roaming around the wood?"

"Yes, in part," replied Piak. "But it's more about my friend, Tiuri, actually Sir Tiuri. After Sir Ristridin and his men routed the rob... I mean, chased away your friends, they went deeper into the wood, to the west."

"That's right," said Adelbart with a nod.

"They were looking for the Men in Green," continued Piak.

179

"The Men in Green?!" exclaimed Adelbart. "If you're looking for them, you won't find them. They never get involved in anything and they harm no one unless, of course, you tread on their toes."

"How do you know that?" asked Piak.

"Yes, hmm, how do I know that?! I... I've heard it from various people – maybe the monks at the Brown Monastery. Leave them alone, and they're no trouble."

"I don't believe a word of it!" cried Piak. "Did you know Sir Ristridin has disappeared without a trace and his men have been killed? Treacherously slain by enemies! And Tiuri, my friend, was ambushed and captured. That's why I need to go to King Dagonaut as quickly as possible to get help and to tell him what's happened."

He stood up, suddenly realizing how little time he had to stop and talk.

"Well, I'll be...!" exclaimed Adelbart. "And it was the Men in Green who did it?"

"They were there," said Piak. "Along with others. And the night before we were ambushed, we heard the beating of drums, a terrible sound."

"Drums?" repeated Adelbart.

"Have you ever heard them?" asked Piak. "Do you know anything about them?" He suspected that was the case.

However, Adelbart shook his head. "I've long known that other people live in the wood," he said. "But I've never gone looking for them or bothered about them, and neither did my friends. There are some things you're better off not sticking your nose into!"

"There's something mysterious going on," whispered Piak, "and no one is allowed to find out about it. But Sir Fitil knows, Sir Fitil of Islan. Have you ever met him?"

"No," said Adelbart. "I never go south of the Dead Stone."

Piak shivered when he heard that name. "I had to flee from Sir Fitil's men," he explained. "That's how I ended up here. Pursued by Islan's warriors, who were supposed to be going to Deltaland."

"Deltaland?"

"Yes, there's been an invasion, from Deltaland," said Piak. "But perhaps that's not even true. Sir Fitil could have made it up... but no, the messengers came from Sir Arturin."

"I can't follow this at all," said Adelbart. "An invasion... knights captured, killed, vanished! All manner of things have been happening while I was daydreaming in my Forgotten City. Well, I fear that's the end of my peaceful solitude. Would you like anything else to eat?"

"Thank you," said Piak. "But I really should go. Could you tell me the quickest way to the Green River and where I might be able to find help?" As he spoke, he grew even more worried. The City of Dagonaut was still so far.

Adelbart gave him a questioning look, then laid a hand on his forehead and said, "Fine, I see that I can't stop you, even though I'd rather you stayed another night. I'll take you as far as the river, on my donkey. Yes, I have a steed. At least I have one if it doesn't refuse to budge." He thought for a moment and continued, "The king's city is far away, and you say there are enemies in Islan. The Brown Monastery is nearby – not that the monks will come to your aid with a sword, but they know a great deal, have friends everywhere, and will surely be able to send a message to the king or to Castle Mistrinaut."

"Castle Mistrinaut?!" Piak almost yelled.

"Calm down, my boy! You startled me!"

"I know that castle!" said Piak. "Is it really that close?"

"From the monastery it's a day's ride on horseback," replied Adelbart. "And from here to the monastery won't take any more than a day. I should imagine that's welcome news."

Piak looked at him, his eyes gleaming. "It certainly is!" he said.

Castle Mistrinaut! A mighty man with a long name lived there, who was one of Sir Ristridin's best friends. He was also a friend of Tiuri's, as was his daughter, Lady Lavinia.

"Oh, Adelbart," said Piak, "show me the way to the Brown Monastery. Then I shall ask for help from Mistrinaut, which I am sure to receive!"

4 To the Brown Monastery

It was late in the afternoon when Piak, Adelbart and his donkey set off.

"I would have liked to show you my city," said Adelbart. "It's beautiful, when you take the time to look. When I think how old it must be and about all the people who must once have lived there, I feel very small and insignificant. Which I am, all things considered."

"Not for me, you're not!" said Piak. "Whatever would I have done without you?"

Adelbart nodded thoughtfully. "The ways of fate are strange," he said. "Or the providence of heaven. I so often thought myself a sluggish coward, just getting on with my life in the Forgotten City, while all kinds of things were happening elsewhere in the world. But now my lonely life turns out to have been good for something: I was able to help you. And who knows what consequences that will have?"

There was no path from the Forgotten City to the Green River, but Adelbart said he knew the way blindfolded. He insisted that Piak should sit on his donkey, and Piak was secretly glad he didn't have to walk. The effects of the fever and the exhaustion had still not entirely left him.

As they travelled, they talked to each other, mostly about Piak's adventures. But as evening fell, Adelbart said they had better be silent.

"You never know who might be listening," he said.

"Do you mean my enemies could be near?" whispered Piak.

"I've heard a few strange footsteps..." replied Adelbart.

They both fell silent. Adelbart strode without hesitation, and after a while he said, "Now let's sleep. The river is nearby and we'll be at the monastery in good time tomorrow."

It was a glorious morning when they reached the Green River. There was woodland on the opposite bank, too – pine trees on low hills – but it was no longer the Wild Wood. To their left, on their side of the water, they saw the roofs of houses.

"Some woodcutters live in that village," said Adelbart, pointing, "but we're not going over there. We can cross the river here. Giddy up, Neddy!"

The donkey stuck its head forward and brayed indignantly.

"Keep your mouth shut, beast," said Adelbart irritably. "Get along now. On you go!"

A man came hurrying towards them from the village; his face was red and angry. "That's my donkey!" he yelled.

Adelbart cursed to himself. "That's all we need," he muttered, giving the reluctant animal a push.

As the red-faced man reached them, Piak saw he was armed with a stick. "Now I've got you, thief!" he said. "That's my donkey, the one you stole!"

"Calm down, calm down!" shouted Adelbart, glancing uneasily at the stick. "I didn't steal it. The creature was wandering around in the forest and I only took it so I could keep it safe until I found the owner."

"Lies!" said the man. "I know you, Adelbart! You're a good-for-nothing – you can't even steal something without getting found out. I'm taking my donkey back, of course – but I'm taking you, too! There are other folks in the village who would like a word with you."

"I haven't done anything!" said Adelbart. "You can have your donkey back, but there's no need to act like an ass yourself. You'd do better to thank me for taking good care of the stupid animal.

And if you want to talk to me, you can come and visit me in the Forgotten City."

"Not likely!" the man shouted angrily. "And you're coming with me whether you want to or not."

Piak, who so far had listened in silence, decided it was time for him to speak up. "Adelbart is coming with *me*," he said. "Our business is more important."

"And who might you be?" growled the man, jabbing his stick at Piak.

Piak put one hand on the hilt of his sword. "I am the squire of Sir Tiuri with the White Shield," he replied. "And Adelbart must come with me to the Brown Monastery. Take your donkey and let us go."

His manner seemed to make an impression on the man, even though Piak didn't look too impressive after all his adventures. The man looked at him with some surprise and then said grumpily, "Suit yourself." He took his donkey by the bridle and walked away.

"That was nicely done," said Adelbart, after they'd crossed the river. "Thank you."

"Oh, you're welcome," said Piak.

"It was true, you know, what I said," Adelbart continued. "The donkey just came wandering my way."

"I believe you," said Piak, but he didn't mean it, because he was starting to think Adelbart had a rather relaxed attitude to the truth.

"That's not what your face says!" cried Adelbart. "All right, I stole the creature. I already told you I'm no good! I always really want to do the right thing, but before I know it I've done something wrong again. I'm weak. The best thing I can do is hide myself somewhere far away from temptation."

Piak laughed. "You're an odd one," he said, "but I still like you! And what you do is none of my business."

"But if you like me, it *is* your business!" Adelbart objected. "So far I've broken only a couple of commandments, but sometimes I'm scared that one day I'll do something truly unforgivable. And what then? We're on our way to the monastery now, where I lived for a year as a lay brother. I'd like to try it again but I wouldn't be doing it for the right reasons. A man must be a monk because of his convictions, not because he wants to hide away from the dangers of the world."

They were now walking along a path that took them first through the wood to the north and then to the west. Hills hid the Green River from sight.

Adelbart continued his musings. "I could go on a pilgrimage," he said. "At the source of the Blue River, in the mountains, lives a wise hermit, or so I've heard."

Piak stopped in his tracks. "Menaures!" he exclaimed.

"You know everyone I mention," said Adelbart in surprise. "It really is destiny that we should meet. Have you ever visited him?"

They went on walking. "Have I ever been there? Oh, yes!" said Piak. "I was born in the mountains and I lived with Menaures for some time." He sighed. Suddenly he felt homesick.

"Yes, now I understand," said Adelbart. "Now I understand why in spite of your youth you seem to know what you need to do, without confusing right and wrong. You have lived with Menaures! I think I shall go to see him one day, too. Would he give me advice, do you think?"

"Certainly," replied Piak. "But he'll tell you that you need to find your own way in the world. That's what he always said to me."

A little later, Adelbart asked, "You're not getting tired, are you? The monastery isn't far now, just at the end of this track."

Piak was tired, but he didn't say so. He was thinking about Tiuri and the Fool. He didn't know Tiuri had also walked along this road, months ago, when he was taking the letter to King Unauwen.

"Good. We'll be inside before sunset," said Adelbart, as he rapped the knocker on the door of the Brown Monastery.

A short gatekeeper opened up for them. "My, my!" he cried. "If it isn't Adelbart!" He didn't seem too happy to see him.

"It is indeed Adelbart," said Adelbart. "But please pay no attention to me. This young man has come a long way and been through a great deal. He is looking for help and strength here, Brother Julius."

The gatekeeper let them in.

"Slide the bolts," said Adelbart. "And be careful who you admit. Worse rogues than I might follow."

"What nonsense is this?!" cried the gatekeeper. "There's always something with you. Why have you come back here to bring more turmoil and disruption?"

"If anyone is bringing turmoil and disruption, it's my friend here, Piak," said Adelbart calmly. "Now welcome him, Brother Julius, and take him to see the abbot."

The gatekeeper turned to Piak. "You are, of course, welcome," he said warmly. "Adelbart just confused me for a moment. Who are you and what brings you here?"

"I am the squire of Sir Tiuri with the White Shield," replied the boy, "and he is in great danger."

"Tiuri," repeated the gatekeeper, as he walked with Piak and Adelbart across the courtyard, where a garden was planted. "Tiuri... I know that name. So you wish to speak to the abbot, do you?"

"Yes, please, reverend brother," said Piak. "As soon as possible."

"Just wait inside," said the gatekeeper, "and I'll ask Father Hyronimus if he can receive you."

A few minutes later, they were taken to see the abbot. A young monk was with him; he was introduced as Brother Martin.

"Please sit down," said the abbot after greeting them.

"Shall I... I'd probably better go, had I not, reverend father?" asked Adelbart a little shyly.

"No, of course not," said the abbot. "I thought we would see you again, Adelbart." He turned to Piak and continued, "I have heard you are the squire of Sir Tiuri, whom I know. He was also here, last year, when he was just a squire himself. But first tell me why you have come. I understand it's a serious matter."

Piak took a deep breath. Then he told the abbot everything that had happened in the Wild Wood, as concisely as he could.

"Then our enemies took Tiuri and Marius," he concluded. "They went along the Black River, towards the Owl House. They need help as quickly as possible – soldiers to free them. Lots of soldiers, because the enemy's numbers are great."

"Sir Ristridin rode out with twenty men," said Brother Martin quietly. "Are none left alive?"

"I fear not," said Piak. "Except for Sir Ristridin himself, but no one knows where he is." And he added, "Tiuri instructed me to tell all of this to the king."

"Of course," said the abbot. "King Dagonaut must receive these ill tidings as soon as possible. We shall send a messenger immediately."

"But the king is so far away!" said Piak. "And Tiuri and the Fool remain prisoners in the meantime. That's why I thought of the Lord of Mistrinaut."

"It was a good thought indeed," said the abbot. "Brother Martin will go to Mistrinaut. He's an excellent rider and he can leave at once."

The young monk rose to his feet. "Certainly," he said. "I shall borrow a horse from Farmer Roldo. And I shall tell him to prepare more horses. Perhaps his son can ride to the king."

"Yes, indeed," said the abbot. "I shall commit to paper the essentials of what Piak has told me. And Brother Martin, have Mistrinaut send a messenger to the capital, too. This message must not be lost."

"As you wish, Father Hyronimus," said the monk. He gave Piak a nod and disappeared.

"And what can I do, reverend father?" asked Piak.

"Tonight you can sleep, my son," replied the abbot. "Brother Martin is leaving at once, but even so we can't expect the Lord of Mistrinaut to be here before tomorrow afternoon – probably later if he still needs to equip his men."

"I'd really like to..." began Piak.

"There is nothing you can do until tomorrow but use your patience, my son," said the abbot. "We will ensure that help arrives as soon as possible. The Lord of Mistrinaut will certainly want to help. And all of us here will pray that the dangers in the Wild Wood may be averted and that you'll see your friends again soon." He turned to Piak's companion. "Stay here tonight, too, Adelbart," he said. "We really should talk, don't you think? Goodnight to both of you, and may God bless you."

5   MEN OF MISTRINAUT

The Brown Monastery was usually an island of calm, but turmoil and disruption had indeed accompanied Piak within its walls. The Wild Wood, which had always seemed so far away, even though the monastery was practically on its borders, now felt threateningly close.

The Lord of Mistrinaut arrived the following day, and Piak was immediately summoned to him.

Sigirdiwarth Rafox of Azular Northa, the Lord of Mistrinaut, was a large man with red hair. He barely seemed to fit inside the abbot's small cell. Piak felt rather shy in front of this powerful lord with his stern face and those penetrating eyes beneath bristling eyebrows. But he told him what he had to say, and he kept it brief and clear.

"I have twenty-five men with me," said the Lord of Mistrinaut. "They have set up camp outside, reverend father. I did not wish to impose too much on your hospitality. The rest of my men are coming this evening. Brother Martin will be in their company. I have also sent word to the Lord of Westenaut and asked him to send men, and of course there are messengers on their way to the king."

Piak nodded with satisfaction. The Lord of Mistrinaut was a man who could be trusted, as he had always known. A burden seemed to have lifted from his shoulders now that this man was here to help.

"I believe it would be best to act as quickly as possible," the Lord of Mistrinaut continued. "The rest of my men will be here soon, so we can enter the Wild Wood tonight or tomorrow morning."

"Yes!" exclaimed Piak.

"I can take sixty men," said the Lord of Mistrinaut. "And Brother Martin also wanted to join us, Father Hyronimus, with your permission."

"You have my permission, Lord Rafox," said the abbot. "Brother Martin has been into the wood a number of times. I am sure he will be of assistance."

"Sixty-three men in total, then," said Lord Rafox. He turned his sharp gaze on Piak. "Of course you will be with us," he said. "Is our number sufficient, do you think?"

"I believe so, my lord," Piak replied. "But I cannot know for sure. As you are aware, Sir Ristridin had twenty men with him. I have seen only the enemies who ambushed Tiuri – there were about fifteen of them. And of course the men of Islan."

"Sir Fitil!" muttered Lord Rafox, with an angry scowl. "Well, I will most certainly set off soon! The soldiers of Westenaut will be unable to get here until the end of the week. I shall leave orders for them with you, Father Hyronimus, if you do not mind. And one more thing – the Wild Wood is unknown territory for me. I should like to know as much as possible about it before I leave."

"I have already thought about that, Lord Rafox," said the abbot. "Piak, who has just come from there, and Brother Martin can certainly tell you something about it. And Adelbart may know more about the Forgotten City than he has told me so far. I also have a map here – it is very old and has been in the possession of our monastery for years. The situation has changed somewhat since then. The Second Great Road, which has fallen into disuse, is still marked on this map. But perhaps that is just as well, because it would appear that the wood is no longer as untrodden as we believed and that it has paths once again, just as it did long ago."

He spread out the map on his desk. Piak and Lord Rafox leant over to study it.

"I do not know if the distances are accurate," the abbot continued, "but at least they will give you an impression. Look, here is the Green River, where we are now. There is Terraverdis, now in ruins, known as the Forgotten City. That is the Black River, where the Second Great Road once ran. There is a castle, probably the Owl House, where Tiuri was ambushed. And there you see the Tarnburg. I thought it had disappeared long ago, but what Piak told me has made me doubt. Maybe it is now inhabited."

The castle Lady Isadoro sang about? thought Piak. *But why did she sing that song if we were not supposed to know anything about it?* He did not ponder the answer to this question, but looked at Lord Rafox, who was indicating on the map which route he wanted to take.

"I think we must cross the Green River and follow it to the south," he said. "To here, where it turns to the west. If we proceed to the south, we should come out by the Black River, about halfway between the Owl House and the Tarnburg. Our route from there depends on what we find. Perhaps we will have to go to the west, perhaps towards the Unholy Hills, or to Islan."

He raised his head and asked, "These Men in Green seem to live near here, between the Green Hills and the Green River. Do you know anything about them, reverend father?"

The abbot shook his head. "Little more than a few strange stories that are oddly contradictory," he replied. "Old tales mention them, but often not in human form..."

"The enemies Piak has spoken about are most certainly human," said the Lord of Mistrinaut drily.

"Yes," said the abbot, "but I would advise you not to be too disbelieving about creatures – which may indeed be people – and situations that you have never come across before. I rarely go beyond the walls of the monastery, but I know the world still hides many secrets."

"As do I," said Lord Rafox, looking thoughtfully at the map. "I have been to many strange parts, for I have travelled far and wide. And as far as this Wild Wood is concerned, there is something else about it that makes it dangerous. These are regions that have been abandoned by people and then shunned. Wicked weeds can take root in such places."

"That's why Sir Ristridin wanted to go there," whispered Piak.

The Lord of Mistrinaut looked at him, a sudden smile making his stern face much friendlier. "And your friend, Tiuri," he said. "With God's help, we shall find him, my boy."

An hour later, Piak was sitting with Adelbart on the edge of the small well in the monastery garden. The gate was open and soldiers were walking in and out. Lord Rafox was still inside, in conversation with the abbot.

"Why don't you come with us?" Piak asked Adelbart.

Adelbart looked thoughtful. "I could come," he said. "If only I knew I was doing the right thing."

"Why not?" said Piak. "You know your way around the forest and you can use weapons, too."

"Yes, but that's not always a good thing," replied Adelbart. "I'm scared I might use them against the wrong person. It's just the kind of thing I'd do."

"Come on, you know who you'll be up against now," said Piak.

"You may think you know – but I don't! There are all kinds of strange folk running around the forest, that's for sure. The creatures that live there see every intruder – good or bad – as an enemy."

Piak took a good look at him. "Adelbart," he said, "do you know more than you've told me?"

Adelbart answered his gaze with big, surprised eyes. "I already told you," he said, "that I had no inclination to go out investigating and interfering in other men's business. But," he continued after a pause, "I think that time's over now. I've made my decision. I'll come with you, if the Lord of Mistrinaut does not object."

"That's excellent news," said Piak and he sneezed.

"I'd go inside if I were you," Adelbart advised him. "The air's chilly."

"Ask Lord Rafox right away if you can come," said Piak. "I'm sure he can use every man."

"Even a man who was a robber?" said Adelbart with a doubtful look on his face.

"I haven't told him about that," said Piak. "And Father Hyronimus will be only too pleased to hear that you're going to do something good."

"Oh, the abbot has already had a few stern words with me," murmured Adelbart. "Fine, I'll ask him. Perhaps this is better than going on a pilgrimage." Then, a little more loudly, he added, "Do you know that lad over there?"

"Who do you mean?" asked Piak.

Adelbart pointed at a spot in the cloister. "One of the squires from Mistrinaut," he said. "He's been watching you for a while."

Piak saw a slim figure, dressed in blue – the colour of Mistrinaut. He was half hidden behind a column and he was beckoning to Piak.

"He's calling you over," said Adelbart. "Go on. I'll pay the soldiers a visit and see if I can talk to Lord Rafox."

It was rather dark in the cloister and the squire had retreated to a far corner.

"What is it?" asked Piak, approaching him.

"Where is Lord Rafox?" the boy asked quietly.

"Inside, with the abbot," replied Piak, a little puzzled.

He saw a boy of about his own age – he didn't think he'd ever met him before, but he seemed familiar somehow.

"You don't know me," said the boy, as if he'd read Piak's mind. "But I know who you are – Piak, Sir Tiuri's squire."

"And who are you?" asked Piak.

"My name is Fox," came the brief reply.

"What do you want from me?" asked Piak.

"Can you tell me what Lord Rafox is planning? When are we setting off?"

"I'm sure you'll be told if you're coming with us," said Piak. "You are one of the men of Mistrinaut, aren't you?"

"Yes, that's right. But... All right, then," said the boy. "I have to trust someone. I call myself Fox, but my name is actually Sigirdiwarth Rafox."

"Is the Lord of Mistrinaut your father?" said Piak.

"Quiet!" whispered the boy. "But yes, that's right."

"Now I know who you reminded me of!" said Piak. "Lady Lavinia, your sister. You are so very much like her."

"It's not the first time I've heard that," said Sigirdiwarth Rafox and he continued, "Listen, my father doesn't know I'm here – and he mustn't find out either."

"Why not?" asked Piak.

"I am a squire," said Fox, "and I want nothing more than to go along and help free Sir Tiuri. But my father does not approve. He says it's too dangerous. I'm not allowed to go, just because I'm... just because I'm too young. How old are you?"

"Nearly fifteen," said Piak.

"Then I'm older than you. Don't you think it's ridiculous? I don't like the thought of staying safely behind at Mistrinaut and only hearing all the stories later. I want to go. And I *will* go. So I'm going to join the company. One of my father's men is in on the secret – and once we're in the wood, they can hardly send me back... Why aren't you saying anything?" he asked, when Piak remained silent.

"Oh, I completely understand," said Piak. "I wouldn't want to stay at home either if I were you. But your father doesn't seem like the sort of person I'd want to disobey."

"You're right," said Fox, "but having to stay at Mistrinaut is even worse. I might not look strong, but I'm brave – really! You won't give me away, will you, Piak?"

"Of course not," said Piak. "Do you know Tiuri?"

"Lavinia has told me a lot about him," replied Fox.

"Lady Lavinia, how is she?" asked Piak.

"She's well," said Fox. "She sometimes regrets she is a woman, though, as it means she cannot go out and about like us – exploring forests, fighting enemies…"

"Lavinia's lovely," said Piak. He was thinking about Tiuri and Isadoro. He could only see the Daughter of Islan as a traitor. But did Tiuri know that?

"What are you thinking about?" asked Fox.

He was so like Lavinia! And Piak knew better than to say anything about Isadoro. "Oh, just about Tiuri," he replied.

"Tell me about… about your adventures," said Fox. "Or no, wait. I think I can hear the second group of soldiers arriving. My father will be out here any minute now. We'll see each other later, in the forest."

"We're leaving tonight," whispered Piak, "or tomorrow morning. If you need my help, just call me."

"Thank you, Piak," said Fox.

6 Fox

They left at daybreak the next morning. Piak travelled on one of Mistrinaut's horses, riding with Lord Rafox and Brother Martin at the front of the group. The weather was mild, but changeable; rain and sun kept trying to chase each other away. Piak felt just the same: full of worries one moment and brimming with confidence the next.

Having crossed the river, they followed a path upstream along the bank. Piak was riding beside Adelbart now, who told him that this road was used by woodcutters and finished in a dead end not too far away. Brother Martin looked around and said he had once seen a Man in Green somewhere around here.

"I was looking for herbs on the opposite bank," he said, "and suddenly he was standing there in front of me. Even his face seemed

194

green in the shade of the trees. He looked furious and he pointed with his spear to the east, as if to say I should go back that way. The next moment, he was gone."

"Did you really see him?" asked Adelbart. "Or could you just have imagined it?"

"Sometimes I wonder," replied Brother Martin. "But no, it was real."

"You should have made the sign of the cross, Brother," said Adelbart. "Then you would have known for certain if the man was real – and whether he was good or bad."

"Have you never met one?" asked Piak.

"Oh, let's not talk about my strange visions," said Adelbart. "I have a vivid imagination and many is the time I've seen things that weren't there."

They looked at the opposite bank, the territory of the mysterious Men in Green. It was densely overgrown and the leaves already had more foliage than elsewhere in the wood. A sudden gust of wind made the trees rustle and a flurry of rain swept over them.

"Here, wrap yourself in this cloak," said Brother Martin to Piak. "Catching cold once is enough."

The path became narrower, and the Lord of Mistrinaut remarked, "I think we shall soon have to go on foot. But I wanted to take the horses because our enemies have them, too. Let's gallop for as long as we can."

"Quiet!" said Piak suddenly.

"What is it?" asked the Lord of Mistrinaut.

"I think I heard something..." Piak reined in his horse and the others did the same.

"I can just hear the raindrops," said Brother Martin, "and thunder rumbling in the distance."

"I thought it was something else," whispered Piak. "But it's gone now." He didn't say what exactly he'd thought, because he wasn't sure he'd really heard the sound of a drum.

As they rode onwards, they let their horses set the pace. Piak looked back from time to time. The line of men was long; he couldn't even see its end because of the twists and turns in the path. He thought about Fox. Was he riding with them? He was probably at the back of the line. After a while, he stopped his horse and allowed the others to go past. It was some time before he saw Lord Rafox's son; he was indeed almost the last.

Just then, the Lord of Mistrinaut gave the signal for a short rest. The men dismounted, and food appeared. Piak lost sight of Fox, but finally found him by the river. He was sitting close to the water, in a spot where they couldn't see him from the path.

He jumped when Piak came to stand beside him. Then he quietly said, "Oh, it's you. Sit with me."

Piak did so.

"It's so beautiful here!" said Fox, with a hint of surprise.

The sun had broken through the clouds again, even though drops of water were still dripping from the branches. The rapidly flowing river was clear, with silvery fish darting about. Flowers grew here and there alongside the path. Fox picked one and idly played with it. He had pale, narrow hands, and Piak frowned for a moment as he looked at them. What did they remind him of?

Fox cast a sideways glance at him and threw the flower into the water. "Well, well, so here we are, then!" he said cheerfully, but it sounded rather forced to Piak. There was something peculiar about this boy. "So, talk to me!" Fox continued. "You were going to tell me about your adventures. I've only heard the most important parts, and always from other people."

"What would you like to know?" asked Piak.

"Everything," said Fox.

"I don't know if everything's worth telling," said Piak with a laugh. But he started anyway. He spoke first about meeting the Fool and then described their journey to the Owl House.

"So the Fool was right," whispered Fox. "Did you believe him from the start, too, just like Tiuri?"

Piak had to think about that for a moment. "I believed Tiuri," he replied, "and so I believed the Fool."

"If only more people had listened to Tiuri," said Fox. "Then perhaps he would not have been taken prisoner. Poor Marius! Oh, but I do not like that Lord of Islan!"

Piak didn't want to respond to that last remark, as then he would have to mention Isadoro. So he quickly explained how the men of Islan had looked for him and then told him about what had happened near the Owl House. As he told his story, though, he got more and more into it, and it felt as if he were reliving many of the events.

But then he faltered. The face of his engrossed listener, gazing at him with wide-open eyes, threw him into confusion.

It was the face of Lady Lavinia!

"Why are you looking at me so strangely?" said Fox, blushing. Then he turned away and looked at the river. "So what did you do after you had read Sir Ristridin's message?" he asked.

"Tiuri said we should return immediately," Piak said slowly, "and so we did..." He was still looking closely at his companion. That delicate profile... it was definitely the face of a girl, even in spite of the helmet that was hiding her hair.

Lavinia!

Somewhere behind them Adelbart called out, "Piak, where are you? We're moving off!"

Fox leapt up and, with his hands on his hips, he looked down at Piak. "Onwards!" he said, trying to make his voice sound manly. And more quietly he added, "Don't let on to anyone that I'm Sigirdiwarth yet. We're still too close to the monastery and to my home."

Is he – or she – Lavinia? Yes or no? thought Piak, also getting to his feet.

Fox turned around and darted ahead of him, small and slender. No, he was not Sigirdiwarth, but his sister, the young lady of Mistrinaut. She clearly wanted to keep playing her role. So Piak thought he had better say nothing, even though he was sure she had noticed his confusion.

As he rode onwards, however, he did not feel entirely comfortable. If Fox was Lavinia, he could understand that her father wanted her to stay at home. A young lady dressing as a squire so she could go out to face dangers and enemies... Piak had never heard anything like it! And yet he admired her. She was so courageous; there was no one else like her. *Is she doing it just for Tiuri?* he wondered. She kept asking about him... She was so different from Isadoro, who had used her wiles in an attempt to keep Tiuri away from the Wild Wood, but who had still not wanted to warn him openly. Isadoro, who did not even dare to stroke Ardanwen, but who had enchanted Tiuri with her beauty...

"You look so serious, Piak," said Brother Martin suddenly appearing beside him. "Do not worry about tomorrow, for tomorrow will worry about itself, my boy."

"I'm not worrying about tomorrow. I'm worrying about today!" said Piak. A little later he said, "Brother Martin, do you know the Lord of Mistrinaut well?"

"Quite well, yes," came the reply. "I have often visited his castle."

"And do you know his children, too? He has a son and a daughter."

"Yes," said the monk, "Sigirdiwarth and Lavinia. Sigirdiwarth is the younger of the two, about your age."

Piak began to have his doubts again. "Why did he not come with his father?" he asked.

"Sigirdiwarth is not at home at the moment. He is serving as a squire with a knight in the far north," said Brother Martin. "So you've never met him?"

"No," said Piak, "but I've met his sister. Does he look much like her?"

"Not in the slightest," replied the monk. "He's the image of his father, robust and red-headed. Lavinia resembles her mother. But why are you asking these questions?"

"Oh, no reason," said Piak vaguely.

So he was not mistaken; Fox was Lavinia. If the Lord of Mistrinaut were to find out! And Tiuri! Ah, Tiuri, where could he be?

Towards evening, they stopped once again. Nothing out of the ordinary had happened all day; they had seen no one. But still Lord Rafox ordered his men not to make any fires. "A group such as ours can hardly ride through the forest unnoticed," he said, "but the light of a fire can warn enemies far away, and seems like an unnecessary risk."

Piak went in search of Fox. Everyone was busy, preparing the meal and places to sleep. Everything was going very smoothly and calmly, as the Lord of Mistrinaut was walking around and keeping a close eye on his men.

An elderly soldier came up and whispered to Piak, "My squire wishes to speak to you."

Piak followed him to Fox, who had found a good hiding place behind a couple of large trees. Fox – no, Lavinia – smiled at him and said, "What an adventure! Don't look so worried. This man, Bronno, is taking good care of me. He knows who I am, as do you."

"Indeed I do, Lady Lavinia," said Piak, sitting down opposite her.

"Shhh!" said Fox, staring at him with wide eyes. "Whatever made you think I'm Lavinia?"

"Well, I'm not blind... You're sitting there right in front of me!" replied Piak.

"Oh," she sighed. "It would seem my disguise is not as good as I thought! These clothes belong to my brother, but I shall have to keep my face hidden or behave in a more manly fashion. I fear that the other men will soon notice I'm not one of them. Do you think they'll count us?"

"Most probably, my lady," said Piak. "Which group are you in?"

"Why are you suddenly calling me 'my lady'? My name is Fox! I think I'm in the last group."

The Lord of Mistrinaut had divided his small army into four groups, each with a captain who was responsible for his men.

"But even if they realize who I am," continued Lavinia, "they won't dare to betray me, not if I forbid it. After all, I am their lord's daughter."

"But they owe allegiance to their master before all others!" Piak pointed out.

"You're not going to stand against me, are you?" she said, leaning closer to him. "Everything I've said to you is true. I cannot stand by and idly wait. I want to help! Why should that be forbidden just because I'm a woman?"

"Yes but Lavin... I mean Fox, it's dangerous," began Piak.

"I'm older than you, and I really am very capable of helping. I'd rather not use my sword, but I'm a better archer than my brother. But that's not what really matters most. Would you let anyone stop you from going to help your friend?"

"Of course not!" said Piak. "But it's different for you."

"Because I'm a woman? It's precisely because I'm a woman that I feel even more strongly compelled to come along. I..." Lavinia suddenly fell silent, as if she'd said too much.

Piak was silent, too. Whatever did she mean? She must care a great deal about Tiuri – yes, that was it.

Lavinia interrupted his thoughts. Taking him by the arm, she looked at him intently, almost sternly. "Piak," she said, softly but urgently, "forget what I just said. Try to see me just as Fox, a squire like you. And when... when we find Tiuri, don't tell him anything about it. Don't let him find out who Fox is. He won't see Fox either."

"Why not?" whispered Piak.

"Because... I'm going because I want to be there. But I don't want Tiuri ever to think I'm running around after him. Because I'm not!"

Yes, you are, thought Piak, but he felt only admiration for Lavinia.

"When we find him – which I'm hoping and praying for – I shall disappear," she continued. "If he wishes to come and visit me later, when I'm Lavinia again, then he is welcome. I just want to be Lavinia for him. He must never hear about Fox."

Then suddenly her seriousness melted away and, with a laugh, she added, "All this talking makes things far too complicated, don't you think? Come on, Piak, shake Fox by the hand and speak a wish with him for the success of our adventure!"

Laughing, yet still uneasy, Piak did as he was asked and he promised solemnly that he would tell Tiuri nothing. He had realized it was not easy to resist Lady Lavinia.

He planned to keep a close eye on her, though, so that he could protect her if needed. He only wished that the thought of Isadoro didn't keep nagging at him. *Ah*, he thought, *Tiuri will forget Isadoro as soon as he sees Lavinia.* But when would Tiuri see Lavinia?

7   THE DRUMS SPEAK AGAIN

The next day, Lavinia was the first to wish Piak good morning. She looked rather pale.

"Oh, I'm so stiff!" she sighed. "Like a plank."

Piak felt just the same, but he said casually, "That's because you're not used to it. Would you really not rather turn around and go back?"

"How dare you ask that?" she said indignantly. "I'm allowed to complain to someone, aren't I? The worst of it is having to wear this helmet again. I only dared to take it off when it got dark. But it's my own fault. If I weren't too vain to cut off my plaits, I'd be able to feel the wind in my hair right now."

"It would be a shame to lose your lovely long hair," agreed Piak.

"And so I'm walking around in helmet, boots and spurs," said the lady. "Quiet, there's Father. Make sure he doesn't come this way."

Piak walked towards the Lord of Mistrinaut.

"Good morning," he said to Piak. "This is where our journey really begins. Adelbart just told me that the path comes to an end around fifteen minutes' ride away. After that we'll have to find our own way through."

"How far is it to the Black River?" asked Piak, still standing firmly in front of him.

"According to the map, a day or two," replied Lord Rafox. "I have a copy of it here, which one of the monks made for me. But, as you know, there's no guarantee that the distances are correct." He told Piak that he'd carve markers on the trees for the men of Westenaut, who would follow them in a few days. "I left instructions with the abbot," he said. "Let's hope they don't get lost."

Then they spoke about Sir Ristridin. Around them, the men made ready to set off.

A sudden noise made everyone fall silent.

A thud! A rattle... *Boom! Tok-tok-tok-tok*. It sounded something like that. Soon it was repeated. *Boom! Tok-tok-tok-tok...*

Someone was beating a drum.

Piak had heard the sound before, but this time it was much closer. And although it was daytime now, it sounded just as ominous. It was coming from the west, from the other side of the river.

The men began to talk excitedly, all at once.

"Silence!" ordered the Lord of Mistrinaut.

"Boom!" came the sound again.

Then another drum began to sound, softly in the distance. *Boom! Tok-tok-tok-tok... Boom! Tok-tok-tok-tok.*

They all listened, holding their breath.

Another *Boom!*, and then the drum in the distance was silent. *Boom!* said the drum closer to them.

They waited tensely to see if the drums would sound again.

"They've stopped," said one of the men.

"No, listen!" whispered Piak, who had sharp ears.

Very far away and dull, he thought he could hear a third drum, like an echo. *Boom, tok-tok-tok-tok... Boom...*

The second drum answered clearly: *Boom!*

Then it was silent.

"The drums are in the trees and they speak to one another," whispered Piak. "That's what the Fool said."

"That's very much what it sounds like," said the Lord of Mistrinaut. "I wonder if they are passing on a message."

"What kind of message, my lord?" asked Piak, although he had a suspicion.

"That we are approaching, for instance," said the Lord of Mistrinaut.

The men began talking once again.

"Stay calm!" their leader commanded. He called the four captains together and withdrew with them.

There was a tugging at Piak's sleeve; it was Lavinia. "What does it mean?" she asked. "Is it the enemy? The Men in Green?"

"I think so," replied Piak. "We suspect they're passing on a message."

"About us?"

Piak nodded.

"And what should we do now?" asked Lavinia. "Are we going to head there, in that direction?"

Some men came over to stand with them. Adelbart was among them, and Bronno, Lavinia's protector. Everyone was trying to guess what the sound of the drums might mean. Only Adelbart said nothing. He looked around the group and suddenly drew attention to Lavinia by peering at her quizzically, then looking her up and down, from head to toe, and stroking his beard in surprise. One of the men followed his gaze, whistled through his teeth, and then said rudely, "Hey, who are you?"

Piak made a move, but Lavinia answered coolly, "Me? I'm just a squire from Castle Mistrinaut."

Bronno gave the soldier a shove. "Do you not see who is standing before you?" he chastised him.

The soldier turned red and took a step back.

Lavinia raised her head proudly, smiled and said, "My name is Fox. And my family is well known to you. Let that be enough."

The soldiers, except for Bronno and Adelbart, slunk off.

"I am sorry I gave you away," Adelbart said politely. "I should never have made it so obvious. But it took me by surprise when I saw you were a woman."

Lavinia put her finger to her lips. "It does not matter," she said warmly. "As long as you've recovered now."

"From now on, my face will reveal absolutely nothing," Adelbart promised. He looked as if he were about to make a bow, but then thought better of it, and walked away.

"The first danger has been averted!" whispered Lavinia. Her eyes were gleaming with excitement. "I am curious to hear what Father's war plan is," she added.

Piak left her in Bronno's care and headed to where Lord Rafox had just been talking with his captains. The lord was walking away now, in the company of Brother Martin.

"What has been decided?" Piak asked one of the captains.

"Lord Rafox is sticking with the original plan," came the reply. "But he may send a few men to scout the other side of the river. We are about to set off."

Piak walked on; he wanted a quick word with the Lord of Mistrinaut. He had disappeared from sight, but it did not take Piak long to find him. He was standing with Brother Martin on the riverbank, some way from the rest of the company. As Piak approached, he heard him say, "I do not like this."

He did not catch the monk's reply.

"Oh, no," said the Lord of Mistrinaut. "If it's a fight out in the open, I can certainly take them on. But they have an advantage over us."

Piak stopped, hesitating, afraid that this conversation was not meant for his ears. *No*, he thought. *What could there be that I am not allowed to hear?*

Brother Martin spoke now, but still he could not make out what he said.

Lord Rafox's voice, though, was deep and clear: "Exactly! Then they have hostages! That's been my concern since the start. If it comes to a clash, I fear greatly for the fate of Tiuri and his friend."

Piak stood perfectly still.

There was more mumbling from the monk and then, quietly this time, Lord Rafox spoke again, "I do not know what they want. May heaven grant that I meet this challenge with success, but young Tiuri and this Marius are in their power. Best not mention any of this to Piak, eh?" he added.

But Piak had already heard. He turned and hurried away. He heard Lord Rafox call his name, but he paid no attention.

"Oh, what a fool, what an idiot I am!" he raged to himself. "I've been so blind! How could I not think of that?!"

He walked through the bustle of men and horses, and then turned his back on them to gaze across the river.

He had been worried all that time, but even so he had been full of hope as he set off in the company of the mighty Lord of Mistrinaut and his valiant men. Now the terrible truth dawned on him: Tiuri and the Fool had fallen into the hands of the enemy! And if those enemies were as wicked as the Fool had said, they would have no qualms about using them to their advantage – by holding them as hostages and killing them if they feared an attack. And yet these enemies had to be fought.

Tiuri had probably realized right away. He had been so serious when he said that he hoped at least one of them would escape the forest alive. Ristridin's men had been killed. Would Tiuri share their fate? Would the Fool never return home to his cabin?

"No, no," prayed Piak, "don't let that happen. Don't let any fate worse than capture befall Tiuri!"

PART FIVE

—

THE BLACK KNIGHT
WITH THE RED SHIELD

1 RED RIDERS AND MEN IN GREEN

Tiuri and the Fool had been captured, and Red Riders from Eviellan were awaiting them at the Owl House. They were forced to enter the ruins, where they found even more Red Riders. Their captain came and stood before Tiuri and said, "What is your name?"

Tiuri looked at him. All he could see of his enemy's face were his eyes. In his mind, though, was a different image: the tree and Ristridin's words. Treacherously slain by enemies... Yet he answered proudly, "I am Sir Tiuri with the White Shield."

"What about him?" asked the Red Rider, pointing at the Fool, who was trying to hide behind Tiuri.

"This is my squire," said Tiuri. He really hoped Marius wouldn't give the game away. But the Fool seemed too scared to say anything at all.

"Squire..." said another horseman. "That may be so, but he has been here before!"

Tiuri knew he had to draw their attention away from the Fool, so he said, quickly and angrily, "Yes, Sir Tiuri and his squire. But who are you? And by what right have you taken us prisoner?"

The Red Riders gave no response. They whispered among themselves for a moment. All he caught was one word, his own name: Tiuri.

Then the captain turned back to him and sneered, "By what right, sir knight? The right of might!"

Then he left the ruins and the others followed him. One of them turned back and shouted to the prisoners that they must stay inside, at least if they valued their lives.

Yes, we are still alive, thought Tiuri. *Shouldn't I be happy about that?* Yet he was filled with worry and uncertainty. Soldiers from

Eviellan – the situation did not look good. Sir Ristridin had been one of their greatest enemies... Had Ristridin really gone to Deltaland? And the invasion – what was he to make of that?

"Now they've caught you anyway," the Fool said tearfully, "and me too. Again!"

"I'm so sorry, Marius," Tiuri said softly. And he really meant it. Hadn't he promised to take him back safely home to his cabin?

"Oh, it's not your fault, Friend," whispered the Fool. "We had to come and see. That was what you wanted..."

Yes, that was what Tiuri had wanted. And he had found out a great deal, but that knowledge would be of no benefit unless he could escape.

But there was still Piak. Piak had not been captured, as far as he knew. He couldn't bring himself to face the thought that something worse might have happened to him.

"Marius," he said, "listen to me! We have been captured, but you are not alone this time. I am with you, and..."

The Fool nodded. "That is true," he said. "I'm not so very afraid when I'm with you. Will you stay with me?"

"Yes, of course," replied Tiuri.

"And are we going to run away?" the Fool asked in a whisper.

"Sssh, don't say too much, Marius," said Tiuri. "Don't let our enemies hear you. They mustn't find out that there were three of us... and that Piak escaped."

"Piak..." whispered the Fool. "Yes, he isn't here."

"I hope he got away," Tiuri whispered into his ear. "He will go to fetch help for us. Do you understand, Marius? But the Red Riders mustn't find out, or they'll start looking for him."

"They won't find out," whispered the Fool. "He's run away, but we won't tell them."

"And that's why we're pretending you're my squire," Tiuri continued. "Remember that, Marius! You are my squire. Don't say too much. Keep our secret!"

"I am your squire," said the Fool, nodding. "Not really, though. Piak's your squire. But he got away."

Tiuri sighed. If only he could be sure that Piak had escaped! Piak, his faithful friend, so brave and resourceful.

He thought about Islan, too. He wondered if he could have been mistaken when he saw the colours of Islan among his attackers. He could hardly doubt it, though: Sir Fitil had something to do with what was going on in the wood. And Isadoro, too. She had probably used her charms just to stop him from investigating. But then later she had warned him! No, he still didn't understand Isadoro. On the one hand she had acted as if she knew nothing about the wood, but then she'd also drawn attention to it by singing that song. How did it go again...? *I heard tell of a fortress grim...*

She had sung another song, and Sir Fitil had become angry. Perhaps the solution to the mystery lay in the relationship between the lady and her father.

"But whatever the truth is," he said to himself, "she never felt anything for me." That was a painful thought and he dismissed it. Now was not the time to think too deeply about that subject. It was more use to consider how they might possibly escape.

Followed by the Fool, he walked around the Owl House, but at every exit, through every window, he saw the same: soldiers on guard. The enemy had surrounded the house.

As night fell, the Red Riders returned. They pointed at a corner of one of the rooms and barked at their prisoners to stay there. Then they lit a fire in the same room and cooked some food, but gave none to Tiuri and the Fool. Tiuri hoped Piak had managed to find their own bag of supplies.

The men talked among themselves in hushed tones. Now and then they glanced over at the prisoners, as if they were discussing them.

Then one of the men leapt to his feet and cried out, "What's that noise?"

"It's just the owls," said another.

"Really?" said the startled Red Rider, eyeing Tiuri as if he suspected him of having made those strange, fluttering sounds.

"Are you scared of a few owls?" his companions jeered.

"Maybe he's right to be afraid," Tiuri called over to them. "Who says it's just owls? Have you never heard of spirits that linger in places they once lived... tortured souls, unable to accept their fate?"

The Fool beside him made the sign of the cross. The Red Riders all looked at Tiuri. By the flickering firelight he could see their faces were threatening, but also fearful. The one who had first mentioned the owls drew his dagger and walked over to Tiuri.

Undaunted, the young knight looked at him. "You've no need to fear them," he said, "as long as there's no blood on your hands."

The Red Rider cursed, but turned around and sat back down with his fellow soldiers.

Tiuri had a brief feeling of satisfaction; he had paid back one of his enemies just a little. Not long after that, though, the Red Riders tied up Tiuri and the Fool, and they spent a miserable night together.

The Red Riders did not sleep much either. Occasionally one of them headed outside, and towards morning there came the sound of horses' hoofs moving away. Soon the prisoners were untied and pulled roughly to their feet.

"Time to go," said the captain. "Come on."

In the cold and misty light of morning, the horses were ready and waiting. Ardanwen, too, was with them.

"That beast is dangerous," the captain said to Tiuri.

"Not for his master," Tiuri replied calmly.

"Then you will ride him," said the captain. "But be sure you don't get up to any tricks on the way."

Tiuri climbed up onto Ardanwen, and a Red Rider tied his hands behind his back. The same happened to the Fool, who quietly protested.

"Get going!" ordered the captain, and the procession moved off. Tiuri looked around; all he could see was Red Riders. He counted eight of them. There was no sign of the men who had ambushed them.

They rode along the path to the west. The water of the Black River was covered by a white haze, and pale patches of mist hung between the trees.

Could I maybe escape now? Tiuri wondered. If he could just get away, they wouldn't find it easy to track him down in the wild, tangled wood on either side of the path. He looked at the Fool, who was riding behind him, with an expression of mute misery. The captain was riding beside Tiuri, and he leant over to him and said, "Abandon any thought of escape, sir knight! Your horse is fast and fiery, as I've seen. But before you could disappear from sight, your squire would be dead, felled by our swords."

Tiuri gave him a look of disgust. Those words brought home to him what kind of enemy he was facing. But he already knew that he was bound to them more because of his friend than because of the ropes around his wrists.

"There's a reason why we're going to the trouble of escorting you," the captain continued. "We tolerate no one else's presence on our roads, but we are taking you with us because of your white shield."

"My white shield?" Tiuri repeated

"Yes. Our master gave us an order: 'You must keep everyone away from our roads, but if you encounter a knight with a white shield, do not kill him, but bring him to me.'"

"Why's that?" asked Tiuri. "Who is your master?"

"I will not answer your questions," said the Red Rider. "And only my master himself can tell you who he is." He turned his eyes to the road again and did not speak another word.

A knight with a white shield... *But I am not the only knight with a white shield*, thought Tiuri. *And all the others are knights of King Unauwen...* The Red Riders of Eviellan were enemies of everyone

213

in the Kingdom of Unauwen. Did they take him, too, for a knight from the west? What lay at the end of this road, and what fate awaited him there?

The path continued to follow the river and was so wide that they could ride two abreast. None of the Red Riders spoke to the prisoners, but they didn't treat them badly. They allowed them to share their food, and even untied their hands so that they could eat. But they did not let down their guard for a moment. Tiuri and the Fool said barely a word to each other. They wouldn't have been free to say what they wanted, anyway.

In the afternoon they saw other people: men who were cutting down trees. A Man in Green with a black cap was with them, giving instructions. The Red Riders stopped their horses and had a quick word with him.

A Man in Green, thought Tiuri. *But he doesn't look like the man we saw a few days ago.*

They rode on. But suddenly there was a disturbance among the horses and riders at the front. They stopped again. Tiuri peered ahead to see what had happened.

A number of men had appeared on the path, Men in Green. And these ones looked exactly like the man he had seen sitting in a tree. Then Tiuri realized with a shock that they were sitting up in the trees here as well. There were Men in Green all around – in the trees and on the road! They all looked the same, dressed entirely in green, tight-fitting clothes, with beards and tanned faces. They were armed; most of them with long spears, some with bows and arrows. Tiuri gazed at them in surprise. There was something magical about the way these men could appear so unexpectedly. They looked back at him, more curious than threatening. No one said a word.

The captain of the Red Riders dismounted and walked up to the men on the path ahead. He spoke quietly to them, and then turned, got back onto his horse and gave the command to ride on.

As they did so, a Man in Green stepped forward and took hold of Ardanwen's bridle. To Tiuri's amazement, his horse immediately stood still, without any sign of protest. The Man in Green looked up at him. His features reminded Tiuri of the face of a wooden statue he had once seen: angular, weathered, and with no expression at all. The man looked at him for a long time, and appeared to be scrutinizing him, but his deep-set eyes revealed nothing. Tiuri had never met anyone who seemed so impenetrable, and that made him feel uneasy.

The Man in Green released Ardanwen and motioned with his spear.

"Ride on!" said the captain of the Red Riders for the second time. Tiuri thought he heard a trace of fear in his voice.

The Man in Green walked into the wood and, in a moment, he was gone. Then the others melted away into the undergrowth.

They rode onwards, but soon stopped again. There was no one else in sight. But the Men in Green could still be watching them...

They are such strange creatures, thought Tiuri. *I can understand the Fool being scared of them.* Even the Red Riders seemed to fear them. That one man in particular had been an impressive figure. Ardanwen had thought so, too...

The Red Riders were conferring in whispers. Then the captain spoke out loud, "We'll take a different route," he said, "and it must remain secret. Blindfold the prisoners!"

Blindfolded, too?! thought Tiuri.

But, even with the blindfold, he could still tell that they crossed the river soon afterwards. He thought they were riding south. That meant they should be leaving the river behind, but after a while he thought he could hear the sound of water again. *A tributary?* he wondered. *Or has the Black River looped around? Are we still following it?*

They didn't ride for long, but after they'd made him dismount and taken the blindfold from his eyes, he couldn't see any clues to work out where they were. It was dark by then and they were surrounded by black trees. There was no sign of a river, although he could still hear the rush of water.

Tiuri and Marius spent the night surrounded and watched by the Red Riders, their hands and feet tightly bound.

The next day brought nothing new. They rode on. The prisoners, blindfolded once again, saw nothing and heard very little. Tiuri was aware that they sometimes passed other people, and he suspected they were still riding south, but he was not certain. He tried not to give in to his feelings of fear and gloom as he was taken helplessly in the hands of the enemy to an unknown destination.

In the evening, their blindfolds were removed again. This time they slept in a small wooden hut and any thought of escape was pointless. *And even if I saw an opportunity*, thought Tiuri. *I couldn't use it. I can't abandon Marius, can I?*

The next morning, no preparations were made for departure. They were simply blindfolded and led out of the hut.

"Sit down here," came the voice of the captain. "And don't touch that blindfold, or you'll never see daylight again."

2   THE MASTER OF THE RED RIDERS

"I know where we are," whispered the Fool. "I hear it, I smell it, I feel it, Friend! I don't need to see it. If you could see with your eyes, you would see what I know."

"And what's that?" asked Tiuri.

"The river is in front of us," said the Fool. "The dark river – do you hear the water? There is a bridge over it, a low bridge made of wood. On the opposite bank you would see a tower, a stone tower, an old tower, a wicked tower in the woods. And there's the road to the castle, to the castle by the mountains, the house that belongs to *him*, to the Master of the Wild Wood."

His voice grew quieter and quieter and Tiuri had to lean in close to hear what he was saying. All around them were other sounds: hoofs, footsteps, the voices of the Red Riders. But suddenly, silence fell.

Then someone spoke: "You may remove their blindfolds," said a rather muffled voice, one that Tiuri had never heard before. "We might as well let them see everything," it continued in a mocking tone. "One of them is clearly looking through his blindfold and neither of them will ever be able to tell anyone else about this place."

Rough hands tugged off his blindfold and then Tiuri was blinking up at the man who had spoken.

He was standing just a few steps away – a knight, clad from head to toe in black armour, but the shield on his arm was as red as blood.

Tiuri rose to his feet. The view in front of him was just as the Fool had said: a river, a bridge and, on the opposite bank, a tall tower and a dark wood. But he paid little attention to the view. He was looking at the knight – a Black Knight with a red shield! His face was hidden behind the closed visor of his helmet. Around him stood the Red Riders, silent and submissive, servants of a feared master.

Tiuri felt a hand slide into his own; it was the Fool's. He, too, had been released from his blindfold and was standing right beside him.

"So this..." said the Black Knight, "is Sir Tiuri with the White Shield."

"Indeed it is, my lord," said Tiuri in a firm voice.

"And who is this other man?" asked the Black Knight.

Tiuri gave his friend's hand a comforting squeeze.

"Marius," he replied, "my squire."

One of the Red Riders said, "That one's been here before."

"I see," said the Black Knight. "Careless of you, foolish of him. That's all I have to say."

Tiuri knew for sure that he was facing a dangerous enemy. Who was this Black Knight? He did not recognize his voice and yet there was something familiar about it – but it was not Kraton of Indigo or Melas of Darokitam, he was certain of that, and he knew no other knights with red shields.

The Black Knight gestured towards the Fool and his next words felt like a fist in Tiuri's face: "There are plenty of trees around. Hang him!"

The Fool let out a cry and clung to his friend. Two Red Riders strode towards them.

Tiuri said loudly, "I forbid it!"

The two riders were so astounded that they stopped.

The Black Knight took a step closer and said, almost laughing, "You, young man, are really in no position to forbid anything."

"I most certainly am," said Tiuri, putting one protective arm around the Fool. "This man is my squire and I am responsible for him. That is still true, even though I am your prisoner. And, as long as I am here, I forbid anyone from harming even a hair on his head." He spoke confidently, but inside he was terrified. Would he really be able to prevent anything happening to the Fool?

The Red Riders had still not moved, but he knew it was not his words that had stopped them. They were waiting for a sign from their master.

He turned back to the Black Knight. "My lord," he said, "Marius has done nothing to you – and neither have I, for that matter – and he has acted only on my orders. If that means he has done something wrong, then the responsibility is my own."

"You who come as a friend, tread this path in peace..." said the Black Knight. "Well, the wood has not devoured you and so I may assume you are a friend – are you not?"

That voice! It was terrifying and yet somehow captivating. People would listen when this knight spoke.

"I make friends only with people I know, sir knight," said Tiuri as haughtily as he could, but at the same time he wondered if such an attitude might further endanger the Fool.

"Ah, but do you really know them?" asked the Black Knight, in a whisper. "How fortunate to feel so certain; that's only possible for one as young as you. But your friends will disappoint you one day, young man. Tell me, what was your name again?"

"Sir Tiuri," he said abruptly.

"Sir Tiuri with the White Shield," said the Black Knight. "Please forgive my discourtesy. But I am many years older than you and even if I were to open my visor, you still would not know me."

His voice, which had sounded soft and almost friendly in spite of his mockery, now changed. "What good is this squire to you, Sir Tiuri?" he said. "He trembles and shakes and does not even dare to look at me! He must surely have been a burden on your travels rather than a boon."

The Fool let go of Tiuri.

"A faithful friend..." Tiuri began.

"Ah, a guide perhaps?" said the Black Knight, interrupting him. "Then he should know, this Marius, that the paths in the Wild Wood may be travelled only in one direction. There is no return, Sir Tiuri with the White Shield. And if you do not wish to go back on your word, then you must place your life in service to his. Let your deeds support your words!"

Tiuri raised his hands, palms up. "Just tell me how," he said.

The Black Knight gave him a penetrating stare. "Ah, Sir Tiuri, the champion of oppressed innocence!" he said. "Give him a sword and let him fight. Who will stand against him? A duel, with the life of this pathetic fool as the stake!"

A murmur went up among the Red Riders and one of them asked, "His own sword?"

"Of course," said the Black Knight.

"No, don't!" the Fool cried. "Don't fight, don't fight!"

"Hush, Marius," said Tiuri. "This will be a fair duel."

"Do you think I don't understand why you want to fight, Friend?" said the Fool. "For me, for me! No one has ever fought for me, and no one will ever fight for me. Not you either, certainly not you!"

A Red Rider handed Tiuri his sword.

"Marius," said Tiuri, "be brave. Come, give me my shield."

"N... no," whispered the Fool.

More men came running. "To the tourney field!" they cried.

Tiuri paid no attention to them. "Do as I ask you, my friend," he said to the Fool. "Do you not remember what I promised you and what you promised me?"

Tears welled up in the Fool's eyes.

One of the Red Riders called out, "Here is the shield!"

The Fool walked over to him and took it from his hands.

"To the tourney field," said the Black Knight. "And as my champion I choose someone who needs to make amends to me... Jaro." He raised his voice: "Bring Jaro here!"

Tiuri, who was just taking the shield from the Fool, was surprised to hear that name again. Jaro! But it had to be a coincidence; lots of people must share the same name.

Surrounded by Red Riders, he walked with the Fool to the tourney field, which was south of the river. Behind him came the Black Knight with the Red Shield, who was riding a large grey horse. Tiuri held on firmly to his sword and offered up a silent prayer. He had to win; heaven would surely be on his side – Marius must not die!

They soon came to a large open field in the forest. "Behold the arena!" said the Black Knight.

It flashed through Tiuri's mind that this could be the place where Red Quibo had watched his ghostly tournament.

"Jaro!" called the Knight with the Red Shield.

A man dressed in green with a black cap on his head pushed his way through the crowd. He bowed and said, "At your service, my lord."

Tiuri froze. He knew this man.

3   THE DUEL

Yes, it was him, Jaro, with his menacing glare and his piercing pale-grey eyes. Tiuri had met him in the mountains when he was travelling with the letter for King Unauwen. Jaro, who was a spy and belonged to the Red Riders, had been sent to kill him. But Tiuri had saved his life and, out of gratitude, Jaro had helped him.

Now the young knight stared at his opponent, with mixed feelings of surprise, anger and disappointment. He would never have expected to meet Jaro here. He was sure the man had said farewell to his life of wickedness.

Jaro calmly answered his gaze. If he was surprised, he didn't let it show.

The Black Knight had climbed down from his horse.

"You know each other," he said slowly. "Isn't that right? Good. Jaro, I have chosen you for the duel with Sir Tiuri, so that you can finish what you failed to achieve last year."

"My lord," said Jaro humbly, "that was not my fault."

"But still you failed," said the Black Knight coldly.

Something flickered in Jaro's eyes. "My lord," he said with a slight tremble in his voice, "I thank you! If I defeat him, may I once again wear the armour and symbols of your Red Riders?"

"Do not request a fanfare before the victory," said his master.

"But I *shall* be the victor!" cried Jaro. He looked at Tiuri and said, "You weren't expecting this, eh, that you'd meet me again? Now I can finally settle our score! You tried to cast me into a ravine, and now I shall plunge you into the morass of death! And then I shall be a Red Rider again, as I was before." He came and stood close to Tiuri. "You were disguised as a pilgrim!" he hissed. "Do you remember? Bah!" He spat in front of Tiuri's feet. "I still remember every word we said to each other. Do you? Every single word! And now I'm going to pay you back and..."

"Silence!" commanded the Black Knight. "Prepare yourselves. A duel for the life of this... squire."

Jaro drew his sword and asked one of the Red Riders to lend him his shield.

Tiuri nodded at the Fool. Confused thoughts were whirling around his mind. Jaro, he had to fight against Jaro. Why had he told such wicked lies? But then he'd also said, "I still remember every word..."

"Ready?" called a Red Rider.

Now Tiuri was facing his opponent. The Black Knight raised his hand.

How can I fight? thought Tiuri, lifting his sword for the ritual salute. He suddenly felt very young and inexperienced among all of these warriors, and he really didn't know what kind of opponent he was up against. "But," he said to himself, "I have to win. I'm fighting for Marius."

The swords tapped against each other a few times, as in a practice fight, calmly and without passion. Both men wanted first to get the measure of the other. They made a few feints. Then Jaro lunged and Tiuri parried, before going on the attack, which was likewise repelled. The young knight regained his composure. If the fight continued like this, maybe it would end well.

But the crowd was disappointed. "Isn't this supposed to be a fight to the death?" one of them shouted.

Jaro's attacks grew a little fiercer. His sword clashed against Tiuri's shield, but did not injure him. So Tiuri also fought back with more fire. The swords clashed together, and then Tiuri made a lunge that Jaro could only just parry.

I must act quickly! thought the young knight, *and disarm him before he knows what's happening...* He let fly with a series of attack movements that he'd often practised with his father. One, two, three... nearly got him! One, two...

And then he stumbled.

The Fool shrieked.

But Jaro stepped back and waited until Tiuri was back on his feet. "Ready?" he said. "I'm going to make this difficult for you."

At least Jaro was behaving like a knight. But now his attacks became more dangerous, and all of Tiuri's thoughts were swept away, except for one: *I must not lose!*

His beautiful white shield soon received its first dents.

Click, clack, clang!

The Red Riders whistled and jeered.

"Take that!" cried Jaro, lashing out, but his aim was slightly off and Tiuri escaped the blow.

The crowd roared.

"And that!" yelled Jaro, and now it seemed as if he really would defeat Tiuri... No, he lost his balance, and the young knight had some time to recover.

Tiuri realized that he had been reduced to defending and he'd have to go on the attack in order to win. But a moment later Jaro made the first strike. Tiuri barely felt it – just a scratch – but it ignited his desire to win. He was fighting for Marius!

All around him, the Red Riders were cheering for Jaro, but some of them were whistling their disapproval and one shouted out, "You could have had him long ago, Jaro!"

No, no, thought Tiuri. *You won't have me.*

For a while, they both fought quite calmly, to recover their strength.

Then it was Tiuri who was driving Jaro back, and in just a few quick movements he knocked the sword from Jaro's hand.

Silence fell.

Tiuri stood there, panting. Jaro gave a quick smile, before picking up his sword and returning to the duel.

Tiuri had not been expecting that. *Keep a cool head,* he thought to himself. *You have to force it to a quick end now. He's a good fighter. If this goes on for a long time, he'll have the advantage...*

He allowed himself to be pushed back a little way, but all the while he was preparing for his next attack. It was so sharp and unexpected that it took Jaro by surprise.

Now! thought Tiuri. A few lightning-fast strikes... blood was flowing over Jaro's hand... They were close together now... their swords were right up against each other... then a movement from Tiuri... and for the second time Jaro dropped his sword.

This time, Tiuri quickly stood on it.

Jaro lowered his shield and looked at him. There was no sign of fear on his face.

The Red Riders were silent.

"Kill him," came a voice.

Jaro knelt. Tiuri turned to the Black Knight. It was he who had spoken.

"I have won, my lord," he said breathlessly.

"Indeed you have. Now finish it," he said.

But Tiuri could not even contemplate killing Jaro; he knew he simply wouldn't be capable of it. "It is finished," he said. "I have won."

"I would have killed you!" cried Jaro, but his expression made it clear that he feared no such fate from Tiuri.

"I will not do it," Tiuri said curtly. "Do you acknowledge me as victor?"

"Yes..." replied Jaro, as he got to his feet. He glanced at his master before saying, "No, it wasn't fair. I... I had the sun in my eyes. I... Oh well... Yes, you have won."

"You were not at your best today, Jaro," said the Black Knight coldly.

"I want to fight again!" cried Jaro. "I have sworn that I will be the one to defeat him."

The Red Riders laughed scornfully.

"It's too late now," said the Black Knight. "You missed your chance and I doubt you will ever have another one. Now hand back that red shield. And begone!"

Jaro bowed, turned around and walked away, dragging his feet.

The Fool came over to Tiuri and whispered, "You are a good knight, Friend!"

The Black Knight turned to the Red Riders and spoke brusquely to them in a language Tiuri did not understand. It was the language of Eviellan, rather than the more familiar tongue of the Kingdom of Unauwen, which was almost the same as that spoken in Dagonaut's land.

Tiuri's sword and shield were taken from him again. Then the knight beckoned to him and they walked back to the river. The Fool followed, and two Red Riders went ahead with the master's horse. The others spread out in all directions.

"You could become a good swordsman, Sir Tiuri," said the Black Knight. "Why did you not kill Jaro?"

"Why should I kill him?" he replied. "I won... isn't that enough?"

"A man must eliminate his enemies," said the Black Knight. "And I take it that Jaro is your enemy."

Yes, that was true. Wasn't it? In a flash, Tiuri relived the whole fight. It dawned on him that, at a few points, Jaro had had him completely in his power...

Had Jaro let Tiuri win on purpose? He could see the Black Knight was waiting for an answer. Of course he mustn't let him suspect anything!

"Yes, my lord," he said. "He has tried to kill me before."

"And you him," said the knight.

"I had to defend myself," said Tiuri quickly. He knew for certain: this was the knight who had lured Edwinem of Forèstèrra into a trap. The Black Knight with the Red Shield, whose knights had chased after Tiuri when he was on his mission to deliver the letter.

"Friend, you are bleeding!" came the horrified voice of the Fool beside him.

"Oh, it's nothing," said Tiuri. But still he realized that he'd like to sit down for a moment – not because of the scratch, but to calm his emotions. His first real duel, the encounters with the Black Knight and with Jaro...

His face revealed nothing, though, and he calmly walked on. Although he stared straight ahead, he could feel the presence of the Black Knight.

"Now we shall go to my castle," the Black Knight said when they had reached the river. He pointed at the road heading north on the other side of the bridge.

Tiuri looked around. To the west, a section of the forest had been cleared; wooden huts had been built there, with slopes rising behind them that grew higher and steeper before giving way to the summits of the Great Mountains. To the north and south he could see the forest, with the road running through it.

"The Wild Wood Way," said the Black Knight. "It leads from my castle to what people refer to as civilization."

"Where does it come out?" Tiuri asked in spite of himself. He didn't actually want to talk to this knight at all.

"At the edge of the forest, by the mountains and the Grey River," came the reply. "For those who know it is there! If you are travelling from Eviellan, or from the Kingdom of Dagonaut, or from the Great Mountains, and you wish to find the Wild Wood Way, you must first know one of the three secret access routes – I call them the Three Ways to One Goal. That goal can be reached along the Wild Wood Way and across the Low Bridge..." He pointed again to the north. "My fortress by mountains and by rivers wide!"

An image of Isadoro flashed through Tiuri's mind. Those were the words of her song...

By the bridge stood a number of guards, dressed in green like Jaro, with black caps on their heads. Another man came towards them, leading a reluctant black horse by the reins.

"And here is Ardanwen," said the Black Knight with the Red Shield. "Once he would allow only one rider on his back."

That rider had been Edwinem, known as the Invincible, Edwinem of Forèstèrra, who had been murdered by...

Tiuri looked at the knight, who seemed captivated by the sight of Ardanwen. The horse had flattened back his ears – did he recognize the knight?

Then the knight suddenly turned his head towards Tiuri, who felt as if his thoughts must be written all over his face. He tried to keep his expression as blank as possible and not to lower his eyes. He wished he knew what the knight looked like. Anything would have been better than looking at that closed visor.

The knight spoke, almost to himself it seemed: "A black horse and a white shield..." A little more loudly, he continued, "Climb onto this horse, Sir Tiuri, so I may see if it is truly yours. Then you shall enter my territory as befits a knight." He called one of his men over and gave him an order, "Return his shield to him, but not his sword."

Tiuri did not know what to make of this. Why did he have to cross the bridge on Ardanwen, with his shield, as if he were a guest – but without his sword, like a prisoner? Should he refuse? But Ardanwen came to him and bowed his neck. He loved Night Wind and was proud of him. No one else would ride him, certainly not this dishonourable knight. So Tiuri climbed onto Ardanwen and rode to the bridge without saying a word. Then he looked around and called, "Marius!"

The Fool came running and took Ardanwen by the bridle. They walked over the bridge together.

The Black Knight followed after them; he too was on horseback now. "Ride on beside me, Sir Tiuri," he said, "to my castle, the Tarnburg."

But Tiuri said: "How can I ride beside you, knight whose name I do not know? Can you and I ride beside each other, as if our goal is the same?"

"I am not riding beside you, Sir Tiuri," came the reply, "but beside a memory, a ghost of long ago. Even your squire – so unlike any other squire – is a good match."

227

"You speak in riddles," said Tiuri curtly. "Why do you not treat me as what I am? Your prisoner!"

"Am I not doing that?" sneered the knight. "I shall speak in riddles if it pleases me, and have you ride beside me on Ardanwen if I so choose. You know what you are, Sir Tiuri: my prisoner! But I, the man to whose whim you must submit, will remain a stranger. I am a secret of the Wild Wood, a place about which you became too curious. Now come with me."

4 THE TARNBURG

Tiuri rode in silence beside the Black Knight with the Red Shield. The Fool trotted alongside; he kept patting Ardanwen, as if it gave him courage. All around was dark forest and the track seemed to be leading towards the mountains, as the ground was becoming more hilly. Now and then they encountered people, Red Riders and men wearing green and black, who greeted the Black Knight with respect.

The Black Knight did not say another word and Tiuri was glad of that. *If only Bendu knew!* he thought. But Bendu was far away; he was fighting against Deltaland in the south. Tiuri was getting further and further away from his friends; perhaps he was now beyond their reach. But Piak... where might Piak be? Had he escaped? Was he on his way to King Dagonaut to tell him everything and to fetch help? Just as long as he hadn't been captured, too...

"I mustn't lose heart," Tiuri said to himself. Arwaut, Ilmar and other brave men had been treacherously slain, but he was still alive. He wondered what plans the Black Knight had for him; he certainly hadn't spared him out of kindness.

They rode onwards for a long time. The forest thinned out and Tiuri saw that lots of trees had been felled and piled up in stacks.

In the afternoon, they came to a clearing. And there was the castle, a large building of reddish stone. The mountains were very close now; their lower slopes were covered with pine trees, but above that they were bare and snow lay on the peaks. As they approached the castle, Tiuri saw it was in a very dilapidated state. A wooden house had been built up against it.

"The Tarnburg and the House with the Red Shield," said the Black Knight – the first words he had spoken since they had set out. "My home in the Wild Wood."

The Fool stopped for a moment, panting and exhausted, because he had not wanted to ride with Tiuri on Ardanwen. He gazed open-mouthed at the castle. It certainly did look impressive, in spite of its age – or perhaps because of it. The house was new; a large red shield hung on a pole in front of the gate.

The Black Knight held out his arm and said, "That mountain, to the north-west, is the Tarntop."

Tiuri had already noticed the mighty peak. *Now we are at the foot of the Great Mountains*, he thought, *the border of the Wild Wood.*

To the north, though, were trees, just as there were to the south and the east. He could hear the sound of water; it must be the rivers that were mentioned in the song.

They rode up to the castle. There were guards all around.

"Welcome to my home, Sir Tiuri," said the Black Knight. "Dismount and enter, never to leave again."

Tiuri did not respond to his mockery. But little room remained for hope. The Tarnburg looked as if there must be many dungeons below, and the entire surroundings seemed designed to thwart any plans of escape. There were impassable mountains, wild forest, and many, many armed men encircling the castle and walking across the clearing.

Ardanwen snorted restlessly as a number of servants attempted to lead him away.

"Take good care of him," ordered the Black Knight.

"May you fare well, Night Wind," whispered Tiuri. "Walk beside me, Marius," he said to the Fool, as the guards escorted them into the House with the Red Shield.

The Black Knight did not go with them.

Tiuri and the Fool found themselves in a large hall, where Red Riders sat at long tables. Some were eating; others were talking, or checking their weapons. The two prisoners were told to sit on a bench in a corner and then left to their own devices. The Red Riders ignored them – a few of them glanced over with spiteful grins, but that was all. Tiuri gently tried to raise the frightened Fool's spirits. For what must have been an hour or more, they just sat there. They were both hungry, but no one thought to bring them any food.

Men came walking in and out; not only Red Riders, but also men in green clothes and black caps. Some of them brought in weapons and handed them to the Red Riders – they must have been cleaning them. One of those men was Jaro.

It looks as if he has a lower rank now, thought Tiuri. *He used to be one of the Red Riders, and they're clearly in charge here.*

One Red Rider started shouting furiously because he found a mark on his sword. Another gave Jaro a scolding. "Why have you brought all those spears in here, you idiot? Put them where they belong!"

Jaro carried the spears through the hall. Then, close to where the two prisoners were sitting, he dropped them and they clattered onto the floor. He picked them up, without looking at Tiuri, and walked away.

Then the Fool leant over to Tiuri with an anxious look on his face and whispered, "He put something in my boot!"

"What? Who?" asked Tiuri.

"That man... He's gone now. The man you fought, Friend!"

"Quiet!" whispered Tiuri. "Don't let the Red Riders hear you." He looked at the Fool's feet; his boots were indeed big enough to hide something in. "Can you feel what it is?" he asked.

"No... He dropped something into my boot. It's hard and cold and sharp."

"Just keep looking straight ahead. Act as if nothing's going on," Tiuri said quietly.

"I can feel it by my foot," said the Fool.

"Don't say anything. Don't give anything away, Marius. It could be something good; perhaps that man wants to help us," whispered Tiuri, looking at the Red Riders, but they were still paying no attention to them.

Something hard and cold and sharp... a knife maybe? Had Jaro not in fact forgotten their encounter in the mountains and his conversation with the hermit? Tiuri's heart was once again filled with hope.

More men came inside. Two of them came over to the prisoners and ordered them to go with them.

Please don't let Marius give anything away! thought Tiuri. No, the Fool was quietly following them, and limping only slightly.

The servants of the Black Knight led them through a door into a dark room with walls of stone. *Now we're inside the castle itself,* Tiuri realized. Then they passed through other rooms and along corridors and up a spiral staircase, which opened into a long hallway. At the other end was a guard; the men opened a heavy door nearby.

"In here," one of them said.

When Tiuri and the Fool were inside, the door slammed shut and the bolts creaked.

"What now?" whispered the Fool.

"We're locked up, Marius," said Tiuri. "Prisoners in the Tarnburg."

He looked around the room. There were two windows opposite, with bars on them.

"May I take off my boots?" asked the Fool.

"Yes, of course," said Tiuri. "Yes, quickly, take them off!"

The Fool did so, and a moment later he held up something for his friend to see. "Look," he whispered. "Here it is."

It was a file.

A file! Jaro really does want to help us, Tiuri thought happily. He took the file from Marius and walked over to one of the windows. He inspected the bars; they were made of hard, strong iron, but were no longer an impossible barrier. Looking outside, he saw that they were quite high above the ground, but it would still be possible, if...

Then his gaze fell on two soldiers in green and black who were slowly walking up and down beneath the windows.

"What's this for, Friend?" asked the Fool, who had come to stand beside him.

"You can use it to file through the bars," said Tiuri. "But the castle's guarded. Look down there."

"File through the bars," whispered the Fool. "And break them! Let me file the bars, Friend!"

"Not now," said Tiuri. "The guards can see us." Yes, one of them was looking up. "We'll have to wait until it's dark."

They were somewhere at the back of the castle. To the left, in the distance, they could see the Tarntop; to the right, their view was blocked by a protruding bastion. In front of them was a grassy area that sloped downwards, with rocks and boulders lying here and there. At the bottom of the slope, to their left, was a bridge and they could hear water. So there must be a river down there. *The Green River maybe?* thought Tiuri. For a long way into the distance, all he could see was forest.

He turned away from the window and said, "First we need to hide this file."

The room was dark and neglected, yet spoke of past glory. The floor tiles, although now cracked, had been laid in a beautiful design. On the walls, the remains of paintings could still be seen. There were just a few pieces of furniture: a table with a candlestick on it, two chairs and a chest. On one side was a doorway, which led into a small windowless room with two narrow beds.

"I think this is a very miserable place, Friend," said the Fool.

So did Tiuri, although their prison was not much like a dungeon. He hid the file under a loose tile by the fireplace and surveyed the room. There was only one escape route: through one of the windows. And they'd be best off taking the window on the right, as it wasn't immediately visible to anyone who came in.

The Fool had sat down; he looked at his boots again and then he gasped. "There's something else in there!"

Tiuri was by his side in an instant. It was a piece of bark with some lines scratched on it. The message wasn't easy to decipher. It was made up of stiff, clumsy letters, which formed three words:

THE THIRD NIGHT

"The third night..." Tiuri muttered.

"What does that mean?" asked the Fool, "the third night?"

"Perhaps it means we can escape on that night," said Tiuri quietly. "That would be the night of the day after tomorrow. As it is now, we'd never make it, not with all those guards. We'll have to make sure we've filed through the bars by then."

The Fool looked as if he wanted to start filing right away, but Tiuri said, "No, Marius, wait until it's dark. Be patient for just a little longer."

The Fool nodded. "Why is he helping us?" he asked. "Do you know him? Yes, you know each other, but you fought. How can that be?"

"It's a long story," said Tiuri, thinking back to his first encounter with Jaro. "I don't understand Jaro entirely. But he is thinking of us and he wants to help us; that's for sure."

"Not all enemies are enemies," whispered the Fool. "I never knew that, Friend."

"Have you met the Black Knight and his Red Riders before?" asked Tiuri.

"Not the Knight, never," replied the Fool. "But the Red Riders, yes. They were riding through the forest. There are many of them,

233

so many! But they do not let themselves be seen very often, like the Men in Green."

"Do they live here, too, the Men in Green?" asked Tiuri. "Is that the Green River we can hear?"

The Fool furrowed his brow. "I don't know," he said. "I haven't been here before, at the castle, in this house. I wasn't allowed to come here. I was over there," he said, pointing to the north-east, "and I also lived by the Low Bridge. You know, by the tower. There are houses there, too – didn't you see them?"

"With your brothers," said Tiuri.

"Yes, but I didn't see them today. Perhaps they ran away, too. But no, I don't think so. They wanted to go with the Red Riders, to come here. But they're scared of the Men in Green, just like me."

"Why's that?" asked Tiuri.

The Fool shrugged. "I have never spoken to them," he whispered. "They don't want to talk to me. They speak only to the Red Riders. And their master is the lord of a castle by the mountains."

"The Black Knight with the Red Shield," muttered Tiuri. "Who is he? The knight that Bendu was looking for... cruel, deceitful, dangerous... What is he doing here, so far from Eviellan?"

"I wish we were somewhere else, Friend," said the Fool. "It's a long time until the third night."

Tiuri's gaze fell on the chest in one corner of the room, a worm-eaten box with iron bindings. He opened it up to see if there was anything inside.

Yes... a black and white checked board and a dusty box of chess pieces. He stood there for a moment, holding it in his hands. He thought of Castle Ristridin, where he had played chess with Tirillo and Sir Idian. Prince Iridian... was he back in his father's kingdom by now?

"What do you have there, Friend?" asked the Fool.

Tiuri placed the board on the table and laid out the pieces – they were beautiful, made of ivory and ebony. "This is a chessboard," he said. "Chess is a game for two people; one person plays with white, the other with black. Whichever player checkmates the other is the winner."

"Checkmate? What does that mean?" asked the Fool.

"It means dead," replied Tiuri. "You can defeat each other's pieces, and they all move in their own way. Look, this is the king. He stands here, with the queen beside him. And these small pieces are called pawns; each player has eight of them." He went on talking, even though he soon realized the Fool didn't understand much of what he was saying. But he was looking at the board with great interest.

"There are horses," he said, "and towers. Play with them, Friend, and I shall watch."

"Then I shall have to play against myself," said Tiuri, making the opening move with white. Perhaps this game would help to make the time pass more quickly. What time was it now? It was already getting dark.

He left the chessboard and went to look outside. The guards were still walking up and down, and a Red Rider galloped past. Tiuri shivered; it was chilly in the room and there was no fuel to make a fire.

Then the bolts creaked and two servants came in. Silently, they placed some food on the table, lit the candles, and left.

"This is welcome, eh, Marius?" said Tiuri as cheerfully as he could. "Look: bread, meat and red wine."

The food did them some good. One of the servants came to take the plates away. When he left the room, he did not close the door. But a moment later, another man appeared in the doorway.

The Black Knight, Lord of the Tarnburg.

5 A GAME OF CHESS

He was still wearing his black armour, with the visor of his helmet closed – he was even still wearing his gloves. His red shield was all he had left behind.

"I have just come to see," he said, "if your accommodation is satisfactory and that you are lacking nothing... except, of course, your freedom."

The Fool leapt up and retreated to the adjoining room.

The Black Knight closed the door, stepped into the room and said, "Yes, you go to your bed, squire, and keep out of my sight. Goodnight!"

The Fool sat down on one of the beds. Tiuri could see him anxiously huddled there. Then he turned back to the Black Knight and silently waited for him to leave.

The Knight remained there, however; he crossed his arms and looked at the chessboard. "Ah, I see you've started a game," he said. "With your friend? No, I'm sure he's no chess player."

Tiuri said nothing.

"It is a fine thing to have oneself as an opponent," the knight continued calmly. "Inside every person there are many different beings... did you know that?" Slowly, he moved a black pawn forward. Then he pulled up a chair and sat down, rather stiffly, because of his armour. "I want to play chess with you," he said, "with a black horse as the stake."

"Which horse would that be?" said Tiuri, breaking his silence.

"There is only one black horse we could play for," replied the knight. "Ardanwen, or Night Wind. He is your horse, is he not?"

"Ardanwen chose me as his master," said Tiuri, "but that does not mean I can play for him, as if he were some object that could be given away!"

"He will also accept me as his master if you command him to do so," said the Black Knight. "Is that not so?"

"Perhaps," said Tiuri. "But I refuse to play with him as a stake."

Anxiously, he waited for the knight's reply.

"For another stake, then?" the knight said calmly. "I once heard a story of two men who played a chess game with a life as the stake. Perhaps one of them was Death himself. I no longer remember."

He paused.

Tiuri heard the Fool's bed creak. Someone outside shouted an order.

"The game of chess is the only fair fight in the world," the knight said then. "Both parties have the same number of pieces; both have an equal chance. Only white has the privilege of making the first move... and I have left that privilege to you." He seemed to be looking at Tiuri. "So?" he continued. "How about playing without a stake? For the sake of the game alone?"

Tiuri did not like the idea of playing chess with this stranger, whom he could see only as an enemy. Deep in his heart he was afraid of this knight, even though he did not wish to admit that even to himself. He glanced at the window, saw the black lines of the bars, and thought of the file. Then he came up with an idea.

He said to the knight, "Yes, let's play with a stake, after all, my lord!"

"And what stake would that be?"

"Your face," replied Tiuri. "I would like to see your face."

The Black Knight put one hand up to his helmet and paused for a moment. "Fine," he said slowly. "If you win I will raise my visor so you can look at my face." There almost seemed to be a hint of amusement in his voice.

Tiuri was filled with uncertainty. He was surprised that the knight had immediately agreed to his challenge. He must be a good chess player. *But so am I*, thought Tiuri. *I have to play to win! He's right. This fight gives us both an equal chance, and it's impossible to cheat.*

After pondering for a moment, he made his move.

The Black Knight immediately moved his own piece and said, "But we haven't discussed what will happen if I am the winner. What is your stake? You cannot change your mind now, as our game has already begun."

What a cunning opponent he was!

"I don't know, my lord," replied Tiuri. "I have nothing I can call my own and neither do I have anything to hide."

To Tiuri's relief, the knight did not bring up the subject of Ardanwen again. "If I win," he said, "I shall oblige you to play another game with me... when it pleases me."

And what will be at stake then? Tiuri wondered, as he looked down at the chessboard. He wanted to win, but all kinds of thoughts were disrupting the calm concentration he needed to consider his strategy. Who was this knight? What did he want? Why had he settled in this forest? Eviellan, he came from Eviellan...

He heard the Fool moving and silently wished for him to stay where he was. He looked again at his opponent, who was like an iron statue, a creature of darkness with no face at all.

I have to see him, thought Tiuri. He felt that only then would he know what attitude to take, what plans to make... I don't want to play another game later, for whatever stake he might choose.

"Then play!" said the Black Knight.

Someone else had once said that to him. Tirillo! The jester's words echoed in Tiuri's mind: "Then play," and "Please be so kind as to concentrate on our game." Back then he had tried for Tirillo's sake; now he had to try again, for a very different reason.

Tiuri closed his eyes for a moment and focused on the board. He made his move and then it was only the game that existed for him: moves, countermoves...

After a while, the Black Knight spoke, "You play well."

"I could say the same of you," replied Tiuri truthfully, as he captured a black pawn.

238

The knight took one of Tiuri's bishops and said, "See, you have to be prepared to sacrifice a pawn to win a greater battle. It's the same in life. Sometimes a man has to push others aside in order to reach a great goal."

Tiuri suddenly thought of Arwaut and Ilmar. Fury rose within him. "Life is not a game," he said coldly, "and people are not pawns."

"But you would not hesitate to defeat your enemies, would you?" said the Black Knight. "Although... you are still far too kind-hearted. What about Jaro? In your place, I would have known what I had to do."

"I am sure you did not hesitate to kill Sir Arwaut and Ilmar and all those others!" cried Tiuri. "But why were they your enemies? What had they done to you?"

"Arwaut? Ilmar?" repeated the Black Knight. "Who are those men? I do not know them."

"That is a lie," whispered Tiuri. Then, more loudly, he added, "And what about Sir Ristridin?"

"Ristridin of the South," said the knight. "I swear on my word of honour that I never hurt a hair on his head!"

"So where is he?" asked Tiuri.

The Black Knight laughed softly. "Do you not know?" he asked. "Well, I shall not tell you."

"Why did you take me prisoner?" asked Tiuri. "What are you doing here in the forest?"

"This is my home, my castle, my land," replied the knight.

"This is not your land!" said Tiuri. "The Wild Wood belongs to our kingdom, to King Dagonaut."

"This wood belonged to no one before I came!" said the Black Knight, sitting up straight. "What did you people know about it? Nothing! You knew it only from some old stories. You have not entered it for years – you even allowed the Second Great Road to the west to grow over! You and your compatriots have lost any right to call this land your own."

239

"King Dagonaut sent out Sir Ristridin to learn more about it," Tiuri began.

"Too late," said the Black Knight.

"That is not true!" said Tiuri angrily. "You have no right to be here or to attack those who come here."

"Ah, you speak like a knight of King Dagonaut," his opponent countered.

"I am indeed a knight of King Dagonaut."

"I am pleased to hear it," said the Black Knight. "I thought at first that I should see you as a knight of Unauwen, with your white shield and your hatred of Eviellan." He held up one hand. "Let me finish," he continued. "I assure you I am no enemy of you and your king. As a citizen of Eviellan I want only friendship with your land! I have chosen to live in the Wild Wood because no one else wanted to dwell here, but I mean no harm and wish to hinder none."

"So why did they disappear, the men that King Dagonaut sent here?" asked Tiuri quietly.

The knight did not answer immediately. Then he said, "Who says they have disappeared? They never reached the Tarnburg, but there are many paths in this wood. I know only that Sir Ristridin left the wood of his own free will. I think he gave up trying to unravel its secrets. One of those secrets is my presence here – and it must remain a secret, for a little longer, just a little longer..."

Tiuri thought, *He is lying! He doesn't know Ristridin left a message on that tree by the river.* And he asked, "So where did Sir Ristridin go?"

"Do you not know?" said the knight again. "Perhaps he is now sleeping soundly in the castle of a friend."

"I do not believe you," said Tiuri.

The Black Knight leant forward. "You speak rashly, Tiuri!" he said. "What right do you, a boy who knows nothing of me, have to judge me? Confine yourself instead to our game of chess, though it would be better for you if you did not win."

His tone was flat, yet menacing. "It's your move," he said. "Do not hesitate to sacrifice one of your pieces if you wish to checkmate me. Or do you not dare?"

When Tiuri did not respond, he gestured towards the room where the Fool had taken refuge.

"A few days ago, it was serious and not a game, and then, too, you did not dare," he said. "I heard from my men that you could perhaps have escaped if you had not gone to help your squire! Now you are both prisoners – do you think that is something to be pleased about?" Again he laughed and said, "Now I have given you something to consider tonight. And you may also ponder your next move. We shall finish our game tomorrow, Tiuri!"

He rose to his feet and stood, tall and dark, facing the young knight. Then he turned on his heels and left the room.

A moment later, the Fool was standing beside Tiuri. "What have you done, Friend?" he said in horror. "You must not speak to him. You cannot listen to him. He is wicked. He is evil!"

"I am only playing a game of chess with him, Marius," replied Tiuri. "And if I win, I shall know who he is."

"Do you not already know who he is?" said the Fool. "He is the Master of the Red Riders. He is playing with you and he wants you to lose!"

Nonsense! Tiuri wanted to say, but he did not. Maybe without even realizing, the Fool had found words that hit home and shocked him.

He is playing with you...

Had he unintentionally done exactly what the Black Knight wanted of him? Tiuri had certainly spoken to him, even though he had planned to remain silent and aloof, and he had listened to him, although he knew his words were lies. And even if he were to win the game... what did it matter if he saw his enemy's face? *He is playing with you, and he does not care if you win or lose...*

241

"Perhaps I am doing the wrong thing, Marius," said Tiuri with a sigh. "But now that I have started, I must keep going – and I must try to win."

He walked over to the window on the right, pressed his burning face against the bars and let the evening breeze cool it down. He suddenly felt hopelessly imprisoned; the world outside the Wild Wood seemed so far away that it was beyond reach.

At that very same moment, on the other side of the Wild Wood, Piak was staring at the Forgotten City in the moonlight and trying to remember the goal of his journey.

The Fool brought Tiuri back to reality. "Here!" he whispered, holding out the file.

Ah yes, of course! Their situation was far from hopeless. *And what's the point of worrying about decisions that have already been made?* thought the young knight. *Should I have abandoned Marius to save myself? I could never have done that!*

He smiled at his friend and quietly said, "First blow out the candles. If the guards are still there, they'll be able to see us by the light."

Yes, they were still there. When the room was dark, he could see them quite clearly. "We have to file through at least two bars," he whispered. "Let's see how it goes." He took the file and started to move it at the bottom of one of the bars – slowly, so as to make as little noise as possible.

"They can't hear us," whispered the Fool. "The water outside is making more noise. Can you hear it?"

After a while, he asked, "Shall I do it?"

"Yes," said Tiuri. "But don't file the bar all the way through. Just do it like this, around the outside."

"Why?" asked the Fool.

"When the Black Knight returns tomorrow, he mustn't see that we've been filing through the bars. I think we'll have to wait until the third night to escape."

"Look how quickly I'm doing it," said the Fool. "I'll soon be able to snap this bar with my hands. I'm strong."

"Shhh!" whispered Tiuri. "The guards!"

More men were coming, down below; one of them was carrying a lantern. Someone shouted an order. He soon saw what was happening: the changing of the guard.

"Well, it doesn't look as if the fortress and our prison will ever be without guards," said Tiuri. "Look, these bars are thinner at the bottom now, Marius. We'll have to work on the top of the bars next! But we can do that tomorrow evening. It's time to go to sleep."

"You sleep, Friend," said the Fool. "I already lay on the bed, and you are tired. You should sleep. I will go on filing and I will wake you if I see anything."

Tiuri looked at the bars, then at the chessboard, and shook his head. But the Fool was so insistent that he finally agreed, even though he was sure he wouldn't be able to sleep a wink. However, it was fine. Tiuri soon dropped off and slept without dreaming.

6 THE ROAD OF AMBUSCADE

"Look at the bars," whispered the Fool the next morning. "If you want, these two will soon be gone."

Tiuri blew away some iron dust and said, "Excellent! No one will notice they've been filed through, unless they go and stand with their nose right up against the bars."

"But the guards are still there," said the Fool.

"We'll still escape anyway," said Tiuri. He was as cheerful as any prisoner could be.

He walked over to the chessboard and considered his next move. The creak of the bolts made him look up at the door, and there was the Black Knight again. This time he even had his red shield with him.

"I should just like to wish my guests good morning before I begin my daily rounds," he said in a mockingly polite tone. "Have you had a good night's rest? Your breakfast will be brought soon." He glanced at the chessboard and then walked towards the window.

The Fool stepped out of his way, but Tiuri dashed across to stand beside the knight, just in front of the bars they'd been filing.

"What fine weather," said the Black Knight, as he looked outside. "I am sorry the circumstances prevent you from enjoying it. The water of the rivers is wild and high, as the snow in the mountains is melting. Everything in the wood is budding and growing, and my men will soon have their work cut out for them as they try to keep the roads open – the Wild Wood Way, the Road of Ambuscade..."

"The Road of Ambuscade?" repeated Tiuri. He had to make sure the knight didn't look at the bars.

"It's over there, right in front of you, although you cannot see it from here. You can see the High Bridge that leads to it, though. The Road of Ambuscade runs east to west on the other side of the Black River."

"So that's the *Black* River?" said Tiuri, rather surprised.

"The castle is situated between two arms of the river, which define the Tarnburg's territory," replied the knight. And he said, "You followed the Black River for some way. What took you there?"

Tiuri replied, "I wanted to know if it was true that the Second Great Road to the west had entirely disappeared."

"And you found that it hadn't," said the Black Knight. "From the Owl House, the road has been cut open again and it runs to the Great Mountains, as it once did. But it has a different name now, one you have already heard: the Road of Ambuscade."

Tiuri had taken hold of the bars and now he was gripping them so tightly that his knuckles had turned white. He was shaking inside. Because suddenly he thought he understood why the road had that name... and so he also knew what the Black Knight was doing in the wood! Ambuscade... That meant an ambush... A surprise attack...

"Would you like to play some more chess, my lord?" he asked, hoping that his voice sounded natural.

"Have you already made your move?" came the reply.

"I shall do so now," said Tiuri. He walked over to the chessboard and moved one of his knights.

"Now it is my turn," said the knight, "but I shall wait for this evening. Until then."

When he had gone, Tiuri went back to stand at the window. The two guards had just been relieved. A group of Red Riders was rushing towards the bridge.

The Road of Ambuscade...

Everyone knew there were two roads to the land of King Unauwen. But few could suspect that there was now another road – that the old road through the Wild Wood had been opened up: a route leading through a pass in the Great Mountains, and giving access to the kingdom in the west. The Knight with the Red Shield and his army could use that road to invade the Kingdom of Unauwen and take the country by surprise. No one would expect any attack from Eviellan to come from that direction.

There was friendship between King Dagonaut and King Unauwen, so how could anyone have known that a knight of Eviellan had established a stronghold in the Wild Wood? He was most certainly planning a surprise attack from the Tarnburg!

"Perhaps," said Tiuri to himself, "he truly means King Dagonaut no harm. I think he wants first and foremost to conquer the Kingdom of Unauwen. And there's a very good chance that he'll succeed if he takes that route."

"You have such a strange look on your face, Friend," said the Fool. "Has something shocked you? What is it?"

"Do you see the mountains, Marius?" said Tiuri slowly. "Do you know what's on the other side?"

"It's where the sun goes down," said the Fool.

"There's a magnificent land over there, Marius, the land of the great King Unauwen, who lives in the most beautiful city in the world."

"Have you been there?" whispered the Fool.

"Yes, I've been there," said Tiuri. "And the Black Knight with the Red Shield wants to conquer that kingdom and destroy it. That is his secret!"

The hours crept by. Tiuri tried to fathom the problems of the chess game, but he kept thinking about the Road of Ambuscade.

In the evening the Black Knight's servants brought not only the meal, but also his bag of belongings. He took a look inside; only his money had been taken. And at the bottom of the bag was a glove.

Tiuri looked at it for a while. It was the glove given to him by Lavinia, the young lady of Mistrinaut. He had said he would wear it when he was knighted and was allowed to take part in tournaments. Now he was a knight, but at Castle Islan he had forgotten Lavinia. Yes, now he was a knight, but everything he thought he was doing right had gone completely wrong. The Fool was further from home than ever and the two of them were prisoners. Instead of fighting in a tournament, he was playing chess with a man who was an enemy of everything he held dear. He was not worthy of owning Lavinia's glove.

He closed his eyes and saw her before him as she had first appeared to him. He had been a prisoner then, as he was now. But beside her loomed the image of Isadoro and he heard her say once again, "Travel to the east, but avoid the west."

With a sigh, he put the glove back into his bag. Why was it that lately he seemed to have lost any feeling of certainty? Old Waldo had been right, "Before you know it, you'll be in all sorts of trouble that you never asked for." He and Piak had been so carefree, so eager to set off on their journey. Now he was locked up, and Piak... Oh, where was Piak?

After Tiuri and the Fool had eaten, the Black Knight came again. Tiuri did not realize it was him at first, because this time he was not wearing armour, but a black robe with wide sleeves over a red undershirt. His face was concealed behind a black mask and he had a cap that almost entirely covered his hair. Tiuri could still see that it was blond, though. The knight seemed to be unarmed and perhaps he didn't look at all frightening without the mask. Perhaps... But who knew what kind of face was hidden behind that black velvet?

Just like the previous evening, the Fool hid in the bedroom; just like the previous evening, the knight sat down in a chair beside the chessboard. As he regarded Tiuri, the expression in his eyes was impossible to read; they looked dark, and that was all.

"It is good to sit here with you," he said. "You are my guest, and I am your host. And we shall settle our dispute – in a fair fight." His voice sounded pleasant and friendly.

But Tiuri could still feel the bars on the window, even though he did not look at them. "It's your move," he said simply.

The knight did not make his move. Instead he said, "How old are you?"

"Seventeen," answered Tiuri.

"Then you must not be annoyed if I address you by your first name," said the knight. "I am twice your age, and what I have lived through sometimes makes it feel as if my youth was a whole lifetime ago. Seventeen years old and already a knight. You're at an age when you should be excelling at games and tournaments or swooning over some young lady, rather than sitting behind bars playing chess with... me."

Tiuri just stared at him.

"Was even the Daughter of Islan unable to prevent you from entering the forest?" the knight continued.

Isadoro! Do you know her? were the words on the tip of Tiuri's tongue, but he pressed his lips together and remained silent.

"Ah, it was better that you left Islan," the knight added, speaking more to himself than to Tiuri.

Tiuri could no longer hold back. "Do you know Sir Fitil?" he asked.

"Had you not already guessed as much?" said the Black Knight, leaning over the chessboard, as if putting an end to the conversation.

"Then I was right. Sir Fitil is a traitor!" Tiuri muttered to himself.

The knight looked up and said sharply, "Do not speak that word! Sir Fitil is no traitor and has betrayed no one."

"No," Tiuri responded angrily, "he certainly said nothing about your presence here! According to him and... According to him, there was nothing of interest in the Wild Wood."

"And that was true," said the knight. "You can view my presence here as in the old song. Did the beautiful Isadoro not sing it for you?"

Tiuri suddenly felt an almost uncontrollable urge to throw a chess piece at his head. But he held himself back and did not move.

The Black Knight continued, "In a castle on the Black River there once lived a knight who loved peace. He expressed the wish to be left alone. Then trees grew up around his castle and hid it from the eyes of men. Hundreds of years went by and he was forgotten. But now he lives again. I am that knight!"

He stood up, paced the room, then turned back to Tiuri and said quietly, "You are the youngest knight of King Dagonaut – not of Unauwen. On what do you base your judgement of Eviellan, my country? No, it is not entirely my country. I am an exile, born in the Kingdom of Unauwen. Have you heard the history of the king and his sons?"

"Yes," replied Tiuri.

"King Unauwen had two sons, born on the same day," the knight began in a singsong tone, as if reciting a poem. "The elder son was crown prince, successor to the throne, while the second was to receive nothing. But he was only very slightly younger than his brother, and in many respects identical to him. Can you not feel some sympathy for that younger prince? Do you not understand that he conquered Eviellan to become what he was destined to be: a king, a ruler? Ah, it is a sorry tale, the story of Prince Viridian, King of Eviellan."

He sat down again. Tiuri was silent. Fascinated, he stared at the knight.

The knight continued, "Eviellan shares your borders and there should be friendship between your land and mine. But some of Dagonaut's knights dare to make judgements about the discord between Eviellan and the Kingdom of Unauwen. They call Eviellan wicked. But what do they know about it?" His eyes, glinting in the candlelight, were fixed on Tiuri. "What do *you* know about it?" he asked. He did not wait for an answer, but moved one of his pieces forward, and then said abruptly, "It's getting late. The victor must be decided."

They played on. Tiuri felt as though some other fight were being fought between the two of them, one that had nothing to do with chess. *I think*, he pondered, *he wants to persuade me to come over to his side.*

He became aware that he was no longer paying enough attention to the game, but he soon noticed that the Black Knight was also playing with less concentration. It was the knight's turn now, and he moved his queen – an ill-considered move! A ring sparkled on his finger.

Tiuri stared at it, wide-eyed.

A ring with a white stone, which gleamed like a star. He knew that ring! Not so long ago he had been sitting opposite another knight at a chessboard, a knight who wore the same kind of ring. Prince Iridian. And much longer ago, someone had told him, *There are only twelve such rings in the whole world. King Unauwen gave them to his most faithful paladins.*

How was this possible?

The Black Knight seemed to notice Tiuri's surprise. He quickly pulled his hand away and hid it in the sleeve of his robe.

Tiuri stared at the chess pieces with unseeing eyes. A knight from Eviellan, the enemy of King Unauwen, and yet one of his most loyal paladins?

"Well?" his opponent said quietly. "I believe you are thinking more about two kingdoms than about the game we are playing. But those two lands are no more different than the white and black sides before us."

But that's not true, thought Tiuri. Indeed, he knew little about Eviellan, but what little he knew was not good. He thought about Sir Ristridin, about the words "so treacherously slain" carved on the tree, and about the Fool, who had been taken from his home. He pictured the opponents of Eviellan: Evan, Tirillo and Prince Iridian, the son of King Unauwen.

King Unauwen had two sons... and he had given two of those twelve rings to them. That was it! A ring to the crown prince and a ring to the King of Eviellan...

Play! he thought feverishly. *He just made a foolish move. Remember Prince Iridian's lessons. This fight could almost be over...*

"Check," he said a little later, in a clear, firm voice.

After a few moves he spoke again, "Check!"

"Checkmate! You've won," said the Black Knight, slowly laying down his king.

The ring sparkled again as he raised his hand to the mask.

Tiuri now suspected who he was, but still, as he looked at him, he was full of anticipation.

The knight removed his mask, and Tiuri saw a pale face in the candlelight, a handsome, friendly, rather melancholy face.

It was the face of Prince Iridian.

7   Unmasked

Startled, Tiuri jerked back, knocking over a chess piece.

"You...!" he whispered.

The expression on the other man's face changed.

"You do not know me!" said the Black Knight sharply. His eyes narrowed, and for one moment there was nothing but fury on his face. But then he smiled, melancholy and slightly mocking.

But Tiuri knew now that this was not Prince Iridian – no matter how much he looked like him. And so his suspicion had been correct: his opponent was Iridian's twin brother, the King of Eviellan.

"Well?" said the knight, as he looked curiously at Tiuri. "My face seems to surprise you. Have we perhaps met before, after all?"

"No... no, my lord," said Tiuri.

"Are you sure about that?" asked the knight. He now looked so much like Prince Iridian that Tiuri could not help pausing briefly before he answered, "I am certain of it, my lord."

"And I am not so certain of it," said the Black Knight. "I knew you before I met you at the Low Bridge."

Again, doubts began to rise within Tiuri. Was this Prince Iridian, whom he had so admired... or was the Iridian with whom he'd played chess at Castle Ristridin in fact the Black Knight with the Red Shield? How could two such different men look so very much alike?

"What is your name, my lord?" he managed to say.

"Master of the Tarnburg is my title, but before that I was Lord of the Seven Castles. I am the Knight in Black, exile, wanderer... You consider me your enemy, but I am not. You do not need to remain a prisoner in my castle! You may be my guest, my friend, if only you will trust me." The knight fell silent for a moment and asked, "Do you have a suspicion who I am?"

"You are the prince..." replied Tiuri, his voice trembling a little. "The King of Eviellan." He began to rise to his feet.

251

"Remain seated," ordered the knight. "I am here incognito. I understand that you have met my... that you have met Prince Iridian." He leant back in his chair and added, "So now do you understand me better? You did not even know for sure which one of us you were talking to! Do you dare now to make a distinction between us? To follow one of us and to reject the other? Yes, I am the King of Eviellan, but I am also a son of King Unauwen. Forget the discord between Unauwen and Eviellan for a moment and listen to me. I could have killed you, but instead I have talked to you and played chess with you."

How can someone with a face like that be evil? thought Tiuri and he whispered, "Why... sire?"

"You are so young – and it is not your fault that you consider me an enemy," replied the king. "But as I have already said, I feel only friendship for the knights of King Dagonaut."

What about Ristridin? thought Tiuri.

"I also love my father, King Unauwen," the prince continued. "Why else would I still wear his ring on my finger? Do you think it was ever my intention to start a war, to bring about death and destruction? Have I not caused Eviellan to flourish and subjugated the cruel lords who live there to my will? And yet I do not feel at home there. I long constantly for my homeland, which I love." He leant closer to Tiuri.

"Look at me," he said, almost whispering, "and tell me I would not look like a paladin of King Unauwen if I were to cross the mountains to the west. Would the people not greet me as their lord, their prince?" He smiled at Tiuri and continued, "And you could ride in my company, a knight on a black horse and with a white shield. You could ride beside me, for you are valiant and could become a great knight..."

Tiuri moved as if he were trying to shake off a spell. He knew he could not trust the prince and yet, looking at him and listening to him, he could hardly believe that this was the wicked King of Eviellan.

The king continued to speak, softly, almost pleading, "I shall tell you everything about myself, so that you will know what I am like and what I wish for. I want only to do good, and any evil I have done was only because I was driven to it through no will of my own. I am, like you, a prisoner, and I want to be free. Do you trust me?"

Tiuri said nothing. To his amazement, he felt the urge to say yes. Now he understood why the King of Eviellan had so many loyal followers.

"Silence is agreement," said the prince.

"That is not true!" whispered Tiuri.

"But you did not say no... Even Sir Ristridin believed me when I told him that an attack on your kingdom was being planned from Deltaland. It was for my sake that he kept silent about the paths in this wood."

Could that really be true? thought Tiuri.

The King of Eviellan continued, "You are perhaps surprised that I, a king, would take the trouble of talking to you like this. But you deserve to be free! This is no man's land, and no one will find you here... or even look for you."

Was there a threat in his voice now?

"To be honest," he continued, "I rather think your friends have abandoned you. Why else did they not accompany you into the wood? But you had the courage to go anyway, a true knight, on your black horse, with your white shield..." and, half to himself, he added, "Just like Sir Edwinem."

That name brought Tiuri to his senses. Edwinem of Forèstèrra – he had been murdered, treacherously lured into a trap by a black knight with a red shield, the knight Bendu had been seeking but had not found. How could Tiuri have forgotten that? It was this knight who had committed that infamous deed, the masked Knight with the Red Shield, the King of Eviellan himself!

"You murdered him!" said Tiuri.

He was startled by the effect of his words. The man opposite him sat upright. His features twisted and changed and his face became terrifying, wicked!

Then the king wiped his hand across his brow and the anger melted from his face. But Tiuri knew now he would never be mistaken again. This knight was nothing like Prince Iridian.

The King of Eviellan looked at him for a long time, with his cold, piercing eyes. Tiuri felt all his courage fading away beneath that gaze.

"I should not have spoken the name of Edwinem," the king said. "But it was you who made me do it."

"Me? How?" asked Tiuri.

The King of Eviellan stood up. "I saw him in you," he said, "as he once was, before the war came. He rode on the black horse Ardanwen, his shield was white, and a peculiar squire followed him wherever he went. In you he could have returned, but this time at my side. I can say that to you now, as it is not going to happen."

His voice grew colder and colder.

"It no longer matters," he continued. "Sir Edwinem will not return. I killed him; that is true. There will be not one single white shield in my retinue when I cross the mountains along the Road of Ambuscade."

To conquer the Kingdom of Unauwen... thought Tiuri.

The King of Eviellan was wicked, and yet for a moment Tiuri felt some sympathy for him. He would never know happiness, this prince, who killed anyone who stood in his way, who would even destroy the land he wanted to rule.

Now the king was looking down at him, his face devoid of expression. "Not one single white shield," he repeated.

And suddenly Tiuri saw very clearly what his own fate would be. He would have to die, just like Edwinem, like Ilmar and Arwaut. The King of Eviellan knew Tiuri would never follow him... And the land of King Unauwen would be destroyed.

But that couldn't happen, could it?! It mustn't! Evil could surely not be allowed to win?!

The King of Eviellan leant forward and swept away the pieces that were still on the board. He said nothing, but his gesture said enough.

I don't want to die! thought Tiuri.

He realized that no word, no plea would help him. Was there truly no way out?

Kneeling down, he hastily gathered up the pieces. He put them back on the board. *The third night!* he thought. *Just give me time until tomorrow night.*

The King of Eviellan turned away from him and walked slowly towards the door.

Tiuri's voice stopped him in his tracks. The young knight had stood up and said, in calm and measured tones, "I challenge you, sire, Prince Viridian."

And when the king turned around, Tiuri pointed at the black and white board and said, "I challenge you to one last game of chess."

The King of Eviellan looked at him coolly and gave no response.

"A game for life – or death," Tiuri added.

8 LIFE OR DEATH

"Do you think I would tie my fate to the outcome of a game?" said the King of Eviellan. "There are no equal chances in life."

Tiuri picked up a black pawn and a white pawn, one in each hand. He closed his fingers around them and took a step forward. "For my life alone, sire," he said. "You may choose which colour you wish to play with."

Luckily, the king did not leave. "For *your* life... or death?" he said slowly. "Now suddenly you trust me! I could kill you anyway, even if I lose."

"I shall have to take my chances," replied Tiuri, holding out his closed fists.

The king looked down at Tiuri's hands. "I have long since dismissed notions such as chivalry and abiding by oaths," he said. Again he looked at Tiuri. "This game is nothing to me," he added. "While you, Sir Tiuri, are putting everything at stake."

"I know," said Tiuri. Only later did he realize that the King of Eviellan seemed to be addressing him with more respect now and using his title. They were facing each other as two adults, who knew what they were up against.

The king appeared to be thinking. "Ah, why not?" he said, with a short laugh. "Your life as our stake, sir knight!" He touched Tiuri's left fist. "This one," he said.

"White!" said Tiuri quietly. Eviellan had drawn white. Was this an ill omen?

The king also looked rather taken aback. "It would seem our roles are reversed," he said. "I shall play with white."

They both looked at the chessboard, where their two small, motionless armies stood facing each other.

I have tied my fate to this game, thought Tiuri, rather surprised at how calm he felt.

The king sat down, and Tiuri followed his example. Then there was silence, broken only by the quiet "tick" of a piece being moved.

Then there came another sound. The Fool had got up from his bed and come into the room. He stood by the window, watching them play. He did not speak a word, but Tiuri was very aware of his presence.

I am playing not only for myself, he said in his mind, *but also for you, and perhaps for even more.*

He found it reassuring to know that Marius was near – his peculiar squire, as the King of Eviellan had called him. He also realized that meant the king most probably knew nothing of Piak's existence.

And if Piak had escaped, then he would certainly do everything he could to help!

But Tiuri knew he could not count on that now; he had to concentrate only on the game. This was another duel, and it was even more of a challenge than the previous one.

He looked at his opponent, who glanced over at the Fool and seemed annoyed by him. Then he stood up and barked, "You have more time than I. We shall continue our battle another day." And he left the room.

The Fool went over to Tiuri and said quietly, "You haven't forgotten, have you, Friend?"

"What?" asked Tiuri.

"That we were going to run away? Or do you mean to stay here, between walls, behind bars? He has sat opposite you and talked to you. He has a handsome face, and he is a king... That's right, isn't it? But he will not speak to me."

"May God forbid that he should ever do so!" said Tiuri, jumping to his feet. "Do not listen to him, Marius! He is dangerous, and more cruel than the Red Riders."

"I listened to him," whispered the Fool, "but I did not understand everything the two of you said. He is Master of the Wild Wood. At first I thought that was another man, but now I see it must be him. Is that not true, Friend?"

"No, it is *not* true!" responded Tiuri, feeling something close to anger as he realized that not even the Fool had escaped the King of Eviellan's influence. "Do you not understand that he is deceitful and that, if I lose this game, he will kill both you and me?"

The Fool licked his lips nervously and fear came into his eyes. "I understand now, sir knight," he said. "Now I am glad he did not speak to me. Now I know why I was afraid that the third night was such a long time to wait. That night is tomorrow, but the bars are still in place."

They walked together to the window. "It won't take us any longer than an hour," said Tiuri, "to remove these two bars."

"And then?" whispered the Fool.

"Then there are still the guards," replied Tiuri. "But, one way or another, we have to escape tomorrow night."

He had an idea. "We could use the bars as weapons," he whispered.

Climbing out of the window, with a heavy, iron bar in their hands... jumping onto the guards and taking them out of action... Each of them would have to take on a guard, and Tiuri did not know if the Fool would be able to do that. The chance of one of the guards crying out was high, and it was unlikely that such an escape would succeed. There were soldiers everywhere. And yet it was the only way... unless they heard something from Jaro on the third night.

There was still the matter of the game of chess, too. When would that be decided? When would his opponent return? On the third night? Then he would have to force the game to a quick conclusion... But what if he were to lose?

Tiuri lost his calm. "Whatever happens, we need to escape as soon as we see a possibility," he said to himself. "This game is only a ruse, a stay of execution. Perhaps I shall never finish it, although I should be sorry about that. But I can never fight him as a prisoner, and fight him I must, as long as the Road of Ambuscade runs to the west."

The candles had almost burnt down and it looked as if the two armies were advancing across the black and white squares of the board. Tiuri rubbed his eyes.

"Why don't you go to sleep?" the Fool asked quietly. "Do not be afraid, Friend. You are a knight, a knight with a beautiful white shield."

"A knight!" muttered Tiuri. He sat down and leant his head against the back of the chair. The King of Eviellan had compared him to Edwinem – Edwinem of Forèstèrra, the Invincible, Paladin of King Unauwen! If he knew how very different Tiuri felt! "I am just a pawn," he whispered, and dreamily he went on:

I am just a pawn.
I followed paths
over fields of white, through woods so dark.
The earth seems to me
like a chessboard of ivory.
North and east and south and west.
Castles, with towers at the corners.
Guards standing watch, hear their drums.
Horses jump from black to white.
Black horses, white horses.
Knights ride with white shields.
Red Riders are on the hunt.
Two armies face each other:
battling night and day,
by light and dark, sun and moon.
In the midst of each army a king –
a white one,
a red one,
forging plans,
deliberating –
moves and countermoves.
Where shall I go?
How can I win?
I look at the stars through iron bars.
My candle burns dimly,
and the chessboard gleams.
How the white shines,
how the red glows.
These fields are so narrow yet wide,
black and white, fields of black and white...
Dreams, schemes.
Which way lies my path?

He did not know if he had thought those words or spoken them out loud. The Fool looked at him quizzically and then blew out the candles. Grey half-light filled the room; dawn was near.

Tiuri closed his eyes and slept.

He was awoken by noise. It was completely light now. The Fool was standing at the window again, and he let out a cry. Tiuri leapt up and was beside him in a second. Blinking, he looked outside.

Men with sticks and whips were running all around, and Red Riders on horseback were shouting loudly. A man lay on the ground, writhing in pain.

"The black horse!" said the Fool.

And then Ardanwen came into view, mane flowing and tail swishing. He was trailing a rope behind him. The soldiers and the Red Riders tried to stop him, but whenever he came close they jumped fearfully out of the way. Ardanwen raced around, disappeared from sight, then came back again. A man had seized the rope now, and he was dragged along for some distance before letting go. The black horse reared up, magnificent and terrifying. Then he galloped towards the bridge.

The Red Riders dashed after the horse, howling and hollering, with the other soldiers following behind.

"Ardanwen!" yelled Tiuri, but only the Fool heard him.

A moment later, another horseman came riding by, surrounded by men in green and black. It was the Black Knight with the Red Shield, the King of Eviellan. He gave a loud cry and rode to the bridge. A few soldiers bent over the wounded man, who was still lying on the ground, before carrying him away.

"What have they done to Ardanwen?" whispered Tiuri. "Someone must have tried to ride him."

He gazed at the bridge. There was no sign of Ardanwen and his pursuers now, but he could still hear shouting in the distance. The Black Knight returned; he was in his full armour, with the visor of his helmet closed. He raised his head for a moment to look at the two prisoners standing at the window, before riding around the castle walls and disappearing.

"He has run away, your black horse," said the Fool. "They won't catch him. They'll never catch him!"

"Oh, I hope you're right!" said Tiuri. "But Ardanwen was injured. I saw it."

"He is wild. And he is fast!" whispered the Fool. "And they will not catch him!"

It was a while before the men returned. They were talking animatedly as they rode by, but the prisoners could not tell how the hunt had ended. But Ardanwen was not with them.

Tiuri sat down at the chessboard and said, "Whatever has happened or will happen, this is all I can think about now."

Head in hands, he pondered matters. He did not look up again until the door of his prison opened, and then he rose to his feet.

The King of Eviellan clearly did not want to wait long to settle their fight. He stood before Tiuri in the guise of the Black Knight and did not raise the visor of his helmet.

"Ah, I see that you are keen to win!" came his voice, muted and mocking. "But you have time, while I can stay for only a few minutes. Not that I begrudge you the opportunity to reflect upon your position. Life or death... Have you really thought about it? Sometimes death is preferable to life..." He continued after pausing for a moment, "I'm sure you do not believe that, but just imagine: a dark dungeon... a crypt where daylight never comes. Locked away forever, lying on slippery stone, listening to the dripping of the drops that fall. Nothing else! Would you call that 'life'?"

He bent over the chessboard. With his hands resting on the table, he stared at the board for minutes. Then he made his move. "Your turn," he said, taking a step back.

Tiuri had stood motionless all that time, trying not to think about his opponent's words. Their contest was already hard enough. The King of Eviellan, however, seemed to be doing his best to disturb Tiuri's concentration, because when it was his move, he started talking again.

"Yes, sometimes death is preferable to life. Do you know what pain is, and fear? Do you know shame and disgrace?" And he continued in that vein, his monotonous, subdued tone making what he said even more horrifying.

But Tiuri kept his eyes on the chessboard and did not react.

"It is better to fall in battle than to remain alive and die a slow death," said the Black Knight, raising his voice. "Did you see your horse?"

Tiuri made even more of an effort to act as if he could not hear him.

"Ardanwen is dead," said the King of Eviellan.

Tiuri did not move, but he felt tears smarting behind his eyelids. *Why are you crying?* he thought to himself. *You didn't cry for Ilmar and Arwaut. And that was worse. Don't cry now.* But he saw the chessmen through a blurry haze and had to swallow hard to regain his composure.

Ardanwen died a good death, he thought to himself. *He was free, and no enemy could tame him.* Tiuri took a deep breath, raised his head and looked at his opponent with something like a smile.

"It's your move," he said.

"Anyone who will not accept a master is dangerous," said the King of Eviellan, "to others and to himself. Anyone who will not submit when he has lost must die."

Tiuri nodded calmly. "That is true," he said.

"As far as our game is concerned," the king continued, "I shall wait a while before making my next move, and give you more time for reflection, Sir Tiuri. One last word of advice: Do not think yourself too lofty, too noble, too strong! It could prove your undoing one day."

A moment later, the door slammed behind him.

9 THE THIRD NIGHT

If he moves his last knight forward, I can take his bishop with my queen. He could check my king then, but... Tiuri yawned. Had he considered all of the possibilities now?

The third night had begun, but the King of Eviellan had not yet appeared. The Fool was looking out of the window. It was quiet in and around the castle; all Tiuri could hear was the rushing river.

If the game is decided this evening, what will happen? If I lose, will the king put me to death immediately? And if I should win, will I be thrown into a dungeon to die a slow death? Tiuri shivered. Suddenly he thought of Ristridin, who had sworn to find the Black Knight with the Red Shield and to punish him. *Would Ristridin have done what the king wanted?* he thought. *I don't believe it for a moment! Perhaps he is locked up in a dungeon beneath this castle even now, a prisoner for all these months.*

The Fool turned to him and whispered, "He is coming again, Friend."

Yes, the muffled sound of footsteps was approaching, and then came the familiar creak of the bolts. Tiuri stood up as his opponent entered the room, in his black armour, but without a helmet this time.

For a short while, they played without saying a word. Then the other man broke the silence by saying, "Your king is in check."

Outside, an owl hooted. Tiuri pricked up his ears. Then he focused solely on the game and brought his king to safety. They both had only a few pieces left now, and they were evenly matched. The outcome of the battle would soon be decided.

But the King of Eviellan did not seem particularly keen to end the game yet. Perhaps he was taking pleasure in playing with his opponent and leaving him uncertain of his fate. He stood up and left the room without a word or a sign of farewell.

Tiuri sighed with relief and blew out the candles. The Fool took out the file and set to work again on destroying the bars.

Tiuri took another quick look at the game. He would not finish it; he was about to escape and leave their battle undecided. In a way, he regretted it... But he had no choice. He had to get away, not only to save himself, but also so that he could try somehow to foil the enemy's plans.

The owl hooted again... but was it really an owl? The Fool stopped filing and peered outside. Tiuri looked, too. He could see the guards. One of them was looking up, but he could not make out his face. Cautiously, Tiuri put his hand out of the window and gave a quick wave.

The guard turned to his companion and said something. Then, suddenly and silently, he attacked him! Holding their breath, the two prisoners watched the struggle. It did not last long. After a few seconds, it was obvious that the man who had been attacked was either unconscious or dead. The victor dragged him away and soon both had disappeared from sight.

"Quickly!" said Tiuri. "Keep filing!"

"This bar's ready," whispered the Fool. "Look out. I'm going to break it."

Down below, the helpful guard had reappeared; it had to be Jaro. He waved at them and, for the third time, they heard the hooting of an owl.

Tiuri waved back before helping the Fool with the bars, which had now been filed almost the whole way through. Perhaps it was only a few seconds, but it seemed like an eternity before they gave way... one of the bars almost fell to the floor and everything sounded so terrifyingly loud. It was a long drop to the ground below the window and Tiuri wondered if it might be a good idea to tie the bed sheets together and use them as a rope. But the guard whispered urgently, "Hurry! Drop down onto the ledge and then move in this direction."

Tiuri climbed out of the window.

"Can you put the bars back?" came the guard's voice.

Yes, then their escape wouldn't be noticed quite so soon. Tiuri pulled himself up and whispered to the Fool, "The bars need to go back. Give them here... yes. I'll do it. You go first."

Now the Fool clambered outside and made his way along the wall like some giant insect.

Down below, the guard whispered instructions. "All the way to the bastion. Now down to here, and then jump."

As he spoke, Tiuri, standing on the ledge outside the window, was busy trying to put the bars back. One was in place, but the other wouldn't stand up.

"Leave it!" said the voice from below. "Just hurry."

The jump they had to make was still from quite a height, but they both landed well. The guard was indeed Jaro. "Back into the shadows," he whispered. "Over there, in that archway, there are some things for you – clothes, weapons. Put them on and wait for a sign from me."

The Fool seemed to be able to see in the dark, like a cat. He found the clothes straightaway and he was the first to spot the figure lying there – the other guard. He moved and groaned, so he wasn't dead, but he was firmly tied up and out of action.

"They're the same clothes that the men here wear," whispered the Fool. "They don't fit me."

Tiuri's eyes had now grown somewhat accustomed to the dark as well. His friend did look rather odd in his disguise. Then he looked at Jaro, who was leaning on his spear, pretending he was still on guard. Jaro beckoned Tiuri over.

"Good, now it appears as if there are two guards again," he said quietly, when Tiuri was standing beside him. "Your friend should stay in the shadows for a moment. Listen and I'll explain the plan. It's all gone well so far, but we're not finished yet. You were so late!"

265

"The... the Black Knight was with us," whispered Tiuri.

"I see. Well, the guards change an hour after midnight. It's about an hour before midnight now, so we have two hours until anyone raises the alarm. We have to get across the field, to the river – that's the most dangerous part. It's so light tonight."

Indeed, the moon was shining brightly and there wasn't a cloud in the sky.

"Do you see that boulder over there?" said Jaro. "That's where you need to head first. Then take a look around to make sure the coast is clear and walk straight to the river. Don't run or they might notice you. If you should happen to meet someone, try to act like you're one of us. The password for tonight is 'pawn'."

"And what then?" whispered Tiuri.

"When you get to the river," continued Jaro, "drop straight to the bank. There's a path down there. Be sure they don't see you from the bridge; it's heavily guarded. We have to cross the river some way downstream... but you'll see that when we come to it. We'll go now, one at a time. You first, then your friend, and me last."

"You're coming, too?" asked Tiuri.

"Yes, what did you expect? No, don't say anything. We don't have much time. I've done my best to prepare everything as well as possible. You just have to do as I say. I know how things work here. Have you got it all?"

"Yes," whispered Tiuri. "Thank you, Jaro!"

"Then go – and tell your squire to come here. Wait... You need to wait for me by the riverbank, but you'll have to know where to cross, just in case... It's past the rapids and the bend. I've hung a rope at the right spot. But I'll be there. Go on!"

Tiuri shook Jaro's hand, beckoned the Fool over and, in a whisper, told him to do exactly as Jaro said. Then he crossed the field to the boulder.

He stopped in the shadow of the large rock... and looked around. There were lights on the bridge and inside the castle. Tiuri could see the window they had escaped through, and Jaro and the Fool standing beneath it. There did not seem to be any danger, but still his heart pounded frantically as he walked in a straight line down the slope from the boulder to the river. The rushing of the water sounded louder and louder and he thought he could make out voices, too. He had to resist the urge to start running. He was almost there now... no, not quite! He looked back. The towers of the Tarnburg were silhouetted sharply against the sky and he could no longer see Jaro and the Fool. He wondered if Marius was already following him.

Then, finally, he reached the river... would the guards on the bridge see him? With any luck, they would think he was one of Eviellan's servants, a man in green with a black cap on his head. It was a strange bridge and it seemed to be made from ropes. Tiuri took another look around, crouched and then quickly dropped down to the bank.

He found the path straightaway, and as he headed along it he felt much safer. He was hidden in the darkness now and only had to be careful not to stumble. Much of the river was in shadow, but the far side was white and frothy in the moonlight.

Soon he was at the edge of the water and could feel droplets splashing him. He thought of Jaro, who had put himself in danger for his sake. Then the Fool made his way along the path. Now they only had to wait for Jaro – where had he got to?

It seemed like an age before Jaro joined them. "That went quickly," he whispered in Tiuri's ear. "It can't be any later than a quarter after the eleventh hour. So it'll be some time before they discover the escape – unless a patrol comes to check."

Had it really been only fifteen minutes since they'd left their prison?

"Follow me!" said Jaro, setting off downstream. Tiuri and the Fool obeyed without speaking. The darkness protected them, but also meant they made slow progress.

The water had carved out a deep riverbed. When they looked back, they saw the bridge high above it, looking very fragile. Ahead of them, the river made a gentle bend.

Just past the bend, Jaro stopped. "Can you swim?" he asked.

"Yes," replied Tiuri. Then he repeated it more loudly, to make himself heard above the rushing of the water. The Fool grabbed hold of him and said, "Well, I can't!"

"It's shallow enough to stand," said Jaro. "As long as you have a firm footing!"

They watched the swirling water. Rocks jutted out above the surface here and there.

"To the other side, then!" said Jaro. "From the bridge they can only see us for the last part, and they'd have to be looking very hard. If you fall, just let the current carry you along. Come on!"

The water was very cold, but they were trying so hard not to be swept away by the river that they soon didn't notice the chill. They stayed close together and, half swimming, half wading, they struggled to the other side – and to freedom.

When they reached the opposite bank, their teeth were chattering, but Jaro immediately started walking, now in the full moonlight. To their left, a rocky wall rose upwards, full of crevices and protrusions. When Tiuri looked back, he could no longer see the bridge.

Jaro stopped beside a rope that was hanging down. The Fool was the first to climb up, and Tiuri followed him.

The ascent wasn't easy, but all three of them arrived safely at the top, among trees and undergrowth. Jaro undid the rope, which was tied around a tree, coiled it up, and said, "I put it here yesterday. Now they'll never know where we crossed the river." He really had set everything up perfectly. "And now be careful," he continued. "We're close to the road, and people come along here quite often."

"The Road of Ambuscade?" Tiuri asked quietly.

"That's right," said Jaro. "We'll cross it and then we'll have to make sure we put our head start to good use."

"I want to go to the west," whispered Tiuri.

"Are you insane?!" said Jaro. "Going along the road that way is impossible."

"But it leads to the pass, over the mountains..."

"Yes. But you can't escape by heading in that direction," whispered Jaro. "You might as well go straight back to the Tarnburg. The road is guarded day and night, from the fork in the river to the Tarntop, and the forest to the north is crawling with Men in Green. Our only chance is to the east, as far as possible from the Black River and not too close to the Green River. But let's not waste time talking. An hour after midnight they'll sound the alarm and then even the eastern route won't be safe. What are we waiting for?"

Tiuri sighed. He might have known the Road of Ambuscade would be guarded, but still...

"Let's go!" said Jaro impatiently.

"Are you coming with us?" whispered Tiuri, as they crept towards the road.

"Yes, what else can I do?" replied Jaro.

"Why are you helping us?"

"I'm sure you can figure that out for yourself," said Jaro. "No, don't thank me. Quiet!" He stopped and Tiuri saw his eyes glinting as they looked at each other. "Perhaps we can talk and make plans later," he said. "But now we need to get out of here. Do you know how many soldiers there are in this wood? Not a hundred, more... maybe a thousand. To the east and out of the forest... And just pray that we make it."

The road was fairly wide, and the shadows of trees lay across it in black stripes. They darted over and Jaro took the lead as they headed into the forest. He walked slowly at first, but after a while he started to run. They continued like that for some time, along a narrow path, until Jaro stopped and signalled that they should proceed more cautiously. Tiuri and the Fool soon realized why; they could hear people talking. "A guard post," Jaro whispered once they had passed it.

After that, they moved on quickly. They came to a clearing, where Jaro looked around and gazed up at the sky for a moment. Then he abandoned the path and continued straight through the forest.

They could not see much, but they could hear plenty: not only their own hurried breathing, but all kinds of other sounds; the wood was full of noises. Flapping and fluttering, crying and calling, rushing and rustling; everything that lived here seemed to be awake. But they heard no people, and they could no longer hear the river.

I wonder what time it is, thought Tiuri. "Look, there's another path over there," he whispered.

"I'm just acting on instinct now," said Jaro. "I don't know the paths around here."

"We mustn't follow this path," whispered the Fool. "It's the track of an animal, this path – wild animals. They have their young now and they're dangerous."

"We're better off avoiding every kind of path," muttered Jaro. "I can barely see my hand in front of my face. We wouldn't be the first to end up walking in circles."

"Where are we going?" asked the Fool.

"To the east," said Tiuri, "where the sun comes up."

"Then we're going the right way, Friend," whispered the Fool. "I don't know for sure, but I believe it's so."

"Then let's get going," said Jaro.

Suddenly there was noise all around them! First a horn rang out, high and piercing – one, two, three, four short blasts. Other horns answered in turn, from every direction. A brief silence, and then came the sound of a drum.

They froze.

"They know we've gone," Jaro said quietly when everything was silent again. No, not silent; startled animals were flying and fleeing all around them.

"Well, we knew this would happen," Jaro continued. "We'll just have to take greater care now."

A horn sounded again, not too far away.

"That will be the guard post we passed," whispered Jaro.

"Are there many guard posts?" asked Tiuri.

"Yes. They use horns to pass on messages. Others do it with a drum, just like the Men in Green..."

"The Men in Green... They're with you, aren't they?" whispered Tiuri.

"They've made an alliance with the Black Knight. They always sound a warning when a stranger is approaching. We need to be even more wary of them than of the Red Riders. They suddenly appear, right in front of you, and once they have something they don't let it go. But I'm talking too much," Jaro said. "Any sound could betray us."

As quietly as possible, they continued on their way. At first they heard nothing untoward, but soon there were voices shouting in the distance.

"Perhaps we'd better look for a hiding place and wait for it to get light," Tiuri suggested when they came to a stop in the middle of a dark and almost impenetrable wilderness.

Jaro agreed.

They dropped to the ground, crawled beneath some overhanging vegetation, and sat in silence for a while.

"If either of you feels sleepy, you must tell me," whispered Jaro. "We mustn't all fall asleep at the same time."

"You two can sleep," said the Fool. "I'll stay awake. I shall tell you if they're coming."

"Yes. I've noticed that you're very good at seeing in the dark," said Jaro.

Tiuri knew the Fool was smiling.

"We have run away," Marius said, "and they will not find us. Go to sleep, both of you."

271

Tiuri did as he was told and dreamt that he was playing chess again. Then he awoke with a start to hear the sound of hoofs nearby. It was still dark, but he saw lanterns moving past.

"We have no need to fear such noisemakers," Jaro whispered a little later. "Only the ones that sneak and stalk."

Tiuri thought again about the Men in Green. He couldn't get back to sleep; he kept hearing suspicious noises, and there was so much to worry about. Hiding in the forest was easy enough to do, but it was just as easy to get lost. Maybe the King of Eviellan had already ordered his men to surround the area and to form a cordon so that they would be unable to pass. *That's what I would do if I were him*, Tiuri thought. *He has so many men, who all know their way around the forest. He is aware that I know his plans... an attack along the Road of Ambuscade. But when...?*

He could hear his companions moving and knew they were not asleep either. All three of them were longing for dawn.

PART SIX

THE MEN IN GREEN

1 THE GREEN RIVER AND
THE WATCHTOWER

I *have to escape,* Tiuri had thought. *Somehow I need to find a way to foil our enemy. I must try to defeat him, as long as he continues to plan his surprise attack along that road to the west.*

But they were running to the east; they had no choice. And it was unlikely that they could escape the enemy's clutches even then. Until now, they had been able to avoid the Red Riders, but they were close to the lands of the Men in Green, and Jaro had said they were more to be feared than the men who served the Tarnburg.

They moved as quickly as possible, constantly glancing around in fear, covered in scratches and with their clothes torn. They barely stopped to rest, pausing only occasionally to hide from pursuers, both real and imagined. But eventually, they sank down to drink from a pool and to eat some of the dried meat that Jaro had brought with him.

Nearby was a tree in blossom. Tiuri looked at it for a moment, marvelling that something so beautiful could exist in this terrible forest. Jaro yawned and wiped the sweat from his face. There was a dirty bandage around his hand.

"I did that," Tiuri said quietly.

"What?" said Jaro. "Oh, my wound. It was my own fault. Your last attack really did take me by surprise."

"Did you let me win on purpose?" whispered Tiuri.

"I was planning to," replied Jaro. "But that didn't make the fight any easier for me. I couldn't arouse the Black Knight's suspicions. If I had fought as I once did, just as all Red Riders fight when they want to win, maybe I would have overpowered you. I say 'maybe' because I no longer dare to say with any certainty that the stronger man must always win."

The Fool whispered, "Tiuri was fighting. But what about you, friendly enemy? Were you fighting for me, too? Not against me?"

"Hush!" said Jaro. "I no longer know who I should be fighting for or against. That's why I went on the run."

"But you..." Tiuri began.

"Don't say anything," Jaro interrupted him. "Do you remember what you once said to me? That you and I owe our lives to each other, including all we might do in the future. I thought our paths would never cross again, but when they did, I knew that I..." His voice trailed off and he fell silent.

Tiuri didn't say anything else either. Later, when they had reached a safer place, he would have a conversation with Jaro. A safer place... when would they ever be safe?

When the day was over and it became dark again, they knew they had still not come very far. But the enemy had not found them.

Jaro swore under his breath. "Look!" he said.

Tiuri and the Fool came to stand beside him. Down below, at the foot of an overgrown slope, they could see clear water flowing.

"The Green River," whispered Jaro. "Just what I was hoping to avoid."

Yet the surroundings did not look at all dangerous in the early morning light. They could see only part of the river; to their right, it curved to the north. On the opposite bank was a narrow strip of white, and the forest that bordered it stood motionless; not a leaf was moving.

"We'll carry on to the east," said Jaro, "until we're some way past the bend. Then we can head north."

They did as he said and after a short while they came to a path that seemed to lead to the river.

"We shouldn't be here," whispered Jaro, his voice faltering.

Then something darted through the bushes opposite them, parallel to the path. Was it a wild boar? But a moment later another figure followed, more slowly. It stopped and looked at them.

A Man in Green!

The Fool was about to run, but Tiuri stopped him and whispered, "Act like there's nothing wrong!"

They stood looking at one another for a moment, the Man in Green and the three runaways. The man took a step towards them; then he seemed to change his mind, and turned around and disappeared into the trees.

"Going straight on would, of course, be foolhardy," Jaro said quietly, "because then we'll be following him. We don't want to turn back and the path seems dangerous, too."

"But we can't stay here either," said Tiuri. "Let's hope he took us for servants of the Tarnburg."

"He's sure to be spying on us," said Jaro. "And if you see one of them, there are usually more nearby. So he'll have help."

By then they had stepped out onto the path and they followed it for a while. Then Jaro stopped again.

"No!" he said. "We're going to end up at the river and we definitely don't want to be there."

"They're coming after us, too," whispered the Fool. "Along this path."

Then they were startled by a soft cry that came from somewhere behind him. They looked back to see another Man in Green, who was calling something to them.

Jaro's hand flashed to the hilt of his sword. The man pointed down the track and said something else, but they couldn't catch his words.

As if by agreement, the runaways walked calmly onwards. When they glanced back, the Man in Green was no longer there. Only then did they start running. The road went downhill and the river could not be far. Now they could all hear what the Fool had noticed earlier: the sound of hoofs!

"We'll have to go right," Jaro panted as they ran. "We can take on one, two, maybe three men. But there are more men than that coming after us."

But suddenly, on their right, lots of green figures were moving among the trees. They had no choice but to head straight on.

Tiuri cast a glance over his shoulder. There they were! Red Riders came riding towards them. One of them blew his horn and answers came from all sides. The hunt was on.

And there, in front of them, was the river! The path came out at the bend, before taking a right turn and running beside the water. But they saw the Men in Green approaching from that direction. The Red Riders were racing up behind them. They couldn't go left either, as the riverbank rose so steeply.

They were being driven into the river.

As he ran towards the water, Tiuri realized it was shallow; it would be possible to wade through.

"Stop!" cried a Red Rider.

"That's it. We've had it," panted Jaro. But, like his companions, he ran on, into the water.

The Red Riders yelled, but by the time they had reached the bank the runaways were almost on the other side.

Jaro got there first; he stopped and waited. Some of the horsemen had now also entered the water. Others raised their bows, and an arrow narrowly missed Jaro's head.

"Keep going!" Tiuri yelled at Jaro. Jaro leapt into action and ran from the bank. Then Tiuri and Marius also reached the other side. Only a few steps separated them from the shelter of the forest.

As they darted into the trees, Tiuri stumbled. Getting back to his feet, he saw a pair of legs... then the whole man... a Man in Green had appeared in front of him, armed with a spear.

Tiuri gathered his last strength to attack him. But the Man in Green stepped aside and walked past him to the water's edge.

"Tiuri, Tiuri!" cried the Fool.

Only then did Tiuri realize that lots of Men in Green had appeared; they were standing in a line on the bank. However, they were barely looking at him or at the Fool. Their eyes were fixed on the Red Riders, who were approaching across the river.

Tiuri did not allow himself the time to be puzzled. In an instant he was beside the Fool and running with him into the forest, where he collided with Jaro. Jaro said something, but Tiuri didn't hear what it was, as so much noise was coming from the river.

The Red Riders and the Men in Green were fighting!

"They're stopping them!" the Fool cried hoarsely. "They're not allowed to come across."

Jaro gave Tiuri a nudge. "Come on!"

They ran onwards. Tiuri's heart was in his throat; he could hardly take anymore.

Again, though, they were stopped by a Man in Green with a spear. The three runaways looked at him, gasping for breath and ready to drop. Jaro drew his sword, but the man raised his hand and smiled. He pointed towards the river, where the sounds of fighting could still be heard, shook his head and indicated that they should follow him.

They're helping us! thought Tiuri, but he didn't have enough breath to say the words. His companions were in the same state, and they all followed the man in silence. Jaro looked most suspicious, though, and he kept his hand firmly clasped around the hilt of his sword.

The Man in Green stopped and pointed at a path. Then he hurried away.

"They're helping us," Tiuri said, out loud this time.

"I don't believe a word of it," growled Jaro.

The Fool said nothing, but just headed along the path.

"I don't trust them," Jaro added.

It had become quieter down by the river, and someone was speaking in a loud voice.

"All we can do is keep on going," said Tiuri, following the Fool.

"And where will this path take us?" said Jaro. "Into their territory!" But he went anyway, because the sound of fighting had started up behind them again.

The Fool glanced back at Tiuri with a look of surprise and fear on his face. "Look!" he whispered.

The path took a turn and they found themselves standing in front of a strange structure, a kind of scaffold made of tree trunks.

"A watchtower!" exclaimed Jaro.

The tower was very high and consisted of a platform resting on four thick poles that stood at an angle, which were braced with thinner beams for support. A rope ladder hung down to the ground.

As they gazed up, they saw men standing on the platform. One of them came down to join them. Half sliding, half climbing, he reached them in a second. It was another Man in Green; he looked at the three of them as if meeting them here were the most natural thing in the world. Without a word, he motioned at them to climb the tower.

"Not likely!" said Jaro, taking a step back.

The man repeated his gesture. They could hear riders approaching from the river now, which removed any doubts for the Fool. He jumped onto the rope ladder and climbed up. Tiuri followed his example, and then Jaro did the same. The man stayed down below.

Up on the platform, there were two more Men in Green. One was sitting with his back towards them and didn't even turn around to look. The other, who was standing beside the low railing, signalled that they should sit down.

The sound of horses' hoofs came closer and closer, accompanied by the sound of angry voices.

"Lie down!" gestured the man by the railing.

The runaways did as they were told; it was all they could do. Two resounding booms right next to their ears startled them. Now they could see that the man who had not looked at them had a large drum in front of him. His friend leant over the railing and said a few words in a language Tiuri did not know.

Lots of men had gathered at the foot of the watchtower. There were wide gaps between the planks of the platform and Tiuri peered through them. He could see Red Riders down below, and Men in Green. The horsemen were talking all at once, angrily and impatiently.

"Where are they?" Tiuri heard someone say. "Let us pass..." "... escaped prisoners..."

Then the man at the railing spoke again. He was calm and composed. Even though Tiuri didn't understand a word, his language didn't sound entirely unfamiliar. One word was repeated a few times, spoken with emphasis, "Tehalon."

The Red Riders were still muttering.

The Man in Green gave a brief reply and Tiuri could tell from the tone exactly what he was saying: "Go away!"

The drum gave a quick roll, as if to reinforce the words.

There was silence beneath the tower, followed by whispering – and soon the Red Riders departed, back to the south, back to the river. The Men in Green who were down below followed them.

The men on the platform turned and studied each of the fugitives in turn. They had sat up by now, and they met the men's searching looks with some surprise.

Whoever they are, thought Tiuri, *they saved us from the Red Riders.* Hesitantly, he spoke up. "Thank you," he said, "for your help! Who are you and what..." He stopped speaking, though, as the men showed no reaction to his words. They just went on staring blankly at him, as if he'd said nothing at all.

The drummer picked up a jug and handed it to the Fool, who was briefly startled. When the man smiled at him, though, he took the jug, raised it to his mouth and drank from it. As he returned it, he smiled back at the man, a little shyly. The man then offered it to Tiuri, who also drank a few gulps – it was tangy and refreshing, and it did him good. "Thank you," he said again. But when it was Jaro's turn, he refused to take the drink.

Then the drummer looked at his companion with a question on his face. The answer was a nod. The drummer nodded back – they appeared to understand each other without having to say anything.

Tiuri would have liked to speak, but these men gave him the impression that speech was unnecessary and superfluous.

The drummer bent over his drum again and began to tap it with his fingers, quickly and in an ever-changing rhythm. It was, thought Tiuri, as if he were telling a tale through the sounds he made – a mysterious tale that Tiuri would have liked to understand.

But as he listened to it for longer, a vague suspicion took hold of him. Now it felt as if he and his friends were in danger of being trapped within some sort of spell that would render them powerless. The sky filled with clouds, the sun disappeared, wind rustled the leaves, and fat drops of rain began to fall. He could almost imagine that the sound of the drum had brought about this change in the weather. He had heard of beings who could control the elements and summon wind and rain at will... but perhaps they weren't just stories. Perhaps they really existed – here in the Wild Wood!

The drumming ended abruptly with a loud boom.

Tiuri jumped to his feet. The Fool was cowering; he seemed to be frightened again. Jaro moved as if he, too, were trying to shake off an enchantment. Tiuri cleared his throat and said loudly, "We're very grateful for your help, of course. But now we should like to..."

Both men frowned and put a finger to their lips.

And then a response came from afar: more drumming. The men listened carefully.

*

Somewhere along the Green River, Piak reined in his horse and said to the Lord of Mistrinaut: "Quiet! I think I heard something."

Tiuri stood beside one of the Men in Green at the railing on the watchtower and looked around. He could see the river through the trees, and noted that the path they'd taken continued to the north; he could see along it for quite some way. The drumming came from that direction. It stopped with a short bang.

"Boom!" went the drum on the platform, and then all was silent once again.

The Fool let out a shaky sigh. The man on the drum leant over to him and gave him a friendly nudge. This seemed to put the Fool's mind at rest, as he smiled again.

"I want to leave!" said Jaro defiantly.

The man beside Tiuri nodded understandingly, beckoned at them to follow him and quickly climbed down from the platform. The fugitives followed. When they were at the foot of the tower, Tiuri said, "Why did you help us? Who are you? Can you understand what I'm saying?"

The Man in Green just shook his head. "Tehalon," he said slowly, pointing to the north, where the path led. He was clearly telling them it was where they should go.

"He is showing us the way, Friend," whispered the Fool.

Tiuri had realized that, too, but where did the path lead? He knew, though, that they had little choice but to go the way the man had pointed. In the other direction were the Green River, the Tarnburg and the Red Riders.

"Tehalon," the man repeated, pointing once again. His friend on the tower leant over the rail and made the same gesture.

"Come on," said Tiuri to his companions, and the three of them went the way they'd been asked – or ordered – to go.

The Men in Green watched as they walked away.

2 SENT TO THE NORTH

"I don't like this at all," grumbled Jaro. "We're heading deeper and deeper into their territory – and I know how dangerous it can be to set foot there."

"They did help us, though," said Tiuri.

Jaro muttered something. Then he said, "From the frying pan into the fire. I don't know what's behind it all, but I'm sure they didn't help us because they liked the look of our faces."

"What do you know about the Men in Green?" asked Tiuri. "I thought they were on your side!"

"So did I," said Jaro. "They are under the command of my... of the Black Knight with the Red Shield, but they don't come from Eviellan." He stopped and turned to look at the tower. "They're still watching us," he remarked. He walked on and continued, "They were here long before us. I think they've always lived here."

"It is as you say, friendly enemy," whispered the Fool. "They belong here. And their master is the Master of the Wild Wood."

"Their master is the Lord of the Tarnburg, the Black Knight with the Red Shield," said Jaro. "The Lord of the Tarnburg is Master of the Wild Wood; it has always been that way. The Men in Green handed the Tarnburg over to the Black Knight when he came to the forest."

"How long ago was that?" asked Tiuri.

"I don't know exactly," Jaro replied. "About three years ago, I believe. But it is only since last year that the Black Knight has spent more time here. He has fortified the castle and is gathering a large number of men."

"And when will the attack begin?" Tiuri asked.

Jaro slowed his pace and looked at Tiuri with a frown. "What do you know about that?" he asked.

"He is preparing to attack the Kingdom of Unauwen," said Tiuri, "via the Road of Ambuscade. As I'm sure you must know..." As he spoke, he was overcome by a feeling of uncertainty. Jaro may have saved him, but that didn't necessarily mean he wanted to help foil his master's plans!

"Of course he created this stronghold in the forest for a reason," said Jaro. "And the war with the kingdom to the west is fully underway. We all know he is preparing an attack."

"Don't you know when it will take place?" asked Tiuri.

"No," said Jaro. "And I don't think I would tell you even if I did know. I may no longer wish to serve the Black Knight with the Red Shield, but I'm no traitor!" He walked on more quickly, looking straight ahead. Tiuri cast a sideways glace at him and said, "I know who he is. The Knight with the Red Shield, I mean."

Now Jaro stopped and stared at him with wide eyes. "You know?" he whispered. "But how?"

"He told me himself," replied Tiuri, who had also stopped. "He told me that he plans to cross the mountains with his army. He said he lured Sir Edwinem into an ambush and killed him. He, the..."

"Do not say his name!" whispered Jaro. He lowered his eyes and turned away. "Perhaps you know more than I...," he said. "And if you have spoken to him, then maybe you understand how difficult it is for me to disobey him, even though I fear... no, I *hate* him."

"So why did you return to him?" asked Tiuri.

"Why? I didn't mean to, but..."

Behind them came a sound on the drum. They looked around; the man on the watchtower was signalling at them to move on.

Jaro cursed. "You see, we have to keep going," he said. "They can order us around without even saying a word!"

They walked onwards in the pouring rain. "As soon as the path takes a turn and they can no longer see us, let's head off in a different direction," said Jaro. "I'm not planning to let them send me to this Tehalon like some meek little lamb."

"Who is Tehalon?" asked Tiuri.

"No idea! It could be a place, or a person, or something else... something worse. Only the king... the Black Knight speaks their language, or so I've heard. He is free to enter their territory whenever he wishes. But we are forbidden."

"It is not the language of Eviellan," said Tiuri. "I don't understand a word of it, and yet there's something familiar about it."

"Oh, they understand us, too, you know" said Jaro. "But they don't want anyone to realize. They're always sneaking around and spying. If anything happens in the forest they're usually the first to know and to pass on the news." He lowered his voice and added, "The Red Riders are the elite troops of Eviellan, but I have thought at times that the king seems to expect even more from the Men in Green..."

"Do you really think so?" whispered the Fool. "You don't know their secrets. Oh no, you don't."

"The king is the only one who knows their secrets," said Jaro. "Look," he continued, changing the subject. "The tower's out of sight now and here's something that looks like a side trail. You don't want to keep travelling on to the north either, do you?"

"No," said Tiuri hesitantly, "but I don't like the thought of meeting the Red Riders again."

"And I really don't like the thought of being at the mercy of the Men in Green," said Jaro.

Tiuri could sympathize, but he was still not sure, as they left the road and headed east, that they were doing the right thing.

Soon, though, he was spared the worry. Four of the Men in Green approached them and told them, silently but most firmly, to turn around and continue along the road to the north. The fugitives thought it would be a bad idea to defy the order. The men were armed and, besides, the three of them were exhausted.

And so, reluctantly, they walked onwards, heading more and more slowly, yet still deeper and deeper, into the mysterious region between the Green River and the Green Hills.

*

"I really do need to stop for a little rest!" said Jaro a while later, dropping down onto the moss. His companions did the same, and the three of them lay there with their eyes closed.

"Who would like something to eat?" asked Jaro. "I have a little food left. And as for drink, I've had enough of water. Thank goodness that rain's finally stopped."

"They gave us a drink," said the Fool, "back there, at the tower. Sir Tiuri and I had a drink. Why didn't you, friendly enemy?"

"Please, just call me Jaro," said Jaro. "Yes, I'm sorry now that I refused their drink. The two of you don't look too good, but you're still alive enough, so there probably wasn't any poison in it." He sighed. "What I wouldn't give to know where we're going to end up!" he added. "Shall we just stay lying here on the moss, somewhere between Tehalon and Tarnburg?"

Tiuri sighed, too. "I don't feel able to decide what we should do for the best," he said.

"You see," said Jaro, "those Men in Green have a bad influence on our ability to make decisions. Maybe they're peering out at us now and having a good laugh. But still, I'm going to try to get out of this wretched wood. I wish I'd never set foot in it."

"How long have you been here?" asked Tiuri.

"Oh, so you want to know how I ended up back with the Black Knight, do you?" said Jaro. He turned onto his stomach and picked at the moss.

"I wasn't planning to," he began, "not after everything that happened in the mountains and my conversation with Menaures. I didn't want to go back to Eviellan, but of course I couldn't go to the Kingdom of Unauwen either. And there were Grey Knights roaming the Kingdom of Dagonaut who were looking for me. 'Go and work,' Menaures told me. 'Find some hard, honest work.' But it wasn't easy!" He looked at Tiuri with an expression that was somehow surly and apologetic at the same time. "No, it wasn't easy," he repeated. "Not after the life I'd led. I have no wish to say anything more about that now, but one ill-fated day I met a man who needed woodcutters. It was too late by the time I noticed that the work was in the Wild Wood and, even worse, that it was for the master I'd escaped from, the Black Knight with the Red Shield! Well, of course, his men recognized me immediately and all I could do was act as if I'd returned of my own free will. Otherwise I'd surely have paid with my life! The Black Knight was already angry enough with me; he stripped the symbols of the Red Riders from me because I had not done as he had commanded. From then on, I was one of the lower ranks – they are dressed in green, but wear black caps to distinguish them from the men who live in this part of the forest."

"What happened then?" asked Tiuri.

"Then? Nothing!" said Jaro. "I had to stay. I knew I was serving a bad master, but I was too fond of my life to defy him again. Besides, it was winter when I came to the forest, and I didn't know my way here well enough to risk an escape attempt."

"But now you've done it anyway!" said Tiuri.

"Oh, I'd been planning to give it a try," said Jaro. "And when I recognized you, when you were being led along the Black River, captive and blindfolded, I knew the time had come. I succeeded in freeing you and I shall never return to the Tarnburg."

Tiuri held out his hand and shook Jaro's.

"Oh no," Jaro said a little shyly. "I should thank you. Finally I've found the courage to escape. Although... I fear we are still prisoners..."

Tiuri asked Jaro if he knew anything about Sir Ristridin. But there was nothing Jaro could tell him. Most of the time he had been made to work in and around the castle and was not allowed to ride freely along the paths in the forest, as the Red Riders were. All he knew was that the Black Knight had ordered his men to ensure that no one who entered the forest would ever leave it again.

"I think all the intruders have been slain," he said. "It was only the knights with white shields who were to be brought to him alive."

"Why is that?" whispered Tiuri.

Jaro sat down. "I can only guess," he replied. "He considers those knights his mortal enemies – perhaps he wanted to question them first to find out more about King Unauwen's plans for war. Maybe he wanted to kill them himself, in his own way. But you are the first and only knight with a white shield ever to come here – and you're not even a knight from the west."

I have lost my white shield, thought Tiuri, *and the sword King Unauwen gave me, too.* He felt very low at that point; Piak was not with him and Ardanwen was dead. He closed his eyes and sighed again.

But the Fool gave him a shake and said, "Knight, Friend, shouldn't we keep going?"

"Where to?" Jaro grumbled. "Onwards to the unknown, to Tehalon?"

Tiuri got to his feet. "I think Marius is right," he said. "We can't just stop and rest. We have to take one path or another – it doesn't matter which, as long as it takes us out of this forest."

3   THE DEEP LAKE

The only road they could see, though, led to the north, and for a short while they followed it without saying anything, sometimes going slowly uphill, then back downhill for a while. Then, suddenly, they emerged from the shade of the trees.

On their left was a grassy valley with just a few very young trees. At its centre was a small, deep-green lake. Beyond, the forest began again, dark and dense, and in the far distance they could see slopes and mountain peaks.

Tiuri blinked; he had just looked up at the sun, which was already in the west. But he went on looking, not at the valley and the lake, but at the mountains, the Great Mountains. How very close they seemed – and on the other side lay the realm of King Unauwen!

"That's where I need to go," he whispered.

"What do you mean?" said Jaro. "I don't like the look of that lake at all. It's so still and it looks very deep."

"I meant the mountains," said Tiuri. "I don't know how to get there, but I know that I must. I have to reach the Kingdom of Unauwen before the attack that's coming via the Road of Ambuscade."

"You must be mad!" said Jaro.

Tiuri looked at him. "Now that I know, it's my duty to warn them," he said, his voice trembling slightly. "I have to attempt it, even if it seems impossible. And you mustn't try to stop me," he continued. "The King of Eviellan is a wicked man and you no longer wish to serve him. So do you really want the Kingdom of Unauwen to come under his rule?"

"Calm yourself!" said Jaro. "No, believe me, I don't want that to happen."

Tiuri thought he sounded sincere. He sat down by the side of the path and his friends did the same.

"You're right, Jaro," Tiuri went on. "We can't keep on walking along a path that we were ordered to follow without knowing our goal. Oh, if only I knew when the attack was going to happen!"

"Listen, Tiuri," said Jaro. "I don't agree with your plans at all! And for a number of reasons. Firstly because, even though I happen to have escaped, I don't like the thought of being a traitor..."

"You have to do one thing or the other," Tiuri said firmly, even though he barely raised his voice. "You were born in the Kingdom of Unauwen, and the King of Eviellan is bad. You can't run away from him and yet refuse to fight him."

"That sounds true enough," said Jaro, "but there's something you don't understand. Maybe you're not able to understand. The King of Eviellan is a wicked man, and I know that. And yet still I can't bring myself to turn against him. I would be the first man to say that everyone should fight against him, but still I don't want to play a part in his downfall. I just can't do it!" He looked at Tiuri with something like desperation in his eyes. "You can't understand," he said again. "You haven't known him and served him for years as I have."

Tiuri didn't know how to respond. But he did understand – had he not spoken to the King of Eviellan himself and listened to his words? But he had met Prince Iridian first... He felt a sudden sympathy for Jaro, who no longer wanted to follow the path of evil and so had nowhere to go.

"I'm not saying you have to come with me," he said finally. "I am the one who came upon this information." *And I'm not the only one*, he thought, *but I could be the only one who can still tell someone about it*. "And because I know," he added, "I have to try to foil Eviellan's plans."

"How are you going to get across the mountains?" asked Jaro. "You can't take the Road of Ambuscade, and there is no other way over. There truly isn't."

Tiuri didn't answer. *I've no idea either*, he thought miserably.

"You want to fight the King of Eviellan," Jaro continued. "But you are no more his match than I am. Whole armies have failed to defeat him! You have met him, so you must realize it's madness to think you could take him on."

For a moment, Tiuri was back in the Tarnburg, sitting across from the Black Knight, with the chessboard between them – the game they had not finished. "Yes," he said quietly, "that's true."

"I think there is only one man in the world who could stand up to him," whispered Jaro. "Someone who is just as strong as him..."

"Prince Iridian," said Tiuri.

"But I doubt he would ever want to take up his sword against his twin brother," Jaro added. "I mean in a one-to-one duel."

They fell silent. But Tiuri noticed now that the silence was full of life. A cricket chirped in the grass, and small creatures were moving all around. He shivered; suddenly he felt cold.

"In any case we have to get away from here," said Jaro. He struggled to his feet and held out a hand to help Tiuri up. "I am afraid this could be the Deep Lake," he continued, "and I've heard nasty stories about that place. The Deep Lake, where sacrifices were once made to the evil spirits of the forest. I don't want to say another word about that, but you know that the King of Eviellan also rules over the Men in Green. You are still on his land, Tiuri, and so you must flee with us from this place!"

When Tiuri did not move, Jaro added, "You can only fight against him once you have placed yourself beyond his reach. Outside of this forest there are better roads and you have friends who can help you."

"That is true," Tiuri agreed.

Now the Fool spoke to him. "Stay here, Friend," he said. "This man Jaro is afraid, but he does not know the secrets. I have already told you that. Stay here and wait."

"What for?" asked Tiuri, rather puzzled. The Fool had always been afraid of the Men in Green.

"I... I... I don't know," the Fool replied.

"Well, what I know is that we're wasting precious time!" said Jaro impatiently. "We have to head to the east and make sure we get to the other side of the Green River. Perhaps we'll reach civilization that way."

"You can't!" said the Fool. "Look, there's another one. Down by the lake."

"The devil take him," said Jaro. "I'm leaving."

"Don't say that," whispered the Fool, going after Jaro. "He's calling us."

"Let's pretend we haven't seen him," said Jaro, without stopping. Tiuri went with him.

"There are two of them now," said the Fool. "They're both calling us."

Yes, they were standing by the lake, beckoning to them. Tiuri and Jaro stopped and looked at each other.

"We can't just run away," whispered Tiuri. "They'll be sure to stop us!"

"We have to go to them," said the Fool.

"Then we shall do that!" said Tiuri, suddenly decided. And to Jaro he added, "It wouldn't be the first time Marius has been right about a situation. Without him I would never have found out who lives in this forest. Besides, I see no other possibility. Right now we just have to do what they want!"

They walked slowly down into the valley, the Fool leading the way, and Jaro bringing up the rear. Tiuri looked up at the mountains again. "If only I knew how much time we have left," he said to himself.

Jaro heard his words and said, "I don't know when the attack will happen. But I think it will be late spring or early summer, when the pass is free of snow and the road is passable for an army with horses."

Tiuri thought of Piak. His friend knew all about the mountains; he could have told him when that would be. Oh, Piak...

"Are you not scared of anything else?" asked Jaro beside him.

"What do you mean?" asked Tiuri.

"An army by the Black River, closer to your own land than to the Kingdom of Unauwen. It actually *is* your own land! You are a knight of King Dagonaut, after all!"

Tiuri looked at him aghast. It was true; he had hardly thought about the danger that might be threatening the Kingdom of Dagonaut!

They soon reached the shore of the lake. The two men had greeted them without speaking, but did not seem unfriendly, and they asked them in their usual, silent way to walk with them to the opposite shore. But Tiuri said, slowly and clearly, "You are telling us where we must go... but why? We are fugitives and mean no harm. Do you hear what I'm saying?" The men nodded, their faces serious.

"But do you actually understand, too?" asked Tiuri. "We don't want to do as you say until we know what you plan to do with us."

"That's right," said Jaro. "You tell them!"

One of the men pointed at the sun, slowly lowered his arm, and said, "Tehalon."

"That again!" growled Jaro.

"Who or what is Tehalon?" asked Tiuri. "Is it a person?"

The man nodded again. He frowned and seemed to be thinking for a moment. Then his face brightened and with a solemn gesture he laid his weapons – spear, bow and arrows – at Tiuri's feet. Then he looked at Tiuri and gave him a cheerful grin. He reminded Tiuri of Tirillo for a moment – the same wry, pointed face – and suddenly the man had a personality of his own. Until then, the Men in Green had all looked the same to Tiuri.

This man appeared to read his mind. He grinned again, pointed at himself, and said, "Twarik." Then he put a finger on Tiuri's chest and said, "Tee-ooh-ri."

Tiuri looked at him, a little surprised, although he shouldn't have been too astonished that his name was known to the Men in Green. After all, Jaro had said they knew everything.

The other man now followed his companion's example. He put down his weapons and introduced himself as "Lian." He was small and slender, and had no beard.

"Delighted to make your acquaintance," said Jaro sarcastically.

The Fool said with a shy laugh, "The Fool in the Forest is what they call me, but my name is actually Marius."

Tiuri suddenly felt lighter. "I have to believe that you mean us well," he said. "We will follow you."

The men loped ahead of them around the lake shore. When they reached the other side, they were made to sit down beside a pile of wood, and Twarik lit a fire.

"It would seem that we're supposed to stay here," Jaro remarked.

"It just occurred to me that they allowed us to keep our weapons," said Tiuri. "That shows they have good intentions."

"Don't be too sure of that! There are so many of them. There's no way we could take them all on," replied Jaro. "I'd rather not be sitting here, but as things stand, I think we should just rest and eat. That's if they have any food for us."

They did. The Men in Green brought them wild apples and hunks of meat, which they cooked over the fire. They joined them to eat, but then disappeared into the trees, where it was already getting dark.

The Fool stood at the edge of the lake, peering into the water, and said, "It is deep, so very deep! But it is not a lake of evil spirits, not as Jaro thought. Not anymore. It makes me sad, not scared."

"Don't the Men in Green make you scared anymore either, Marius?" Tiuri asked quietly.

"N... no," replied the Fool. "Not now. They speak to me – not with words, but still they speak." He stretched out in the grass by the shore and continued thoughtfully, "For the first time I am not longing for my home and my cabin, Friend. And that is good, because you cannot take me there yet. If I cannot go there, then I want to stay here. I have never been here before, so I did not know what it was like."

"Is this place... good?" asked Tiuri.

"Yes..." said the Fool slowly, and he yawned.

Tiuri went for a wander around the valley. He stopped by a path that led to the west. There was a large stone there, with words carved into it. It was exactly the same kind of stone as the one by the path to the Unholy Hills, and the words written upon it probably meant the same.

> *You who come as an enemy,*
> *now retrace your steps*
> *or may the Wood devour you!*

Was the language of the Men in Green, which had sounded so familiar to him on the watchtower, the same language as this, the old secret language of the Kingdom of Unauwen?

He thought about Isadoro. He wished he had asked her more questions when he'd had the chance. He tried to picture her, but she remained hazy, like a dream that leaves a strange feeling upon awakening.

The sound of a voice made him look around in surprise. A woman's voice... how was that possible, here in this forest? A man's voice replied, and it was two men who came walking down the track: Lian and Twarik. Lian said something to his companion, but fell silent when he saw Tiuri.

He...? Lian was not a Man but a *Woman* in Green, a woman, dressed and armed like a hunter. Tiuri stared at her. There was no doubt about it, although he'd never heard of such a thing before, except in stories.

Lian and Twarik both smiled and walked past him, to the place where Jaro and the Fool were sitting by the fire.

Tiuri followed them. *They belong together,* he thought. *They must be husband and wife.* And he wondered if more of the Men in Green were actually women.

The sun sank behind the trees and mountains. Lian stamped out the fire. Tiuri looked at Jaro; would he notice she was a woman, too? But Jaro wasn't paying attention to anything; he looked as if he was working on an escape plan.

Then Twarik signalled at them to follow him beneath the trees, where they found three hammocks.

"Do we have to sleep in those things?" said Jaro. "Like birds in a nest?"

Tiuri laughed. "They're high and they're dry," he said. He looked at Twarik and said, "When will we be free to come and go as we please?" He used gestures to make his words as easy as possible to understand.

Twarik shrugged and simply replied, "Tehalon."

"So we have to wait for Tehalon," muttered Jaro. "Then I'll just crawl into this hammock and hope he doesn't see me."

A moment later they had climbed into their hammocks. They were actually comfortable, Tiuri realized. Twarik and Lian went away again, but he was sure they would remain nearby.

Now he realized just how tired he was, and finally he would be able to have a peaceful night's sleep. He could not imagine that the King of Eviellan was the ruler here as well – and that he might appear and take him prisoner once again.

He dreamt he was drifting in a boat on the lake. Slowly he sank into its depths, but he was not afraid. All around him was green half-light; ragged plants waved to and fro, and fish looked at him with dimly gleaming eyes. He sank still deeper, darkness enveloping him... but suddenly it was torn apart by a bright light that shone in his face.

He awoke slowly and reluctantly. Someone was leaning over him with a lantern. Startled, he tried to sit up, but the hammock rocked and he fell back into it.

The figure held up a hand to block the light. Now it illuminated the figure's face instead, which looked down at Tiuri like a ghostly mask, angular and weather-beaten. But still Tiuri recognized him. It was the Man in Green he had seen by the Black River, the man against whom not even Ardanwen had dared to protest. In the flickering light, his face looked even more mysterious, and not a little frightening.

"W-what... is it?" stammered Tiuri.

"Do you want to sleep? Or are you awake?" came the quiet response. "If you are awake, I would like to speak to you."

"I'm awake," said Tiuri. He scrambled out of his hammock and stood swaying unsteadily.

"Quietly, then," whispered the Man in Green, taking Tiuri by the arm. "Come with me."

They walked for a way around the lake. The man blew out his lantern and Tiuri realized it was not completely dark. He could see the water, the slope on the opposite shore and the outline of the trees against the sky. As he looked at his companion, it dawned on him that he had spoken to him in his own language.

299

"Who are you?" he asked. "And what do you want to tell me?"

"We have seen each other before," said the man. His voice was low and he spoke slowly and deliberately. "You were a knight with a white shield and you rode along the Black River on a black horse, captured by the Red Riders. You escaped the Tarnburg, with one of your companions. But the third man who is with you now is not the one with whom you came into the wood, but a servant of the knight who lives in the Tarnburg. The other one was not captured. Where did he go?"

Piak! thought Tiuri. Oh, if only he knew what had happened to his friend. "I do not know," he said. "But who are you?"

"I watched you while you were sleeping," came the reply, "and I decided to speak to you. Can you not guess who I am?" He stopped and let go of Tiuri's arm.

"Are you... Tehalon?" Tiuri asked quietly.

"Yes, Tehalon, that is what the Men in Green call me. In your language that simply means 'Master'. I am the Master of the Wild Wood."

4 THE MASTER OF THE WILD WOOD

"**B**-but surely..." Tiuri stammered in surprise, trying in vain to see more of the other man's face. "You... Tehalon... the Master of the Wild Wood? I thought that was the Lord of the Tarnburg."

"The Lord of the Tarnburg!" said Tehalon contemptuously. "You thought the knight who lives in the castle of my forefathers was the Master of the Wild Wood? Perhaps he thinks that himself, but he will go away and disappear. My sons will not even know his name. I have always been here. I was here when he came. I allowed him to take up residence in the castle I had abandoned... what did I care? He may call himself the Lord of the Tarnburg and imagine he is king here and ruler of this place. But it is I who am Master of the Wild

Wood. I shall remain here and my sons after me, when he is long gone and forgotten."

Tiuri fell silent. Tehalon's formidable personality made his words very believable, but still he had to take a moment to let everything sink in. It was not the King of Eviellan who commanded the Men in Green! And the Master of the Wild Wood had not spoken very kindly of him – and was anything but subservient.

"Does this surprise you?" said Tehalon. "Strangers recently started to come into the Wild Wood, and they are all amazed to find out who lives here. And yet we have been here since time immemorial! But history becomes legend, and legends are forgotten. The song of the fortress by mountains and by rivers wide has not been sung outside this area for a long time."

"But it has!" said Tiuri. "I have heard of it. And about the lord who lived in the Tarnburg..."

"And the wood that grew up and hid his castle," Tehalon said, completing his sentence for him. "He forgot about the world and the world forgot about him. He was my ancestor. He came from the kingdom beyond the Great Mountains, at a time when they still spoke the language I speak, the language that has been forgotten now by everyone, except the Men in Green."

"No," whispered Tiuri, "that language still exists, as the old secret language of King Unauwen and his paladins."

"You know more than I would have expected from someone of your age," said Tehalon. "Well, now you also know that the Master of the Wild Wood never ceased to exist. His son and grandson lived on after him in the Tarnburg. But castles decay and become ruins, as trees grow and forests turn wilder. When I became Master of this forest, I left the Tarnburg and chose to live in the Green Grottos, near the source of the Green River. I do not live there alone. Many Men in Green are descendants of the followers of the first Lord of the Tarnburg. Others came later, seeking what I have found: peace, far from the wicked world."

"So what about now?" whispered Tiuri. "Now that the Red Riders have come here, and the Black Knight with the Red Shield?"

"That will pass," said Tehalon. "Their stay in my wood is for them only a stop on the way to somewhere else."

"But do you know why they are here?" asked Tiuri. "And what they want?"

"I know everything that happens in my forest," replied Tehalon. "That is why I said they will leave."

"And go where?" whispered Tiuri.

"That is no concern of mine. They will not be here much longer – and that is as it should be, for they are filled with cruelty, anger and vengeance, and they have disturbed the peace of this place."

"So why did you tolerate their presence?" asked Tiuri.

"I shall never use violence and lower myself to their way of behaving. We Men in Green wish to live in peace. We take up arms only to defend ourselves if attacked."

Tehalon looked at the trees, where Tiuri's friends were sleeping. Two silhouettes crouched nearby on the shore of the lake: Lian and Twarik. Then he slowly climbed the slope and Tiuri walked with him, in silent wonder. In the east it was already getting light; the morning star was the only one still shining brightly.

They stopped on the path, looking down at the valley. The lake lay down below, a patch of gleaming blackness. "Behold part of my domain," said the Master of the Wild Wood, "part of the realm that still remains our own, between Green Hills and Green River. None may enter it without our permission and remain unpunished. But we will not turn away anyone who is pursued and seeks refuge. You and your companions are safe here. The power of the Red Riders counts for nothing in this place."

"Thank you, my lord," said Tiuri softly. So the Men in Green really did mean them well. And yet he was still not entirely sure about them and he had many questions to ask.

"Let me finish," said Tehalon. "I am not saying we are pleased that you have come here. For you are entangled within the threads that have been spun in the Tarnburg – threads that are connected to the world outside the wood. And that world must remain outside of this forest!"

"Why, my lord?" asked Tiuri. "You can't prevent the world from entering the forest, can you? King Dagonaut..."

"King Dagonaut lives far from here," said Tehalon, interrupting him. "He rules over a large kingdom and the Wild Wood is a part of it – on his maps! In truth he cannot be the ruler here, because he does not even know of our existence. Understand me, young man, I do not wish to dispute Dagonaut's power. I make no claim to a royal title. I am the Master of the Wild Wood. I know this place. I am part of it! The Men in Green have lived here for as long as the House of Dagonaut has existed."

"And when Dagonaut's knights came into the wood, you allowed them to be murdered without raising a hand!" Tiuri began furiously.

"No. *We* were not their enemies," said Tehalon simply. "And we have nothing to do with other people's fights. We wished only that it had not taken place in our wood, which should be a place of peace."

But Tiuri could no longer feel any sympathy for the peaceful Men in Green. "But you have allowed the Knight with the Red Shield to create a stronghold here," he said. "You know who he is! He is wicked, dangerous – an enemy."

"*Your* enemy perhaps," said Tehalon, "but not ours. We were wary when he came, although we did nothing. After a while, however, we made the condition that his men could not set foot in our territory between the hills and the river. That way we still had our peace. And we knew he would soon leave, or we would have had to drive him out. He does not like this wood; he longs for power over many people, over castles and cities of stone."

Tiuri stared at him. He could now vaguely see the hard, angular face. "And do you think it would be a good thing for him to gain that power?" he whispered.

303

"I do not think it good," said Tehalon calmly, "but I know the world cannot be changed. I know it! Always, war has just finished or is newly begun – even the realm of King Unauwen has been touched by its rot since his sons have come of age." He gestured at Tiuri to remain silent. "I wanted to speak to you because I wished to find out more about you," he said, "and now I know enough. You intend to fight the King of Eviellan, even though you have only just escaped from him. You're caught up in this struggle, involved in a quarrel that is not yours!"

"But it *is* my quarrel," Tiuri began.

"No," said Tehalon. "Let the Black Knight cross the mountains, so that the war between Eviellan and Unauwen can reach the conclusion that has long been written in the stars."

Tiuri was filled with fear. He could tell it would be very difficult to convince the Master of the Wild Wood that he had to choose a side.

"Surely you cannot mean that, my lord!" he said.

"Even before I had spoken to you, I knew you would cause me problems," said Tehalon. He sat down and gave a gentle sigh, adding in a tone that was almost bored, "Go ahead, then. Say what you want to say."

Tiuri dropped down on the ground beside Tehalon and spoke to him. He told him what he knew and what he'd been through, and finished by saying that the King of Eviellan had to be opposed, that he could not be allowed to pass along the Road of Ambuscade.

"What does it matter if he takes this road or another?" said Tehalon. "As long as he leaves the wood without causing any more conflict here? Then we shall soon forget him, and think: *It is over.*"

The stars had become pale, the birds were chirping; day had dawned. For Tiuri, though, everything was still dark and grey.

The Master of the Wild Wood had heard his words, but he had not listened. And, even worse, the man did not intend to let him go!

"If the Road of Ambuscade is blocked on the other side of the mountains, the King of Eviellan will remain here," Tehalon said. "And that would be a disaster for this forest. No, I cannot let you go, because if you tell your king what you know, Dagonaut's knights are sure to come here. They will challenge the threat that resides in the Tarnburg... War will rage in the wood, and I cannot allow that to happen!"

He took a long look at Tiuri, who was still sitting beside him. His face was as impassive as ever, but there was a twinkle in his eyes. "I don't really know what to do with you," he added. "The Men in Green never take prisoners. But we shall have to keep you here long enough for you to realize that your efforts are pointless." He stood up and started to walk.

Dismayed, Tiuri jumped to his feet and followed him. He knew very well that he would never be able to escape from the Men in Green. Jaro had been right after all.

They stopped beneath the trees that lined the southern side of the valley. The Master of the Wild Wood placed his hand on a trunk and said, in a much less measured tone than before, "I cannot act any differently. I love this forest and I want it to remain unspoilt."

He is no more human than the trees of the Wild Wood, Tiuri thought bitterly. *I might as well talk to a log or a stone.*

Tehalon went on speaking: about trees, plants and animals, about hidden springs and secret paths in the forest. Tiuri barely listened to what he was saying but, even so, the tone of Tehalon's voice gave Tiuri hope that maybe he could make this man relent after all.

Tehalon seemed to notice Tiuri's expression, because suddenly he stopped and said, "One day you will no longer hate me. Now return to your companions." He started to walk away.

Tiuri was sure he would never have another opportunity like this to talk to him. So he said – no, he almost yelled, "Tehalon!"

The Master of the Wild Wood paused and waited.

"You want to live here in peace," began Tiuri, "and not interfere with other people. So why are you stopping me from doing what I want? You must..." He faltered for a moment. If only Tehalon's face would show some sign of emotion! He would rather have seen anger than that blank expression.

"You must also allow me, too, to do as I want, freely and without hindrance," he continued, "because..."

He paused, trying to come up with truly convincing words, but instead, to his horror, he burst into tears. He tried to control himself, but it was no good; his sobs welled up until his whole body shook. He turned away and hid his face in his hands, deeply ashamed. There he stood, Sir Tiuri, crying like a child.

After what seemed like an eternity of misery, he felt a hand on his shoulder. It was Tehalon, who forced Tiuri to look at him. Tiuri could hardly see his face, even after he'd briskly wiped his eyes.

"Sometimes it is good to weep," spoke the Master of the Wild Wood calmly. "And you need not be ashamed of your tears."

Tiuri stepped away from him and did not reply. He wished Tehalon would go away. But the man crossed his arms over his chest and did not move.

Suddenly a drum sounded nearby. *Boom.* That was followed by a rapid drumroll. *Tok-tok-tok-tok...*

Tehalon raised his head to listen. *Boom! Tok-tok-tok-tok...*

The sound was repeated from afar – perhaps from the watchtower by the river. The drum nearby went boom once again, and the other drum replied.

Tehalon looked to the north and said, "They say many men are approaching from that direction..."

Only now did Tiuri see a second watchtower, rising up above the trees.

"I must go there," Tehalon said to him. "Follow me later, with your companions. Perhaps our conversation is not yet over." With quick steps, he loped away.

Tiuri leant against a tree and pressed his face against the rough trunk. The tears were over. But still, when he saw his friends coming, he hid behind the tree. He was not ready yet to face them. They walked around the lake, and then towards the watchtower. The Fool was looking around, as if seeking Tiuri. Lian and Twarik brought up the rear.

I'll follow you soon, thought Tiuri.

A couple of minutes later he did just that, but first he knelt down beside the lake and washed his face with cold water. Then he started running and went after his friends.

Suddenly, Tiuri felt light and relieved, and in good spirits.

"Many men are approaching..." Tehalon had said. Perhaps Tiuri could take advantage of the situation, and escape while the attention of the Men in Green was elsewhere. "Many men..." – maybe even friends and allies. They were coming from the north, from outside the wood.

Behind him, another drum sounded.

5   PIAK AND ADELBART

Piak stood on the bank of the Green River. "Don't let any fate worse than capture befall Tiuri," he prayed.

"Over there. That's where they live," said Adelbart from behind him.

Piak just gazed at the water and did not reply.

"You're afraid, aren't you?" said Adelbart. "That they'll harm your friends. But whatever they may be, they are not wicked people. Unless they've changed a great deal." Piak turned to stare at him.

Adelbart acted as if he didn't notice, but looked at the opposite bank, deep in thought. "No," he said. "I'm sure they remain the same, just as they have always been. But the circumstances may have changed, and..."

"What are you talking about?" Piak exploded. "Are you talking about the Men in Green? So you do know them! What can you tell me about them?"

"Not much," replied Adelbart.

In the distance, the drums sounded again. An immediate answer came from nearby.

"Now there's something approaching from the other direction," said Adelbart.

"Ah, is that what you think?" said the Lord of Mistrinaut, walking over to stand beside Piak.

"He doesn't think – he *knows*!" Piak cried. "He knows far more about the enemy than he has told us!"

Lord Rafox gave Adelbart a searching look.

Adelbart shuffled his feet, tugged at his belt, pulled a face, and then said, "To be honest, I've never regarded them as enemies. I know them as peaceful men, even though they know how to use weapons."

"It is time, Adelbart," said the Lord of Mistrinaut sternly, "for you to tell us your story."

Adelbart sighed. "Very well, my lord, here it is," he said. "Some time ago, when I was a good deal younger, I once went into the forest, along this path. Of course, I got lost, became hungry and thirsty, was bitten by beasts... In short, I was in a wretched state and I would surely have died if the Men in Green had not found me. They took care of me, and when I was back to my old self, I stayed with them – a summer, an autumn and a winter. But Piak knows what I am like: one day I longed to see something different, and so I said I wanted to leave. They let me go but made me solemnly promise that I would never, ever say anything about them to anyone else. I have kept that promise – until now. And I don't know which is worse: not saying anything before or saying something now."

"The situation now is so serious that you must speak," said the Lord of Mistrinaut. "What kind of men are they, these peaceful

Men in Green? Come with me. Brother Martin and my captains need to hear this, too. And I am sure your story is not yet finished."

"That really is all, my lord," said Adelbart a few moments later, when they were all seated in a small circle on the ground. "The Men in Green have lived here for centuries, and their home is in the Green Grottos. Once, they say, Tehalon had a castle..."

"Who is Tehalon?"

"He is their leader. They call him the Master of the Wild Wood. He has turned away from the world and is not keen on strangers."

"And did he ever attack anyone?" asked the Lord of Mistrinaut.

"Never, my lord. I spent almost a year with the Men in Green, and I was their companion on the hunt and on many wanderings. If others entered the forest, they knew immediately. They always know exactly what is going on in the wood. They have a great many guard posts, some in trees, others in towers, and they pass on important news by sounding their drums. Every combination of drumbeats means something – they probably just announced your approach."

"And what will they do, now that they know?"

"They used to hide from every stranger," replied Adelbart. "But back then hardly anyone ever came here. After all, most people believe they're woodland spirits." He looked around the circle and then continued, "I don't believe they're wicked, but I do think they may be dangerous. They are master archers, but that's not what matters most. Unlike us, they are so at home in these woods that it is almost uncanny. It is quite possible that, at this very moment, they are listening to every word I say."

He glanced around, and his listeners automatically did the same.

"And now I am coming to the end of my story," said Adelbart. "I returned to them. Only one Man in Green would show himself to me – a special friend of mine. Twarik was his name. He told me that Tehalon would allow me to stay only if I swore never to leave. And well... I did not dare to do that. Twarik told me something had changed in the forest. He and his friends never went south of the Black River now and strangers were less welcome than ever. He would not tell me more, but I had the impression that others had come to live in the forest. After saying farewell to Twarik, I stayed in the wood and headed eastwards. That's where I discovered the Forgotten City."

"Do you know anything else about these 'others'?" asked Lord Rafox.

Adelbart took a deep breath and said, "I lived in the Forgotten City with some friends of mine." He glanced at Piak. "We were hunters. Some of them went along the Black River to the west and never returned – all except one. He told me people were living there, soldiers. He was scared and ran away from them. I once saw a few of them in the distance myself: men on horses, dressed in red."

"Red Riders?" whispered Piak, his eyes wide with shock and amazement.

"Red Riders?!" exclaimed Lord Rafox.

Adelbart was startled by their reaction. "Did I say something wrong?" he asked.

"It is just a pity you did not mention this before," said the Lord of Mistrinaut. "Go on!"

"I have nothing else to say!" cried Adelbart. "I have said everything and told you no lies. Really and truly. I'd happily swear it, if only I knew what to swear upon. Who are these Red Riders?"

"They come from Eviellan," replied Piak.

"Oh," said Adelbart, but it was clear that he was none the wiser.

"Red Riders," repeated Lord Rafox, with a worried frown. "It could just be a few of them, but maybe more. And if that's the case... Oh, Adelbart, why didn't you tell us this right away?!"

"My lord," said Adelbart. "I would like to make up for my mistake. So I have a suggestion. Let me cross the river, as your envoy. I have already told you the Men in Green do not like intruders, and there are many of them. But I know them, I speak their language, I can talk to them. They will not harm me if I enter their territory..."

"And what if they hide from you?" said Lord Rafox.

"I know a certain call," whispered Adelbart, "a signal, a cry that will make every one of them come to me. Twarik taught it to me, and told me to use it only if I had something very important to say." In a louder voice, he continued, "Let me go, my lord! Right away! We will have a better idea of what course of action to take once I have spoken to them."

"Perhaps it's not such a bad idea," said the Lord of Mistrinaut.

"There's a watchtower nearby," said Adelbart eagerly. "I remember the way. It's about a couple of hours' walk. Give me until this evening, or tomorrow morning – whichever you think best. If I'm not back by then... well, then something's gone wrong." He paused and then quickly added, "But that's not going to happen."

"Agreed," said Lord Rafox, standing up.

"And I want to go with him," said Piak.

Both Lord Rafox and Adelbart shook their heads doubtfully.

"Please say yes!" said Piak. "Adelbart doesn't even know Tiuri. He has no idea what he looks like. I want to go. It's always better to travel together and I'm surely the most suitable companion for Adelbart."

"He has a point," said Adelbart. "And I honestly don't think we'll be in any danger."

6   A BLACK SHADOW

Piak and Adelbart were soon on the opposite bank of the river. Adelbart walked first along the water for some way, to a point where a stream met the river. He led Piak along the stream into the lands of the Men in Green. The ground was boggy and the grass and leaves were wet with dew. "Keep an eye out," said Adelbart. "There should be a path somewhere around here that leads to the tower."

"Listen!" said Piak.

"Someone's shouting something," Adelbart replied. "Probably just one of Lord Rafox's men. Their camp's still near enough."

"I can hear someone coming," said Piak. "From the river." Yes, there he came, one of Mistrinaut's men, dressed in blue. "What is it?" he called, trying not to shout too loud.

In just a few moments, the person had reached them.

"Lavinia!" exclaimed Piak.

"Sssh," she said. "I'm Fox." Out of breath, she stopped and wiped her forehead. Piak and Adelbart saw that her clothes were wet.

"What's wrong?" whispered Piak.

"I'm glad you hadn't gone too far," she said. "I had to go back quite a way to find a spot where I could cross the river without being seen."

"But why?" asked Piak sharply.

"I have my reasons," said Lavinia. "I saw something you need to know about. I hope we can still find it."

"What?"

"A black shadow."

"A what?" said Adelbart.

"A black shadow," repeated Lavinia. "Come on, before it's gone."

"Yes, but, my lady..." began Adelbart.

"My name is Fox!" she said. "Please, come with me. It's not far. I saw it when I was on the other bank, and I crossed the river as quickly as I could."

"You swam?" asked Piak, rather impressed.

"Swam, waded, floated," said Fox. "Quickly, or it'll have gone. This way."

"But what is it?!" said Piak, as he and Adelbart walked with her.

"I told you. A black shadow," Fox replied. "I'm not saying any more than that. You need to see it for yourselves. I hope you'll see for yourself what I don't yet quite dare to think. Although... maybe it's better if it's not what I think it is."

"Now I really am lost!" muttered Adelbart.

"It was around here somewhere," Fox soon whispered.

They saw snapped branches and trampled grass.

"So it's not a ghost, this shadow," said Adelbart. "It looks more like an animal's trail."

"Sssh!" said Fox. "Quietly does it... Look, there!"

"Oh... yes," said Piak in a low voice. He could see something dark moving among the trees. And it wasn't a person.

Fox stopped.

"Go and take a look," she said.

"It's not dangerous, is it?" asked Adelbart.

"I hope not," said Fox. "Just go and see if it's him," she continued to Piak. She suddenly seemed doubtful. "Maybe I just imagined it," she murmured. "Oh, I'm sorry I..."

As Piak cautiously walked onwards, the shadow moved away from him. If only he could see what it was... He quickened his pace, afraid of losing sight of whatever it was that was fleeing into the trees. Fox and Adelbart followed behind.

Piak stopped. The vegetation ahead of him was less dense – and there it stood.

"A horse!" whispered Adelbart behind him.

A black horse with a wild mane, looking around skittishly, as if it were about to bolt.

Piak hardly dared to breathe.

Fox came and stood beside him; he felt her fingers gripping his arm. "Do you see him?" she whispered in his ear. And he knew what she really wanted to say, "Is it him?"

Piak looked at her and his lips formed a name.

Ardanwen!

As Piak approached, the horse raised his head and restlessly twitched his ears.

"Whoa. Easy, Ardanwen, Night Wind," he said quietly. Ardanwen must have recognized him, too, but seemed very nervous. "Ardanwen!" Piak repeated. "Good, loyal horse. Easy, boy. Come to me."

The horse gave a whinny and trotted over to him, then bent his neck and allowed Piak to stroke him.

"Ardanwen," whispered Piak, "what happened to you? Your coat is full of scratches and you're all alone. Oh, Night Wind, where is Tiuri?"

"So it really is him," said Fox, coming to stand beside them. "But then... where is Tiuri?" Her voice was trembling.

Ardanwen pulled away from Piak, shaking his mane, but Piak soon calmed him.

"This is Sir Tiuri's horse," Piak said to Adelbart. "The most loyal and intelligent animal in the land. If he is here, Tiuri cannot be far..." His voice trailed off. Again he was gripped by fear for his friend's fate.

Adelbart understood, as his expression was grave and thoughtful.

Lavinia stroked Ardanwen's nose. "If only you could talk," she whispered. "Where is your master? I'm sure you haven't abandoned him."

"The horse has neither reins nor saddle," said Adelbart. "Just a piece of rope around his neck, with a frayed end, as if he somehow tore himself free."

"What now?" asked Lavinia.

"Whatever we do, we have to keep going," said Adelbart, "to find the Men in Green. That's what we agreed. And as far as you're concerned, I think it would be best for you to return immediately."

"I agree," said Piak.

"And you can take the horse," said Adelbart.

"No, Ardanwen should stay with us," said Piak. "He could lead us to Tiuri."

"Let's go on together, the four of us," said Fox. "I'd rather not go back and have to cross that river again, and besides..."

"No, I can't agree to that!" said Piak.

"Why not?"

"They could take you prisoner, use you as a hostage. What will your... Lord Rafox have to say about that?"

"He's right," said Adelbart. "Although the Men in Green won't be surprised to see you, my lady... I mean, young master Fox. Their women and girls often wear such clothing when they roam the forest with their menfolk."

"They do?" said Fox. "Then you can't possibly have any objection to my joining you, can you? Who was it who found Ardanwen? Me! I'm sure I could help in other ways, too."

But Piak was still shaking his head.

"Fine. You can say no if you like," said Lavinia, "but you can't order me about. I make my own decisions. Ever since I've been Fox, I only do what I want to do, and I know exactly what I'm doing now. Let's not talk any longer."

"We've already had quite a delay," remarked Adelbart, "and we still have to get back to the stream. I don't know the way otherwise."

"But you'll have Tiuri's horse Ardanwen with you," said Lavinia. "Go! And I'll take my leave of you here."

"That's most sensible of you," said Piak with relief. "Can you find your way back to the river?"

"Of course I can," said Lavinia. "Farewell." She walked away without waiting for a reply.

"It really is better that she didn't come," said Piak to Adelbart, as they continued their journey. "I wouldn't be able to face Lord Rafox... and Tiuri if anything happened to her."

"Lord Rafox... Fox!" said Adelbart and he gave a whistle. "Oh, so that's how it is." Then he looked around. "Listen," he said. "I can already hear the stream."

"I can hear plenty of other things, too," whispered Piak. "All kinds of creatures appear to be skulking around in the undergrowth."

"It's always like that in a forest," said Adelbart. "But..." he went on a little later, "there is indeed someone wandering around. And this time it's not a black shadow. By my beard, I think it's Fox!"

Yes, it was Fox! They met her at the stream.

"Ah, what a coincidence," she said with a friendly smile. "Fancy you going the same way as me."

Piak tried to look indignant. What now? He couldn't force her to go back, could he?

"Just give up," said Fox. "Pretend you can't see me. I'm setting off on my own." She turned her back on them and walked off along the stream.

Adelbart and Piak followed her with Ardanwen. But after a while Adelbart called out, "Hey, we're crossing the stream!"

Now it was Lavinia who was walking behind; first across the stream and then quickly along little paths through the forest.

"I feel as if we're wandering around in circles," Piak remarked. He looked back and called to Lavinia, "Fox! Please come and walk with us. We all know you're going the same way as us."

"You're right," said Adelbart. "And would you like to put my coat around your shoulders, young master Fox? It's not very elegant, but I suddenly realized you must be cold."

"That's very kind, but no thank you," said Lavinia. "I'm already dry, thanks to the speed we're walking at. I don't understand, Adelbart, how you can be so sure of the direction. I'd have got lost ages ago. And I'd keep stopping to look around in case someone was lying in ambush."

"Oh, I don't really know the way either," said Adelbart. "But I'm sure the Men in Green will come to us. If they don't arrive soon, I'll call for them."

That, however, did not prove necessary. Less than half an hour later, two Men in Green strode towards them, with two more following. With a gesture of their spears, they ordered them to stop.

7   THE ENEMY

Piak and Lavinia stood close together, nervously studying the men. They looked like fighters, but did not seem cruel.

Adelbart placed one hand on his chest and said, "Giaruda!"

"Giaruda!" replied one of the men, an expression of surprise on his face. But the others said nothing. They looked from Adelbart to Ardanwen and then from Ardanwen to Piak and Fox.

"Giaruda," said Adelbart again and then he cleared his throat. There was silence as they all stared at one another.

"Tell them, Adelbart," Piak said quietly, "about us being envoys, and everything else."

Adelbart began to speak their language, rather haltingly. The Men in Green listened to him with no expression on their faces.

"Oh, I know very well that you understand my language, too!" Adelbart cried finally. "We are envoys from the mighty Lord of Mistrinaut and we have come to ask if you know anything about Sir Tiuri with the White Shield. We need to talk to Tehalon himself."

One of the men nodded and replied.

"It seems Tehalon is nearby," Adelbart whispered to Piak.

Another man pointed at Ardanwen and said something.

"He has been following this horse for some time," Adelbart translated. "It was very skittish and kept escaping."

"This is Sir Tiuri's horse!" Piak said loudly. "And I would like to know how it came to be here!"

Adelbart was about to translate, but the Man in Green seemed to have understood, because he shrugged his shoulders, shook his head and indicated that they should go with him.

"And I'm sure we have to obey, don't we?" said Piak. The men nodded vigorously and said, "Tehalon."

"To Tehalon. Lead on, then," said Adelbart.

They walked for some time, at least a couple of hours. Little was said. Adelbart occasionally spoke to one of their escorts, but he hardly received any response, perhaps because he didn't seem to have a very firm grasp of their language or maybe just because the Men in Green were not very talkative.

317

Then another Man in Green suddenly appeared on the path.

"Twarik!" Adelbart cried with delight.

This Man in Green's eyes widened in surprise. "Giaruda, Adelbart," he said.

Now there was plenty of talking – first by Adelbart and Twarik, and then by Adelbart and Piak. Twarik said Tehalon would definitely want to hear their story soon.

"Have you heard anything about Tiuri?" asked Piak. The uncertainty was gnawing away at him and he'd gathered that Twarik could understand what he said.

"Answer him, Twarik," said Adelbart. "You can do it."

The Man in Green looked searchingly at Piak, glanced at Lavinia, and then spoke quietly in their language, "Tiuri and his friends are alive and well. But there is still a great threat of danger. The enemy is approaching. So follow me very quietly and let no one hear you. Not another word!" He turned around and walked ahead of them. Lavinia took hold of Piak's hand; hers was as cold as ice. As quietly as possible, they went onwards; even Ardanwen's hoofs made barely a sound.

Finally, they saw the tower at the end of the path – a tower made of tree trunks, with people moving around on top. One of them waved twice, and Twarik immediately darted off the path. He beckoned at them to follow him through the wood. After a short while, he stopped beside a tree and signalled for them to tie Ardanwen to it. With a few whispered words, Piak made the horse understand that it should stay there quietly.

A short drumroll came from the tower. Twarik leant in closer to Piak, Adelbart and Lavinia. "You can see him," he whispered. "But, no matter what happens, remain silent!"

They crept after him through the bushes and followed his example when he knelt on the ground. Cautiously, they peered through branches and leaves.

Piak's heart pounded with nervous excitement. He could see they were close to the tower; just the width of a path separated them from it. Only the bottom part of the tower was visible, though.

Piak was between Lavinia and Adelbart, and Twarik was kneeling beside them. At first Piak thought there was no one else around, but when he surveyed the scene he spotted lots more Men in Green hiding in the undergrowth and up in the trees. The entire area around the tower was surrounded! He knew there were people up on the tower itself, too, but couldn't hear them. He couldn't hear anyone.

What were they all waiting for? Twarik looked at him and put a finger to his lips.

Someone was approaching – on a horse. Piak could hear him clearly and moments later he saw him, too. It was a knight, a knight in black armour on a big grey horse. A Black Knight with a Red Shield!

The knight stopped at the watchtower and gazed up. The visor of his helmet was closed and he did not say a word. He appeared to be waiting for someone else to speak first.

Then a loud voice boomed from the tower. "Giaruda," the voice said, followed by a few sentences that Piak could not understand.

The Black Knight replied; his voice was soft and melodious. And yet it still made Piak feel unpleasant, even though he didn't know what was said.

The unseen man up on the tower spoke again, and Piak pricked up his ears, because this time his own language was used – slowly and deliberately. "The three you are asking about are here, my lord. Why should they not be permitted to understand our words? Repeat your request."

Piak, Adelbart and Lavinia glanced at each other. Who were these "three"?

"Very well, Tehalon," said the Black Knight. "I have come to claim the prisoners who escaped from me. I note you have not concealed them; I see them up there on the tower with you. Why did you send away my riders, so that I was forced to come here myself?"

"You know, my lord," said the man up above, "that all strangers are forbidden to set foot in this part of the forest, do you not?"

"Indeed, Tehalon," said the knight. "And yet you have kept these three with you. They are not permitted to be here either! I claim them as my prisoners."

"Ah, but why are they your prisoners?" said Tehalon. "They succeeded in escaping, as is every prisoner's right."

"As Lord of the Tarnburg I have the right to demand their return," replied the Black Knight. "We agreed not to interfere in each other's affairs, did we not? And so I ask you to hand them over to me."

"Prove your right to me," Tehalon said calmly.

The knight's voice had a threatening tone when he replied, "You dare to ask too much! The first is one of my own men. The second is a fool, who has fled my territory once before and then was dimwitted enough to return. And with the third – with Tiuri – I am playing a game that is not yet finished."

From the tower came a sound like a sigh, followed by whispering. In the undergrowth, Piak and Lavinia held on tightly to each other.

Tehalon said, "My lord, I cannot comply with your request."

The knight made an angry gesture, but Tehalon continued, raising his voice, "They came here three days after full moon. And by the new moon they will no longer be here. By then they will have stepped onto a hidden path... do I have to tell you which one? Do you not know the rites that take place on the shores of the Deep Lake? These three sealed their fate by stepping onto my soil on that particular day. They are *my* prisoners!"

"What is the meaning of your words?" the Black Knight asked after a few moments of silence.

"This," said Tehalon. "The Deep Lake was once known as the Lake of Death. Do you think it no longer craves sacrifices?"

The Black Knight made a soft, hissing sound. Then he spoke again, saying many words. But only a few got through to Piak.

"And so they will die..."

Piak felt like leaping to his feet and screaming, but managed to hold back. Lavinia slumped against him; for a moment he thought she'd fainted. Then Twarik leant over and put his hand over Piak's mouth.

"It's not true!" he whispered. "Quiet!"

Piak tried to pull away.

"It's not true," repeated Twarik. "We are friends."

Piak couldn't understand what was happening. It had all been too much of a shock.

The Black Knight turned his horse and galloped away.

"And he is the enemy," said the Man in Green.

8   TOGETHER AGAIN

Twarik took Lavinia's hands in his own and soothed her. Adelbart also leant over her. "It's not true," he said forcefully. "Don't be afraid. It was a trick!"

Dazed, Lavinia looked at each of them in turn. "Are you sure...?" she whispered.

Twarik glanced over his shoulder at Piak and said, "Your friends are safe. Ask them yourselves, if you don't believe it."

Piak worked his way through the undergrowth and headed for the tower. Two people were just climbing down; the first was a Man in Green, the second was Tiuri.

Finally, the two friends were together again! They held on to each other's hands and at first they could barely manage to say anything more than each other's names.

"Piak," said Tiuri. "Piak... It's really you!" He squeezed Piak's hand and beamed at him.

Piak took a good look at his friend; there were dark circles under his eyes, and his strange green clothes were torn and stained, but otherwise he was the same old Tiuri. "Is everything all right?" he asked. "You... you're not really a prisoner, are you?"

"Not anymore," said Tiuri with a sigh. "You! Here! I wouldn't have dared to hope..."

"I had the fright of my life," said Piak, suddenly feeling rather shaky. "That Black Knight..."

"The knight believed what I told him," said the Man in Green standing beside them. "Because he is wicked himself, he believes the same of others."

Piak realized this must be Tehalon.

Now two others came to join them.

"Marius!" Piak exclaimed happily. "And... Jaro?!"

"Without Jaro we wouldn't be here," said Tiuri. Then they all started talking at once, excited, happy and emotional. Only Tehalon watched in silence.

Adelbart walked over. "Fox doesn't want to come out," he whispered to Piak. Then he saw Tehalon and greeted him with respect.

The Master of the Wild Wood addressed them. "What brings the two of you here?" he asked, looking at Piak and Adelbart.

"We are envoys," said Adelbart, "sent by the Lord of Mistrinaut." He explained why they'd come, with Piak filling in some of the details.

"The Lord of Mistrinaut!" Tiuri said, eyes gleaming. "And his men. That's wonderful." He turned to Tehalon and asked, "My lord, you surely do not mind if..."

"I should like to speak to Rafox, the Lord of Mistrinaut," said Tehalon. "To him alone. He must come immediately. He can be here soon if he comes on horse. But his men are not to enter my territory."

"The Black Knight also knows they are on the way," said Tiuri, with a frown. "Because of your drums..." He looked at Piak and continued, "Of course, you don't understand much of what is going on. I need to speak to the Lord of Mistrinaut as soon as possible. But the enemy must not suspect that he knows anything about what is happening in this forest... So have Lord Rafox command his men to go to the east, as if that is their goal. They must withdraw from this part of the wood immediately, or they will meet the same fate as Sir Ristridin and his men. Under no circumstances should they go to the south, not yet at least."

"What is in the south?" asked Piak.

"In the south is the Tarnburg, with a thousand armed men," replied Tiuri. "Most of them are Red Riders."

"And the Black Knight with the Red Shield?" whispered Piak.

"He is their leader – the King of Eviellan."

Less than ten minutes later, Adelbart was on his way back to the camp, accompanied by Twarik. They were to make sure that Lord Rafox would join them with all haste.

"The King of Eviellan!" said Piak. "Were you his prisoner? How... how did he treat you?"

"He... played chess with me," replied Tiuri.

"He never did!" said Piak.

"Oh yes, he did, my friend," said the Fool. "They played every night. But we used the file, too, and on the third day we ran away, with him, Jaro."

"Tell me everything," said Piak.

Then he thought of something. Lavinia... where had she got to? And Ardanwen? He wasn't supposed to say anything about Lavinia, but...

"Oh, Tiuri," he said. "We found Ardanwen. He was wandering around the forest. However did he..." He fell silent when he saw Tiuri's face.

"A-Ardanwen?" Tiuri stammered. "But that's impossible. He..."

"He was wandering around the forest and we brought him here," said Piak.

"Ardanwen? But I thought he was dead," whispered Tiuri.

"He's alive – and kicking. Truly!" cried Piak. "Come with me. I'll show you."

But a Man in Green was already approaching with the horse. Tiuri froze. Ardanwen whinnied, pulled away from his escort, and raced towards his master. Tiuri ran to meet him and a moment later they were greeting each other.

"The wicked knight lied," said the Fool. "I told you, didn't I? The black horse ran away and they couldn't catch him."

Tiuri threw his arms around Ardanwen's neck and buried his face in his long mane.

"So," said Jaro to Piak in his usual grumpy tone, "how does it feel to have such good friends and an unexpected reunion?"

That reminded Piak of Lavinia again and he looked around to see if he could spot her. Tehalon came over to him and said in a low voice, "Your third travelling companion is safe in the care of Lian, Twarik's wife. But she wants to see your friends only from a distance."

"Oh yes, I understand," said Piak quietly. "You see, Tiuri's not supposed to know she's here."

"Why not?" asked Tehalon. "Is it because she's a woman?"

"Yes, my lord," said Piak. "That's why."

"A foolish reason," said Tehalon. "But that is her business... Come on," he continued, "call your friends and withdraw to the tower. You are my guests, but I want to have you all in one place and within my sight. I shall say no more until the Lord of Mistrinaut arrives."

"Tehalon wouldn't let you go?" said Piak. "So what's he up to now? Has he changed his mind?"

They were up on the tower – Tiuri and Piak, Jaro and the Fool. A Man in Green was sitting in one corner beside the drum, but he did not join in with their conversation.

The tower was high and they could see a long way. Piak had paid very little attention to the view, though, not even to the peaks of the Great Mountains. He was more interested in his friend.

Tiuri had told him about the dangers hidden within the Wild Wood. He'd also explained how he and the Fool had escaped with Jaro's help. But Piak still hadn't heard nearly enough.

"Yes, Tehalon has changed his mind," said Tiuri. "But I don't know why. I think it's because the Lord of Mistrinaut has come. With so many soldiers in the area he cannot prevent the secret of the Tarnburg being revealed."

"The Knight with the Red Shield, the King of Eviellan," said Piak. "What kind of man is he? What does he look like?"

"He is the man who murdered Sir Edwinem," said Tiuri slowly. "And what does he look like? He looks just like Sir Idian."

Piak wanted to ask more questions, but Tiuri did not give him the chance. "First I want to hear about your adventures," he said. "I don't know what would have happened if you hadn't managed to arrive with help just at the right moment, Piak!"

"Oh, there was a lot of luck involved," said Piak. "And good people who helped me, like Adelbart." He told Tiuri all about what had happened to him.

"I'm so very glad we're together again!" said Tiuri a little later. "And that Ardanwen is here, too." He looked down below; there was his horse. Tehalon himself had fed and groomed Ardanwen.

Just then, the Master of the Wild Wood came out of the trees, accompanied by a young man dressed in blue.

"Who's that?" asked Tiuri.

As Piak looked, he felt his face flush. "Oh, that's Fox," he replied, "a squire from Mistrinaut, who came with us." He noticed that Tiuri stopped paying attention to Fox then, and he didn't know whether to be relieved or annoyed with him. "Aren't we still more or less prisoners here?" he said, changing the subject. "They just ordered us to climb this tower."

"Tehalon has promised I can go wherever I want," said Tiuri. "But he wants us to discuss before we act – him, the Lord of Mistrinaut and us. We must be very careful and consider our plan if we want to take on the enemy in the Tarnburg."

"And where do you want to go?" asked Piak.

"To the Road of Ambuscade," replied Tiuri, "over the mountains."

His intention did not surprise Piak. "I'll go with you," he said.

"That's what I thought you'd say," Tiuri said with a smile. "I obviously can't go into the mountains without you!"

"So you still haven't given up on that plan?" Jaro growled. "How do you intend to get there?"

"And what about me?" whispered the Fool.

"Marius," said Tiuri. "I haven't forgotten my promise to you."

"Oh, I know it'll happen, Friend," the Fool said. "But another day, later."

Tiuri frowned, though, and looked thoughtfully at the Fool and then at Jaro.

"Look, the Master of the Wild Wood is beckoning to us," said Jaro. "See? He is summoning us to him. Well, I hope he's calling us to eat. I'm hungry."

"Me too," said Piak. "I've only just realized." To his annoyance, he saw that Tehalon stopped Lavinia as she went to walk away.

"What's wrong?" asked Tiuri.

"Oh nothing," said Piak. "Goodness, it seems so long ago that I went to fetch that bag and heard you shouting, 'Danger! Flee!'" He went on chattering away, even after they'd reached the bottom of the tower. He hoped it might distract Tiuri's attention from Fox.

Fortunately, his friend headed straight for Ardanwen.

Tehalon called him back, though, "Tiuri, here is someone you have not yet greeted."

Piak stopped talking, in the middle of a sentence.

Lavinia bowed her head and said, "Fox is my name." She clearly had not changed her mind.

As Tiuri walked over to her, she had no choice but to stand there, but she tried to avoid his gaze. That only made Tiuri all the more curious. And for the first time he took a proper look at this stranger, the squire from Mistrinaut.

Piak saw Tiuri's eyes open wide. *He's recognized her,* he thought. The colour drained from Tiuri's face, but he said nothing, just held out his hand. Lavinia took it, and they stood there for a few moments, not moving.

"What... did you say... your name was?" asked Tiuri, very quietly.

"Fox..." Lavinia replied in a whisper. She tried to take back her hand, but Tiuri was holding it tightly.

His face lit up with a smile. "I would like to call you by a different name," he said.

Lavinia looked down at her feet. Blushing, Tiuri released her hand. He stepped back, took a deep breath, and rubbed his hand across his forehead.

"Fox?" he said. "Squire of Mistrinaut? Why?"

"Why?" repeated Lavinia. She seemed just as confused and uncertain as Tiuri. "Because... I... Um... Are you perhaps mistaken somehow?"

"I am not mistaken about what I see," said Tiuri. "You are..."

"My father needed a squire," she interrupted him, breathlessly. "My brother was not there and so I came with him instead. Is that so strange, just because I'm a girl?"

"No... yes," said Tiuri. "All I can say, Lavinia, is that I'm... most surprised to see you here. Please forgive me if I greeted you rather strangely."

Neither of them had been paying any attention to the others, but now they realized they were still standing there. They looked embarrassed, as if they wanted to say more, but both remained silent.

Tehalon introduced Lavinia to Jaro and the Fool and then said calmly, as if nothing had happened, "Come on, let's go. We will wait for the Lord of Mistrinaut nearby, on the shore of the Deep Lake."

"When will he be here?" asked Lavinia, turning to him with a startled look on her face.

"It'll be a couple of hours yet," replied Tehalon. "First we shall eat. And Fox – or Lavinia – you are a lady. Allow Sir Tiuri to accompany you to the Deep Lake, as is the custom in your circles."

They went with Tehalon, Tiuri walking beside Lavinia. Piak thought he looked as if he were sleepwalking.

I'm sure Tiuri was happy to see her, Piak thought. *He was surprised, but happy.* And yet there was something about it that he didn't like... Perhaps Lavinia had been right, after all, and this was not a good time for her to be reunited with Tiuri. But Tehalon had made sure they would meet. He knew Lavinia did not want to see Tiuri yet, but still he had brought them together. Did he have some reason for doing so?

Piak looked at the Master of the Wild Wood. His face was as blank as usual. *But*, Piak said to himself, *I would not be at all surprised if he did it with some hidden intention.* He found it hard to imagine that the Master of the Wild Wood had acted just out of kindness or simply to interfere and meddle.

9 TIURI AND LAVINIA

Tiuri walked beside Lavinia. What a surprise it had been to recognize her! A shock, yes, but a delightful one. It felt as if he were seeing her for the first time and yet as if he'd known her forever – the only girl he could ever love. But when she had tried to pull her hand away and looked down, he suddenly realized that she probably did not feel the same way. And then he remembered that, so very recently, he had thought he was in love with another. He had even left Lavinia's glove behind at the Tarnburg. And then there were her words: "My father needed a squire..." What a fool he was to think for even a moment that she would venture into the Wild Wood for his sake. *As if she'd do that!* he thought. *I'm not worth it.*

He tried to pull himself together, as he really needed his wits about him. He had a vague feeling that it could be dangerous to give in to his emotions right now. Was he truly in love with Lavinia?

But whatever the case, he could not walk beside her in complete silence. He had to say something to her, to speak to her.

Lavinia spoke first. "I hope it did not startle you too much to see me in these clothes," she said. "Perhaps I should be flattered that you still recognized me."

"I would recognize you anywhere, Lavinia," he said. "But it is true that I was surprised... I still am."

"Only surprised?" asked Lavinia. She looked at him out of the corner of her eye and gave him a shy smile.

"No, much more than that," replied Tiuri. "Glad, afraid, and..." He fell silent, worried that he would say too much. Then he added, "But I don't understand why your father would approve of your going with him."

Piak, who was walking behind them with Ardanwen, pricked up his ears.

"He didn't at first," said Lavinia calmly. "But I knew he was very sorry my brother was not there to accompany him. And I did not want to let him go alone. Someone needs to keep an eye on him and to take care of him if anything should happen."

"Well, well," said Piak to himself, "she had an answer all ready for him." And he wondered what would happen when Lavinia came face to face with her father.

Tiuri hesitated before speaking. "Ah... yes," he said. "After all, none of you knew what kind of dangers might be awaiting you. But you really can't stay here too long, Lavinia."

"Lady Lavinia is completely safe in my territory," said Tehalon.

"Would you please call me Fox, my lord?" said Lavinia. "As long as I am wearing these clothes, I would prefer to be treated as a squire. It won't be for much longer, as I'm sure my father will send

329

me back soon. Then you will have your way, Tiuri, and be free of my presence."

"Oh, that's not what I meant at all!" said Tiuri in dismay. "I'm just concerned for you, Lavinia... Fox. Please do not think ill of me. I seem to be saying everything wrong."

"Don't be angry with me, Tiuri!" began Lavinia.

"Angry?"

"Well, don't be concerned, then. Please, talk to me as you would... as you would to a fellow soldier." She glanced back. "As you would to Piak."

"And what a great brother-in-arms she is!" cried Piak. Lavinia and Tiuri seemed to be doing their best to misunderstand each other and Piak was glad to have an opportunity to speak. "Lavinia... I mean Fox, was the one who found Ardanwen." He went to walk beside them and told his friend how they'd followed the horse.

By then they'd reached the valley with the lake. Lavinia said, "If this is the Deep Lake, I don't think I shall ever grow fond of it." She saw that Tiuri's gaze was fixed on her and quickly added, "Are you not happy to have Ardanwen again?"

"And you standing here beside me is..." Tiuri began, but she didn't let him finish.

"Have you ridden him yet?" she asked. "He must be longing to gallop with you."

"As am I!" Tiuri suddenly realized.

He leapt up, even though Ardanwen had neither reins nor saddle. The horse responded immediately to the pressure of Tiuri's knee and the touch of his hand. The two of them raced away, into the valley.

The others stood and watched them go.

"Beautiful!" sighed Lavinia.

"Now he is a knight again," said the Fool, "a rider on the beautiful black horse."

Tiuri rode around the lake and waved at them. Then he galloped westwards and disappeared from sight.

Jaro turned to Tehalon and said, "Are you not afraid that they will run away?"

"No," came the brief reply. Tehalon beckoned to Lavinia and started walking down to the lake.

"Piak," whispered Lavinia, "would you do something for me?"

"Yes, what is it?"

"Would you go ahead to meet my father and prepare him a little? You can tell him everything." She went to walk beside Tehalon.

"Dear me," muttered Jaro. "Whatever is that young lady doing here? She might have disguised herself as a man, but it doesn't help much. It seems to me that Tiuri already has enough on his mind. Now this girl's here, too, to send his head spinning, there'll be no end to the trouble."

"Stop talking nonsense, Jaro," said Piak.

"If you use your sense for a moment," said Jaro, "you'll see I'm right."

When they'd reached the shore of the lake, Tiuri turned back. His cheeks were flushed and his eyes were sparkling. As he reined in Ardanwen, he greeted them cheerfully.

"A magnificent horse," said Jaro.

"No one but Tiuri can ride him," Lavinia explained.

"He let me sit on his back, too," said the Fool proudly.

"Really?" said Lavinia.

"You may also ride him, Lavinia," said Tiuri, bowing towards her. "Ardanwen is your servant, as am I."

"Oh, yes please..." she whispered.

"But he has no saddle," said Tiuri. "Climb up and ride just a short way, together with me... if you wish."

Lavinia hesitated for a moment before nodding. Tiuri helped her up in front of him and they rode away, at a gentle pace around the lake.

"Tiuri won't forget me, will he?" whispered the Fool. "He used to let *me* ride with him."

"You see? Marius thinks the same as me," Jaro said quietly to Piak.

"Ah, hold your tongue," said Piak.

I dreamt about this! thought Tiuri.

He urged Ardanwen to go faster and Lavinia held on more tightly. Yes, he had dreamt about it, about riding Night Wind with Lavinia in his arms. But he'd been going even more quickly, racing towards an unknown destination...

Suddenly he slowed Ardanwen's pace. "I'm sorry," he said a little shakily. "We should return."

Lavinia said nothing, but she smiled at him. Tiuri rode back at walking pace. "Lavinia," he said, "or Fox if you prefer..."

"Call me Lavinia," she said.

"I have a confession to make. Your glove... I lost it."

Lavinia laughed out loud. "Oh, Tiuri!" she said. "You've been through so much danger, you were taken prisoner, and then you escaped... and the first thing you tell me about it all is that you've lost my glove!"

"Yes, but..." Tiuri began. "I just wanted to say that I'm sorry I lost it."

"I'm not," declared Lavinia.

"You're not?" said Tiuri, suddenly afraid once again that he'd revealed too much about his feelings.

"No, I'm not," said Lavinia, "because I can give you another glove now, a nicer one... at least I can if you ask me for one."

By then they'd reached the others and Tehalon was approaching, so Tiuri did not have to reply.

The Master of the Wild Wood looked at Lavinia and said, "You would feel at home among my people."

"Why is that, my lord?" she asked when they had dismounted.

"Because you are able to enjoy the moment and forget worries that are for another day. You could both be happy here, together..." He stopped and said abruptly, "The fire is lit. Come."

332

Lian and some of the other Men in Green came to join them, and they sat by the fire to eat.

In the distance a drum sounded, just once.

"That means," said Tehalon, "that the Black Knight with the Red Shield has left my lands."

Tiuri turned his gaze from Lavinia and sat up straight. He felt so alive right now! But although their surroundings were peaceful, warmongering warriors were not far away.

Piak asked Tehalon if he could ride out to meet the Lord of Mistrinaut.

"You have my permission," Tehalon replied. "I expect him in less than two hours."

He stared at Piak, then Tiuri. "And then," he continued, "we must have a serious discussion about matters that seem important now, but which will soon become history, then legend, and then be forgotten."

10 PLANS AND GOODBYES

The afternoon of that eventful day was drawing to a close. They were once again sitting on the shore of the Deep Lake: Tiuri and Piak, the Master of the Wild Wood and the Lord of Mistrinaut, Lavinia, Adelbart, Jaro and the Fool. Around them, hidden among the trees, the Men in Green watched and waited.

Tiuri had told Lord Rafox everything he knew about the enemy that dwelt within the Tarnburg.

"It is even more serious than I thought," Rafox replied. "The King of Eviellan himself! My men are few in number, but I don't think we'll be able to wait for reinforcements." His expression was grim.

Piak looked at him and thought about the conversation they had recently had, when he had gone to prepare Lord Rafox for the unexpected reunion with his daughter. Lord Rafox had been furious at first! Yet Piak had managed to calm him down so that he wasn't too angry with Lavinia when he saw her again.

And now there were more important issues to discuss.

The King of Eviellan was threatening both the Kingdom of Unauwen and the Kingdom of Dagonaut. Those in the west needed to be informed of the existence of the Road of Ambuscade, of course. Lord Rafox would immediately send some of his men as messengers, along the First Great Road, which lay to the north of the forest.

It was not known when the attack would take place. Jaro thought that more men from Eviellan were expected to arrive and it would certainly be some time before they were all ready for battle.

It was possible, however, that the king would attack sooner than originally planned. He might fear that his stronghold would be discovered.

"That's why I asked you if you could send your men to the east," Tiuri said to the Lord of Mistrinaut. "He knows you are in the forest, because of the drums and perhaps because of his spies. If he thinks your goal is elsewhere – the Forgotten City, for example – perhaps he will not act as yet. Does that give us enough time to warn them in the west?"

"I hope so," said Lord Rafox. "But it'll take eight to ten days for messengers to reach the other side of the mountains. And, of course, the Kingdom of Unauwen will not immediately be ready to resist an invasion."

"It would be faster along the Road of Ambuscade, which is nearby," said Tiuri. He turned to look at Tehalon and said, "This morning, just before Piak came, you said you might know a way to get there quickly."

The Master of the Wild Wood stroked his beard thoughtfully and said, "The Road of Ambuscade is heavily guarded. But there is a hidden path that leads from the Green Grottos into the mountains and emerges close to the pass. That way is also not without dangers, but it is the only chance to get from the Wild Wood into the Kingdom of Unauwen. As I said, it is a hidden path, known only to the Men in Green. One person passing along it, creeping and with cunning, could escape the attention of Eviellan..."

"Would you show me this way?" asked Tiuri.

All was silent for a moment.

"I will," said the Master of the Wild Wood. "But I cannot promise that you will reach your destination. To be honest, the chance is small."

"All I can do is try," said Tiuri. "If I succeed, when could I reach the other side of the mountains?"

"Set off tomorrow morning and you'll be at the Green Grottos by the afternoon. From there it's just over three days to the pass," replied Tehalon. "In less than six days, you'll be in the Kingdom of Unauwen."

Tiuri looked at Lord Rafox, silently asking his opinion.

"Just you?" Rafox said quietly.

"No armies may pass along that path," said Tehalon. "Only a lone traveller stands any chance of crossing the pass unseen."

"Surely two people could do it as well?" said Piak. "Such an important mission cannot be entrusted to one person alone. Two have one more chance of success! And I know the mountains. I'm more at home there than Tiuri. He has to take his squire with him!"

The friends looked at each other and grinned.

"Fine, the two of you," said Tehalon. "If Lord Rafox agrees."

"I believe providence has appointed Tiuri for this task," he said slowly, "and I understand Piak does not wish him to go alone. May heaven grant that you succeed!"

"Thank you," said Tiuri. "But do not forget the other messengers, too."

"So you got your way, after all," muttered Jaro.

The Fool looked around with big, frightened eyes. "I am afraid," he whispered.

"That's the Road of Ambuscade dealt with, then," said the Lord of Mistrinaut.

"One moment, my lord," said Tiuri. "I was actually appointed for another task, or rather, it was a promise I made. I was to take Marius back to his home, to his cabin in the woods. He knows we can't go there now, but I've just realized he doesn't have to wait." He turned to Jaro. "I know, Jaro," he said, "that you are uneasy about being here with us. You'd rather not be listening to the plans we are making to oppose your former master. And you don't know what you should do yourself. So I thought perhaps you would keep my promise for me. Would you take Marius back home?"

Jaro's face lit up. He nodded. "If Marius trusts me, I'd be happy to," he replied.

The Fool nodded, too.

"Then, with Marius's permission, I charge you with completing my task," said Tiuri.

Piak kept glancing at his friend. He'd changed quite a lot since their paths had separated – he seemed to have become older somehow.

"Good," said the Lord of Mistrinaut. "And now this: if the people of Unauwen are warned in time, they can lie in wait for the King of Eviellan and stop him. Then he will most probably retreat back here. No, he definitely will, as there is nowhere else for him to go. What then? Will he not turn his army on us in fury and vengeance? Advance into the east, deeper into the Kingdom of Dagonaut, where they are just as unsuspecting of an imminent attack?"

"I thought of that, too," whispered Tiuri.

"I agree that they need to be warned in the west," said the Lord of Mistrinaut, "but at the same time we must prepare for a war in our own land. Messengers have already been sent to King Dagonaut with the news of enemies in the Wild Wood. But we did not know then which enemies, or how many! And the City of Dagonaut is far; the king's knights and army will take days to get here. So we'll have to take care of the first battle ourselves."

He took out the abbot's map and spread it on the ground. "The nearest castles are Mistrinaut and Islan," he continued. "The Lord of

Islan is in league with Eviellan, so he represents an additional threat. For now we can count only on my men and on the reinforcements from Castle Westenaut, which will be here soon." He looked up and asked Tehalon, "What help can we expect from you?"

"No more than I have already given," he replied in a chilly tone. "The Men in Green will keep out of this and defend only our own land. But," he added, "we will no longer warn the King of Eviellan with our drums. We shall offer him no assistance at all, so you will have every opportunity to foil his plans. Our drums will pass on one more message for him to hear: that you and your men have retreated. The rest of the battle is up to you! Just one more thing: I will tolerate not one single armed man, from either side, in my territory between the Green River, Green Hills and Great Mountains."

"Thank you," said the Lord of Mistrinaut, just as coldly. "So now we know where we all stand."

"Lord Rafox," said Tiuri, "you will be few against many. Of course I want to help you if you wish me to. I do not mean to run away! Perhaps another could..."

"No," said the Lord of Mistrinaut, interrupting him, "as the only army commander in the forest I will take the liberty of giving orders. Someone has to go to the west and you are the right person to do so. One man more or less will make little difference in the battle... You and Piak must go to the Kingdom of Unauwen. I will keep watch in the wood. Now let me tell you my plans."

Those plans were as follows: Lord Rafox was to return to his soldiers immediately and send out some of his fastest men as messengers to King Dagonaut and the Kingdom of Unauwen. Then, with Adelbart as his guide, he would go eastwards with his small army, towards the Forgotten City. He would wait a few days before turning back, to give Tiuri and Piak time to get across the mountains. Then he would approach the Tarnburg again, along the

337

Black River. A number of scouts would be sent ahead to observe the enemy's movements.

"I will give my men the same task," said Tehalon. "They will stay in constant contact with you."

The Lord of Mistrinaut raised his eyebrows. "More help, after all?" he said wryly. "It is, of course, welcome. If the King of Eviellan sets off earlier or attacks us, I will naturally have to change my plans."

For the first time, he turned to his daughter. "Lavinia," he said, "you will come with me, and then return home as swiftly as possible. Perhaps Brother Martin can accompany you."

"She would be safe here," said Tehalon.

"Do you think so? No, now that there is a chance of fighting, I do not wish her to remain in the forest. I'm sure you agree, don't you, Lavinia?"

"Yes, Father," she meekly replied.

It was decided that Lavinia would begin her journey home the next morning. Twarik and Lian said they would take her some of the way.

Lord Rafox stood up. Everything had been discussed, so he was free to leave. Adelbart left with him.

They said farewell to the others, who would be setting off the following morning at sunrise: Tiuri and Piak going with Tehalon to the hidden path, Lavinia back home to Castle Mistrinaut, and Jaro with the Fool to the cabin in the woods.

Lord Rafox made a point of shaking both Tiuri and Piak firmly by the hand. They wished each other good luck and their expressions were grave at the thought that they might not see one another again. Just before he rode away, the Lord of Mistrinaut took Piak to one side for a moment and said quietly, "It is rather premature to speak such thoughts aloud, but I wanted to let you know that I would welcome your friend as a son-in-law."

*

The Men in Green had made sure everyone had a place to sleep – in hammocks or on the ground.

Tiuri and Piak lay next to each other; they were both tired, but still couldn't fall asleep. They whispered together about all that had happened. Piak did most of the talking, and after a while he noticed his friend was saying very little. "What are you thinking about?" he asked.

"Oh, about all kinds of things, all at once," replied Tiuri. He gave a little sigh.

"About Lavinia?"

"Yes, about Lavinia, too..." Then, very quietly, he added. "Do you know something, Piak? I love her. Maybe you don't believe that after... Oh, never mind! But perhaps she doesn't feel the same way about me." He fell silent for a moment and then said, "Why didn't you tell me that she had come with you?"

"Because..." Piak began. "No," he said, "that's something you'll have to ask Lavinia. It's not my secret to reveal."

Tiuri was awake before sunrise; he knew he wouldn't be able to go back to sleep, so he got up.

A huddled figure sat by the lake. It was the Fool. When Tiuri went to sit beside him, he looked up and whispered, "Soon you will leave, Friend, and I am returning home to my cabin. Our paths are going in different directions, taking us further and further apart. You won't forget me, will you?"

"How could I forget you, Marius?" said Tiuri. "Could I forget when you showed me the way in the forest? Could I forget fighting for you? Could I forget being captured and escaping together? Could I forget that we should really have travelled back to your home together? I haven't asked you if you will forget me, have I? And I'll be sure to come and visit you in your cabin... if I can find my way over the mountains and back."

"To where the sun sets..." said the Fool. "You have been there before. And you will return. I will wait for you, in my cabin in the woods."

Time to say farewell... to Marius and Jaro... and to Lavinia...

After a hurried breakfast, Tiuri suddenly noticed that he and Lavinia were alone on the shore of the lake. Had everyone realized he wanted to speak to her in private?

No, not everyone; Tiuri saw Tehalon approaching. He stood beside them, not saying a word. His presence meant their words of farewell were only what friends might have said. *Ah*, thought Tiuri, *but perhaps it's better that way*. His path was uncertain and there would be time enough if he returned.

"Time is passing so quickly!" said Tehalon suddenly. "The messengers sent by Lord Rafox to the Kingdom of Unauwen will be there soon. You, Sir Tiuri, hope to arrive before them by travelling along the hidden route. But perhaps it is not hidden enough – you could be betrayed by your haste and come to the end of your life's path before the battle has even begun. Why do you want to risk it? Do you wish to follow the example of those fearless knights who have perished at a young age? Songs are sung of their daring deeds, but they can no longer hear those songs themselves! What good is that to anyone?"

Tiuri was silent. He saw a flash of fear on Lavinia's face and turned away from her. He noticed that Tehalon was watching her. Then he understood that he had deliberately chosen to speak those words while Lavinia was present. The Master of the Wild Wood surely hoped she would agree with him, so that he would abandon what he considered his duty.

He closed his eyes for a moment. Oh, if only Eviellan did not exist! If Lavinia loved him, too, she would not wish him to go, and saying farewell would be unbearably hard. And yet he had to go.

340

Tehalon was undoubtedly acting out of self-interest; he probably still hoped the enemy would disappear forever along the Road of Ambuscade. But Lavinia... Oh, Lavinia...

Tiuri's reflections took no more than a moment, and were interrupted by Lavinia.

"Last night I thought of a song," she said, "a song I once sang for Sir Tiuri. Also about a knight who..." She did not complete her sentence but looked at Tiuri, her eyes gleaming. "About Edwinem of Forèstèrra, do you remember? I thought of a verse I did not sing for you.

> *The slopes, they are so high and steep,*
> *deep and dark the gorge below,*
> *rough and grey the rocky cliffs,*
> *with lofty peaks of bright white snow –*
> *as white as the shield of Forèstèrra...*

She paused for a moment before continuing:

> *as white as the shield of Sir Tiuri the good,*
> *who with Piak, his friend and squire,*
> *sought out the secrets of the dark Wild Wood.*

"There," she said, "now I can sing it for you, too. Farewell, Tiuri. Have a good journey and take care... until we meet again." Her voice trembled, but she did not cry.

Tiuri did not concern himself anymore with Tehalon. He put his arms around her, kissed her and said, "Thank you, Lavinia... and farewell to you, too, until we meet again. I will return... for your glove... and for more than that."

For a moment, they held each other tightly as if they would never let go. Tiuri was unspeakably happy and deeply sad at the same time. But he knew he could not have one without the other.

11 Tehalon's Secret

Soon Tiuri and Piak were moving westwards through the forest. They took it in turns to ride Ardanwen, while the Master of the Wild Wood went ahead of them.

"Every step takes us closer to the mountains!" said Piak. "We'll be up there in a couple of days. I'd never have expected to go climbing again so soon."

"But it's not like before," said Tiuri, "when you knew every path and could avoid every danger."

"Oh, but I'm always at home in the mountains," said Piak. "I can just smell any dangers in the air! And I have a friend beside me who knows how to handle a sword. Sir Tiuri is his name!"

Tehalon looked back at them now and then, but he did not speak.

"I wish he'd smile for once, or cry, or look angry," Piak whispered to Tiuri. "I almost feel like sticking my tongue out at him, just to see if he'd show any sign of surprise."

"Shhh," said Tiuri.

"He knows everything I say, anyway," replied Piak. "I feel like he can hear everything, even if we don't say it out loud. But I'm sure he doesn't care what we say. I know I talk nonsense, but sometimes I have to say something, even if I don't really know what I'm talking about."

Tiuri smiled; he understood what his friend meant.

By the afternoon they'd reached the Green Grottos, in the foothills of the Great Mountains. The caves were at different heights, with paths winding up to the lowest ones, but those at the top could only be reached by climbing a rope ladder.

"What a wonderful place to live!" said Piak, his eyes roaming around the slopes with their birches and pine trees, and patches of green grass between. There was a lookout post and a Man in Green up there, who waved in greeting. From the caves and from the slopes came more people dressed in green – mainly women and children.

342

They looked curiously at the strangers. Tehalon raised a hand and briefly spoke to them in his own language. Then most of them left.

"You must regret that you cannot stay here longer," Tehalon said to Tiuri and Piak. "This is our home, a better place to live than any castle or town."

"Like the Forgotten City," said Piak thoughtfully.

"That is a place we would not want to live. It is good that it has been forgotten. You have been there, haven't you? And while you were there did you consider that every city will one day fall, perish, or be destroyed?"

"But perhaps it will be rebuilt," whispered Piak.

Tehalon did not reply. "Here we live in safety and happiness," he said. Then he placed his hand on Ardanwen's neck and continued, "Soon you will have to say farewell to your horse, Tiuri, because you cannot take him along the hidden path. But he can stay here and graze on the meadows above. My daughters and grandson will take care of him, and they will not ride him if you do not wish them to."

"Thank you, my lord," said Tiuri. He was not particularly fond of the Master of the Wild Wood, but he was sure Ardanwen would be in good hands until he returned.

"Then follow me now," said Tehalon. "I wish to depart at midnight, so we shall eat soon and go early to bed."

He took them up one of the winding paths, past caves where many people peered out at them, and then climbed a rope ladder to the highest cave, his home.

The cave was large and simply furnished, like a hermit's cell. Pine needles were scattered on the floor, so that the room smelt, as Piak put it, "really green".

Dark openings led to other caves. Tehalon told them there was a whole network of caverns and passageways, and that nearly all the caves were connected. "We have water," he said, "and a supply of food. If necessary, we could withstand a siege."

"Do you think that will happen?" asked Tiuri.

343

"No," said Tehalon. "But if you return here, you will not know this place as it has always been."

He went to stand in the mouth of the cave and looked out for a while over the land he called his own, the green forests between hills and river.

"Whatever happens," he said, "no matter who wins or loses – our days are numbered." He looked at them; there was still no emotion on his face, but his voice sounded melancholy. "Our realm, as it was, is over," he said. "But that too was written in the stars – and I see now that I can no longer resist the change."

Tiuri and Piak remained silent. What could they have said?

"And so I shall give you something, before it gets dark," continued the Master of the Wild Wood. "A secret I did not wish to reveal at first. But it would be bad if I did not, as it is a legacy handed down from my forefather who came from the Kingdom of Unauwen. Perhaps I was given this knowledge only so that I might pass it on to you now."

He went to an old chest, which he opened with a bronze key, and, after some digging around, he took out a number of yellowing documents. "Letters and writings of the first Lord of the Tarnburg," he said.

They sat on the floor, with Tehalon in the middle. He spread out the documents in front of him; they were covered with spidery, faded letters.

"This is the old language, of course," said Tehalon. "Listen and I shall tell you what it says. It is about Vorgóta, which is the name of the river, the forest, and the first castle on the other side of the mountains."

Slowly, he began to translate: *"The Lord of Vorgóta commanded Tongan the smith to make three objects: a sword, a mallet and a gong. The sword has been written about elsewhere; the mallet is for beating the gong. And the gong is hung in such a way that it can be heard for miles around. I shall tell my faithful followers how to find the Vorgóta*

Gong, so that they can warn the guardians of the Kingdom of Unauwen if danger should threaten from the east. To do so, they will have to pass along the Second Great Road, where I will never set foot again."

The Master of the Wild Wood raised his head and said, "The Second Great Road is now known as the Road of Ambuscade. But the Vorgóta Gong still hangs in the same place, one of the western foothills of the Great Mountains. You may have only a small lead on Eviellan, and from the mountains it could take a long time to reach a place where people live. But if you bang that gong, people will come to you. The people of Unauwen have surely not forgotten that any man who bangs the gong is calling upon everyone to rise up against great danger."

"And... where is this gong?" whispered Tiuri.

"That, too, is written here," replied Tehalon. "I shall read it out to you, word for word. I have never travelled that way myself, but I think it is indicated clearly enough."

He spoke the sentences aloud, repeated them, and made Tiuri and Piak say the words after him.

> *Across the mountains, then down below.*
> *Wide path through forest of pine.*
> *Take a right turn into the valley deep*
> *where flow the Twin Cascades.*
> *Follow the stream to where it disappears.*
> *Then find a sign to show the way.*
> *Two paths – one leads to the gong,*
> *hidden song, Vorgóta Gong.*

When they had eaten and rested, Tiuri and Piak were given new clothes, so that they looked just like the Men in Green. They were also provided with everything they needed for their journey: sturdy boots, a fur in case it was cold up on the mountains, provisions and a length of rope. They were both armed, Piak with King Unauwen's sword and Tiuri with a dagger that Jaro had given him. They said farewell to Ardanwen.

In the clear night they began their journey: from the Green Grottos to the south, across the Green River and then up. Tehalon led them without hesitation, slowly in the dark and then more quickly when it became light. A short distance beyond the river's source, the path disappeared into the mountains, and they walked some of the way by torchlight.

They passed through caves of stalactites, so beautiful that the friends couldn't help stopping to look. "Like drops of water turned to stone," said Piak, "and cascades made out of rock."

"This is the hidden path," said Tehalon. "I spoke the truth to the King of Eviellan when he came to claim you, Tiuri!"

Tiuri and Piak misunderstood his words for a moment. They froze.

"I told him you would step onto a hidden path – and that is exactly what you are doing now, even though it is not as he imagined! But I should add that I knew he would misinterpret my words, which I'm sure you have not."

For the first time, Tiuri thought he saw a hint of a smile on Tehalon's lips.

"Does this path go underground all the way?" asked Piak shakily. He preferred to walk along ordinary mountain paths.

"No," said Tehalon. "In an hour you will see daylight again. If we speed up a little, that is."

He was proved correct and Piak was glad to be back outside. Now he was on familiar ground!

"No more trees grow here," said Tehalon. "We have left the Wild Wood behind."

The next morning they found themselves between two mountain ridges. Still some distance away, but seeming closer, the Tarntop stood before them.

Tehalon stopped and said, "Now there's no way you can get lost. If you keep following this path, you will come to the Road of Ambuscade, beyond the last major guard post. From there to the pass it is only a short way. At the pass itself there are also guards, who are changed every day as far as I know. But I can tell you now that your path is not as dangerous as I made it seem at first."

"How many guards are there?" asked Tiuri.

"I do not know," said Tehalon. "Not many, two, maybe three. You'll have to work out how best to outwit them and pass by unnoticed."

"Why have they never found this path?" asked Piak.

"You'll soon see for yourself," replied Tehalon. "The path comes to a sudden end at a precipice. You'll see the Road of Ambuscade down below. You have rope so that you can climb down; as a boy from the mountains, you'll know what to do. Do not speak too much or too loudly, for you are approaching the enemy's territory. That is all. I shall bid you both farewell – and I truly mean what I say. May you both fare well. And be sure to find the gong!"

He turned and hurried off. Before either of the friends could say anything, he was already far away. They stood and watched him go.

"The Master of the Wild Wood!" said Piak. "I'm sure we'll never meet another man like him."

Then, together, Tiuri and Piak continued their journey towards the road that would lead them over the mountains to the west.

PART SEVEN

SIR RISTRIDIN

1 THE PRISONER

The road across the Great Mountains to the west, the Second Great Road that had once again been opened up... When would Eviellan's armies come thundering along it to conquer the Kingdom of Unauwen? When would the wickedness that lurked within the Wild Wood flare up and spread like wildfire, taking everyone to the east and the west by surprise?

"Always the same thoughts," the prisoner said to himself, as he paced his room – six steps from the window to one wall, and then five steps from there to the other. He had already walked miles like this, in this room and in another, and also inside a dark and gloomy cell.

He stopped and looked at the window, which was so high up that he could not see outside. Of course he could have climbed onto a chair but all he would have seen was a courtyard and one or two guards.

What should I do? he thought despondently. He had made every effort to keep his spirits up, so that he would be ready to go straight into action as soon as he was free again. At first, he had tried hard to escape. Once he had attacked the servant who brought him food. But, of course, it had done no good, and since then they had always brought his food in pairs. After that, his escape attempts had become more cunning. He had managed to pull up a floor tile and had started to dig a tunnel beneath, using a spoon and a nail as tools. He knew very well that his chances of getting out of this castle were very low, surrounded as it was by walls and a moat, but at least it gave him something to do. Worst of all was doing nothing. His hard work had been wasted, anyway, as one day they had taken him to a different room. Yes, taken him, like a man with no will of his own, him, Ristridin of the South, the hero of so many adventures.

Him, Ristridin, caught in a trap, a trap he had walked right into! He had survived the Red Riders' attack, escaped their pursuit, and all on his own he had found the way through the winter wilderness – driven onwards by only one thought: to let the world know what he had discovered in the Wild Wood.

But how could he have suspected that the Lord of Islan was conspiring with the enemy?

Sir Ristridin sat on his bed and buried his face in his hands. He was reliving how he had arrived at Islan, exhausted and hounded by the enemy, and how he had blown his horn and been admitted to the castle.

"Close the gate, pull up the drawbridge!" he had panted.

They had done so, and made him a prisoner. Soon after, his enemies had appeared at the gate – men in red, green and black – and asked the Lord of Islan to hand him over.

Sir Fitil had not granted that request, though; he apparently had at least that much honour left.

And now, thought Ristridin, *I am locked up in Islan. Sir Fitil said he would treat me as a guest, but he did not dare to look at me. He has violated the laws of hospitality and betrayed the trust of his king. If only I could just speak to him again, and convince him that what he is doing is wrong. I need to talk to him, or perhaps his daughter...*

He had once spoken to the lady, when he was being held in a room that looked out onto a walled garden. One morning – it was still winter – she was walking there in the snow, and he had beckoned to her through the bars of the window and spoken to her. As she had listened to him, her beautiful face had turned pale, but she had not answered. And the next day he had been taken to another room.

Sir Ristridin looked at one of the bedposts, into which he had carved lines, one for each day. The days had become weeks, the weeks months. And every day was the same... no, once, not that long ago, he had been ordered to go with the soldiers to an underground cell, a damp dungeon, far from the bustling life of the castle. He had wondered why he had been moved, particularly when he'd been brought back here a few days later. Might there have been guests in the castle who could not be allowed to suspect that he was there?

Now it was spring. Time was passing, while he waited... Waited? What for? Again he buried his head in his hands.

They expect me back at Castle Ristridin in the spring, he thought. *When I don't come, they'll go out looking for me.*

That thought was not a new one either, but this time it gave him no hope. He felt as if he had become years older, that his life was over. And if his captivity went on any longer, it would be too late.

Besides, they would be looking for him in the forest. And perhaps they, too, would be attacked, killed like Ilmar, like Arwaut and all the others. As far as he knew, he was the only one to have escaped.

The door opened, but Sir Ristridin did not move. Then he realized that it was not one of his guards who had entered the room. He looked up and saw the lady standing there, the Daughter of Islan. Again he noted that she was very beautiful, but her face was serious and her attitude was haughty, almost defensive. *Surely*, the thought flashed through his mind, *she would rather listen to courtly words of love than to what I have to say to her.*

He said nothing, though, but stood up and waited for her to speak. It was a moment before he heard her voice, a whisper, "Sir Ristridin..."

2 LADY ISADORO AND SIR FITIL

Sir Ristridin did not move and his attitude was just as haughty as hers when he responded, "Yes, my lady?"

She stepped into the room and said quietly, "Once you spoke to me and I would not listen. But now..." She fell silent.

Ristridin said nothing, but merely stared at her until she looked down at her feet. Then she lifted her face and said, "Why do you not answer?"

"What answer do you expect from me, my lady?" said the knight. "I have nothing to say."

She frowned. "Why are you making this so difficult for me?" she said, sounding almost indignant.

"Forgive me, my lady," said Ristridin, "but how can I, a prisoner, make anything difficult for you?" Then he saw her eyes fill with tears and he added a little less coldly, "My words carry no weight at all... in this place. As you must know."

"Yes, I am aware," she said flatly.

She turned away, and he took a step towards her, suddenly afraid she would leave. But she closed the door and said calmly, "I know you have been wrongfully imprisoned. But my father could have handed you over to the... to a Black Knight with a Red Shield, who has been here twice to claim you."

"Shame on your father if he had done so," said Ristridin.

"But he did not!" she said fiercely, her face flushing.

"Do you know who he is, this Black Knight?"

"I will not answer that question."

"But you do know what would have happened to me if your father had done as he asked. And so I must be grateful that the Lord of Islan has locked me up in his castle – Sir Fitil, who serves a master you do not even dare to name!"

"That is..." she began.

"That is the truth," said Ristridin.

"Yes," she said, the haughtiness leaving her face. "It is the truth."

"And what do you intend to do about this truth?" asked Ristridin quietly.

"I don't know!" she said. "That's why I came to see you."

She's still so young, thought Ristridin, and his expression softened.

"If you were free," she said, "what would you do?"

"Free?" repeated Ristridin. That thought made him take a deep breath. Free! But then he added suspiciously, "Why are you asking me that question? What do you want from me?"

"You do not trust me," she said bitterly. "And I do not blame you." She shook her hair back over her shoulders, all uncertainty gone. "Listen to me," she continued. "My father has promised to keep you prisoner here until... I don't know exactly when."

"To whom did he promise that, to the Knight with the Red Shield, the Master of the Tarnburg?"

"Yes. If we let you go, he will never forgive us. And you – if you were free – could you ever forgive us?"

"I cannot answer that question right now, my lady," said Ristridin. "Again, what do you want? All I can say to you is that I am being held here because I know too much about the Wild Wood and about the danger that threatens us all."

"That threatens the Kingdom of Unauwen!"

"Is that not enough? Do you truly know nothing about that land, which is known far and wide as the most beautiful land on earth? But the danger threatens us, too. The King of Eviellan is the enemy of all those who strive for good."

"Sssh!" she said.

"Why do you fear him so? He is not yet in power. Or is he?"

"No..." she whispered.

"But he will come and he will triumph. Unless the Black Knight is unmasked and his identity is revealed to all. And when I am free, I intend to do exactly that!"

The fire vanished from Ristridin's voice as he added, "If it is not too late."

"Perhaps there is still time," she whispered. "Perhaps you can persuade my father to let you go. That's why I came here. I want you to speak to each other. Oh, I pray that he will let you go! You are the only one who can erase some of the shame we have brought upon ourselves. Oh, please forgive us!"

Ristridin held out his hand, but she stepped back, her face suddenly pale, and cried out, "Do not say anything! Do not look upon me with such pity. You do not know what has happened!"

A wave of anxiety washed over Ristridin. "Tell me," he said sharply.

"Friends of yours... They came here, asking about you..."

"Who?"

"Sir Bendu, and Evan, and Sir Tiuri with his squire."

"Did something happen to them?"

"Tiuri is... Sir Bendu and Evan left, for Deltaland."

"Deltaland?" exclaimed Ristridin. "But Tiuri... was it the young Tiuri?"

"Yes, Tiuri with the White Shield. He went into the forest with his squire... and someone else, a friend..."

Ristridin roughly grabbed her hand. "And?" he growled. "Have they disappeared, too? Were they attacked, like my men? Are they... dead?"

She pulled her hand away. "No!" she cried. "Not dead! But captured. The squire escaped, though, and no one knows where he is. The Black Knight doesn't even know he exists."

Ristridin rubbed his forehead.

"So, somewhere out there, someone is wandering free, a squire who also knows about the secrets of the Wild Wood," he said slowly. "Now I understand! Take me to your father. This instant!"

*

Soon after that, Sir Ristridin was standing before the Lord of Islan – and it was the prisoner who was in charge of the situation. Various emotions flashed across Sir Fitil's face: fear, anger, shame... Lady Isadoro stood beside him, more composed than her father.

Ristridin had now heard what had happened – that Tiuri and his squire had gone into the wood with a friend, a peculiar vagabond who seemed to know something about what was going on. Sir Fitil had sent his men to capture them and bring them back to Islan. But the Red Riders had beaten them to it, and had taken Tiuri and his friend to the west. The squire had not been with them, though. The men of Islan had chased after him, but he had escaped. They had informed their master about the events a few days ago.

"And so," said Ristridin caustically, "you have realized it may well be pointless to keep me imprisoned. After all, there's a chance that someone else will betray your secret! And the King of Eviellan will still hold you responsible."

"The Lord of the Tarnburg knows nothing about this squire," said Sir Fitil. "He was not with his friends when they were captured."

"So he has a better chance of reaching civilization," said Ristridin. "But the others... do you ever think about them? You are also to blame for their fate! Tiuri... I know him. He was destined for greatness... he was a knight even before he was knighted..."

"I only wanted to keep him prisoner here," began Sir Fitil, "until..."

"Until your master has made his move!" Ristridin interrupted him.

"He is not my master!" cried Fitil, turning even redder. "And he is also well disposed towards the Kingdom of Dagonaut. The fight is between him and King Unauwen alone! I never meant any harm..."

"I could kill you for those words!" said Ristridin, his eyes flashing. "You meant no harm? But you allowed Eviellan to take up residence here and grow in power. You meant no harm? But when I told you that my men had been slaughtered, you turned a deaf ear. You meant no harm? But you allowed Sir Tiuri to go into the forest, and your only excuse is that all you would have done was hold him captive. I would rather hear you say that you did in fact mean harm!"

"You are sorely tempting me," said the Lord of Islan, with a threatening frown.

"Oh, be quiet!" cried Isadoro, coming to stand between the two men. "What good will it do you to rebuke us, Sir Ristridin? We were complicit in everything that has occurred in the Wild Wood – and if we let you go, it is only to protect ourselves."

"Isadoro..." her father began.

"Or are you scared of *his* revenge?" she sneered. "Do you think we can ever expect anything good from a ruler who does not value a man's life, or that it really matters if we obey him or not? Let Sir Ristridin go! We have not known a moment's calm since he came here."

"Quiet, Isadoro," said Fitil. He looked at Ristridin. His fury was gone. "Yes," he said dully. "It is madness, but for her sake and in the name of God, go – and leave me in peace."

Ristridin turned away for a moment from the despair in Sir Fitil's eyes. But he pulled himself together and said, "Your own conscience will perhaps be a better judge of you than I. You are setting me free, but I will not go until you have told me more. How did you keep my disappearance a secret? Where are knights Bendu and Evan?"

As he was speaking, Isadoro silently left the room.

Sir Fitil recovered sufficiently to look angry. For a moment it seemed that he would refuse to answer. Then he growled, "False rumours are easily spread. Your friends will be in Deltaland by now, or at the border."

"Why?"

A look of something like triumph flashed briefly across Fitil's face. "To repel the invasion," he replied, "Deltaland's invasion of the Kingdom of Dagonaut. But, believe me, that is not a false rumour. Deltaland is indeed invading, and Eviellan has rushed to the aid of our land! I am sure I do not have to add that it was actually Eviellan who planned that invasion. Deltaland is, of course, dependent on that land. An insignificant little incursion, which has probably been repelled by now. But the goal has been achieved: Dagonaut's knights have been lured to the border and attention has been diverted from the Wild Wood. The case for an alliance between Eviellan and Dagonaut grows stronger. Oh, by the way," he added, "another rumour has been spread, to say that you, Sir Ristridin, had already set out for Deltaland."

"So," said Ristridin slowly, "I have no friends nearby to help me. You have done your work well, Sir Fitil."

"No," said the Lord of Islan. "If I had done my work well, you would no longer be alive. And," he continued with bitter self-mockery in his voice, "it was not my own work I was doing, but Eviellan's donkeywork! Please, go now."

Sir Ristridin remained where he was. "And still I dare to place some trust in you, Sir Fitil," he said. "It is not yet too late! You have men, soldiers who could..."

"No!" said the Lord of Islan, and he clearly meant it. "I am a traitor through and through, but I cannot and will not choose a different course. Begone from my castle and look after your own affairs."

"Fine," said Ristridin. "But listen, Fitil! Keep your men at the ready and fortify your castle. For this is what I predict: the enemy in the forest will soon turn his fury upon our kingdom, and Islan will be his first target! If you have not yet forgotten your oath to Dagonaut, then prepare yourself to resist him."

"I do not believe that," said Fitil in a monotone.

"You know I am right," said Ristridin, and he looked at Isadoro, who had just returned, with her arms full. She was carrying his sword, his shield, his silver horn and his torn cloak. "You should send your daughter to a safer place," he added, taking his sword, horn and cloak from her.

"No," she said proudly. "I will remain here, where I belong."

In spite of all that had happened, Ristridin felt admiration for her, and he bowed silently.

"Here is your shield," she said.

"Permit me to leave it here," he said. "I intend to abandon my name here for now and to travel as an unknown knight. But if you should have a horse for me..."

"Take everything you want," growled Sir Fitil, "and begone."

Ristridin asked, "When will the attack on the Kingdom of Unauwen begin?"

"I do not know," replied Fitil. And then, suddenly, he roared, "I told you I was just doing their donkeywork, didn't I? Now, please, go!"

So Ristridin went.

3 RED QUIBO

Sir Ristridin left Castle Islan, and the gate was shut behind him and the drawbridge raised. Sitting on his horse, he thought for a moment. Back to King Dagonaut, who had sent him on his mission, it was almost a week's journey. And he had little time... maybe no time at all. And he would have to gather many, many men if he wished to make a stand against Eviellan. He knew there was only one place he could go: Castle Ristridin. That was the nearest castle, and he could trust his brother Arturin. A moment later, he was riding south as fast as an arrow, without a shield and with his visor closed. The enemy did not know he was free and could not be allowed to find out. That meant there was still a chance to bring about his downfall!

The day was drawing to a close as Ristridin set out. As the next day dawned, he reached the village on the southern edge of the Forest of Islan and stopped at an inn, the very one where Tiuri, Piak, Evan and Bendu had spent a night on their journey to Islan. Ristridin did not want to delay, but his horse was tired. He would need a fresh one if he meant to reach Castle Ristridin that day.

The inn appeared to be closed so early in the morning, but, after a few knocks on the door, the innkeeper came out. He looked up in surprise at the tall knight with the closed visor.

"What do you need, sir knight?" he asked.

"A moment's rest and a fresh horse," replied Ristridin. "I must ride onwards as soon as possible."

"A horse, sir? Yes, sir!" said the innkeeper. "Come on in."

The inn was not very welcoming. Last night's dirty cups and glasses had not yet been cleared away, but were cluttered across a large, stained table, and among them lay the red-haired head of a man who was probably sleeping off whatever he'd had to drink the night before. As Ristridin came in, he looked up and stared at him with dull eyes.

"What would you like to eat, sir knight?" said the innkeeper, noisily pushing aside the dirty cups and so preventing the redheaded man from going back to sleep.

"I don't mind," replied Ristridin. "A little bread and some water. I'd rather you looked into finding me a horse."

"H... horse?" said the redheaded man. Then he gave a loud yawn.

"Why don't you just get out of here, Quibo?" said the innkeeper irritably. "You're no credit to my establishment."

"I most certainly am!" Quibo objected. "I made a fine display of finishing off your brandy last night, didn't I? And I feel too wretched now to..."

"Ah, hold your tongue," barked the innkeeper. He quickly put down a plate of bread and mug of water in front of his anonymous guest and said in a solicitous voice, "I shall ensure you have a horse, sir knight."

"Huntsman Bas has good horses," said Quibo, with another yawn.

The innkeeper's face lit up. "I shall go and see him at once," he said, and he left.

Sir Ristridin was about to open his visor to eat. But as he looked at the other guest, he thought better of it.

The man was rubbing his eyes. His voice sounded less sleepy when he next spoke, "You have no need to fear my keen gaze, sir knight! I see nothing and hear nothing until the sun has reached its highest point. And by then I'm so sleepy that I spend my afternoon pondering and resting until evening comes."

He reached out a hand for Ristridin's mug, then seemed a little startled by his own boldness. He went on, "Oh, if I could just get my thoughts in order... Who are you?"

"Why do you ask the very question I cannot answer?" said Ristridin abruptly, but not unkindly.

"Ah, a thousand times forgiveness, noble sir! I shall bid you farewell and humbly take my leave," said the redheaded man. He staggered to his feet and immediately fell back down onto his chair. "Just get my breath back..." he mumbled.

Ristridin stood up, walked to the door and looked outside. But, of course, the innkeeper couldn't possibly be back yet. He sat back down at the table and noticed that the young man with the red hair was now completely awake and was watching him closely.

"I beg you," he said, "do not wait to eat on my account, Sir... Ristridin."

"Sir Ristridin?! Wherever did you get that idea?" asked the knight, trying to conceal his surprise.

"You do not know me, but I know you," came the reply. "I do not need to see a face to know who I'm talking to. I have often seen you riding and watched you with admiration. But of course you never noticed me. Red Quibo is my name."

Ristridin did not respond.

"And now you are finally returning from your journey through the Wild Wood," the strange fellow continued. "In secret, with your visor down, and maybe even feeling a little shocked and surprised. Did you see them, too, the men in red, green and black, holding their tourney in that quiet and lonely spot?"

"Hush!" said Ristridin. He rose to his feet. Large and threatening, he towered over Red Quibo.

Red Quibo looked up nervously at Sir Ristridin. "I..." he began.

"Be silent," said Ristridin, sitting down beside him. "Not another word!" He raised his visor and looked sternly at Quibo. "It is not a joke that I wish to remain unknown," he added. "It is true I am shocked and surprised that you know what is in the Wild Wood. But in the name of God, be silent, and pretend you do not recognize me, until I have had the chance to talk to you properly. You are sober now, aren't you?"

"As a judge," said Quibo. "But..."

"Not another word," repeated Ristridin. His voice and manner had the desired effect, as Quibo kept his mouth closed. Ristridin pulled the plate of bread towards him and started to eat. He offered some to Quibo, who just mumbled, "I couldn't swallow a bite."

As footsteps approached, the knight quickly closed his visor. The innkeeper came in and said, "There are two horses outside, sir knight. I shall saddle whichever one you prefer."

"Can you ride?" Ristridin asked Quibo.

"I can," he replied.

"Then saddle them both," Ristridin said to the innkeeper. "This young man is coming with me."

"Quibo?! Fine, sir. Yes, sir," said the innkeeper and he walked off with a puzzled look on his face.

"Me? Coming with you?" exclaimed Quibo. "But I..."

Ristridin interrupted him. "No objections, if you please."

"But why?" cried Quibo.

"I need a squire," Ristridin casually replied. "And besides, you and I have to talk."

That was true, but Ristridin had another reason for wanting to keep Quibo in his care. The man looked as if he enjoyed a good few glasses of brandy – and Ristridin was sure that once he'd had a few, he might easily say too much.

"Come with me," he ordered, heading outside.

Red Quibo obeyed him without any further objections, but he wore an expression of disbelief as he followed the knight and waited for the horses to be saddled. "I could be dreaming, of course..." he muttered to himself as he climbed onto the horse.

Ristridin pressed some coins into the innkeeper's hand and said, "The owner of these horses will have them back as soon as possible. My thanks for your help. And mark this: by the crown of King Dagonaut and the swords of his knights, I implore you to remain silent about my visit. Farewell."

"Nicely spoken, sir knight!" said Quibo with a sigh.

Ristridin mounted his horse and rode away, followed by his reluctant squire.

"I haven't even had any breakfast!" whined Red Quibo.

"You weren't hungry," said Ristridin. "Now onwards, at a gallop."

"On an empty stomach? It'll make me sick," wailed Quibo. "Me? A squire... It's outrageous, ridiculous!"

But Ristridin noticed that he sat well in the saddle and, before long, they were racing along the road to the south.

After a while, Quibo yelled out, "Sir knight, please, can't we rest? Just for a moment?"

He could not see that Ristridin was smiling when he stopped and said, "Fine. It's quiet here. We can go more slowly and talk."

Red Quibo ran one grubby hand through his hair and said grumpily, "I am your servant, my lord, although I still do not understand why you disturbed my sleep and dragged me along to... I don't know what... slavery, or some castle or a battle."

"There could be more truth in your words than you realize, Quibo," said Ristridin. "Great dangers threaten this land and another. What do you know about the Wild Wood?"

Quibo sighed. "I shall tell you if you wish," he said. "But allow me to sit safely on the ground while I do so."

Ristridin gave him permission, and Quibo then repeated the story he'd told some weeks ago to Sir Bendu, Tiuri and their companions.

"So this happened to you a while ago!" said Ristridin. "Why did no one hear about it before?"

"No one believed it before!" cried Quibo. "I told the story to anyone who would listen. About the tourney, and about that sinister valley among the hilly slopes."

"Well, right now it's best if they continue to see your experiences as just a story," said Ristridin. "But what you saw is the truth, Quibo, and those warriors at the tourney were not ghosts or phantoms, but men."

"Really?" whispered Quibo. "I can't say that's a reassuring thought. What manner of men could they be?"

"They come from Eviellan," replied Ristridin.

"Oh, so that's why you're in such a hurry. Not to return to your home, but to catch up with him!"

"Him? Who are you talking about?"

"The knight who rested at the inn last night. A knight in raven-black and red – I mean in black armour and with a red shield."

This was news to Ristridin. "Tell me more!" he said.

"There is no more to tell, my lord. I... I was not entirely clear-headed, if you catch my meaning." Red Quibo scratched his head and grinned apologetically. "He reminded me of something..." he added, "and now I know what it was: the wood!"

"And he went this way?"

"My memory is a hazy fog... I believe he came from the north and was going south." Quibo pulled a face as if it were painful for him to think.

"Then we shall swiftly move onwards," decided Ristridin, getting to his feet. He walked some way down the track, looking carefully at the ground. "A knight has ridden this way recently, in the same direction as us," he commented. "Come on, Quibo!"

"Sir knight," he replied, "I have told you everything I had to say. Can I go back home now?"

"And to your inn?" said Ristridin.

"I shall not breathe a word of what I know."

"Even if you've been drinking brandy, Quibo?"

"Even then! And what I drink is not your affair, knight," said Quibo with a flash of anger.

"If it loosens your tongue, it is my affair," said Ristridin gravely. "So my answer is no, Quibo! You are coming with me, for as long as this knowledge must remain secret." He grabbed Quibo by the shoulder and pulled him to his feet. "Do not bother objecting," he continued. "You are staying with me, whether you like it or not."

"I shall only be a millstone around your neck, my lord!" Quibo cried. "I'm the strangest rogue of a squire ever to ride a horse."

"That may well be," said Ristridin, "but that is how it is." As he remembered Ilmar, young, cheerful Ilmar, his squire who had been killed, he sighed.

"Sir knight..." said Quibo.

Ristridin looked at him and saw that his face was actually bright and kind-hearted, even though it was grimy and showed signs of too much drinking.

"Yes?" he said.

"What must be must be," said Red Quibo solemnly. "With my empty stomach and my weary head, I will follow you into... unto... until the day I'm allowed to go home."

"Good," said Ristridin with a smile. "Then let's ride on."

"May I say something else, my lord?" said Quibo. "Would it not be better to keep your horn in your saddlebag? I can see it glinting and glimmering through the rips in your cloak."

"So that's how you recognized me!" cried Ristridin.

"No, that wasn't it – that just confirmed my suspicions. One doesn't come across such a fine silver horn every day."

"Or such an observant pair of eyes as yours," said Ristridin. "My thanks for your good advice. I shall follow it immediately."

"It is not far to go now," said the knight a little later. "A few more bends in the road and we shall see the castle."

"As long as it's not too many bends!" muttered Quibo. "I'm already feeling dizzy. I don't want to go tumbling from my horse."

Ristridin pretended not to hear his complaints. "And there," he said, as they went around the first bend, "is the knight you were talking about, a Black Knight with a Red Shield."

"Let him ride on," said Quibo dully. "We're too tired to catch up with him."

The horses were indeed weary, but still Ristridin urged his steed on. A knight from Eviellan who had come from the north... maybe from Islan or from the Wild Wood. He wanted to find out more.

The Black Knight looked around, before reining in his horse and waiting for Ristridin to reach him.

"Greetings, sir knight!" he called. "Travelling companions are always welcome." He had raised his visor and Ristridin saw a face that, in spite of its smile, seemed gloomy and grim.

He did not know the man, but then he had never looked his mortal enemy, the Knight with the Red Shield, in the face.

"And greetings to you, sir knight," Ristridin replied. But he did not lift his own visor.

4   SIR KRATON OF INDIGO

"There is only one road, so we can ride together for some way," said the Black Knight with the Red Shield. "Is that man with you?" He pointed at Quibo, who was slowly trudging along.

"My squire," said Ristridin.

"Oh! I am travelling alone, as you can see. I am Sir Kraton of Indigo."

Ristridin gave him a nod and said, "I know your name, Sir Kraton."

"Of Indigo," said the other man, with a frown. And when Ristridin said nothing, he went on, "Or are you disputing my right to call myself by that name?"

"I am not disputing any right, Sir Kraton," said Ristridin, rather surprised.

"Of Indigo!" repeated Kraton. "My castle may have been destroyed by the elder son of King Unauwen, but I shall rebuild it! And the name of Indigo cannot be destroyed, even though that is what your refusal to utter it was intended to suggest."

"I was not suggesting anything," said Sir Ristridin coldly, "Sir Kraton of Indigo!"

The other knight looked him up and down, and said, "I have come from the City of Dagonaut and am on my way to the south. And you?"

"I, too, am heading south," replied Ristridin.

"Where did you come from?"

"From the north."

"And your name?"

"Will remain unknown," said Ristridin. "But we can travel together, if you have no objections to the company of a knight with no name."

"But I do object!" cried Kraton. "I told you my name, and you are insulting me if you do not tell me yours and raise your visor!"

"My apologies," said Ristridin without moving.

"Are we not in the Kingdom of Dagonaut, where peace reigns?" Kraton continued. "There are no conspiracies here, no assassins, no robber barons and others who choose to lurk in shadows, are there? So whatever possesses you to ride around like that?" Again he studied Ristridin closely.

"That is my business, Sir Kraton of Indigo," he said brusquely, pulling at the reins of his horse.

But Sir Kraton blocked his way. "That is not good enough," he said.

"Hell, heaven and all the saints," sighed Red Quibo. "This is all we need!"

There was no way out of the conflict, though. Ristridin knew he and Kraton could not let each other go. This knight from Eviellan must not be allowed to discover his identity; the enemy had to believe he was still imprisoned, harmless, locked away in Islan. Perhaps Kraton already had his suspicions about who he was dealing with – and even suspicions could be dangerous if he shared them with his king. The only solution was a duel.

"I see. So that is not good enough for you, Sir Kraton," said Ristridin. "Please continue. I am at your disposal."

Kraton did not respond immediately. He suddenly seemed more hesitant.

"I am waiting!" said Ristridin, raising his voice.

With an angry gesture, Kraton pulled off his glove and threw it at Ristridin.

"I am pleased to accept your challenge," said Ristridin calmly. "What are the conditions?"

"Your name!" barked Kraton. "And I want you to raise your visor."

"If you win... fine. But what if I should win?"

"I have nothing to hide," said Kraton sarcastically. "Just tell me what you want from me."

"If I win, you must come with me to my destination."

"A fine condition!" cried Kraton. "A goal that is unknown to me!"

"I shall reach it today," said Ristridin. "But if you wish to be the only one who imposes a condition..."

"Fine. I accept!" cried Kraton. "I do not expect to be defeated by some ragged knight with no name. How will we fight?"

"I have no weapon but my sword."

"With the sword, then," said Kraton, putting aside his dagger and battle-axe. "And on horseback, until one of us is disarmed and lying on the ground."

"Agreed," said Ristridin. He looked at Quibo and said, "Wait, and watch."

"Yes, sir knight," said Quibo.

Ristridin thought, *If this turns out badly, will he be bright enough to ride on to Castle Ristridin and tell them what has happened?* He could say nothing else now to his travelling companion. But, drawing his sword, he thought this could not, *must* not, turn out badly. He was definitely as strong as his opponent; only Kraton's horse seemed superior to his own.

Sir Kraton threw his shield to Quibo. "There," he said, "and now we are equal." So he was a man who fought with chivalry, as a true knight should.

He was also a formidable fighter, although he'd met his match in Ristridin. But Ristridin was fighting for the future of two kingdoms. Perhaps Kraton sensed that, because his attacks were fierce and fast, designed to bring the fight to a quick end.

But Ristridin parried all of his slashes and blows, and hit back all the harder. His horse really did put him at a disadvantage, though – not only was it tired, but it was untrained for combat. His opponent's steed was far more agile. So he redoubled his efforts, pressing close to Kraton and dealing him a blow that glanced off his helmet.

The Black Knight swayed in his saddle, and Ristridin seized the chance to pull him from his horse. Both men fell, but Ristridin had already slid his feet out of the stirrups, and he was the first to stand up again.

He heard Quibo's voice, high and shrill, "Hit him, stab him!" But Ristridin waited for Kraton to get back to his feet.

Now they really were equal. Dust flew up as the clashes of metal on metal rang out, and both men were slightly wounded.

Then Ristridin raised his sword and struck so powerfully that Kraton's sword broke. Ristridin cast aside his own weapon, pounced on his opponent and threw him to the ground. "I win," he said, panting as he leant over him.

Kraton moved a little and mumbled something. Ristridin helped him to sit up.

"Yes, you win," Kraton growled. "You can let go of me. I'm still alive."

But then he allowed Ristridin to help him to his feet; he walked up and down a few times with his broken sword in his hand.

"Have you recovered sufficiently to continue?" asked Ristridin.

"Certainly, Knight with No Name," said Kraton. "Lead me to your unknown destination."

Quibo came closer.

"Take Sir Kraton's battle-axe and dagger," Ristridin ordered him.

"I am still capable of carrying them myself," said Kraton.

"You will not need them on our journey," said Ristridin. "Mount your horse, Sir Kraton of Indigo."

Kraton glared at him. "I know one thing now," he said. "Your name must be very well known indeed! Otherwise I would not be riding with you now, against my will."

"Stay close to my side," Ristridin said. He did not like the flicker in Kraton's eyes. This knight surely suspected he was an enemy and could well try to escape.

"How many more bends?" Red Quibo shouted from behind them.

There, before them, was the familiar outline of Castle Ristridin on the Grey River.

"Is that your goal?" asked Kraton.

"Indeed it is," replied Ristridin.

"Well, that is indeed convenient," said Kraton. "As it happens, I was also heading to the castle. I stopped there on my way to the City of Dagonaut, too. It's a most hospitable place. Does that surprise you?"

"No, Sir Kraton," said Ristridin. "Why should it surprise me?"

"I thought you might be one of those knights who have something against me and my compatriots," replied Kraton. "Sir Arturin is not like that. He knows there is peace between Dagonaut and Eviellan."

Ristridin did not reply. He had already decided what he was going to do, and though he didn't like the prospect it was unavoidable. There was no peace between Dagonaut and Eviellan; soon the gloves would come off.

Kraton watched him out of the corner of his eye and remained silent. But he seemed to understand that he was in danger, because as they approached the castle he reined in his horse and said, "We have reached our goal."

"Not yet," replied Ristridin. "We are going inside."

They rode on and stopped at the closed drawbridge. Ristridin had always sounded his silver horn in the past, but now he merely asked in a loud voice to be admitted. With a grinding creak, the drawbridge descended.

"I have accompanied you to your destination," said Kraton, "and now our ways must part."

Kraton was about to spur on his horse, but Ristridin held it by the reins, drew his sword and cried, "What? You wish to flee? Dismount and come inside with me."

"And what then?" said Kraton, angry and uneasy. "Is this a trap? What can I expect from you, Knight with No Name?"

"Exactly the same as I can expect from Eviellan," replied Ristridin. "Dismount!"

On foot, they made their way onto the bridge. Soldiers came towards them and asked in surprise what was going on.

"This knight has lured me into a trap!" cried Kraton.

"We both request your hospitality," said Ristridin. "Allow us to enter and announce our arrival to Sir Arturin."

He took the reluctant Kraton by the arm and marched across the bridge with him. The soldiers walked with them, but made them stop inside the gateway.

"What is your name?" they asked Ristridin.

"Do not allow him in!" cried Kraton.

"This is the castle of my forefathers," said his escort, now raising his visor. "So I am sure you must know my name! I am Ristridin of the South."

5 RISTRIDIN'S HOMECOMING

Sir Kraton raised his arms and then dropped them at his sides in a gesture of resignation. The astonished soldiers all talked at the same time. "Let us in," said Ristridin, "and close the gate."

A moment later they were in the courtyard. Others came running towards them; cries of delight and surprise echoed around the walls: "Sir Ristridin has returned!"

And then Sir Arturin, his brother, came out to meet him, with outstretched hands. "Finally!" he cried.

The welcome was a warm one, but brief, as Kraton drew his broken sword. "And what about me?" he asked.

"You, Sir Kraton, are my guest," said Ristridin coldly. "Just as I was the guest of the Lord of Islan."

Sir Arturin looked surprised. "What is the meaning of this?" he asked.

By then another knight had appeared in the courtyard; it was none other than Bendu.

"To put it simply," said Ristridin, "Sir Kraton is my prisoner."

"Ristridin!" cried Bendu.

Then his eye fell on Kraton. "So we meet again, Sir Kraton." The knight merely growled.

Ristridin greeted Bendu warmly. Then he gave the guards an

order: "Lock him up. He is to have anything he wants, except his freedom."

"I refuse to accept this," said Kraton angrily. "You got me here by trickery. I do not understand your reference to Islan. Sir Arturin, I appeal to you as the lord of this castle! Today I will be your guest, but tomorrow I must leave."

"You shall not go until I release you," said Ristridin.

"When will that be? You are acting without honour and you have no right..." began Kraton.

Ristridin interrupted him. "When?!" he cried. "Only after Eviellan has launched its attack."

Those words silenced Kraton. His face froze and he said not another word. But the look he gave Ristridin was one of impotent rage.

"What does all this mean?" asked Arturin again.

Ristridin looked around the circle of astonished faces and said, loudly and clearly, "For the love of God, do as I say. No one must know I have returned home, and you may tell no one Sir Kraton is here. Guard this castle as if it were under siege."

Then he pointed at Quibo. "This man is my squire," he said. "Look after him. Give him food and a good glass of wine – but no more than one glass, even if he begs you."

Turning to his brother and Bendu, he said, "At last. Come with me. I have so much to tell you."

"So it was the Wild Wood, after all," said Bendu after they had spoken for a while.

"Yes, indeed it was," said Ristridin. "Oh Bendu, if only you had listened to Tiuri!"

"I am sorry," muttered Bendu. "But you mustn't hold it against me. Tiuri is so young, and that Fool seemed completely unreliable."

"Out of the mouths of babes, drunkards and fools..." Ristridin muttered to himself. "But Tiuri is no longer a child and he has previously shown the courage to defy prevailing opinions and customs." He sighed.

"I am sorry about the boy," said Bendu. His face was dark with anger. "And Arwaut, my nephew," he continued. "And Ilmar and... I swear, here and now..."

"Wait a while before you start swearing oaths," Ristridin said in a gentle voice, cutting him off. "Maybe you will be given another task first, Bendu! Where is Evan?"

"He left here the day before yesterday," replied Arturin. "Bendu arrived the day before that, and the messages he brought convinced Evan he could wait no longer for you. He had to warn King Unauwen."

"What messages?" asked Ristridin. "What have you done, Bendu, since you left for Deltaland?"

"Well, the invasion did indeed take place," said Bendu, "although I am not surprised to hear it was just a diversionary tactic. Evan and I joined the forces of your brother and the Lord of Warudin. Within a few days we had driven most of the attackers back beyond the border. It was only then that Eviellan finally came to our assistance, with an army led by Sir Melas of Darokitam. Too late to help. But of course that was all part of their bluff. They just wanted to strengthen the case for an alliance between our countries and to draw our attention away from the Wild Wood. But all the time they were actually behind the invasion. Hmm, well, then Evan returned to Castle Ristridin, as he could hardly fight side by side with his declared enemy. After that, there were a few little skirmishes, but I did not take part for long. I headed into Deltaland with a few men, and then I only had to cross the river to get to Eviellan. You see, I had my doubts about the situation – and from what you tell me, I was right to have them."

"And what did you do in Eviellan?" asked Ristridin.

"Oh, they were not pleased to see me, but of course they had to keep up the pretence of friendship that exists between our two lands. So I was relatively undisturbed as I travelled westwards on the other side of the Grey River, past Darokitam and Agfarod." Bendu fell silent before continuing, "There I discovered that they were very busy indeed. Soldiers were approaching from every direction, some openly, others in secret. Entire armies had been mobilized, and they were nearly all on their way to the west. A large force must already have been gathered where the Great Mountains meet the Southerly Mountains; a gorge there leads to the Kingdom of Unauwen."

"An attack on two fronts," said Ristridin thoughtfully. "Yes, that's quite likely. In the Kingdom of Unauwen they know of that weak spot in their border; there has often been fighting in that place. But a large attack at that point, and at the same time, or shortly afterwards, an invasion from the Wild Wood, across the pass of the Second Great Road... That attack would come as a complete surprise to the Kingdom of Unauwen! And there would be no chance to resist it, as Unauwen's forces would be concentrated in the south."

"If only we knew when it was!" said Bendu. "Sir Kraton..."

"I don't think you will learn anything from Sir Kraton," said Ristridin. "But I do not believe it will be soon. If that were the case, he would have not have been quite so furious when I told him he'd remain a prisoner until after the attack. We may still have time." He turned to his brother. "Arturin..." he began.

"I am ready, along with all my men," he said.

"Messengers first of all," said Ristridin. "They must be sent with haste to King Dagonaut, to Castle Mirtelan, Warudin, Griudin, Igrudin..." He looked at Bendu. "You must be a messenger, too," he said. "Evan is not here, so you must travel along the Grey River to the Kingdom of Unauwen to inform them about the threat from the Wild Wood. The Kingdom of Dagonaut has a duty to Unauwen, as we have unwittingly allowed this evil to take root and grow in our land."

"How did the King of Eviellan find his way into the Wild Wood?" Arturin wondered.

"Along the Grey River somehow," said Ristridin. "It's probably been going on for years. And more men will have joined his forces while our attention was on Deltaland."

Bendu faced him. "You want me... to go to the Kingdom of Unauwen?" he said. "Fine. I shall leave tonight."

"No, early tomorrow morning," said Ristridin. "A departure at night could suggest to Eviellan's spies that your mission is secret and important."

Bendu nodded.

"For now, our enemy must not suspect that we know of his plans," Ristridin continued. "Arturin, you must ensure that no more men from Eviellan cross the river to join the army in the Wild Wood. The southern border of the wood must be placed under close watch, but not immediately, as that would also arouse their suspicions. Bendu must first cross the mountains."

"And what about you?" asked Bendu.

"I am preparing myself for the war on our own territory," replied Ristridin. "The battle between Unauwen and Eviellan has gone on for years, and it seems as if its outcome will be decided on our soil, in the Wild Wood."

6   BACK TO THE WILD WOOD

The messengers had been sent out. Arturin's men had been ordered to prepare for battle. But Sir Ristridin's face was serious when he considered how long it would take him to gather an army that was large enough to resist the mighty forces of Eviellan.

"You can count on assistance from at least one quarter before too long, that's for sure," Arturin said to him. "He went to Deltaland for the battle and Evan spoke to him before returning here. Sir Tiuri of Tehuri. He was planning to head here."

"Tiuri the Valiant!" exclaimed Ristridin. "He will be a strong brother-in-arms! But I don't relish the prospect of explaining what has happened to his son."

"Do not be too downhearted," said Arturin. "You have heard only that the boy has been captured – not killed."

"But he is in the hands of the man who rules the Wild Wood," said Ristridin. "A knight with black armour and a red shield, whom I suspect is also the man who killed Sir Edwinem." At that point he looked at Bendu. "The Black Knight with the Red Shield is the King of Eviellan himself!" he told him quietly. "I think, Bendu, that this knight is not destined to fall at your hand. And how do you expect such a man to treat Tiuri, son of Tiuri?"

Sir Bendu left at dawn, riding along the Third Great Road to the west.

Sir Arturin prepared his men for their task.

Sir Kraton was locked up, cursing the fate that had made him lose to Ristridin.

Sir Ristridin walked restlessly around the castle, burning with a need to act and yet knowing he had to wait. He sent for Red Quibo, gave him weapons and chainmail and said, "The men are practising out in the courtyard. Go and join them."

"Me?" said Quibo. "My lord, I truly wasn't born to handle weapons! I am your prisoner because you do not trust me, but you cannot force me to carry such things, or to act bravely until I meet a bloody end! My courage is lacking, my health is poor..."

"Well, I'm sure it will improve now that there is no inn nearby," said Ristridin wryly. "Do as I command. My squire must be able to use a weapon."

"Why do you hate me, sir knight, just because I recognized you?" cried Quibo. "You are mocking my pain, laughing at me, lazy coward that I am!"

"It's time to put an end to that laziness," said Ristridin. "Hold your impudent tongue and go and play your part!"

Two hours later he found Quibo, covered in sweat and dirtier than ever, crouched in a corner of the courtyard.

"Get up," he ordered, "and go and wash."

"Have pity, my lord!" groaned Quibo. "I am defeated and as good as dead."

"A little cold water will do you some good," said Ristridin without pity. "Hurry or you'll miss your lunch."

"Lunch!" spat his reluctant squire. "I am thirsty! I want to drink until I'm drunk!"

Ristridin pulled him roughly to his feet and cuffed him around the ears.

"Oh, mercy," sighed Quibo, as he stood reeling. "Why don't you just lock me up, like Sir Kraton? Then I'd have some peace."

"No, you're coming with me," said Ristridin. "Perhaps you can be of some use. After all, you know your way around the Unholy Hills."

"Unholy? It was an unholy day when I met you!" wailed Quibo. "Must I again be dragged along without a little drop to strengthen me? When are you leaving, my lord?"

"Very soon," said Ristridin. "I think Sir Tiuri will not want to wait for long before heading into the Wild Wood."

"Sir Tiuri?"

"Yes, I expect him here today or tomorrow."

"Yet more knights," muttered Quibo. "Intrepid knights, valiant and true, and me, poor Quibo, stuck in the middle." And Quibo hurried off for his lunch.

Towards the end of the following day, a line of knights rode onto the Plain of Islan. At the front was a knight with a shield of azure and gold, Tiuri the Valiant, the father of Tiuri with the White Shield. Beside him rode Ristridin, with his visor closed. Red Quibo was also with the company, properly fitted out as a squire, but with a most disgruntled look on his face.

They reined in their horses and gazed at Castle Islan in the distance, formidable, the drawbridge up, the gate shut.

The knights, too, looked most formidable.

"And yet I feel it is better to leave Islan to its own devices for now," said Ristridin.

"Hmm, that is where Tiuri departed from," his companion said.

Ristridin thought of Lady Isadoro for a moment and wondered how she and Tiuri had got along. He looked at Tiuri's father and said, "You understand, though. We cannot provoke a confrontation too soon. Bendu should reach the Kingdom of Unauwen within about six days. And men from many castles will soon be on their way here..."

"I understand completely," said Sir Tiuri the Valiant. "But no one will be surprised that I choose to head to the wood."

"A father in search of his errant son," said Ristridin in a weak attempt at humour. "Of course. We will enter the Wild Wood at Stoneford, heading first in the direction of the Forgotten City, and then to the west, as swiftly as seems wise." They rode onwards.

Then Quibo piped up from behind Ristridin, "Sir knight, forgive me, but I heard we're missing out the Unholy Hills. Could I..."

"Silence!" said Ristridin impatiently. "Who says we will not go there another day?" Again he looked with sympathy at the knight beside him. He could tell that Sir Tiuri was thinking about his son.

Part Eight

Final Moves

1 THE PASS

Tiuri, son of Tiuri, lay on his stomach, looking out over the edge of the steep drop where the hidden path ended. Down below he could see the Road of Ambuscade. Piak lay beside him and whispered in his ear, "Do you see that plume of smoke, to the right of the Tarntop? That must be where the last guard post is."

Further to the west was the pass, where Tehalon had said soldiers were also standing guard. A high rock was blocking their view, so they could not see how they might be able to get past. But, whatever they did, they would have to get down to the road below first. Piak had already worked out the best route.

They heard footsteps approaching along the road below them. The friends pulled back their heads, but then peeped over the edge again, very carefully, to take a look. It was two Red Riders, heavily armed, but on foot. They walked past, slowly, as the road was slippery with melting snow, and headed westwards, disappearing behind the rock. Voices came from that direction. The two friends waited in silence. After a while the men returned... no, it was two different Red Riders, who were going back to the east, towards the Tarntop.

"They've changed the watch at the pass!" whispered Tiuri, when they had gone. "That's good. Now there's a chance that no one will come by for a while. Let's go."

Piak uncoiled the rope and tied the two ends together. He looped it around the rocky outcrop he had chosen. It was so long that even as a loop it hung nearly all the way down to the road. "You first," he said quietly. Here in the mountains he felt like a guide again, who had to take charge and bring up the rear during a descent.

It took Tiuri a moment to pluck up the courage to go over the edge, but down he went. His friend was better at this kind of undertaking. But he reached the bottom in one piece. He flexed his fingers, which were red and sore from the rough rope, and then held his breath as he watched Piak, who was down and beside him in a split second and then tugged at the rope until he held the knot in his hands. He untied it and pulled. "Good!" he whispered, coiling the rope back up again. "The last part of the hidden path is behind us and we're on the Road of Ambuscade." Then he let Tiuri take over again. "So what do we do now?"

Tiuri didn't know either. They couldn't see the pass from here and they didn't know exactly where the guard post was. But there was nothing else they could do except head in that direction – creeping and with cunning, to use Tehalon's words. The road was wide and climbed gradually. Steep cliffs stood on either side and, to the left, around the corner, were the guards. It would be best, of course, if they could slip past unnoticed.

Piak nudged Tiuri and whispered, "Please, take my sword. I'm not very good with it. I prefer this." He brandished the stick he'd found along the way.

Tiuri accepted his offer, knowing his friend was right.

Shortly after that, they were peering around the rock that had blocked their view for so long. They could see the road to its highest point – the pass. Some way beneath it was a hut, built of blocks of stone. Smoke curled through a hole in the roof, and the door was open. It was so close that they could see the horn hanging by the door. Someone was moving inside and they quickly stepped back when a Red Rider came out, then waited for a moment before looking again to see that the man was making a fire at the side of the road. He stood up, with his back towards them, and gave a loud cry. The second guard appeared over the pass.

When the two friends plucked up courage to look again, one of the men had disappeared. The other was sitting by the fire, grasping a spear that he'd planted in the ground beside him.

As quietly as possible, they walked back to the spot where they'd climbed down. They didn't dare to speak until they got there, and still only in whispers.

"We'll never get past without being seen," said Tiuri. "We have to follow the road to get over the pass, and it looks as if one of the two is always on guard outside!"

Piak nodded. "You're right," he said. "But what about when it gets dark?"

"Do you think that'll make much difference?"

"I don't know," said Piak thoughtfully. "We can only go along the road, and there's a guard sitting next to a fire that's lighting up the whole area. He might not see us straightaway, but he's sure to hear us."

"So," said Tiuri, "we'll just have to let them see us."

"And how's that going to work?"

"We'll have to go as soon as possible. We might as well go right now, if it's not going to make any difference anyway."

"But how?"

"We'll pretend we're Men in Green. That's what we look like, after all."

"But do you think they'll just let us through?" asked Piak.

"No," replied Tiuri after pausing to think. "But they won't see us as enemies, so we'll be able to get closer."

"And then?"

"Then it's two against two. We'll have to overpower them."

"Ah!" sighed Piak and then he added, "Well, I've got enough rope to tie them up tightly."

"But we can't give them any time to raise the alarm," Tiuri continued. "If we take them out of action, it won't be discovered until tomorrow, when the next guards come to relieve them. That's why we have to do it now – then we'll have more of a lead."

"Yes..." whispered Piak, his voice trembling slightly. "Just tell me what you want me to do. And I'll do it!"

Once again they walked up the Road of Ambuscade, not skulking along the rocks this time, but casually striding up the middle of it.

The guard rose to his feet when he saw them coming; he stood in the middle of the road and held up his spear to bar the way. The friends walked onwards, outwardly calm but their hearts were beating faster.

The guard barked something at them.

Tiuri and Piak stopped, bowed their heads in greeting and said, "Giaruda."

Tiuri cast a glance at the hut; the other guard was standing in the doorway. Then he looked again at the soldier facing him. He had a hostile expression, with small, beady eyes that stared suspiciously at Tiuri. He spoke again, asking something in the language of Eviellan. The meaning of the question was clear enough: "What do you want?"

Tiuri pointed from east to the west and indicated with sign language that he and Piak wanted to cross the pass.

But, just as Tiuri had feared, the guard shook his head and made it very clear that the answer was no.

Tiuri repeated his gestures. But the guard kept on shaking his head and giving them threatening glares.

Tiuri placed one hand on his chest. "I come from the Tarnburg," he said slowly, pointing in that direction. "The Black Knight with the Red Shield... Eviellan..."

Piak helped him. "Tehalon," he said.

"Tehalon," nodded Tiuri, pointing at the pass again.

He had been keeping a close eye on the hut, which was just as well, as the other guard had become curious and came over to see what was happening.

Now the two Red Riders were standing together, grim and forbidding, but also rather puzzled. Tiuri repeated his gestures and made sounds whose meaning he didn't know himself. He ended with, "Let us through!"

Those were the last words he would say, just as he and Piak had agreed. When the guards began to answer, he gave the signal: "Now," and they both attacked at the same moment.

Their plan went better than expected. The guards' initial suspicions did indeed seem to have been eased. It took them a second to recover from the surprise and try to defend themselves, but by then they had both been relieved of their weapons. Tiuri wrestled on the ground with his opponent, who was knocked out when he hit his head on a rock. He stood up in time to see Piak hit the other one with his stick and trip him up.

"Your rope, quickly!" panted Tiuri. Then he gasped. Another Red Rider had appeared from the hut. There was a third guard!

Tiuri drew his sword and ran towards him, slipping on the icy surface. The guard took out his sword and reached for the horn beside the door.

"Duck!" Piak cried from behind him, and a stone went whizzing past his ear. It hit the guard, who recovered only to find Tiuri standing before him.

Tiuri immediately went on the attack, determined not to lose this fight; it had to be done quickly and quietly. He was met with fierce opposition but the fight was soon over – incredibly soon, with a grim, but inevitable, conclusion. Without thinking, Tiuri seized his moment and thrust – a powerful, deep strike... The man swayed, his face turned pale, he grimaced... and then fell.

Tiuri took a step back. For a moment the world stood still.

But a stifled cry from Piak made him spin around. One of the other guards had come round and grabbed his spear, and he was approaching Piak, on the attack. Tiuri leapt at him and let his sword descend on the man's head. He, too, collapsed and moved no more.

The two friends looked at each other for a moment, and then Tiuri followed Piak's gaze to the bloody sword in his hand. Suddenly he felt sick. But he pulled himself together and bent over the fallen man.

"We have to tie them up," he heard Piak say. His voice was trembling and seemed to come from a long way off.

"Just the one who's lying there, on the road," replied Tiuri. "This one's dead, too." His own voice sounded strange, as if someone else were speaking. *Maybe I should kill the last one as well*, he thought, as he walked over to him.

But as he looked down at the defenceless man, he knew he couldn't do it – in a fair fight, yes, but not now. "Bind him tightly," he ordered Piak, "and put something in his mouth, so he can't shout for help when he comes round." He knelt down and helped his friend. "We'll put him in the hut," he said. "Along with the others..."

Quickly and without speaking, they did what had to be done. Then they stood on the road again and looked around. There was no sign of danger. Tiuri wiped the sword as clean as he could with some snow.

"It's your sword," he said. "Do you want it back?"

"No," replied Piak. "You can keep it for now."

They started walking up to the pass.

I've killed a man, thought Tiuri. *Two men.* Could he ever forget? Stabbing and pulling back his sword? The blood gushing from the wound?

What else could you have done? he thought to himself. *You knew when you were given a sword that this would happen one day.*

As he walked faster, he wondered what Piak was thinking now. He'd hardly said anything. Would he regard him later with horror in his eyes?

When they had reached the top, Piak broke the silence. "The pass!" he said. Tiuri looked at him and saw only companionship on his face.

"Yes, we've made it," he said quietly. "And now we have to head down."

2 THE DESCENT

It was not the first time Tiuri and Piak had made their way across the Great Mountains and down into the Kingdom of Unauwen. They had travelled along a different road before, across a pass that was much higher, along a path that was narrower and more difficult. The Road of Ambuscade was an easy enough walk, even though it was still early in the year. It was cold, but the weather was fine, so they could travel quickly.

And yet still Tiuri felt gloomy and apprehensive, because of what had just happened, and also because he was not sure they'd reach their destination in time. The bleak landscape around them did not improve his mood.

The slopes, they are so high and steep,
deep and dark the gorge below...

Those were the words Lavinia had sung, adding the lines about his own white shield. But even the snow up on the mountaintops looked cold and grim, rather than the glorious white of the shields of Unauwen's knights. There were no beautiful vistas ahead, only grey slopes and ranges of hills stretching out until they vanished in the distance, hiding their destination from view.

They walked very quickly, Piak leading the way to set the pace. Now and then they looked back at the pass, half fearing that threatening figures would appear there. But after a while a slope blocked their view of the highest point of the road.

Tiuri went to walk beside Piak and said, "We have almost a day's lead. That's if Tehalon is right and the guards don't change sooner."

"What do you think they will do?" Piak said. "Come straight after us? But they won't catch up with us, not even on horseback. Still, a day isn't all that long..."

"We just need to make sure our lead doesn't become any smaller," said Tiuri. "The Tarnburg is quite a way from the pass, so it'll be a while before they hear about what's happened, but even so..."

"Yes, we need to keep moving," Piak said in a whisper.

"And by the time they mobilize..." Tiuri did a few calculations. "Yes, if we're lucky we should have enough time to warn Unauwen."

The light took on the colour of mother-of-pearl, and their surroundings were bathed in a strange, almost unearthly glow.

"You would think nobody ever comes here," Piak remarked. "But they must, as the road is so well maintained."

"But what is there to maintain?" said Tiuri. "Nothing grows here."

Piak pointed at a nearby slope. "Look, a load of stones have tumbled down over there," he said. "Do you see them? But there's not a single one on the road itself. Someone's neatly stacked them up on the roadside. Though," he continued, "it could have been done a while ago, I suppose."

"That's true," said Tiuri. "But you're right. It's likely that people often pass this way. And we may well meet some of them..."

"At least the good road means we can make quick progress," said Piak. "And the lower we go, the easier it'll be. We should aim to walk at night, too." He looked around and said anxiously, "I just pray we don't have any snow."

Piak's prayers were heard, and until noon the following day their descent went without incident. It had taken a lot out of them, though, as they'd had to face enemies including cold and exhaustion, fear and thoughts of despair.

That afternoon they saw the first sign of people: a dilapidated mountain cabin close to the road. The hut looked uninhabited, but of course they couldn't be sure.

"I wouldn't like to live there," whispered Piak as they walked by. "There's no good meadow for grazing and..." He paused.

392

A shadow moved across the road in front of them. Tiuri and Piak peered up to see an eagle, slowly beating its wings as it flew over. As they looked at each other, they tried to smile.

But that nervous, apprehensive feeling remained.

The day went by and was followed by another night with far too little rest. But the next morning brought a little cheer. It was not as cold, the road was dry, and the landscape became green and more welcoming.

But then something spoiled their good mood. They heard a cry and saw a man standing on a hill, waving at them and beckoning. Not wanting to make him angry or suspicious, they waved back, but then walked on quickly.

"Maybe it was foolish of us," said Piak, "to be so nervous. He wasn't even dressed in red. But he was armed. Did you see his bow? I don't trust anyone around here. How about you?"

"Me neither," replied Tiuri. "If we could, I'd take a different road."

"There must be other paths at this height," said Piak. "But we can't take them..."

"Or we'll miss the gong," Tiuri said, completing his sentence for him. He watched as the man walked away.

A little later, they passed another mountain cabin; there was definitely someone living in this one. Two grumpy-looking men were standing in front of it. They eyed Tiuri and Piak suspiciously, and didn't respond to their friendly greeting. As Tiuri and Piak walked past, though, one of the men approached them.

"Hey," he said, "wait a moment!" He was armed with a bow and arrows and may well have been the same man they'd seen earlier. He and his companion were shabbily dressed. Perhaps he was a hunter who eked out a living up here. But the two friends did not like the look of him.

"Is there a problem?" Tiuri asked in a calm tone.

"What are you doing here?" came the question in return.

"We are walking along the road," replied Tiuri coolly, "and heading down the mountain, as you can see."

The man looked him up and down, as if weighing up an opponent. Then he said gruffly, "Oh, no offence meant! I wish you a good journey. Be careful you don't take a tumble."

He turned around, walked back to his friend and the two of them disappeared into the hut.

"Phew!" said Piak quietly. "That's him dealt with." He didn't speak the thought that these men could quite easily follow them, or take other paths and wait for them somewhere down below. But he held tightly onto the stick in his hand, and Tiuri reached for the hilt of his sword.

3   THE WAY TO THE VORGÓTA GONG

Across the mountains, then down below.
Wide path through forest of pine.

"This must be it!" whispered Piak, as the road led them between tall pines. The day was already drawing to a close and it was dark beneath the trees, and not the most pleasant of places to walk. There was a hushed silence and their footsteps were muffled by the pine needles underfoot. But high above them the wind whistled in the treetops.

"I'll be glad when we can take that right turn that Tehalon told us about," said Piak.

Me too, thought Tiuri. He could hardly believe they'd be able to complete their journey without any opposition from the enemy. Eviellan would surely be guarding the road in the western part of the mountains, too.

That night they did not keep walking for long, but spent it in the forest, some way back from the road. And yet they could not rest properly, because they had to take it in turns to sleep and neither of them could settle. Twice they thought they heard something, but no one came near. At sunrise they went on their way and soon left the wood behind.

The road here was not nearly as well maintained. It twisted and turned even more than it had high up in the mountains, and every turn revealed a different view. They caught glimpses of the flat land at the foot of the mountains – the east of the Kingdom of Unauwen. It looked inhospitable and was covered almost entirely in forest. But their destination could not be far now.

How much longer? thought Tiuri. He could not shake off the feeling that they were being followed.

They passed streams and green ravines and sunlit meadows. They heard water flowing and, as the sound grew louder, they thought of the words Tehalon had taught them.

> *Take a right turn into the valley deep*
> *where flow the Twin Cascades.*

The rushing became a roar... and there they were: two waterfalls plummeting alongside each other down a steep cliff before joining to form one river below, which flowed to the west.

"That's it! The Twin Cascades!" said Piak excitedly. "Now quickly, down into the valley."

It took them a while to find a path that led down below. The track was very narrow, and almost entirely overgrown. The valley, too, was full of lush growth, and the stream they had to follow danced through the vegetation, splashing high over white stones.

There was no path as such, but it was not too difficult to walk alongside the water, hopping from one bank to the other.

At around midday, they had the stream to their right; the side of the valley rose up steeply beside them, and their path took a turn to the left. Tiuri was walking in front; he was warm and tired, but he'd decided not to rest until they'd reached the place where

Tehalon's instructions had promised they would find a sign. He turned a corner; perhaps he would see it now...

Follow the stream to where it disappears...

In a flash, he caught sight of a man standing on the slope ahead... Then he felt a hard blow to his chest, followed by an intense, stabbing pain.

And Tiuri fell, struck by an arrow.

Piak did not realize what had happened. He raced to his friend's side and saw, to his horror, an arrow sticking out of Tiuri's chest; it was just under his left shoulder. Then he heard a swish – and a second arrow tore past his ear.

"Run!" gasped Tiuri. He pulled himself up and knelt on the ground, supporting himself with one hand and clutching at his wound with the other. "Take cover!"

Now Piak saw the man on the slope; he was aiming his bow to take another shot.

Piak ducked, but the arrow stopped some way ahead of him, quivering among the stones. Gently, he put his arm around Tiuri. His friend was alive – thank God! – but he had to get him to safety... back around the corner...

"Get away, away..." Tiuri panted.

"Can you walk?" asked Piak, holding him around the waist. "Lean on me." All of his attention was on his friend and he didn't dare to breathe again until they were beyond the reach of the enemy's arrows.

Tiuri had sunk down against the rocks, his eyes closed and his face as white as a sheet. Fear gripped Piak when he saw the cruel, feathered arrow, and the trickle of blood seeping through Tiuri's clothes.

But then his friend looked up at him and whispered, "Make sure that... that he doesn't... hit you."

"He can't hit us here," said Piak. "But you..."

Tiuri slowly turned to inspect the wound. "I don't think," he spoke haltingly, "it's as bad as it seems..." He tried to sit up straight, and managed to do so with some help from Piak. "Is it sticking out of the other side?" he asked in a whisper.

"No," said Piak, looking in concern at Tiuri's face, which was contorted with pain.

Again they heard that familiar swishing sound.

"Look out!" gasped Tiuri. "He's still there. Leave me..."

"I'm not leaving you here alone," said Piak. Carefully, he leant his friend back against the rocky slope, then he quickly crept down the path to locate their enemy. He was still in the same place, with his bow, but he was no longer looking in their direction. And then he turned, walked away and disappeared from sight. Piak did not take the time to wonder why, but returned to his friend.

"He's gone," he said, as he knelt down, wishing he knew more about how to treat this kind of wound. "That arrow..." he began.

"It has to come out," said Tiuri with a much firmer voice. He grasped the shaft, but his face turned whiter, even his lips. "I... don't dare," he whispered. "I think it has barbs."

Piak remembered the arrow he'd just seen on the ground. "You're right," he said. He took his friend by the shoulders, as he seemed about to faint.

Tiuri soon recovered a little, though. "I feel better now," he whispered.

"Do you want me to do it?" Piak asked quietly. "I don't know if I'll do it right. But if I have to..."

"No," said Tiuri after a brief pause. "Not yet. I fear it would only make matters worse. Leave it there for now. It'll stop the bleeding. Don't look so frightened! It really is the best thing to do. I'm scared I won't be able to take another step if I pull it out, and we can't have that, not now. But..." He gritted his teeth, grasped the arrow more firmly and snapped the shaft with his other hand. "Give me a moment," he mumbled, leaning forward. "We have to get away from here... Where is he?"

"Disappeared," said Piak.

"He can't have done," said Tiuri weakly.

"No, really. I saw him leave," said Piak, putting his arm around Tiuri again. "Maybe he ran out of arrows... How are you feeling now?"

"I want to stand up," said Tiuri.

A few moments later, he was on his feet. Piak held onto his friend, supporting him.

"We have to sound that gong," said Tiuri, "and so we need to keep going. It's the only way."

"It could be nearby," whispered Piak. "Can you walk?"

"Yes. Shall we? You can let go of me. Honestly, I'll be fine." Slowly, Tiuri took a few steps.

"Wait..." said Piak. "I'll take a look first, to see if there's any danger."

"One of us has to get there," said Tiuri. "Do you understand, Piak? I... Just be careful nothing happens to you too..."

The valley was still just as sunny as before, and there was no sign of anyone around. But the deadly danger must still be lurking and lying in wait – if only they knew where. They couldn't walk alongside each other and Piak insisted on taking the lead. He kept glancing back to check on his friend and he stayed on the lookout for anything suspicious. Tiuri wasn't as alert; he needed all his strength and concentration just to keep on walking. But after a while he became more used to it; the stabbing pain eased a little and he began to think he could keep on walking for hours, as long as nothing out of the ordinary happened. The world around him felt unreal somehow, even though the stream still babbled along beside him and the white rocks flashed away. But Piak was real and close to him, and he answered his questioning looks with a weak smile.

Then they found themselves walking in the shade. The stream went to the right and they had to struggle through high undergrowth. Tiuri stepped into a hole and a jolt of pain brought him back to reality. A cliff rose upwards, completely covered in climbing plants. At the bottom was an opening into which the stream disappeared.

Follow the stream to where it disappears.
Then find a sign to show the way.

"Now you need to rest a little," said Piak. "And I'll look around for this sign."

That wasn't the first thing he did, though; before starting his search, he gave his friend a drink from a cup that he skilfully made by folding a few big leaves together, and gently mopped Tiuri's damp brow with cold water from the stream.

"Thank you," said Tiuri, nodding at Piak. Whatever would he have done without his faithful friend? Then he looked around. "I don't see any sign," he said. "How about you?"

"Give me a moment, I'll find it," replied Piak. He walked around and then disappeared. It was a while before he returned. "There are two paths," he told Tiuri. "One of them goes up along the side of the valley and then back down; you can see it over there. The other one's lower down. The first part has been swallowed up by plants, but I found the path again where the rocks begin. Both of the paths go to the west."

Two paths – one leads to the gong,
hidden song, Vorgóta Gong.

"It has to be one of the two," he continued. "But I can't see any sign to indicate which one."

"Follow the stream to where it disappears..." mumbled Tiuri. He struggled to his feet and walked with his friend to the point where the stream went into the mountain. What kind of sign? What should they be looking for? Would it be a signpost, like the ones beside the paths in the Wild Wood?

"See if you can find a stone," he said, "with something written on it." But any stone would be buried beneath all those plants after so many years.

Piak searched everywhere, but after a while he said, disheartened, "I can't find anything. No stone beside the paths either. But that sign must be here somewhere."

"Perhaps it's disappeared," whispered Tiuri. "The gong was hung such a long, long time ago." He stared at the cliff and thought, *We have to move onwards, and quickly. I'm afraid I won't be able to keep on going for much longer...* Then he said, "Do you think the sign might be carved onto this rock face?"

Piak immediately tried to find out, nimbly clambering up the steep slope and tugging away the plants. He removed the greenery from a few areas, but they couldn't see anything of interest beneath. Perhaps there had been something there, once upon a time, but it had been erased by the passage of time.

"I give up!" he said, panting as he went back to join his friend. "No, no, I don't. Let's think about this..."

But Tiuri shook his head. "Who knows how much time we have?" he whispered. "Whether the gong's here now or not... both paths go to the west. We'll each take one of them."

"I was afraid you'd say that," mumbled Piak. "Are you sure you can manage it, Tiuri?"

"I'd rather you told me I *have* to keep going!!" replied Tiuri. "Do you have a better plan?"

"No..." sighed Piak. He took a good look at his friend and frowned at the broken shaft of the arrow.

"It hurts a bit. Of course it does," said Tiuri, "but see, the wound's stopped bleeding. Which path shall I take?"

"The lower one," said Piak immediately. It was the easier one, as far as he could make out.

"Fine. Whoever finds the gong has to sound it. The other one will hear it – and then he can come back, and we'll see each other again."

"But..." began Piak.

"I'll see you at the gong," Tiuri said, gently interrupting him.

Piak took Tiuri's hand and shook it firmly. "Good luck!" he said.

Without any more words, they each took a path – and so their ways parted.

4   THE VORGÓTA GONG

Tiuri first had to struggle through the undergrowth and the effort made him dizzy. But, once he was through, it was easy enough to find his way. The path descended between two cliffs and then alongside a deep valley. The stream reappeared at that point, flowing in the same direction as he was heading – westwards. He looked down into the valley as little as possible, as the drop was making him even dizzier. Fortunately, the path soon took a turn and descended, twisting and turning through surroundings that became more grey and barren. After a while Tiuri could no longer tell which direction he was going in. The sense of unreality returned, even more strongly than before. It actually made it easier for him to walk quickly, in spite of his wound, as if he were sleepwalking. At a certain point, he had to become more awake and alert, as the path led him into the mountain, and he knew he might stumble or bump into something in the darkness. But before long, he saw light again and, soon after that, he came to a stop.

As he gazed around, he realized he was looking at something quite extraordinary. For a moment, he was reminded of the Green Grottos. These were not caves, though, but actual rooms, halls inside the mountain! They were connected to one another and to the world outside, and the sun shone through them. Above his head was a high vaulted ceiling; it was almost impossible to believe it had been formed by nature. Blue sky peeped in here and there through holes in the rock.

Tiuri leant against a wall and struggled to fight his rising dizziness. He spoke out loud, drawing strength from the sound of his own voice. "Here ends my path... The world has such wondrous places in it! Does the Gong of Vorgóta hang here?"

Slowly, Tiuri walked onwards. He stopped again when he saw a large, round, flat metal disc hanging on two iron chains.

He had found the Vorgóta Gong.

The gong was made of bronze, grown dull over the centuries it had hung there. Beneath it was a polished stone with letters carved into it; he made out the word VORGÓTA. Across the stone lay a staff – the mallet for beating the gong.

Tiuri knelt down to pick it up; it was heavy, almost impossible to lift. Then he stood, swaying. Twice he tried – and twice he failed – to raise it high, breaking out in a sweat at the thought he might lack the strength to complete his mission after enduring so much. The third time, he managed to lift the mallet up, and, though it only brushed against the gong, it still conjured forth a sound: a deep boom, an ominous drone, which echoed before dying away, as if the rock walls had voices and were responding – voices that reverberated around the rocky vaults, in a dreamy singing tone.

Something began to vibrate inside Tiuri, too, and without hesitation he swung the mallet back and hit the gong as hard as he could. A booming, penetrating, almost deafening sound rang out... and was repeated by hundreds of echoes.

Tiuri cringed away from the sound, as pain shot through him and the arrow in his wound seemed to twist around. Strange shadows danced before his eyes, surrounding him, grabbing at him...

When he came to, he was lying on the ground. He gazed up at the roof, where the shadows were still dancing, patches of black, as if the echoes of the gong, still buzzing and vibrating, had taken on a life of their own. But then he saw that they were just bats, flying around anxiously, startled by the noise.

Piak should have taken this path, he thought. *I cannot hit the gong again...*

The gong... it had been hung so that people would hear it for miles around, if the Kingdom of Unauwen were threatened from the east. One bang of the gong would surely not be enough! He sat up and carefully touched his wound. His fingers came away wet with blood. Then he desperately struggled to his feet and would surely have fallen again if he had not had the mallet for support.

Then he stood before the gong once more, leaning on the mallet and praying for strength. *Let me hit it enough times*, he thought, *before I fall and cannot stand up.*

Again he raised the mallet and let it fall. He did not wait, but struck again – and again!

The blows boomed, one after the other, beating against his temples, singing in his ears – and each blow was a stab of pain. The rocks quivered, the air vibrated, the ground shook. Then everything around him seemed to collapse, burying him in darkness.

Piak heard the sound of the gong. He was already a long way down the other path, which also led west, but not to the gong. First he heard one crash and then many more, one after another, strong and clear. Echoes came from all around, and he couldn't work out quite where the sound was coming from. Immediately he retraced his steps, running, racing, and, as he darted along, the echoes died away. The way back seemed endless, and then he had to follow the entire length of Tiuri's path, too.

Panting, he finally entered the amazing halls – which were now filled with absolute silence. He found the gong, but Tiuri was not there. A mallet lay on the ground; he picked it up and headed onwards and outside.

In front of him, a weathered stone staircase led down to a road. The day was already drawing to a close and there was no one around. He studied the mallet and noted there was blood on it, and his throat clenched in fear. Where was Tiuri?

Then he saw a man walking along the road, who paused briefly when he spotted Piak and then quickly started climbing the stairs. Piak grasped the mallet more tightly, but the man did not look hostile. He was tall and blond, with a friendly face.

"Are you Piak?" he asked, when he was almost at the top of the steps.

"Yes..." said Piak, still rather suspicious of him.

"Then I got here in time," said the man. "I am Wila, the forester of Vorgóta. Your friend asked me to come and meet you."

"Thank goodness!" exclaimed Piak. "Where is he? How is he doing?"

"I shall take you to him," said the man.

But Piak backed away. The forester did not appear to be dangerous, but how could he be sure?

"I understand," said Wila. "But I have nothing that would convince you I am to be trusted. All I can say is this: Eviellan is my enemy, and the gong has awoken us all. Just listen!"

Now Piak could hear voices shouting in the distance, and the sound of hoofs somewhere nearby.

"Some are coming now, and others will arrive later," said the forester. "Sir Tiuri called them and he sent me here."

"Where is he?" cried Piak, whose instincts told him he could trust the man. "What happened?"

"That's what I'm about to explain," said the forester. "When we heard the gong, my friends and I, who live nearby, naturally ran straight here. We know where the gong is, even though we'd

404

never entered the cave ourselves. It's a kind of holy sanctuary, you see; no one ever goes in there. When we got here, your friend was sprawled on the ground, in front of the gong, with the mallet still in his hand. I'm sure you can imagine just how shocked we all were! We carried him out here, loosened his clothes, and brought him round with a little brandy. Luckily, my friend Markon always carries some with him."

"And then?" asked Piak.

"Then he told us... that Eviellan is coming over the mountains..." The forester paused before continuing, "What a brave young man! He sat here, as white as a sheet, but his eyes were gleaming – no, they were glowing – as he told us that we must make ready to resist the invasion and... well, of course, you know all about that already..."

Piak's doubts had vanished. "Please, take me to him," he said. "Where is he?"

"In Anto the shepherd's hut. Come with me. No, leave the mallet here. We'll put it back with the gong." Wila the forester went and did just that, and on his return he said, "That mallet has not been touched in human memory, and the words on the stone threaten anyone who beats the gong for no good reason."

He walked down to the road with Piak; it was the big road down from the mountains.

"Tell me more," said Piak.

"Well, my friends Markon, Anto and I were the first ones to arrive," said the forester, as they headed westwards. "But soon more people who had heard the gong came. Most of them are already heading up into the mountains to start making barricades. Markon the hunter has nocked his sharpest arrow for the wretch who shot Sir Tiuri. He came across him earlier this afternoon and was already suspicious when the man ran away from him, and..."

"Oh, so that's why he disappeared so quickly," said Piak. "And what about Tiuri?"

"In the midst of all the excitement, your friend fainted again, and of course we couldn't leave him there. So we carried him to Anto's hut, because he lives closest."

Piak started walking faster and asked anxiously, "How is Tiuri?"

"We laid him on the bed, but none of us dared to pull out the arrow... Oh, don't be concerned. There is a good physician in Vorgóta. The knight is weak with pain and loss of blood, but he came round soon enough to start asking about you – which is why I returned to the gong." The forester gave Piak an encouraging nod. "We're nearly there," he said.

It couldn't be close enough for Piak, but they still had to walk quite a way, along a stream and through a wood. They came across a group of men who were armed with pitchforks and scythes; the advance guard of Unauwen's army was already on the move.

"The gong must have been heard in the castle, too," said Wila. "The men of Vorgóta will already be on their way. Luckily, a knight is currently visiting the lady down at the castle. I saw him riding out when I went to meet you."

Finally, they saw Anto the shepherd's hut. A soldier stood outside with a fine white horse.

Piak began to run; what he'd heard hadn't eased his fears for Tiuri's well-being. Pushing open the door, he entered the cabin.

A number of people were inside, but he paid no attention to any of them. All he saw was Tiuri lying on the bed, with a tall, dark-haired man sitting beside him.

Tiuri's face was pale and still, as if he were asleep. He was asleep, wasn't he? He surely wasn't...

"Tiuri!" whispered Piak.

His friend's eyelids trembled and then opened. "Tiuri!" said Piak again and he was not ashamed of his tears.

"Everything is going to be fine," said the dark-haired man, as he stood up.

Now Piak realized who he was. With surprise, and happiness, he recognized Sir Ardian, the toll master of the Rainbow River. Tiuri and Piak had met him the previous year, first fearing him as an opponent, then trusting him as a friend.

The knight laid his hand on Piak's shoulder. "I have removed the rest of the arrow," he said, "and now all he needs is rest." He leant over Tiuri again and gave him something to drink from a cup. "Now you'll forget your pain and enjoy some peace," he said. "Close your eyes and sleep!"

His melodious voice made the words sound like a friendly command that must be obeyed. Tiuri did so, his face relaxing.

Sir Ardian looked down at him. Then he beckoned Piak and took him outside.

"Well, it seems the two of you are destined for great things," he said, looking at him with a searching gaze. "This is the second time you have come from the east with news for King Unauwen."

Then he started to ask questions. Piak answered, finding it easy to tell the knight everything he needed to know.

Then Sir Ardian said, "I shall take command of all the able-bodied men I can gather. Messengers are already on their way to the king, the crown prince and the paladins at the Rainbow River. You have nothing else to worry about now."

"What about Tiuri?" asked Piak.

"His wound is not life-threatening, but beating the gong did make it worse."

"I wish I could have done it!" said Piak. "I thought he had the easier path."

"Such things are a matter of destiny," said Sir Ardian. "Tiuri is young and healthy and is sure to recover quickly. And I believe that you need some sleep, too, not to mention a good meal." He turned to a bearded man who had come out of the cabin, together with Wila the forester.

"Anto," he said. "Let me introduce you to your new guest. His name is Piak."

The bearded man bowed and said, "Sir Tiuri and Piak will be the most honoured visitors ever to sleep under my humble roof."

"I shall see you later," said Sir Ardian.

Then he rode away on his white horse.

"Lord Ardian of the Toll, Knight of the Rainbow Shield," said Wila the forester. "There's not another man like him in the kingdom, except for the crown prince, but he is, of course, the son of a king."

"He is skilled in combat and knows the wisdom of books," said Anto the shepherd. "He can defeat the enemy in battle, but also knows how to heal wounds. A true knight! Now come with me, Piak. Welcome to my home."

5   Echoes

The night was full of sounds – many people had heeded the call of the gong. Piak woke whenever he heard someone passing by, and then he would quietly get up to take a look at Tiuri, even though Anto, his host, had told him that was not necessary, as he was sitting at Tiuri's bedside. But Tiuri went on sleeping until Sir Ardian returned the following morning.

The knight examined Tiuri and did not seem dissatisfied. Then he turned to Piak and said, "The two of you need to leave this place, especially Tiuri! When the battle begins, this house will most probably be in the middle of the fighting. I don't think it would do any harm to have Tiuri taken to the Castle of Vorgóta today. Anto can get hold of a cart and the lady of the castle is expecting you."

Piak nodded. "And I'm sure you're staying up here," he said.

"Yes," said Sir Ardian. "The barricades are almost ready and my army is growing by the hour."

He looked at Tiuri, who was now wide awake and who said in a whisper, "I'm sorry there's nothing I can do."

"Your job is done," said Ardian. "But Piak still has work to do. He must take care of you and ensure that you do not move until the physician declares you healed. Goodbye for now to you both, and may the heavens bless you."

Piak accompanied him outside, where his men were waiting. "Sir knight," he said, "I wish you the very, very best."

"Thank you," said Sir Ardian. "I have placed a guard by the gong. When the attack begins, you will hear it. It will sound twice. Farewell."

Later that day Tiuri and Piak set off in a covered cart for the Castle of Vorgóta. Anto sat up front; he was driving very carefully, so that Tiuri would be troubled as little as possible by the jolting of the cart.

The young knight managed well at first, but after a couple of hours Piak asked if the cart could stop for a moment. The wound had opened up and needed to be bandaged again. Then they travelled onwards, even more slowly.

Piak looked in concern at the flush on his friend's cheeks, which had been so pale before. Tiuri's face was glowing. Tiuri did not notice, though; he just frowned as if he could hear something that was disturbing him.

What Tiuri could hear was the Vorgóta Gong: bronze crashes reverberating from wall to wall – over mountains and valleys, through the trembling air. Echoes sounded, fading into the distance, dimmer and dimmer, but still audible. Then they rebounded, coming closer and closer; the sound clattered all around, metal on metal. It boomed inside his head!

He looked at Piak and stuttered, "The gong, the Vorgóta Gong... Make it stop!"

"It has stopped, Tiuri," said Piak quietly. "It's other sounds that you can hear. Are you awake? Lie still. There's nothing to worry about."

But Tiuri turned away and peered out at the sky through the back of the cart. The sun would go down soon, and in the reddish clouds he saw flames and smoke. When he closed his eyes again, it was as if he were in the heart of a scorching fire. He heard the crashing gong and an oncoming army in the sound of wheels and horses' hoofs. Tiuri was fighting in the battle. Again he raised his sword to kill a man, and again he felt only disgust for himself.

Perhaps they were not just fever dreams, but echoes of a real fight that was taking place at the same moment, far from the Vorgóta Gong, in the Kingdom of Dagonaut on the other side of the mountains.

There, between the Green and the Black Rivers, a horn rang out, the silver horn of Sir Ristridin. He had entered the forest with Tiuri's father; they had heard the sound of battle from afar. The first skirmish took place at the bend in the Green River where Tiuri and his friends had fled into Tehalon's territory.

"For the Lord of Mistrinaut!" cried Ristridin, throwing himself into the fray, side by side with Tiuri the Valiant. Red Riders had almost entirely encircled Lord Rafox and his men, and it was looking bad for them, even though they were bravely defending themselves. The help came just in time.

The Red Riders were quickly routed; they spread in every direction, fleeing the fury of the knights, startled by the sound of the horn.

"Ristridin has returned!" they cried. "Ristridin of the South!"

The knight heard their words and knew they would be back with more men. Other horns sounded from the direction of the Tarnburg, challenging his own. But there was enough time to tend to the wounded and to prepare the uninjured men to fight again. There was little chance to talk, but Lord Rafox was able to give Sir Tiuri the good news that his son had escaped and travelled to the west with Piak.

"If everything went as planned," he said, "they are now in the Kingdom of Unauwen."

Yes, they were indeed in the Kingdom of Unauwen, at the Castle of Vorgóta. Piak was sitting beside Tiuri's bed. His friend looked at him with wild eyes. He kept talking about the gong, asking for his sword and trying to sit up, so Piak had to hold on to him.

"It's your move," whispered Tiuri. "Quiet!" he said in a tortured voice. "How can I play chess if that gong keeps sounding?"

Pawns, castles, kings... knights! Tiuri was back in the Wild Wood. He saw them coming and screamed out, "The battle has begun!"

The Battle between the Rivers, the Green and the Black... on one side the forces of the Tarnburg, on the other side three of Dagonaut's best knights: Ristridin, Rafox and Tiuri the Valiant. But Eviellan's men outnumbered them by far, and more were arriving every minute. The forest to the south of the Black River was full of soldiers – there must have been thousands of them.

Ristridin led Dagonaut's men, because he knew his way around the forest. However, they could do little more than weaken their enemy, hindering him and slowing his movements. And the moment came when their situation seemed hopeless. They had pressed on, been driven back, advanced and been attacked once more. Many of them were wounded or dead, and the remaining men were at risk of being encircled by the Red Riders again.

Then suddenly Men in Green leapt from the trees and threw themselves into the fight, bringing death and destruction to the men of Eviellan!

In a brief pause for breath, Ristridin, Tiuri and Rafox came together; they leant on their swords and Ristridin said, "Now we must try to take the High Bridge and destroy it. Then the link between the Tarnburg and the Road of Ambuscade will be broken."

They advanced again, this time with the Men in Green. A day later they had captured the watchtower, which gave them a view of the bridge.

Blood-red banners flew on the towers of the Tarnburg, and armies rode over the bridge, armies of Red Riders. The Black Knight led them; the attack had begun in earnest! Eviellan was marching unopposed along the Road of Ambuscade to the pass.

Not all of the men followed their king; many stayed on the other side of the Black River to guard the area around the Tarnburg. And others launched a new attack against Ristridin and his men.

Again the silver horn rang out, and the Men in Green beat their drums. The Master of the Wild Wood joined the knights and, step by step, they fought their way along the Black River to the west. They could no longer stop the army that had headed into the mountains – the knights of King Unauwen would have to do that. But they could attempt to cross the High Bridge and conquer the Tarnburg. More creeping through prickly bushes... more weapons clashing in the wilderness... whinnying horses, cries and groans... But the High Bridge was still in the hands of the enemy. More Red Riders crossing the bridge... The sound of drums... more drums... louder, threatening, frightening...

Then the fighters saw smoke rising above the trees and a red glow in the west. There came a cry: "The forest is on fire!"

Ristridin saw Tehalon's face, dirty, stained, with glinting eyes.

"Eviellan has moved into the Kingdom of Unauwen," he said. "But the king has left my wood in flames!"

"The forest is on fire!" whispered Tiuri. He groaned as he tossed and turned. Piak spoke to him in calming tones, but none of his words reached his friend. For days, he had been in a delirious fever, which persisted in spite of all the good care he received. Piak had barely moved from his friend's bedside, even though there were plenty of others who wanted to watch him. The lady of the castle often sat with Tiuri, and the physician, an old monk, came several times a day. He always gave encouraging responses whenever Piak asked what he thought of Tiuri's condition. But it was obvious that he was not telling the truth. The patient was not improving. On the contrary, he was clearly becoming weaker. Piak wished for the presence of Sir Ardian; he felt that he would be able to help his friend recover. But Ardian was with the soldiers at the foot of the mountains. Every day, more armed men came from the west to join them. They rode past the Castle of Vorgóta to the place where the attack could be expected any time now.

"They are on the way and they will be here soon," said Tiuri in a clear voice. His eyes were wide open, but there was no recognition in his gaze. "They set the forest on fire," he continued in a whisper. "Can't you feel it? Can't you smell it? Everything scorched, burnt..." His voice faded into an unintelligible murmur.

Piak soaked a cloth in water and carefully dabbed his friend's face. That calmed him, as it always did. But a few moments later it started again.

"Now they're beating the gong. Listen!"

The Vorgóta Gong always pursued Tiuri in his fever dreams, and stopped him from sleeping soundly for even a minute.

"Tiuri!" said Piak, almost pleading with him. "Listen to me. The gong is silent. Silent!"

"No," whispered Tiuri. "I can hear it." He closed his eyes and mumbled, "One, two... Two times."

Worried, Piak watched him. His friend looked exhausted, grimacing with pain, as if the sound of the gong were too much for him to bear.

Then he heard it, too. Once, and then again... twice! He thought for a moment he must be imagining it, influenced by Tiuri's words.

But then he realized that someone really had banged upon the Vorgóta Gong.

And that could mean only one thing: the attack had begun!

Can they hear the sound everywhere? wondered Tiuri. The wind carries the echoes of the gong all the way to the sea, the sea where the sun sets...

He felt as if he were in a dungeon; through a barred window he saw shadows flitting past, men with spears and bows. The Red Riders were moving along the Road of Ambuscade; the battle was in progress and he could not take part.

Suddenly, though, the dungeon vanished and he was standing on a huge chessboard that stretched out in every direction. He was all alone, but the sound of battle went on. Then a figure approached, striding across the black and white squares – the closer he came, the larger he grew: the Black Knight with the Red Shield!

"Now," he said, "Sir Tiuri and I will finish our game. I am the king."

Then other figures appeared on the board, all of them life-size. And they were alive, too... There were pawns with black caps on their heads and horses carrying Red Riders. And as Tiuri stood there in the middle of the chessboard, unable to move, they came closer – an army that meant to trample him underfoot.

Behind him he heard others but he could not turn to see who they were.

A horn sounded. With a sob of joy, he recognized it as Sir Ristridin's silver horn. That broke the enchantment; now he could move and see which army was approaching from the other side. Knights with white shields!

The chessboard transformed into the Road of Ambuscade. Again he had to fight with the guards at the pass and he relived those moments of horror. Then the battle flared up again and raged for a long time.

Tiuri heard not only the ever-ringing gong, but also the same sounds as Piak, who was sitting at his bedside: shouts and crashes and the hiss of boiling pitch.

The Castle of Vorgóta was under attack.

After a while Tiuri realized the soldiers were gone. But the forest was still burning and he had to flee from the heat of the flames. He found himself on the shores of the Deep Lake.

He leant forward; finally there was coolness, and under the water he would no longer hear the gong. He saw his reflection... no, it was Lavinia beckoning to him. He held out his hand, but the water rippled and her face disappeared. Someone else took hold of his hand and wouldn't let go, dragging him into the depths... Or were they pulling him up, away from the coolness and silence, back to the heat and the horror?

Then someone grabbed hold of him and called out, "Tiuri, Tiuri!"

Through a smoky red haze, he saw Piak's face, and it was Piak who was saying to him, "Tiuri, can you hear me?"

He tried to hold on to his friend and did his best to understand his words. But he could not, and darkness enveloped him.

"Tiuri, Tiuri!" said Piak. "Eviellan has been driven back! Tiuri, can you hear me?"

But Tiuri was beyond his reach again. It seemed as if he were wandering elsewhere, watching events that Piak could neither hear nor see.

Tiuri was at the Black River, with Sir Ristridin, Lord Rafox and his father. He saw the High Bridge again, and he watched as it collapsed. Smouldering sections of the bridge dropped into the swirling water far below, where they were swept along by the river and disappeared.

6 WAKING UP

The water of the river swirled and whirled; it raced in his ears and, through it all, he heard the echo of the Vorgóta Gong.

Tiuri tried to swim but he could barely manage; he was dashed against cruel rocks and the pain made it hard for him to move. But he had to get to the other side, away from the Tarnburg, and flee from the Black Knight with the Red Shield. It was night and the crests of the water were white with moonlight. He heard a voice – was it the Black Knight calling him?

He opened his eyes; it was still dark. A dim light illuminated a face that was looking at him. The King of Eviellan! The game of chess had to be finished, for life or death... Or was he mistaken? Was it Prince Iridian who was sitting opposite him?

No, he saw now that it was neither Prince Iridian nor the King of Eviellan. It was Sir Ardian, the toll master from the Rainbow River. But he had no money to pay the toll...

Now it was as if he were swimming again, but he could still see the toll master's face. He had to reach the other side, but the river was wide and the current was strong.

"I'm drowning!" he panted.

"No, you're not," said the toll master. "You can swim, can't you? Keep going."

Tiuri did as he was told. Suddenly the water calmed and he could drift along. Someone laid a hand on his forehead; he opened his eyes again and saw that Sir Ardian was still sitting beside him. But now he realized he was lying in bed. There was candlelight, and behind Ardian's head he saw an open window and a sky full of stars. It was very quiet; finally the Vorgóta Gong was silent.

He sighed and slowly moved his head. Then he saw Piak, who was staring at him; his eyes seemed big and dark.

"Piak..." whispered Tiuri.

His friend smiled and the sonorous voice of the toll master spoke, "You have returned to us, Tiuri."

Yes, it felt as if he'd been far away and had survived dangers that he remembered only vaguely now. And he was tired, so tired. His eyes closed again, he felt fingers on his wrist and heard Piak whisper, "Sleep well." And then he slept.

"Lavinia..." mumbled Tiuri. It was not Lavinia, though, but another lady who was leaning over him.

He looked up at her. Her face was beautiful and kind, but she was older than Lavinia and wore a headdress, so she must be married. Her gown was grey, as if she were in mourning.

"You are awake," she said. "Good morning to you!"

"Good morning," he whispered. "Who are you?"

"I am the Lady of Vorgóta," she replied. "How are you feeling now? You are still weak, of course, but your eyes are bright. Soon you must have something to eat and then you can go back to sleep."

"Am I in the Castle of Vorgóta?" asked Tiuri. "How long have I been here? Where is Piak?"

"I have sent your friend to bed," said the lady of the castle. "But you will see him soon enough."

"He's here already!" came Piak's voice, and a second later he was beside Tiuri's bed. "You're wide awake!" he said, his eyes gleaming.

"I thought you were sleeping, Piak," said the lady.

"Oh, my lady, I couldn't go to bed straightaway," said Piak apologetically. "I wanted to say goodbye to Sir Ardian and..."

"Sir Ardian..." mumbled Tiuri. "I dreamt about him."

"That was not a dream," said Piak. "He was here last night and he took a look at you early this morning, too, but you were asleep." He sat down on the edge of the bed and gave his friend a searching look. "No fever now," he said. "What about the pain?"

"Barely..." began Tiuri.

"No, don't move," Piak said, interrupting him. "You have to lie still until you're completely better. May I feed him, my lady? You already have so much to do."

The lady smiled and gave him the bowl of bread and milk before leaving the room.

"Adelbart did this for me when I was sick in the Forgotten City," said Piak, as he fed Tiuri. "But that was nothing compared to you."

"How long have I been lying here?" Tiuri asked between two mouthfuls.

"Over a week," replied Piak. He thought for a moment and then added, "It's been nine days since you hit the gong."

"That long?" whispered Tiuri. "What... what has happened in all that time?"

"Eviellan has been defeated," said Piak. "Well, no, maybe that's overstating it. But the attack from the mountains failed. Many men were killed; the rest fled."

"Where to?" asked Tiuri.

"Over the mountains back to the east. Sir Ardian has gone after them. He got here yesterday and left this morning."

"Ah!" sighed Tiuri. "I'd have liked to see him again."

"What good fortune that he happened to be in Vorgóta when we arrived," said Piak. "He was visiting the lady here and did not intend to stay for long. There is no knight in this castle; he perished last year in the Southerly Mountains. Have you had enough to eat?"

"Oh yes," said Tiuri.

Piak plumped up Tiuri's pillows and said, "I think Sir Ardian is the best knight I know. Although Rafox is also very nice. And brave."

Rafox... what had happened in the Wild Wood? Tiuri closed his eyes and for a moment he saw vague images from his feverish visions. But Piak chased them away by asking with concern, "Have I tired you out with my talking?"

"Not at all," said Tiuri. "Tell me more."

"No, I won't say anything else," said Piak. "You know now that you were in time..."

"That *we* were in time," whispered Tiuri.

"Fine. You can hear everything else later. First you need to rest."

"You're right, Piak," said the lady of the castle, coming back into the room. "And now you can get yourself off to bed, too."

Tiuri saw that his friend wasn't looking too well either. "Oh, Piak! I'm sorry..." he began.

But Piak just laughed. "We're going to sleep so well!" he said. "No more worries to keep us awake or give us nightmares. Sweet dreams!"

Tiuri recovered. The fever did not return and every day he grew stronger. But the physician told him that he had to lie in bed for a few more days before he was allowed to try sitting up and walking. Piak spent as much time as possible with him, but he was also kept busy with work in and about the castle.

Gradually Tiuri came to hear about everything that had happened to the west of the Great Mountains while he had been ill. There had been no news at all from the east as yet. He heard how the army of Red Riders had come storming down from the mountains, and how they had been stopped by the forewarned men of the Kingdom of Unauwen, under the command of Sir Ardian. It was strange, though, that the King of Eviellan had not led his army himself. So it was suspected that the attack had indeed begun prematurely and they had not been entirely prepared. Even so, the fighting had been heavy. The enemy had even reached as far as the castle and had tried to capture it. The siege had lasted only a couple of days, though. Piak had even stood up on the battlements, throwing down pitch and rocks. When Sir Ardian returned, the besiegers had fled. The knight had been able to stay for only a short while, "but," said Piak, "he sat by your bedside all night."

"As did you – almost all the time I was ill," said Tiuri quietly. "The lady told me so."

"Of course I did," said Piak. "And it's proved useful that I know how to take care of sick people."

Many of those wounded in the battle were now at the castle, and Piak and others were helping the lady to look after them.

Tiuri could do nothing now but wait patiently to regain his health. At times it felt like a very long wait indeed, although he did not let it show. Piak sometimes stared at him thoughtfully. He could see that Tiuri had changed again. No, that was not entirely true; he was still the same old Tiuri, and yet there was something different about him. He didn't know quite how to put it into words.

"My goodness!" said Piak, ten days later. "Look how you've grown! You're almost a head taller than me. But you're as thin as a rake," he added.

"That will change soon enough," said Tiuri cheerfully. It was so wonderful to be able to walk around again, to feel that he was alive and healthy! He walked to the window of their room and looked longingly outside, at the mountains in the east. "We will leave soon," he said. "The physician has told me I can travel the day after tomorrow, if I take it easy and don't become involved in any fighting for the time being. Which is fine by me, and as I've lost my sword anyway..."

Piak came to stand beside him and said, "You can have mine."

"The sword King Unauwen gave you?" cried Tiuri. "I have fought with it, but I could never keep it." And he continued in a quieter voice, "I lost my sword when I was captured, but one day I will have another."

Neither of them had noticed the door opening.

"That's right!" said a voice behind them. "And it is not the sword that matters, but the hand that holds it."

The two friends turned around in surprise. "Tirillo!" they both cried.

The jester stepped into the room, followed by the lady of the castle.

"Ah, why am I always greeted with astonishment?" he said. "Is there such a lack of fools in this world?" His tone was light, but his eyes were full of warmth as he shook their hands.

The lady of the castle said, "Tirillo is here as an envoy from King Unauwen."

"I do not come with a letter or message," said the jester. "I have only to say two words on behalf of King Unauwen. And those words are: 'Thank you!' There are many words to be added, and perhaps you will hear them at some point, but that is all fancy frippery. One day you will meet King Unauwen again. He has left his city and is now at the Rainbow River, awaiting news from east and south. I think, though, that it will be some time before you see him, as I have heard that you wish to return home soon."

"Yes," replied Tiuri after a moment's pause. "Back to the Kingdom of Dagonaut... to the Wild Wood."

"When are you leaving?" asked the jester.

Piak looked at Tiuri and answered, "He wants to leave as soon as possible, if not sooner, but..."

"I told you the physician approves, didn't I?" Tiuri said, interrupting him. "I'll go as soon as I'm allowed, and that's the day after tomorrow."

"Then I shall travel with you," said the jester.

"Excellent!" said Piak.

The jester smiled. "You and I will make sure Tiuri takes care of himself," he said. "I can understand that he does not want to wait any longer. I, too, am sorry that I could not take part in the great battle at the side of my knight, Prince Iridian."

"Great battle?" repeated the two friends.

Tirillo told them that the armies of Eviellan had invaded from the south, on the same day that the Castle of Vorgóta was besieged.

The crown prince had led Unauwen's army in the Battle of the Gorge in the Southerly Mountains. "The reports we received are incomplete and confused," he said, "but one thing is sure: Prince Iridian repelled the enemy. And if I come with you, perhaps I shall meet him, somewhere in the Wild Wood."

"In the Wild Wood?" said Piak.

"The warning about the other, more dangerous attack through the pass was heard by Unauwen's men in the south as well," said Tirillo. "So I think the prince will soon head for the Kingdom of Dagonaut, down the Third Great Road, along the Grey River. You were the first to bring the message of the stronghold in the Wild Wood. But you were not the only ones. Sir Bendu arrived a little later with the same message."

"Sir... Bendu?" said Tiuri.

"Do not ask why and how!" said the jester. "Sir Bendu's name was mentioned, as was that of Ristridin, who apparently sent him."

The two friends were most surprised by this news and bombarded Tirillo with questions. But he could not tell them much more.

Then the lady of the castle spoke. "So we shall soon say farewell," she said. "Then this is the right moment to tell Sir Tiuri I wish to give him something before he leaves."

"To give me something, my lady?" said Tiuri. "You have already given me so much, hospitality, care..."

"Hush," said the lady. "Just now, as I came in, I heard what you said. And so... wait a moment."

She left the room and soon returned with a large sword in her hands. Stopping in front of Tiuri, she looked at him with a grave expression.

"This," she said, "is the Sword of Vorgóta, forged by Tongan the smith, who also made the gong. My husband carried it until his death, as did his forefathers before him. I have no sons to inherit

422

it, and I believe you are the right knight to carry it. After all, you beat the Vorgóta Gong with Tongan's mallet. They belong together: gong, mallet and sword. Here, take the sword and may it help you and make you strong in every battle!"

Tiuri bowed respectfully as he took the precious gift. He could not manage any more than those two words either: "Thank you!" But they came from the bottom of his heart.

"I will also give you my husband's white shield when you set off," said the lady. "And so you will once again carry the colour you have earned."

She had still not finished speaking, though, because then she turned to Piak. "You have a sword," she said, "and I have no other heirloom to present to you. May I therefore give you something of my own, as a reminder of your days at Vorgóta?" She took a finely crafted gold chain from her neck. "I shall hang it around your neck for now," she said. "But you can keep it to give one day to the girl you want to marry."

Piak blushed. "My deepest thanks, my lady," he said. "But I think I would rather keep it myself. I don't know anyone I could give something so beautiful to."

"Wait a few years," said the lady, "and see if you still feel the same way."

They laughed, partly to conceal their emotions. They were indeed magnificent gifts.

"The Sword of Vorgóta is famous," said Tirillo. "It is often mentioned in our chronicles."

Later, when they were sitting comfortably together, Tirillo told them some of the stories that were connected to the sword. "So you see," he concluded, "it is a reminder not only of great deeds, but also of good ones, which certainly cannot be said of every sword. All too many weapons have an aura of evil clinging to them."

"Do you know of any evil swords?" asked Piak. He loved listening to such tales.

"Oh yes. There's the Weapon of Woe, for instance, from the Cavern by the Chasm..." Tirillo looked at the lady and continued, "But I don't want to tell you about that now. I hope it has rusted away... Besides," he added, "I think it's probably just about bedtime, don't you?"

When Piak was sitting in bed, he looked more closely at the necklace, and took a moment to think about what kind of girl he would like to give it to. She would have to come from the mountains, like him... but she would also have to be a bit like Lavinia. Then he laughed. *Go to sleep!* he told himself. *You have other things to dream about now.*

7   THE BLACK RIVER AND
THE TARNBURG

A week later, they had crossed the pass over the Great Mountains – Tiuri, Piak and Tirillo the jester. They stopped to rest in the stone hut, which was now guarded by Ardian's men.

As he looked at Tiuri's pale and glum face, Tirillo suggested spending the night in the hut. But Tiuri said he would rather travel on to the larger guard post at the Tarntop. Piak agreed; this place was full of bad memories.

Sir Ardian's men told them that the Road of Ambuscade was occupied by Unauwen's men all the way beyond the Tarnburg. But to the south of the Black River the enemy must still be powerful. The friends also heard that the King of Eviellan had led his army up to the pass, where he had waited to see if the attack would succeed.

"What a coward!" exclaimed Piak.

Tirillo, though, shook his head. "No," he said, "I know many names for the King of Eviellan, but he is not a coward. I think he already suspected that this attack was doomed to fail, and he had other plans."

"It seems they set fire to the wood," said one of the men. "The sky in the east was glowing red."

Piak was shocked and he looked at Tiuri with wide eyes. He recalled what his friend had said in his feverish delirium. But Tiuri seemed to remember nothing about it, and so Piak remained silent.

Soon they travelled onwards. At the place where they had climbed down the rocks, they stopped for a moment.

"Look," said Piak, pointing, "there's the hidden path."

A Man in Green appeared on the precipice. Piak waved at him and he waved back. As they went on their way, they heard the sound of a drum.

"Do you think that's about us?" Piak wondered.

From the large guard post at the Tarntop the road led down along the Black River, which was now not dark at all, but white with foaming rapids. Two days later, they reached the edge of the forest, and what they saw gave them such a shock that they stopped and stared – even though they knew what was coming.

In the distance all was still green, but there was little left of the forest closer to them. Everything was scorched and blackened.

Tiuri frowned. In his mind he could picture it burning... he could feel the heat and the suffocating smoke, hear the crackle of burning wood, the roar of the flames, the sounds of people and animals fleeing. His thoughts were so vivid that it felt as though he had been there. But that was, of course, impossible.

They entered the devastated area. Ash puffed up under their feet as they walked, and the smell of smoke and scorched vegetation still hung in the air. Some of the trees were not completely burnt; they stood like ghosts of the murdered forest, their twisted branches charred and flaking. Silent, saddened and fearful, they walked on.

In the north, from the direction of the Green River, another drum sounded. From the east, along the Black River, a man approached them, leading a horse. The horse was black and the man was green, and, as they came nearer, Tiuri and Piak recognized Ardanwen and the Master of the Wild Wood.

"What I feared has come to pass," said Tehalon, after they had spoken their greetings. "Part of my forest has been destroyed by fire – but not everything, not everything at all. And your horse is in fine fettle, Sir Tiuri. Climb up and ride to the Tarnburg."

Tiuri stroked Ardanwen. "What happened here?" he asked Tehalon in concern.

"There was a battle between the rivers," Tehalon replied. "Two knights came to help Lord Rafox against Eviellan. But they could not stop the army heading to the east. Even so, the attack along the Road of Ambuscade failed; the army fled, battered and beaten. Were you in time?"

"Yes," said Tiuri, "thanks to the Vorgóta Gong."

"I heard it," said Tehalon. "Not for real, but in a dream. Come with me. You will hear all about it in the Tarnburg. Other shields hang there now, but those who are there will not be there forever. And the one who dwelt there before has not yet been defeated."

"He hasn't?" whispered Tiuri.

"He has fled south and has gone to ground, still able to do much harm."

"Tell us more," said Piak.

"No," said Tehalon. "Let another do that."

"You detest this struggle," said Tirillo.

The Master of the Wild Wood looked at the jester as if seeing him for the first time. "Who does not?" he said. "You seem like a sensible man, a man who would understand me."

"Perhaps so," replied Tirillo. "Even so, you still took part, did you not?"

426

"I did indeed," said Tehalon. "We had to! And then came the fire, which we extinguished with great difficulty. And since then, we Men in Green have been working to restore everything. Look!"

It took them a while to see what he meant. As they approached the area where the Tarnburg stood, they saw that almost everything was still green on the opposite bank of the river, but the High Bridge had gone. A few tree trunks had been placed across the river as a temporary measure. Tehalon's men were busy building a new bridge beside it.

Tiuri took Piak by the arm and said quietly, "I saw that, the bridge collapsing and disappearing..."

"It was a spark from the fire," said Tehalon. "Dagonaut's knights were upset at first because it would make it more difficult for them to conquer the Tarnburg. But later their disappointment turned into satisfaction when the King of Eviellan returned from the mountains and found his route of retreat cut off."

They stopped by the bridge.

"You must tell us more," said Tirillo.

"The King of Eviellan rode out ahead of his routed army," said Tehalon slowly, "a Black Knight with a Red Shield on a large grey horse. And he did something I would never have believed had I not seen it with my own eyes. He drove his horse onwards to the river and forced it to jump. He jumped even further himself, out of the saddle, and that's how he made it to the opposite bank. His horse perished. There were Red Riders who attempted to follow him, but they fell to the rocks or drowned. The rest of his army fled to the east, where they were stopped and defeated by the knights of Dagonaut."

"And what about the king?" asked Piak. "He no longer has the Tarnburg."

"No, no longer. But he is alive and he is still powerful. You should cross the river and go to meet the knights who have occupied the castle."

427

"Who are they?" asked Tiuri. "Is Lord Rafox with them? And who are the others? Sir Ardian? And is there... is there a knight with a silver horn?"

"There was a knight with a silver horn," replied Tehalon, "but he has left the forest. Go across the river. You will hear everything there. I shall bid you farewell, as I still have much to do."

The three travellers walked across the tree trunks of the temporary bridge, Tiuri leading Ardanwen by the reins.

The Men in Green greeted them with smiles. There were other men on the opposite bank, soldiers. One of them let out a cry and waved excitedly.

"Adelbart!" cried Piak.

Then a knight came striding towards them. Amazed, Tiuri stopped in his tracks. It was his father!

A few moments later, the two Sir Tiuris were greeting each other very warmly indeed. Sir Tiuri the Valiant looked at his son with a mixture of pride and affection. "I am glad you have returned," was all he said.

Tiuri noticed his eyes were now at the same height as his father's. And yet, as he walked beside him to the Tarnburg, he still felt like the boy he had once been. That feeling did not last for long, however. As they entered the castle, he realized most clearly that he was no longer a child, and it seemed that this was the place where he had become a man.

The castle had not changed much – it seemed more dilapidated maybe, and the red shield had gone. There were now other shields at the entrance: the shields of Tehuri and Mistrinaut.

"You can hang your shield alongside them," said Tiuri the Valiant to his son. "You fought with us, together with Piak, even though your paths led you far from here."

"But fortunately you have returned in good health!" said another man. It was Lord Rafox, who had come out to meet them.

Tiuri and Piak were delighted to see him, too. Piak, concerned, asked after his health, as his arm was in a sling.

"Ah, that's almost healed," said the Lord of Mistrinaut. "We've been keeping a lookout for you. We heard much about you from Ardian. How are you faring, Tiuri?"

"I'm almost healed, too," he replied. "How are you? How is everyone?"

"Where is Sir Ardian?" asked Piak.

"And Sir Ristridin?" said Tiuri.

"And Prince Iridian?" said Tirillo, who had stayed in the background at first, but now came to join them.

"Ah, so you already know the prince is in the Wild Wood?" said Tiuri's father. "Come inside. Then you can rest... and talk."

They went into the hall where once the Red Riders had sat at the long tables. Now there were other soldiers there, who greeted them and then left the room. They sat down together; at first everyone spoke at once. There was so much to ask and so much to say, and it was a long time before everyone knew how everyone else had fared and all that had happened in the three kingdoms.

"Lavinia is back at home," said Lord Rafox to Tiuri. "She managed to find a messenger and sent me a letter full of good wishes... including some for you as soon as you returned. The messenger is returning to Mistrinaut tomorrow. I'm just passing on my greetings, as I'm unable to write at the moment. Perhaps you would write a few words on my behalf, and add a few of your own."

"Oh, I'd be happy to!" said Tiuri, and he blushed as Lord Rafox looked at him with a smile. Then Tiuri asked again about Sir Ristridin.

Now Piak and Tiuri finally got to hear that Ristridin had been imprisoned at Islan, and that he had eventually been released and had fought, together with Rafox and Tiuri's father, between the rivers.

"More men came from the south to reinforce Eviellan's position," Lord Rafox told them. "We wanted to conquer the castle, but we could not get across the Black River. Sir Ardian came from the west and joined us. The night after that, the king suddenly abandoned the Tarnburg and withdrew. Nearly all of his men followed him, and the castle fell into our hands almost without a struggle."

"Why did he withdraw?" asked Tiuri. "Was he afraid that he would be unable to continue to resist your attacks?"

"No, that's not why," said his father. "You probably know that Prince Iridian won victory in the Kingdom of Unauwen at the Battle of the Gorge. Part of Eviellan's army fled to the east, along the Third Great Road, and then along the secret paths into the Wild Wood, to join the forces there. Prince Iridian pursued them, with his company of knights and warriors; men from our kingdom joined him, too."

"Sir Bendu was with them," said Lord Rafox.

"The King of Eviellan was ahead of us," continued Tiuri's father. "That's why he left the Tarnburg; his withdrawal was actually an attack! He rode out to meet his brother and they came to blows close to the Unholy Hills. There was another battle, the Last Battle, which lasted three days."

"But Prince Iridian won, didn't he?" said Piak.

"In a way," said Lord Rafox slowly. "We fought too, along with Sir Ardian. Eviellan lost – at least most of his army was defeated. And yet still we did not truly win victory! When the King of Eviellan saw that he had lost his chance to win, he withdrew from the fight. He fled with his remaining men into the Unholy Hills. That's where he is now, but no one knows exactly where. He and his Red Riders know their way around, and they'll have plenty of traps and hiding places in there."

"But," said Piak, "we're going to do something about it, aren't we? I mean..." He fell silent and looked rather sheepishly at the knights. After all, they knew far more about warfare than he did.

"I'm sure it'll be very difficult to find him there," said Tiuri.

His father sighed. "So far it's proved impossible," he said. "Although we have many more men, we are at a disadvantage. And he has continued the conflict in a different way. His Red Riders are carrying out sneak attacks. They bring death and destruction before disappearing without a trace. Others lie in ambush and attack our men when they venture into the Unholy Hills. It's almost impossible to fight openly there. As you know, they are very familiar with the territory. We are not."

Tirillo asked after Prince Iridian and Sir Ardian.

"They have set up camp by the Wild Wood Way," replied Tiuri's father, "not far from the Unholy Hills. We came back to hold the castle."

"The war is over," said Tirillo, "but the fighting goes on, as is so often the case. Many more fights will be fought in this wood, which is wilder and more dangerous than I had imagined. I will go with all haste to my master, the prince, and support him however I can. I must bid you farewell."

Tiuri and Piak both thought they had never seen the jester look so serious.

"Can't the Men in Green help?" asked Tiuri.

Lord Rafox replied that the Men in Green had not set foot in the Unholy Hills for years. "Besides," he said, "Tehalon has told us that he no longer wants to fight, but will only be involved in the repair work."

"There is someone else who knows his way around the Unholy Hills!" said Piak. "Sir Fitil of Islan. But he..."

Lord Rafox held up one hand to interrupt him. "Sir Fitil of Islan is no longer alive," he said.

"Sir Fitil? Dead?" said Tiuri.

"He fell fighting against Eviellan," said his father.

"Against Eviellan?" repeated Piak. "But... I thought..."

"That he was in league with Eviellan," said Lord Rafox. "Indeed he was. But the King of Eviellan sent a detachment of Red Riders to capture Islan. Why? Perhaps because possession of that castle could prove strategically valuable; perhaps out of revenge because Sir Fitil let Ristridin go free. But whatever the reason, Castle Islan was besieged. The enemy did not capture the castle, though; Sir Fitil defended it valiantly and finally met his end in a counter-attack. Ristridin is there now."

"Sir Ristridin!" said Tiuri. "But he came here to the Tarnburg with you."

"Yes," replied his father. "But then he travelled on to Islan and so did not take part in the Last Battle by the Unholy Hills. He anticipated that Eviellan would attack Fitil's castle, and that is what happened. This news reached us only recently, and Ristridin is planning to remain at Islan for as long as there is chance of a second attack."

Tiuri thought of Sir Fitil, with his loud and cheerful manner and his darting eyes. He also thought of Isadoro. She had stood with her father on Eviellan's side, but she had not done so gladly, he realized. And now sadness had come upon her and she was alone. He had never truly loved her, but at that moment her image appeared so clearly in his mind that it was almost alarming – as she sat in the Round Chamber, singing and playing her harp...

He wanted to ask about her, but he hesitated to do so, as Lord Rafox was sitting beside him, Lavinia's father.

So Isadoro's father was dead, and now Sir Ristridin was at Islan, where he had spent months as a prisoner...

8   THE MISTRESS OF ISLAN

Sir Ristridin stood facing Lady Isadoro in her Round Chamber and thought to himself that she was most definitely a worthy mistress of Islan.

She was not wearing the grey clothes of mourning, as was usually the custom, but a rich green gown with gleaming folds. Her beauty was still striking, although she looked pale and tired. A short time ago he had seen a different side of her: at the siege on the battlements, as she had rallied the castle residents after her father's death.

He had watched her tending the wounded, speaking to them with kind words. He had heard her issue orders, which were obeyed immediately, and he knew everyone who lived at Islan had already accepted her as their mistress. She would only officially become its mistress, though, after King Dagonaut had given his permission. Ristridin was planning to ask him to do so; the Lord of Islan had paid for his guilt with his life and no one was better suited than his daughter to follow him. The king would soon be at Islan – he had left the capital and set out for the Wild Wood.

"You must receive him, Sir Ristridin," said Isadoro. "I do not dare to approach the king."

"And yet you must, my lady," said Ristridin, "and welcome him as befits the mistress of a castle."

"The mistress of a castle?" she repeated. "I have no other home than this, and I would not know where to go otherwise. Yet I feel that I must leave this place, retreat and hide. But where? In the Wild Wood perhaps?" She smiled, but without a trace of happiness.

"Your place is here, my lady," said Ristridin. "You are the Lady of Islan, as you have already proven. King Dagonaut is sure to agree with me. He will not remain here long, and neither will I..."

"Are you leaving?" she asked.

"Yes, there is nothing left for me to do here," replied Ristridin. "And should you need any help, there are many knights here now, in their tents on the plain. I must go; the war is not yet won."

Isadoro turned away; she glanced at her father's chair and laid her hand on her harp for a moment. "Ah," she said, with her back to him, "I understand that you dislike this place. It must still seem like a prison to you. I am already most grateful to you for coming to our aid."

As Ristridin looked at the lady, so proud and so sad, he felt great tenderness for her.

"Isadoro..." he said, "Lady Isadoro, I came to help because Eviellan was threatening the Kingdom of Dagonaut. But I entered this castle of my own free will. I am leaving because I have obligations elsewhere. The danger here has receded, believe me!"

The lady turned to him again and said in a trembling voice, "I wish it were not so! As long as there was danger and the battle was still being fought, I could remain strong and I did not have to think. Now I miss my father – although perhaps I should be glad that he died as a brave man. But I loved him and I helped him, even when he was in league with Eviellan! I hate this castle; all of its rooms seem empty and my footsteps echo on the stairs. Sometimes I wish I were a warrior, so that I could march with an army, into the Wild Wood. But I could head into the forest anyway," she added in a whisper, half to herself. "And then go astray and disappear, as I deserve..."

Ristridin walked over to her and took her by the shoulders.

"Isadoro," he said in a grave tone, "you must not talk like that! You may not run and you cannot go astray. You have one task to perform, and one task alone: to remain here as the noble and valiant Lady of Islan. You will know sorrow, but you must not torture yourself with self-reproach. Be from now on the guardian of Islan, the only stronghold beside the Wild Wood. And if I can help you, I am always ready and willing to do so."

She lifted her face to look at him and smiled through her tears. He let go of her and took a step back.

Isadoro wiped her eyes. "You have already done enough for me," she said. "I thank you and I shall never forget you. But now, please, leave me on my own."

Silently, Ristridin did as she requested. And he had to admit to himself that he was glad to leave her company. The Lady of Islan threatened to rob him of his peace of mind. And that, he thought, was far too foolish for a man of his age.

"At my age it is too late to begin another life," said Red Quibo. "I'll never get used to drinking water, or looking at a king, even from a

434

distance, or being surrounded by knights who make me run when I would rather rest." He glanced up from the silver horn he was polishing and gave Ristridin a gloomy look.

"Don't talk nonsense, Quibo," said Ristridin. "Even in your own village you would have found no peace. They are also being plagued by the enemies who are hiding out in the Unholy Hills."

"It is so close!" muttered Quibo. "My beloved village, my home and my refuge, the spot where my cradle stood, the place where I lived... and I am not even allowed to visit."

"Perhaps you are needed more elsewhere," said Ristridin. "Now stop that polishing and go and pack."

"Off on another journey... Well, enjoy the ride!" Quibo grumbled. "Why are you leaving Islan and its peaceful plain? Are you abandoning the lady who is most probably the kindest – and indisputably the most beautiful – woman in the Kingdom of Dagonaut? I thought a knight was supposed to serve ladies, protect them, love them..."

"Go and pack!" growled Ristridin.

"I'm already doing so!" protested Quibo. "Here is your horn, my lord. Should I pack for myself as well?"

"What do you think? Of course!" said Ristridin. He stood up and paced the room, his brow furrowed.

His squire set to work in silence. But after a while he said, "Sir Ristridin... we have to go into the forest, I know, but do you also want to go into those... hateful hills?"

He faltered briefly as Ristridin stopped and looked sternly at him. Then, timidly, he continued, "I don't know the way from here, my lord! If I can find the way, and I'm not saying I can, then it's only from the tourney field to the east... to that gloomy vale, which you've already made me describe to you a dozen times."

"We're going along the Black River back to the Tarnburg," said Ristridin. "The tourney field is near there. That's all I can say for now."

"When are we leaving?" asked Quibo.

"Today," replied Ristridin. "I have spoken to the king; there is no reason now to delay my departure. So say farewell, Quibo, to Islan."

"Farewell," sighed Quibo, looking around the room. "It's so very beautiful here. Aren't you going to miss this?"

"I have never of my own free will stayed in one place for any length of time," said Ristridin. "I am a knight-errant, with no castle that I call home."

"And do you always wish to wander restlessly?" asked Quibo. "Don't you miss home, hearth and... heart?"

Ristridin snorted. "I am not a young man," he said, "and I cannot change now. Travelling, wandering, that is my destiny, and that is what I have always wanted."

"A life of loneliness, all on my own..." began Quibo.

"Now, please, will you just hold your tongue?" said Ristridin. But it was not long before the same words sounded in his ears once again, as he said farewell to Lady Isadoro.

"You have shown me the way, Sir Ristridin," she said. "King Dagonaut has made me Lady of Islan and charged me with righting my wrongs through my actions here. I shall try to be brave and noble, and to govern my lands justly. An honourable life, but a life of loneliness."

"My dear lady," said Ristridin, and he could not help but smile, "you are young and you are sad, and I understand why you should speak that way. But be assured that you will not feel lonely for long or remain alone." He thought about the knights whose tents were pitched on the plain, and about other knights he knew. There would surely be many gentlemen who, to use Red Quibo's words, would wish to serve her, protect her, and love her.

But Isadoro said, "Even surrounded by many people, one can feel alone – particularly when the person one loves is not there."

"Your father..." Ristridin began gently.

"I am not speaking only about my father," she said quietly, and she blushed. "Ah," she continued in a louder voice, "but it matters little now! Farewell, Sir Ristridin, you have already been too kind to me. Oh, I feel guilty, so guilty... I knew what was in the wood and I warned no one... You were imprisoned and still I allowed others to head into danger..."

"Are you thinking of Sir Tiuri?" said Ristridin.

"Yes, him, too... Please send word to me when he returns from his mission! But I am also thinking of others..."

Is she in love with the young Tiuri? thought Ristridin. *But he seems to have forgotten her for Rafox's daughter.* And he said, "There are many knights in the Kingdom of Dagonaut, young, valiant..."

"Oh, do not speak of them," she said with a shudder. "I know that there is a war. And you... you are the finest of them all."

"Oh, I feel that I've had my day," said Ristridin. He spoke lightly, although he did not feel that way. "Do not think too much about what has been, Isadoro. Look to the future. One day you will meet a knight whom you truly will find the finest knight of all."

"I have already met that knight," whispered the young lady.

"And who is it?" asked Ristridin after a moment's pause. "Tiuri?"

She shook her head and seemed to want to say something, but remained silent. Then she said quickly, "I do not wish to hold you up any longer, Ristridin. The wood is waiting for you. I would like to bid you farewell with the words on the old signpost: 'Tread this path in peace and may you reach your goal.' Do you know who translated those words for me? The Lord of the Tarnburg himself, the Black Knight with the Red Shield. Once I thought he was the first among all knights, even though I feared him. Now I no longer think that, but he is still often in my thoughts. He is so close by, in the Unholy Hills..." She looked at him. "I have promised myself I will speak only the truth from now on," she said, "and so I say this to you: I shall be Lady of Islan and no knight will be permitted to wear my colours."

"Do not speak that way," said Ristridin. "You cannot keep such a promise."

"Fine, then you shall be the only one! You are already wearing my colour, Ristridin, even though it is perhaps without your knowledge and intention."

"How is that?" said Ristridin.

"Yellow and brown are the colours of Islan, but green is my own colour – just as it is the colour of your cloak and of the symbol on your shield."

Ristridin shook his head. "Let your knight be a younger man," he said. "Although I will always be at your service should you request it of me."

Isadoro shook back her hair and said proudly, "I shall not ask your help again, Sir Ristridin. I am certain I shall hear of your deeds – and then I shall ask if you are still wearing my colour. If not, then I will know I will not see you again. But if you are, then perhaps the message will reach you that the Lady of Islan has invited you to her castle. But that will not happen before this war is over and won." Then she held out her hand to him and said once again, "Farewell."

Ristridin would have liked to give her a goodbye kiss, but he did not do so. He just said kindly, "Farewell," and soon he rode away at full tilt.

Red Quibo, who was following him, kept falling behind. He glanced back at the castle several times. "Will we ever see it again?" he asked out loud, when he had finally caught up with his master.

"I do not know," said Ristridin. "I am a knight-errant and my paths are uncertain." But to himself he thought, *Will I continue to wear green? Yes, of course – I have always done so and the symbol on my shield is older than Isadoro, older even than myself. It would make no sense to change it. Besides… she must not think I am not always ready to help her.*

"My paths are uncertain," muttered Quibo beside him. "True words! But wherever they lead, there is always misery and anger… Ah, woe is me… To the Tarnburg we go!"

9 ENDGAME

Tiuri thought how strange it was to be back at the Tarnburg. He was not a prisoner now and was sleeping under the same roof as friends, but he kept thinking about the prince who had lived there for so long.

The first night he slept there, he awoke with a start from a dream in which the King of Eviellan was speaking to him: "And with the third – with Tiuri – I am playing a game that is not yet finished."

He could not get back to sleep and so, after a while, he got up, very quietly, so as not to disturb Piak, with whom he was sharing a bedchamber. He wandered in the darkness through corridors and halls, and finally found the spiral staircase that took him to the room where he had spent three nights as a prisoner – over a month ago now.

He stood in the doorway for a moment, looking at the window on the right, with its two missing bars. Then he stepped within, and felt around for the candlestick and lit the candles. Nothing had changed. The chessboard was still on the table; one pawn had fallen over and lay beside the board. He picked it up and put it back in the right place, remembering the exact position of the pieces. Then he walked over to the window; once again he could hear the rushing river and see the guards down below. They were different men this time, though. He thought about Jaro and the Fool – would they have reached the Fool's cabin yet? He turned away, walked around and found his bag of belongings, with the file lying beside it. He opened up the bag and took out Lavinia's glove. As he thought of her, he forgot the gloomy atmosphere, just for a moment. Then he smoothed out the glove and tucked it into his belt. He knew he really should leave.

But there was the chessboard and it seemed as if someone were standing in the shadows, waiting for the game to finish. But that moment would never come...

Tiuri sat down at the table and hesitantly raised his hand. Then he slowly moved one of the pieces – it was his turn. Frowning, he wondered what move the King of Eviellan would have responded with. He sat there for a while, just staring at the board, thinking and pondering. A shiver ran down his spine; it felt as if he were playing chess with a ghost who was invisibly mocking him. There were so many possibilities; he would never know how the game would have ended had he not escaped. Life... or death? When he left the silent room and went back to bed, he felt as if he were running away again.

In the days that followed, though, Tiuri could not resist returning several times to the room and to the game of chess, to reflect further upon who would have won the game – Tiuri or the King of Eviellan. There was little for him to do at the Tarnburg; he was not yet allowed to go out riding or to help with the repair work.

Tiuri spoke to no one about it, but Piak soon worked out where he disappeared to. Piak was not at all surprised; after his friend's delirious dreams, he already knew the unfinished game of chess was troubling him. So he chose not to follow him or to ask any questions.

On the afternoon of the third day, Prince Iridian arrived at the castle, accompanied by Tirillo, a number of knights and a dozen men. Tiuri was not there to welcome them, however; he didn't even know the prince had come, because he was sitting at the chessboard again.

"You have to stop this!" he said to himself. "There's no point to it, and I don't think it's good or healthy." But still he went on sitting there, his eyes fixed on the pieces.

Outside his prison, he heard footsteps... No, it was no longer a prison; he could stand up and walk around as he pleased. The door opened.

Tiuri looked up – and his heart seemed to skip a beat. Then he realized who was standing before him, and he rose to his feet.

Prince Iridian!

Tiuri bowed and looked at him again; never again would he confuse this prince with his brother. Iridian answered his gaze with a grave smile and held out his hand. Tiuri came closer and shook it. "Your Highness..." he began.

"Your friend Piak told me where to find you," said the prince.

"Forgive me, Your Highness," said Tiuri. "I did not know you were here..."

"I arrived only recently," said the prince, "and I wanted to come and fetch you myself." He looked at the chessboard and said, "Is this the game you were playing with my brother?"

"Yes, Your Highness," replied Tiuri.

"What were the stakes?"

"Life or death."

The prince turned his dark, penetrating eyes on Tiuri. "Did you challenge him?" he asked.

"Yes, my lord. But I was planning to escape as soon as I had the chance." Tiuri paused before continuing, "I have always done what I believed to be right, but I often feel that what I have done was not right at all! Up on the pass I killed two men. I had no choice, and yet..."

"I understand," said the prince. "Even if you are fighting against evil, you can take on a burden of guilt that can be hard to put down. That's just the way it is and there is nothing you can do to change it."

They were silent for a moment. Then the prince asked, "Does it bother you that this game of chess is still here, unfinished?"

"Yes, Your Highness," replied Tiuri.

"Then that must change," said the prince in a firm tone. "Other matters will soon demand your attention. Come."

Tiuri thought at first that he was being told to leave the room and the game, but the prince stepped forward and took his brother's place.

"I have a little time," he said. "Sit down. Whose move is it?"

"The King of... Yours, my lord," replied Tiuri, doing as he was told. He was surprised, but felt that he must do as the prince commanded.

The prince moved a piece and leant back in his chair, his elbows on the armrests, his fingers steepled under his chin. "Now you," he said abruptly. But his eyes were kind.

Tiuri found it hard to concentrate on the game at first, and yet he did his very best, as he knew that was what the prince expected.

He did not know how long they played for; time did not seem to matter. It was not like the other three nights, though; his opponent was a different man.

They played in silence – and Tiuri lost.

"That's checkmate!" he said quietly. "So if we had finished the game, the king would have won."

"If you think about it for a moment, you must realize you'll never know for certain," replied the prince. He rose to his feet and continued, "I took over the game and I beat you. So if the stakes remain the same, your life belongs to me. But," he added, "I return it to you – although you know you are not entirely at liberty to do with it as you please."

Tiuri stood up; suddenly he felt free. He said nothing, as he knew the prince already understood. And he left the room with him, never to return.

10   The Unholy Hills

Prince Iridian had come to confer with Dagonaut's knights about how best to defeat the enemy. His retinue included not only the jester Tirillo, but also Bendu and Evan, who had taken part in the battles. Tiuri and Piak were, of course, happy to see them again, although that joy was overshadowed by the fact that matters were still not settled. Sir Ardian was not there; he had remained with

442

the men who were encamped near the Unholy Hills. Piak was particularly disappointed, although he understood why Ardian could not come. Someone had to stand guard over the place where the enemy was lurking.

The next day, the sound of a silver horn rang out in front of the Tarnburg. Sir Ristridin had come from the east to take part in the discussions on behalf of King Dagonaut.

Tiuri was the first to greet him. Finally he stood before the knight who had been in his thoughts so often. He looked at that lean, weathered face, with the bright blue eyes that studied him both thoughtfully and approvingly.

"I have been looking forward to this meeting," said Ristridin. "You continued my journey where I had to end it." And he added, "Perhaps we shall soon ride out again together, side by side."

Towards the evening, Piak was walking across the clearing in front of the castle. He had helped the Men in Green with the work on the bridge and then spoken to Adelbart for a while, but now he was walking around somewhat aimlessly. The discussions were still going on inside; Tiuri was there, too – he was now considered the equal of the other knights.

It shouldn't be much longer now, thought Piak. As he stood by the shields at the gate, he suddenly saw someone he recognized... Who was that man with the spiky red hair? It was Red Quibo from the inn by the Forest of Islan! He was almost unrecognizable in his smart new tunic.

"Quibo! However did you end up here?" asked Piak.

"Oh, for goodness' sake, don't ask me!" cried Quibo. "I'm here against my will and my wish! That cruel Sir Ristridin dragged me here, defencelessly and unlawfully, refusing to heed my cries of woe. No, now don't you laugh or sneer. I am his squire, although that is poor consolation, and most harmful to my health."

Still, Piak couldn't help but laugh at Quibo. "But why?" he said. "And how?"

"Ah, be silent, before I give in to the weakness of tears," groaned Quibo. "The things I've had to endure! I was dragged into battle, and – oh, horrors! – I even had to fight and brandish a sword! That's the truth, or I would not be here to tell the tale! Now I have only one wish: to relate my adventures in an inn somewhere, to tell a story, not to be part of one myself."

As Quibo was speaking, Sir Ristridin had come outside, together with Tiuri. Piak started to say something, but Ristridin gestured at him to remain silent.

"Let me tell *you* a story, Quibo," Ristridin said. "Almost a year ago, four knights rode out to avenge the death of Edwinem, their friend. In armour of grey they rode along paths beaten and unbeaten, and the men they followed were Red Riders, led by a Black Knight with a Red Shield. They did not yet know who their enemy was: the King of Eviellan... the man who is now in the Unholy Hills plotting our destruction. The knights were four in number: Bendu, Evan, Arwaut and I. Sir Arwaut is dead, but the other three are now together again. And they will ride out once more to search for the Black Knight with the Red Shield. Not to fight him this time, but to talk to him as envoys of King Dagonaut. Four Grey Knights we were then, and now we will be four once again, for Tiuri, here beside me, will take the place of Arwaut and go with us to the Unholy Hills."

Red Quibo had turned even paler. "And how does this story end, my lord?" he asked.

"You already know," said Ristridin. "You are coming with us, as you are the only one who knows his way around the Unholy Hills. You will be our guide; you are to take us to that gloomy vale and it is the last thing you will have to do for me. Then I will let you go!"

"That's if my life's story does not reach its conclusion in the Unholy Hills!" muttered Quibo. He cast a timid glance at Ristridin before quickly striding away.

Piak looked at Ristridin and then at his friend. "Envoys?" he said.

"Yes," replied Ristridin. "This situation cannot be allowed to continue indefinitely. We have no doubt that we can defeat the King of Eviellan, but as the situation stands, that could take months – or longer, and it is sure to cost many lives. The king must realize, beyond any doubt, that his cause is lost. King Dagonaut wants us to inform him that he and all of his men must leave the Wild Wood immediately and retreat to within the borders of Eviellan. That way the conflict can be ended quickly without any further losses."

"Do you think the king will do that?" asked Piak.

"It is the only reasonable course of action he can take," replied Ristridin slowly. "But he is not a reasonable man – and I fear there will be no reasoning with him now. All his plans have failed, and a man who feels so frustrated and disappointed..." He stopped. "I had better not say such things," he said. "Forget my words and try to be hopeful."

"The four of you are going," began Piak. "And Tiuri..." He turned to his friend. "Is your squire allowed to come, too?" he asked.

Tiuri's face made it clear that he'd be only too pleased to say yes, but still he looked questioningly at Ristridin.

"That's something Sir Tiuri must decide for himself," Ristridin said with a smile.

"There's no decision to make," said Tiuri. "Of course Piak should come! Isn't that right?" he asked his friend.

Piak nodded.

Then, deep in thought, they headed back into the Tarnburg, where the other knights were waiting for them, along with Prince Iridian.

Some days later, the envoys headed out into the enemy's territory, from the tourney field to the south-east. Sir Ristridin blew on his silver horn again. Twice: a long blast followed by a short one. It had the same meaning in all three kingdoms: *Lay down your weapons. An envoy approaches.*

Would the King of Eviellan hear it in his hiding place? The envoys looked around and wondered if they would find him.

They saw trees, both straight and twisted, some covered with moss, some grey brown with rough bark, others silver grey with patches of black. They saw leaves, most of them pale green, with dark branches of pine here and there... and leaves on the ground, dry and rotting. There were paths that split, and split again, twisting and turning, leading down and then back up, before splitting once more – and every path looked just like the one before, going past the same trees, the same ups and downs... That was the way through the Unholy Hills!

Red Quibo went first, with the four knights following him: Ristridin, Bendu, Evan and Tiuri. All four of them were on horseback; Tiuri was of course on Ardanwen, with Piak sitting behind him.

Now and then Quibo stopped; sometimes because he seemed not to dare to go any further and had to summon up courage, but often because he had to think about which direction to take. Once he looked up pleadingly at Ristridin and asked, quietly but eloquently, to be relieved of his task. Ristridin shook his head, though, and said, "Carry on."

"Onwards, onwards!" muttered Quibo, tugging at his hair. "But how? I chose left or right every time the path split – left and right in turn... at least that's how I did it back then, after I'd ended up in the same place yet again. Hmm, that was by that hunchbacked birch tree, I think... Or am I mistaken? Onwards!" And onwards he strode.

Ristridin blew his horn once again – it sounded clear and bright in the silent forest.

Ardanwen twitched his ears, but his step remained steady and even. *I am not at all afraid*, thought Tiuri. That was strange, because they could be attacked at any minute. The men of Eviellan would surely not hesitate to attack envoys.

Many of the valleys were deep and full of undergrowth, which sometimes swayed and moved. But they saw no one.

They rode on and the hours passed. They exchanged few words and Ristridin kept blowing his horn. But as the day was drawing to a close, they still hadn't seen a single soul.

They stopped, dismounted and prepared to sleep.

"Now we are in the middle of the Unholy Hills," Red Quibo said in a whisper.

Evan and Piak gathered dry branches and made a fire. They sat around it in silence as darkness fell.

Ristridin blew his horn once again.

"They must know we are here by now," said Bendu, speaking more quietly than was his usual custom.

"Without a doubt," said Ristridin. "But perhaps they have no wish to speak to us or to listen to us. The King of Eviellan is hiding and we must find him. I believe I know where he resides..." He looked at Quibo. But he was silent; all his eloquence had abandoned him.

With daylight, however, Quibo's talkativeness returned. "The Forest Brook is over that way," he said, pointing. "So I think the valley, our goal, must be nearby! I heard many feet last night... sneaking, stealing, skulking stealthily all around. Blow your horn again, Sir Ristridin! I am afraid of this silence; please ease my fears."

There was indeed something comforting about the silvery tone of Ristridin's horn; the horn that – as Tiuri remembered – Sir Edwinem had given to him.

And this time the sound was answered. Men appeared from all around. Red Riders! Most of them gathered on the path, clearly intending to block their passage. One of them, the captain, came closer, with his sword drawn.

"We are envoys of King Dagonaut," said Ristridin. "We wish to speak to your master, the King of Eviellan."

None of the Red Riders responded.

Ristridin repeated his words and added, "Let us pass!"

The captain of the Red Riders silently complied with his request. His men stepped aside and allowed the envoys to pass. But then they followed after them.

Red Quibo looked around. "I don't like this at all!" he said. "Do they want me to show them the way, too? But they already know it!"

"Onwards, Quibo," said Ristridin.

"I'm so confused," muttered Quibo. "Wish me more wisdom – or better luck!" He walked this way and that for a while before leading them up a slope.

Soon the envoys were looking down into a shallow valley. They did not have to ask which vale it was... it was just as Red Quibo had described. They saw the pool and the den built into the slope; smoke curled from the roof.

Behind them someone cried, "Wait!" and the captain of the Red Riders hurried towards them. He looked at Ristridin and said, "What do you want here?"

"I have already told you that," the knight replied coldly. "We want to speak to the King of Eviellan." He lent force to his words with two more blasts on his horn.

"The King of Eviellan!" said the Red Rider. "Do you think this is a residence fit for a king?" The other riders came closer and surrounded them threateningly.

"Fine, then, announce us to the Black Knight with the Red Shield," said Ristridin calmly. "He knows me – he knows all four of us."

"We are envoys of King Dagonaut," said Bendu. "But you may also call us the Grey Knights. I'm sure your master remembers us."

"Then dismount from your horses," said the captain of the Red Riders, "and walk down the slope. I shall announce your arrival to the Black Knight."

He went down into the valley, and the envoys followed him, leading their horses.

11 THE CHALLENGE

They stopped by the pool, which was so dark and dull that nothing was reflected in its surface. The water was covered in a slimy layer of green. On the other side of the pool was the den; it appeared to be built of earth and sheets of moss and turf, with rough grass and branches sticking out here and there. There was an opening in it, like a door, and the captain of the Red Riders disappeared through it and into the darkness.

The envoys waited in silence. When they raised their heads and looked around, they saw Red Riders standing at the top of the slopes around the valley. They, too, were silent; there was not even the clink of a weapon.

Tiuri laid his hand on Ardanwen's neck; he felt the horse twitch and tremble under his fingers. He glanced at Ristridin; his face was pale and serious and he was clutching his silver horn. Red Quibo was standing right next to him; he was clearly frightened.

So this was where the Black Knight with the Red Shield had gone to ground, after so many wrong turns. This gloomy vale was now his realm; this humble dwelling was his residence – the King of Eviellan, once a glorious prince, the son of a king. But he had not given up the fight; here he was powerful, and he still wanted to do harm.

Tiuri held his breath for a moment as the captain came back out. A moment later, the Black Knight with the Red Shield appeared. He walked towards them with slow steps and he stopped, facing them; the water of the pool was all that separated them. He did not raise his visor and his voice was muffled when he said, "What brings you here, knights?"

It was Ristridin who replied: "We are envoys of King Dagonaut and we want to speak to the King of Eviellan."

"Then speak," said the Black Knight, without moving.

Tiuri had a strange feeling, as if something were wrong.

Ristridin said, "We have come here with open visors and I shall tell you our names if you wish. But who are you? Our words are meant only for the black knight who is the King of Eviellan."

"I am the King of Eviellan," said the knight.

He was *not* the King of Eviellan, Tiuri suddenly realized; his voice sounded completely different. He turned to Ristridin and said quietly, "That is not true!"

"I am the ear of the king," said the knight. "Tell me your message."

"No, sir, we will not," replied Ristridin. He frowned thoughtfully and then said, "Now I know who you are: Sir Kraton of Indigo!"

"Bravo! Well done!" said the man, raising his visor. "So we meet again, Sir Ristridin. Are you surprised to see me here? You did, after all, promise me my freedom after the attack had begun, did you not? Your brother Arturin kept that promise and let me go. But soon I will return to Castle Ristridin. I intend to besiege that castle and destroy it as soon as my master issues the command."

"Your master," said Ristridin coldly, "is the one to whom we wish to speak! Not about the oath we once swore, but with peaceful intentions. Tell him so, if he is reluctant to listen to us."

"On the contrary!" an unexpected voice said behind them, a voice Tiuri would have recognized among many. He had walked down the slope unnoticed and was now approaching them; clad in black armour like Sir Kraton, but with a bare head and no shield.

The other envoys stared at him aghast; his resemblance to his brother had taken them by surprise.

"I have already listened to your words," said the King of Eviellan, "and I know what else you want to say. So you can spare yourself the effort of speaking."

He stopped close to them, looking at each of them in turn. Tiuri did not find it easy to meet his gaze, even though he detected barely any sign of recognition in it, and certainly no interest. There was something chilling about the lack of emotion in those fathomless dark eyes – particularly when the king sneered and continued, "King Dagonaut orders me to leave his territory immediately and to retreat within the borders of my own kingdom... Is that not true?" he asked, when the envoys did not respond. "Well, I do not care for Eviellan and this is now my domain. Not that I am planning to remain in the Unholy Hills forever – I rather think I shall lay claim to the entire Wild Wood."

He gestured towards Kraton and the Red Riders. "I still have loyal followers," he continued, "who would go through fire and water for me and who, if it must be so, are willing to share in my fate and my downfall."

Slowly, he looked around the valley before turning back to the envoys. "I have only to give the sign," he continued, "and they will be here. There are many of them. Another command will send them on their way... to set fires in the north and to sow terror in the west, to bring death once more to the east – hmm, is that not where Islan lies? – or to plunder in the south and to breach the walls of Castle Ristridin. They will attack and then retreat here, inside my labyrinth of Unholy Hills."

He laughed again. His resemblance to Prince Iridian was rapidly fading. "That is how it will be," he said. "There will be a patch of darkness within the Kingdom of Dagonaut, a place from which the curse of my anger will spread like a disease. You may try to wipe it out, but some sicknesses last a long time and are hard to cure."

Then he was silent. Ristridin was about to say something, but the king spoke first.

"Let me finish!" he said. "Do not reproach me, do not try to intimidate me or to make me see reason with your wise words. I understand my situation only too well! As far as you are concerned, you have yourselves to blame for this situation. You have chosen sides and now you will have to fight on to the bitter end." Threateningly, he added, "And, if it is down to me, that end will indeed be bitter."

He turned away from them and walked around the pool. When he reached the other side, he stopped next to Sir Kraton and addressed them once again.

"Now heed my words," he said, raising his voice. "You may tell this to King Dagonaut, although he might understand me better if I killed you and threw your bodies into this pool. Heed me! Now the son of Unauwen speaks! This war is not yours, and it is not up to you to put an end to it. This war is between me and the crown prince of the west. You wish to drive me out of the Wild Wood, while you have allowed him to enter it and even supported him. So be it. But this battle is between the two of us, and there is only one man who can and may stand up to me. That man is..." He faltered for a moment, as if he found it difficult to utter the words. "My brother!"

He drew his sword and raised it above his head. "I, Viridian, son of Unauwen, King of Eviellan, challenge him," he said. "I challenge him, my brother, Prince Iridian, son of Unauwen... I challenge him to a duel, to decide the struggle between us once and for all!"

He sheathed his sword again before continuing: "This, envoys, you may tell His Highness in my name. And you may say to him that, should I lose, every man in my army will withdraw from the Wild Wood."

He held up his hand and beckoned to them. "Come here," he commanded, "and I shall tell you my conditions, inasmuch as I can make demands, for I have little to win."

The envoys saw fear, fury and suspicion on one another's faces. Ristridin, though, simply looked serious, as if he were thinking deeply. Then they obeyed the king.

He still had the bearing of a monarch, in spite of the surroundings and the absence of any outward signs of royalty.

"I shall not invite you into my palace," he said. "We shall conduct our conversation standing, under the open sky." Again his voice was light and mocking, but his face was dark and grim.

Ristridin was the one to respond. "Conversation, Your Highness?" he said in a tone of chilly politeness. "You are the only one who has spoken. Why are you challenging the crown prince – what advantage could a duel have, for you or for him?"

"Our battle will be decided," the king responded, just as coldly. "And that will not happen as long as we both live. One of us must die at the other's hand – that is the ultimate consequence of our existence, which by some curse began on the same day. If I lose, my defeated men will immediately leave this place. Sir Kraton of Indigo, here beside me, is their commander, and he will ensure that this happens. If I win, my brother's army must withdraw from the forest, to within the borders of the Kingdom of Unauwen. Otherwise, the situation will remain exactly as it is now: I will keep my base here. It is then up to King Dagonaut to continue the war or to form an alliance with me. Do you understand? The duel will decide which of Unauwen's sons may remain in the Wild Wood with his army."

"Eviellan has already lost," whispered Evan. "This is..."

"Eviellan has not surrendered!" the king interrupted furiously. "And it will not have lost until I am dead." He was silent for a moment, then crossed his arms and said, "I challenge the Prince of the West to a duel to the death. This duel must take place within three weeks at the tourney field by the Low Bridge. Our two armies will pitch their tents there, both ready for an immediate retreat. And as it is two sons of a king who will fight, our judge may be no less than a king. For this purpose, I shall appeal to Dagonaut, who calls himself the rightful ruler of the Wild Wood. Those are my conditions. Convey my words without alteration. We shall wait here and not raise any weapons until the answer reaches us."

It seemed that he had finished speaking and was about to withdraw. But then he changed his mind and, almost in a whisper, he added, "I shall give you a token to take to the Prince of the West. If you hand him this, he will know I am serious."

He slid the ring from his finger, the sparkling ring, only twelve of which existed. Two of them – the finest ones – were identical; King Unauwen had given them to his sons. The King of Eviellan slowly handed the ring to Ristridin. But before the knight could take it, Viridian cast it to the ground.

"Here!" he spat. "And tell him he can keep it."

It was Tiuri who bent down to pick up the ring. As he wiped off the mud, he looked at the king. And he understood: by renouncing this ring, he had broken the last link that connected him to his father, King Unauwen.

As the king met his gaze, his face became so twisted with hate and cruel fury that Tiuri gasped and took a step back.

A while later, on the return journey, he realized that he was still clasping the ring in his hand. He opened his fingers and looked at it.

Piak, who had come to ride beside him, asked in a whisper, "Why does he hate you so much?"

"I don't know," said Tiuri. He handed the ring to Ristridin, who answered Piak's question, "It's because he could see in his eyes what Tiuri was feeling at that moment," he said quietly. "Not just disgust, but also pity."

"Pity!" repeated Red Quibo. It was the first thing he'd said since they'd left the valley. "That man's soul is as black as his armour. I won't set foot on this unholy ground again for as long as he lives, not for all the gold in the king's treasury."

"And now, Quibo," said Ristridin, some time after that, "you may leave us and go your own way. The hills are behind us."

Red Quibo stopped, gave a sigh, shook his head and said, "But the tourney field is still ahead of us, my lord! You don't want to send me away without a conclusion, with an unfinished tale, do you?

Terrible though it is, I feel obliged to remain your follower until the duel has been fought."

"Permission granted," said Ristridin.

Evan asked, "Do you think the prince will accept the challenge?"

No one responded to this question, but Evan did not appear to expect a reply. He bowed his head and remained silent.

Then Ristridin said, "Sir Ardian's camp is close by and he must hear about this, too. Tiuri and Piak, would you like to ride there?"

The two friends immediately agreed and they rode together to the Wild Wood Way.

"This is a false challenge," said Piak. "Eviellan has lost; everyone says so. The king wants only to snatch one last chance to kill his brother. The crown prince will surely understand that, won't he?"

"I'm sure he will," said Tiuri.

"And yet he will accept the challenge," said Sir Ardian when the friends had told him the news. "He will want to face his brother in the arena – even if only to put an end to the war and to prevent further bloodshed." His expression was mournful as he added, "Perhaps it had to come to this, no matter how horrific it is."

"Why?" said Piak. "I mean... why does everyone seem so sad and afraid? Prince Iridian is sure to win – he has to win, because he is fighting for what is right."

Sir Ardian nodded. "Indeed, pray that he will win, my boy," he said. "In any case this will be a fair fight between two equally strong opponents."

"Prince Iridian is better," whispered Piak.

"He will fight with all the strength he has in him," said Sir Ardian. "May God grant that he wins, even though it will give him no joy. He will, after all, have killed his own brother, whom he loved in spite of everything."

12 SINGLE COMBAT

"**N**ot much longer now!" Tiuri said to himself. He was standing, with Piak beside him, at the edge of the tourney field, where the conflict between the sons of King Unauwen was about to be settled.

Their tents stood at opposite sides of the arena, with their banners beside them. The banner of Eviellan was blood red; the crown prince's banner was the seven colours of the rainbow.

Many people were gathered around the field; in their midst was King Dagonaut, who would be judge. It was a strangely colourful spectacle in the gloomy forest – all those knights, horsemen and soldiers. Some Men in Green had also come. Tehalon stood across from King Dagonaut in the shade of a tree.

He must also wish for Prince Iridian to win, thought Tiuri. *In spite of himself, Tehalon chose Iridian's side when it came to it. And only Prince Iridian can bring back peace to the forest and beyond.*

Murmurs and whispers passed through the crowd and then died away. Here they came, the king's sons! They had not yet put on their helmets; the sun was shining on their hair. Both were on horseback. Iridian was wearing a pale-grey suit of armour and carrying his white shield; the King of Eviellan was, as always, in black with a red shield. Prince Iridian was followed by Sir Ardian of the Rainbow River, and his squire was Tirillo the jester. His twin was accompanied by Sir Kraton of Indigo and had a Red Rider as a squire.

The two princes stopped; they stood next to each other before King Dagonaut, so similar and yet so very different. The king stated the conditions again, and the rules of combat, and asked in a loud, clear voice, "Are you ready?"

The brothers nodded. They looked at each other, but did not speak; they had no words left to say.

"Then wait for my signal," said Dagonaut.

The two men rode to opposite ends of the field. They put on their helmets, and their squires passed them their lances.

Sir Ristridin sounded his horn once.

"May God judge over you," said King Dagonaut, raising his staff.

Now they rode, with their lances low. They stormed at each other and met with a resounding crash.

Tiuri couldn't help closing his eyes, but when he looked again they were still sitting upright in their saddles and neither appeared to be injured.

They separated, then approached each other again, fierce and fast. And this time they hit each other with such force that the King of Eviellan's lance shattered and the impact sent him tumbling from his horse.

A murmur ran through the Red Riders.

Prince Iridian calmed his trembling horse. His brother stood up, drew his sword and shook it furiously, as if he wished to kill his enemy's steed. Iridian moved out of the way and cast his lance aside. He sat high on his horse, bright and glorious. Looking down at his brother, he gestured at him to get back on his horse. But the King of Eviellan adamantly refused, so Iridian let go of the reins and jumped to the ground.

Then they were facing each other, on foot, two men, silent and alert. Motionless, they both clutched their swords. And no one could know what thoughts they might be thinking.

Eviellan was the first to attack, but the white shield absorbed the blow. Then Iridian went on the attack; and the clanging clash of swords rang out over the tourney field.

Then they fought furiously. Splinters flew from their shields, the blades glanced off their shoulders; with a great din, they knocked dents in each other's helmets. They whirled around each other, the dust flying up around their nimble feet until they could hardly be seen.

But still the fight went on. And the tension squeezed Tiuri's throat shut, as he watched them with fear and awe.

Then they suddenly parted and stood still again. Leaning on their swords, they looked at each other. But Tiuri did not know what expression they wore, as the helmets hid their faces, which must be dripping with sweat.

Then they both raised their weapons at the same time as if in a final salute, and stepped towards each other, irresistibly drawn together. Again the fighting flared up, and they fought even more furiously, matching blow for blow. Never before had Tiuri seen two knights fight so fiercely, so wildly, but without breaking any rules.

The sparks flew from their swords, their shields started to crack, and blood trickled through their chainmail, as red as the shield of Eviellan.

Tiuri felt as though nothing else were happening in the world but this fight.

One staggered... the other stumbled, but got back up. Now both were covered in dust. Iridian struck, and his brother's shield shattered.

The King of Eviellan grasped the hilt of his sword with both hands and hacked ruthlessly at his opponent. But he missed and, for the first time, he spoke, his voice hoarse and rasping: "My sword is damaged. Squire, bring me another!"

Prince Iridian took a step back and handed his battered shield to Tirillo. He waited for the Red Rider to give Viridian another sword, and opened the attack again.

Now the end is approaching, thought Tiuri. *They have only their swords and both must be exhausted...* The king pounced; he struck his brother between the arm plates... *No, he hasn't won.* But Prince Iridian was only slightly injured, and recovered quickly. The King of Eviellan went on the attack again, but Iridian was stronger now, and his strength seemed to be growing... *Oh, let him win!*

The sword in Iridian's fist was like a flash of lightning; it shone brightly above his dark brother's head, glanced off his helmet and ripped open his hauberk, and went up again for the final blow...

That final blow hit the king in the shoulder, a sharp slash. That final blow cut him deeply, and brought him to his knees.

Viridian fell, and his brother leant over him. The king tried to sit up, but when Iridian knelt to help, he roughly pushed him away. That seemed to cost him the last of his strength, as he fell to the ground and lay there without moving.

Prince Iridian stood up and King Dagonaut walked towards him, with Kraton and Ardian. The two knights looked at the fallen man. Then Sir Ardian removed his cloak – black on the outside, blue on the inside – and covered him with it.

The King of Eviellan was dead. The Prince of the West had won.

King Dagonaut's voice rang out loudly through the tense silence: "The battle is decided, justly and fairly."

Prince Iridian slowly picked up his brother's sword. He would, of course, return it to the dead man, fold his fingers around the hilt, and have him buried with it.

Dagonaut went on speaking, but Tiuri did not hear what he said; his attention was only on Prince Iridian, who was examining his brother's sword.

And suddenly there was silence again; now everyone was waiting for a word from the victor.

But Prince Iridian said nothing; he clasped his brother's sword in one hand and his own sword in the other. He swayed and Sir Ardian put out a hand to steady him. A gasp passed through the crowd, a whispering that quickly died away. But now the prince was standing again, although he was still silent. Sir Ardian took both swords from him, and Tirillo removed the prince's helmet. Iridian's face appeared; he was as pale as death. He turned to King Dagonaut and thanked him. Then he glanced around, but his eyes seemed to see something other than the tourney field.

Tiuri felt Piak's fingers around his own, and he knew everyone else must be holding their breath, too.

A number of Red Riders approached across the field; they stopped beside the defeated man. Sir Kraton was about to join them, but Sir Ardian stopped him with a sharp "Wait!"

Then Prince Iridian raised his voice – that captivating voice that no one could help but listen to.

"I have ended the battle," he said. "The victory is for my father, Unauwen, and now peace may return to the Kingdom of Dagonaut. Eviellan surrenders, and everyone must lay down their weapons."

That was all he said, and so it would happen. Prince Iridian was victorious and the war was over.

No one dared to cheer, though – they all looked at him with trepidation, reverence, awe and fear. His face was calm and serene; there was almost a smile on it, and yet it was full of melancholy. He turned to the knight beside him, Sir Ardian of the Rainbow River, who gravely returned his gaze. They appeared to be having a silent conversation. Sir Ardian briefly shook his head and handed the prince his sword. But he gave Eviellan's weapon to King Dagonaut and he spoke to him, this time out loud. No one could hear what he said, though, except maybe Tirillo, who was standing close beside them, with Iridian's white shield. The jester looked shocked, and the prince laid a hand on his shoulder. Then King Dagonaut gave orders and instructions. The King of Eviellan's body was carried away to his tent, and everyone bowed their heads to pay him their last respects. Everyone – except for King Dagonaut, as Tiuri was startled to see.

Prince Iridian, with Tirillo beside him, slowly walked in the other direction; everyone watched him until he disappeared into his tent.

"Tiuri!" whispered Piak.

The two friends looked at each other. "I'm afraid," said Piak. "And I don't know why. It feels as if it's not over yet..." His words echoed Tiuri's own thoughts.

Ristridin's horn sounded, preventing any reply. It was a sign. The king had something else to say.

King Dagonaut stood in the middle of the field, with Sir Ardian beside him. Ardian beckoned to Sir Kraton and the Red Rider who had been Viridian's squire.

"Hear now my words!" King Dagonaut spoke loudly. "The sons of Unauwen have fought and the best man won. But you should know that the other man did not fight fairly; even his final act was one of wickedness and treachery." He turned to Kraton and the squire. "Here, in my hand, is the king's sword," he continued gravely, "the instrument of his vengeance, as you surely know."

"Sire, what do you mean?" exclaimed the Red Rider. "It is a good sword, one of the two that belonged to him."

Sir Kraton said nothing, but frowned threateningly.

"So you do not know where it came from?" asked Sir Ardian. He took the sword from the king and held it out to the rider, who cowered away. "No!" he exclaimed. "My king gave it to me to keep ready and to give to him if..."

Sir Ardian interrupted him. "I know this sword," he growled. "It is from the Cavern by the Chasm."

The Red Rider recoiled, but Kraton strode up to Ardian and cried, "No! That is a lie!"

"My master, the prince, knows this sword, too," said Ardian. "It is the Weapon of Woe – not perished as we had thought, but still sharp and lethal. This sword is poisoned!"

A few moments of appalled silence followed. Sir Kraton looked as if he had been hit in the face. "No..." he said again, almost inaudibly.

"Prince Iridian is the victor," said King Dagonaut, his voice shaking with fury or pain. "But he will not live to enjoy the peace and he will not see tomorrow's sunrise."

After an eternity – or was it just a minute? – he spoke again. "The King of Eviellan is doubly dead, as he leaves a name that is devoid of honour."

"I did not know," said Kraton. "I did not know!" As he looked in bewilderment at the king, it was clear that he was speaking the truth. "Then I have always served the wrong master," he continued. "Now everything truly has come tumbling down. I am without king, without castle, without land, and my memories are destroyed... May the King of Eviellan be cursed!"

"Silence!" cried Ardian. "You never truly knew or understood your master; even now you do not understand him – or you would feel more pity than fury. Do your duty and take his men back to their land in the south. Be their commander and leader. May you be strong enough to fight the difficulties that will await you in Eviellan."

Kraton did not reply; his face was grey and drawn. But he grimly held his head up and departed.

Sir Ardian quickly returned to the crown prince's tent and was soon followed by King Dagonaut.

Beside the tent hung Iridian's banner, the colours of King Unauwen.

Tiuri and Piak stood together, blind to what was happening around them. They looked only at the banner and at the tent. Prince Iridian lay inside the tent, dying of the slight wound that the King of Eviellan had inflicted upon him. Sir Ardian had said nothing would save him.

They did not know how long they had been waiting when Sir Ardian came back out of the tent. They saw on his face what he had not yet spoken. He stood beside the banner and the two friends watched through a haze of tears as he slowly lowered the seven colours.

13   On the Riverbank

Tiuri and Piak stood beside the High Bridge, which had now been rebuilt and was wider and more handsome than the original. On the other side of the river was the burnt forest. It saddened them to see it.

The war was over, but at what price! Prince Iridian was dead; he had been lying for weeks now in the grave on the spot where he had fought his last fight – buried beside his brother and opponent. Both had been laid to rest with their swords, but only the white shield had been placed on the mound over the grave.

"The Prince of the West lives on in our memory," King Dagonaut had said, "in everything he was and everything he did. What he won shall not be lost!"

The army of Eviellan had left, as had the army of Unauwen. Sir Ardian and Tirillo had returned to the west to tell King Unauwen that from now on he would rule alone in his magnificent city. Here, beside the Black River, they had said farewell to Tiuri and Piak. The two friends could still remember their words very clearly.

"My heart is sad," Tirillo had said, "and yet soon I must try to bring a trace of joy to Unauwen's palace. My king has the heavy burden of government to bear alone once again – until Iridian's son is old enough to help him. And I am a jester; I shall never again be a squire. I am the jester of King Unauwen and I know which song I shall sing first. I think of it constantly. Prince Iridian loved these words and often asked me to sing them for him." And Tirillo had sung the same words for Tiuri and Piak, quietly and in a soft voice:

> Now I'll lay down my sword and shield,
> on the river, by the shore.
> No more for me the battlefield,
> No more the cries of war.

Then Sir Ardian had spoken to them and the last thing he had said was this, "If you can be spared here, then go to visit Menaures, the hermit in the Great Mountains."

Menaures...

He was King Unauwen's brother, although very few people knew that. Piak would have been happy to leave right away. The hermit's cabin in the Great Mountains – how he longed to be there!

And the road to Menaures goes past Castle Mistrinaut, thought Tiuri. Lord Rafox was back there now, and he had promised to go and visit him, him and his daughter. Lavinia – it seemed so long ago that he had said farewell to her.

"What are you thinking about?" asked Piak.

"About everything I have to tell Lavinia," replied Tiuri. "I realized that she never met Prince Iridian. Will she ever know just what he was like?"

He turned around and looked at the Tarnburg. He saw the window of his prison and suddenly felt that he would never be able to play another game of chess.

King Dagonaut had taken up residence in the castle for the time being; he truly was king of this territory now. Yesterday he had summoned the Master of the Wild Wood – and spoken to him for a long time. And now, today, the king would leave and return to his city. That was why Tiuri was there; he and his squire were to see Dagonaut off at the High Bridge. The real farewell had been early in the morning, when they had said goodbye to Tiuri the Valiant as well. He would be riding in the king's company.

Sir Ristridin and Bendu were staying in the forest, as was Evan, the only one of Unauwen's knights who had not yet left. The rightful lord would return to the Tarnburg. Tiuri wondered if Tehalon was pleased about that; after all, he did not like the castle.

The procession of men approached; King Dagonaut in the lead, with Tiuri the Valiant beside him. Adelbart was also in the company; he was to become Guardian of the Forgotten City once again. But that city would no longer be called "forgotten". Other people would most likely go to live in that place, and the roads leading there would become easy to find. The Road of Ambuscade would again be called the Second Great Road, and would be extended from the Owl House to the City of Dagonaut.

The king stopped for a moment before crossing the bridge and spoke a few more words. He also turned to Tiuri.

"Sir Tiuri," he said, "after discussion with Sir Ristridin I give you leave to visit Menaures next week, on a pilgrimage to the Great Mountains. You must report back to my city at the end of the summer."

Tiuri the Valiant nodded at his son and his son's friend again, and then the hoofs thundered over the bridge. King Dagonaut and his company rode to the east.

As Tiuri and Piak watched them go, Sir Ristridin came to stand with them. "I expect," he said, "that the king will command you to return to the Wild Wood."

"Oh, I'm sure we'll be back," said Tiuri.

Red Quibo joined them and asked Ristridin, "And what about you, my lord? What are your plans?"

"Sir Bendu, Evan and I are to remain here," replied Ristridin. "There is still much to do. The wood is just as wild and it may still be dangerous, even though Eviellan has now departed. So much of it remains unexplored. But you, Quibo, know that you are free to return to your own village."

Quibo coughed and said sheepishly, "Sir Ristridin, I am willing to stay with you. To be honest, that is, in fact, my will and my wish!"

"And, also to be honest, it is as I expected," said Ristridin with a smile. "I can put you to good use, Quibo, because I want to ensure that a proper road is made through the Unholy Hills."

"Your mockery almost makes me regret my decision!" cried Quibo. "I do not like those hills! A proper road... With signposts?"

"With signposts."

Red Quibo looked worried, but then his face lit up. "Yes," he said, "I can certainly see one advantage of such a road: it will lead us all the faster to Islan!"

"Your only fault, Quibo," said Ristridin, "is that you talk far too much."

"Oh, but I love words!" cried Quibo. "With words you can say what you are thinking... or hide it..."

Islan... thought Tiuri. *That is where the adventures began.* He looked at Ristridin and asked, "Are you planning to return to Islan?"

Ristridin did not answer immediately. "Who knows?" he said then. "My memories of that place are not so fond, as you know, but I have seen a different side of it. And Lady Isadoro will be a good mistress of the castle. Shall I send her your regards when I am there?"

"Yes, please do," said Tiuri, and he continued hesitantly, "The Lady of Islan... I never truly understood her."

"You are not the only one," said Ristridin. "But," he added after pausing, "that is also true of others. Do you understand Lavinia entirely, or yourself? Probably not, if you take some time to think about it."

"Exactly what I wanted to say," remarked Red Quibo. "Words are often untrue, thoughts so hazy, and..."

"Come, Quibo," said Ristridin, interrupting him. "Bendu and Evan are waiting for me in the castle. Are you two coming as well?"

"We'll be along soon," said Tiuri.

When Ristridin and his squire had left, the two friends stood together for a while, looking thoughtfully at the turbulent water below. Piak sang softly:

Now I'll lay down my sword and shield,
on the river, by the shore.
No more for me the battlefield,
No more the cries of war.

And suddenly Tehalon was standing beside them.

"That is an old song," he said. "It is often forgotten, but then people remember it and sing it anew." He fell silent for a moment and continued, "The High Bridge has been rebuilt, and soon many people will see it, everyone who will travel along the Great Road,

466

from east to west and from west to east. And anyone who wishes may cross the bridge to greet the lord who will live in the Tarnburg."

"The Master of the Wild Wood," whispered Piak.

"No," said Tehalon. "The Lord of the Tarnburg will no longer be the Master of the Wild Wood. He will merely be a vassal of King Dagonaut. But, like his forefather long ago, he will obey the king and love peace. I know that will be so, for he is my son."

"Your son? What about you?" asked Tiuri.

"I will withdraw to the north of the Green River, where there are still places no one knows. Never will all of the secrets of the Wild Wood be revealed!"

Tehalon looked at the two friends. "Farewell," he said. "Do you see that the dry branches are sprouting again? A new forest will cover the scorched earth, and there, too, will be paths I shall tread."

He turned on his heels and crossed the bridge.

Tiuri and Piak stood and watched him go until he had disappeared from sight: Tehalon, the Master of the Wild Wood.

Epilogue

Summer in the Mountains

P iak raised his face to the eternally snow-covered mountaintops, which glistened in the sun.

"Go to visit Menaures," Sir Ardian had said, and now Tiuri and he were on their way – upstream along the Blue River to its source. That was where the hermit lived, in the Great Mountains between the kingdoms of Unauwen and Dagonaut.

It was a warm summer's day and they were walking slowly, Tiuri leading Ardanwen. At the point where the path became narrower and steeper they stopped for a moment and read the words carved into the stone.

> *Pilgrim climbing to the heights above,*
> *may you travel with God's love.*
> *And, dear friend, as you go,*
> *pray for us in the valleys below.*

Before continuing, the two friends looked back at the flat land they had left behind and thought about the people they knew there.

They could see nothing of the Wild Wood now. But the Blue River flowed past Mistrinaut and the City of Dagonaut and on past Castle

Tehuri. They had broken their journey at Castle Mistrinaut briefly and would stay longer on the way back. Lord Rafox also wanted to visit the hermit, but he would set off a few days later, accompanied by Lavinia. So the four of them would journey back to the east together. But now Tiuri and Piak travelled the path to Menaures, just the two of them, as they had gone adventuring before.

Tiuri thought: *A year ago I walked here, too, with the letter for King Unauwen. Then I did not have Ardanwen with me, as he could not come with me across the mountains. And I had not yet met Piak. A year ago... It feels as if I have known him all my life.*

A year ago, thought Piak, *I was sitting up there on a mountain slope. And then I saw Tiuri coming, with Jaro, disguised as a pilgrim. That's how it all began. But now we're going only as far as Menaures's cabin, not over the mountains to the Kingdom of Unauwen...*

And suddenly he was overwhelmed once again by the sorrow that had faded a little since their journey began. A shadow hung over the Kingdom of Unauwen. Prince Iridian, the leader of the knights with the white shields, was no more.

Piak glanced sideways at his friend, whose face was pensive and serious, but not sad. As he saw Tiuri look back over his shoulder, he thought: *His mind's on Lavinia, of course. Later, when we're at Mistrinaut... maybe even on our return journey, she'll make him laugh again. One day – soon – he'll marry her, and he won't really need me anymore.*

Tiuri seemed to feel his gaze and he looked at his friend, with a question on his face.

Piak quickly turned to look at the road ahead and began to sing:

Now I'll lay down my sword and shield...

Yes, he thought, *perhaps I no longer need to be a squire. I could stay here, in the mountains, live with Menaures and tend sheep, as I once did. I could climb and climb again, walk across the glacier and look out over the Kingdom of Unauwen, but only from a distance. If I went there, everything would have changed so much...*

These thoughts continued to occupy Piak, although he did not speak them out loud. And when he finally saw the hermit's cabin on the green slope ahead, beneath the mighty wall of rock, his heart leapt. This was his home!

"Are you pleased to be back?" asked Tiuri.

"Oh, yes!" said Piak. "It's still exactly the same. Nothing has changed."

The twists and turns of the path hid the hut from view at times, but they came ever closer. Then they saw a boy sitting in the meadow above the path.

Tiuri stopped for a moment. "It's true," he said. "It really *is* exactly the same! There you are, just like the first time I came here." He smiled as he looked at Piak and added, "But this boy is not brown as a berry and he is not playing the flute."

Piak did not smile, and his good mood melted away. His place here had been taken by another. This boy was sitting on the slope where he had once sat. And he greeted them with the same words, "You must be here to see Menaures." He told them to head around the bend to the cabin. He did not hurry there himself, though, as Piak had once done, but remained sitting where he was.

Will Menaures understand how I feel? Piak wondered to himself. *Of course he will, because he knows everything.*

Soon he was looking into the hermit's wise eyes and he felt stronger.

"The wickedness of Eviellan has been defeated," said Menaures, "and Prince Iridian is the victor, even though he is no longer in this world. But," he continued, "you must remember that the fight goes on, even if we are not at war. Even the peace in our hearts is something we must always fight for." He nodded at Piak and added, "I am pleased to see the two of you. I am old and one day I, too, will no longer be here."

"Why do you say that?!" said Piak, his voice trembling. "I know

471

it's true, but... oh, why does it have to be that way? One day you will no longer be here, and King Unauwen will no longer be here... and what then? Who will reign over the Kingdom in the West? Oh, I wish I had not said that. I..." He ran out of words.

"The words I spoke were something you already know," said Menaures, "even though you would rather not. But before we talk further, you must first meet my young friend. Would you ask him to come here, Piak? He should be nearby."

Piak was happy to go back outside. In the mountain meadow, beneath the sunny blue sky, he realized it was almost impossible to remain gloomy. But then he saw that was not true for everyone.

The boy was sitting in the same spot, but his head was resting on his knees and his whole posture radiated sadness.

Piak remained at a distance and called hesitantly, "Hey, hello!"

The boy looked up, quickly wiping his eyes, and then stood and turned his back to Piak, as if studying the view. Piak walked over to him and looked out as well. He could see a very long way over the Kingdom of Dagonaut; he saw the river and the towers of Rafox's castle, hills and houses, farmland and dark forests. He did not look at the boy's face, but simply said, "Menaures has sent for you."

The boy pointed one finger and said, "That forest over there. It's not the Wild Wood, is it?"

"No," replied Piak. "The Wild Wood lies more to the south, beyond those hills on the right." Only then did he look at the boy. Was it a coincidence that he had asked about that forest, of all places?

"I'm Piak," he said and then, startled, he fell silent.

The boy was taller than Piak, although he was certainly no older. He stood straight, his blond hair gleaming in the sunlight. His face was calm now and his dark eyes looked questioningly at Piak.

But Piak did not know what else to say; he just stared at that face in astonishment. He had seen it before, although it was much younger now and not yet marked by war and hardship.

"Who are you?" he finally managed to say. "Is your name perhaps Idian... or Iridian?"

"How did you know that?" the boy asked, also surprised.

"It's like seeing the prince standing before me!" said Piak. "You're so... You are his double, my lord!"

"Do not call me that," the boy said. "Call me Idian, like my... Did you know my father?" he said, changing the subject. He looked at Piak with an expression that said, "Talk to me about him! Please!"

Piak understood now why he was sad, this boy, Prince Iridian's son. He took his hand and shook it firmly.

"Yes," he said. "I... Oh, what can I say? I was at the duel, with my friend, Tiuri. And your father won!"

"I know," said the boy quietly. "I only wish I had been there... Tell me about it!"

"Of course," said Piak. "I'll tell you everything I know."

They both stood in silence for a short time, looking at the ridge of hills that the Wild Wood lay behind.

Now I understand, thought Piak. That's why Sir Ardian told us to come here; that's why Menaures said I should come out to call him, this boy. Iridian's son is alive, he is the prince of the Kingdom of Unauwen! He will live here in the mountains and Menaures will teach him everything he knows. Then he will return to the land of his grandfather, the king, and one day he will rule over the kingdom in the west.

Almost in a whisper, he said, "You are sad, Idian, but I am happy to meet you. There is still a prince in the Kingdom of Unauwen; you are your father's successor."

"I am happy to hear you say that," replied the young Idian. "I mean I'm happy that you are happy."

They looked at each other and smiled.

King Unauwen is not alone, thought Piak. *And besides he has many friends... Ardian, Tirillo, Ristridin, Tiuri...*

473

"Come with me!" he said. "My friend has to meet you, too. His name is Sir Tiuri and I am his squire. Come with me, and then we shall tell you everything..." *And we'll also ask you plenty of questions,* he thought to himself.

They walked together to Menaures's hut.

Tiuri had come outside; he was standing with Ardanwen by the spring and waiting for them.

Here I come, with Prince Idian, thought Piak. *Tiuri's going to be so surprised when he finds out.*

But as he came closer, he could tell from Tiuri's face that his friend had already seen and understood.

TONKE DRAGT was born in Jakarta in 1930 and spent most of her childhood in Indonesia. When she was twelve, she was interned in a camp run by the Japanese occupiers, where she wrote (with a friend) her very first book using begged and borrowed paper. Her family moved to the Netherlands after the war and, after studying at the Royal Academy of Art in The Hague, Dragt became an art teacher. She published her first book in 1961, followed a year later by *The Letter for the King*, which won the Children's Book of the Year award and has been translated into sixteen languages. Dragt was awarded the State Prize for Youth Literature in 1976 and was knighted in 2001.

LAURA WATKINSON studied medieval and modern languages at Oxford, and taught English around the world before returning to the UK to take a Master's in English and Applied Linguistics and a postgraduate certificate in literary translation. She is now a full-time translator from Dutch, Italian and German. She lives in Amsterdam. Her translations of children's books have won the ALA's Mildred L. Batchelder Award three times.

PUSHKIN CHILDREN'S BOOKS

We created Pushkin Children's Books to share tales from different languages and cultures with younger readers, and to open the door to the wide, colourful worlds these stories offer.

From picture books and adventure stories to fairy tales and classics, and from fifty-year-old bestsellers to current huge successes abroad, the books on the Pushkin Children's list reflect the very best stories from around the world, for our most discerning readers of all: children.